The Manor

by

Sally Ferla

This is a work of fiction. Names, characters, places, and incidents are either the product of the author's imagination or are used fictitiously, and any resemblance to actual persons living or dead, business establishments, events, or locales, is entirely coincidental.

The Manor

Contact Information: info@thewildrosepress.com

The Wild Rose Press, Inc.
PO Box 708
Adams Basin, NY 14410-0708
Visit us at www.thewildrosepress.com

Publishing History
First Wild Rose Press Edition, 2019
Print ISBN 978-1-5092-2810-2
Digital ISBN 978-1-5092-2809-6

Published in the United States of America

Dedication

The greatest thanks to the houses of Europe and their guiding lights of freedom.

Chapter 1

Worship

The straps hurt her arms, and so her Mistress slightly loosened them with a grimace, obviously angry she was having to do this again. Jennifer couldn't work out why, as she was bent over into the box, why after all this time and being together all these years, she just couldn't completely let go…she did love her Mistress. She trusted her, and she tried to worship her, although she still felt… well, silly at times, like it was, well, silly – and, of course, this could be felt by her mistress, which was why, yet again, she was being put into her punishment box.

Her punishment box, a necessary implement they had both agreed on before they tried to live the lifestyle permanently, when it became clear that Jennifer had a tendency to become not just wayward, but resistant to her Mistress's wishes…..this wouldn't do.

Fortunately, her Mistress was wealthy, a business woman whose reach could tap onto whatever they required; her real problem was time, which seriously added to her frustration when Jennifer seemed to willfully waste it, and with not just disobedience, but resistance, seeming to force her Mistress to endlessly have to keep pushing in order to get the results she had already learned.

Having the luxurious holdings of Kurt Mayer – a master craftsman who specialized in fine artistic bondage furnishings – and having been on such good terms with him over the years, they were lucky enough that he accepted a commission to build their most necessary new piece. 'Expensive' was a good word for how it was made, partly due to her mistress's tastes, and 'awe-inspiring' was another when it was positioned in the corner of the den, their usual nightly place for chatting about their day.

Once it had been unveiled, Jennifer could always feel its presence; even without locking her in it, the effect on her behavior was immediate. Her Mistress was overjoyed, as awkward quirks and silly resistances that Jennifer had made seemed to melt away almost like magic. Their times in their den were so improved, and it became as decadent as their surroundings, the soft magnolia walls leading down to ornate skirtings and onto the soft cream carpet, itself inches thick and seeming to bathe them in comfort, the gorgeous chandelier above glinting down at them into their recessed floor, two steps leading down to their comfort from the entrance, as they were often to be found on the floor, cuddling and laughing and with red wine flowing, the black leather couches in front of them to their right and behind them, looking on in lust. Lust, too, for the huge flat screen television, its contribution from the front left corner adding to their fun as it sat on its ornate dark wooden stand, its many drawers holding more fun collected over the years. Watching what they liked, and learning so much more, the lamps sitting on ornate table stands each matching the flat screen stand, and striding low on each side of the three seater couch on the right wall, bathed their soft light through their cream shades on a familiar occupant in the room.

It sat in a commanding position in the right corner, between the three seater and the one seat couch, the flat screen to the left of that in the other corner; it looked like a fine antique table, cozy and ornate, but that was not what it was for…..

That wasn't why it had been commissioned; the Mistress had many options in dealing with Jennifer's bad behavior, and had great experience in handling it, but she was a very busy woman. Her time was so important that there had even been occasion when her business life had invaded their den through her cell phone, something that made her hideously angry – not at Jennifer, but at the lack of time. She was a very fare Mistress, and Jennifer had understood her anger and cherished their private time together, which was why her Mistress had such trouble understanding her resistance to her wishes, as it took so much of their precious time together away. So much tying and rapping, buckling and paddling, but it did work, and Jennifer was calmed and cured of her wantonness…..for a time. Jennifer, too, couldn't understand it: she loved her Mistress, and was so thankful for this decadent world she provided for her and bathed them in at every opportunity, but somehow, something inside made her pull back, pull away at times. Pull back from her Mistress's wishes, not from the punishments or chastisements, as she actually liked them, but from certain ways of acting, certain ways of carrying herself, and from certain words and phrases that the Mistress insisted on, things that made her feel, well, silly. These feelings inside, these mental blocks she had, caused her to resist and to pause to consider too long, behaviors which, after all the Mistress had done for her, and all her efforts and attentions to give her a good life, simply infuriated her…. There should be no resistance!

Well, now things were different; always in her panties, Jennifer wore wrist and ankle cuffs, and sometimes nothing else but her cuffs, and had become so used to their beautiful design – styled by her mistress for her with soft inner leather holdings – that she truly missed them when they weren't on. It was nice to feel their little golden padlocks, their love-heart shapes gently bouncing off of her cuffs on the outside, like earrings reminding her the cuffs could not come off. So easy was it for her Mistress to take her by her wayward hands to whatever corner of the house and snap her into implements for punishment. Time no longer wasted on tying and rapping endlessly, now the punishment came quick and fast, with Jennifer left in no doubt as to who loved her.

An interruption gave her time to think on it….

She could hear her on the phone; she was angry, angry at the intrusion of the call into her den. Try as she might not to carry that anger into Jennifer's punishment, she knew she would, and Jennifer would feel that anger, making it harder inside…. Why couldn't she just give her what she wanted? 'Worship', she said….'Worship?' The Mistress liked to be worshipped after a long day, and she tried…tried, but didn't know fully what she meant. She wanted Jennifer to stare at her, she'd said, stare at her not with wanton lust, which she'd learned to exhibit on command, but to stare in a way that made her feel worshipped. She was to look at her like she was the most valuable and sought-after woman in the world, the Mistress had explained, like she was an awe-inspiring sunset, a golden glow who drew her attention fully and without equal. Jennifer had tried what she thought was this look, had acted in a way she thought was appropriate to the Mistress's desires, even getting so close that she couldn't resist kissing her soft skin, but none of this worked, and instead brought sharp chastisement…she was not to touch, she was to worship. She'd tried again, as she'd tried many times before, listening to the Mistress's direction and failing again, her instinct to satisfy in a physical way coming forth and irritating the Mistress, and leaving Jennifer hurt. Soon, it became clear they had failed, and the Mistress's frustration – despite Jennifer's obvious anguish at failing her – had her reaching for Jennifer's cuffs. Being taken by the hand was a sure sign of her being led to punishment, but being taken by the cuff was a sign of an angry Mistress; head down and on her knees, Jennifer had been led, half-crawling to the back corner of the room, her eyes just able to make out the Mistress lifting the lid of the punishment box, its red velvet learning waiting inside.

The punishment box… her Mistress and Mr. Mayer had spent a long time designing it, down to Jennifer's exact size. The box itself was rectangular, for Jennifer to enter it length-ways as it sat commandingly, made in mahogany on a wooden base twice the size of the box, and completely covered in thick tan velvet and tapered in at one end, the entrance end. As if to ensure that there was no doubt as to why one would be led up to this tapered end, there were leather buckles waiting for wayward eyes as, head down, they would come into view, two further back on the base, but in line with the box, their deep black ankle holdings in leather taking an unfortunate charge's attention – for just a moment – from the mahogany teaching that lay in front. A charge in servitude, head down, would no doubt see the lid of their punishment as being its lovely smooth-edged deep mahogany finishing, causing its deep red velvet underlid to stand out to bowed eyes. This, though, would almost immediately fall into the background as the true scope of what was coming lay in view: beyond the ankle restraints of the base, on the box's immediate front, lay two low-down thigh restraints, their deep black sumptuous buckles waiting to hold their charge, and above, now in view, was a crescent-shaped recess, its soft black leather curve lined all the way around, meaning only one thing…..

Made with sumptuous padding, this was not for the charge's benefit; it was purely for the Mistress. The padding on the deep soft leather of the recess, joined with the sumptuous buckles, was intended to hold a charge for a busy Mistress, and for as long as was necessary, leaving her free to go about her business without fear of the charge's comfort, knowing full-well that they were in no danger and completely immobile, left to wait for as long as she deemed was necessary….

Necessary, too, was the time they'd spent on the design, for as a charge was led into the leather crescent, all hope of escape was removed with soft leather strapping rapped round their ankles, and buckling falling in place around their thighs, quickly giving them the sense of the box's firm strength as they were secured inside, certain they were caught. Led in at a crawl, this was necessary, not for obedience, but for comfort, the charge to be held for as long as was necessary, so buckling before being bent over was not advisable. The box's front crescent was matched equally by the lid, its elegant design having a crescent of its own, smaller and made by the gentle folding inward of two half-crescent-shaped black leather flaps, obvious connotations signaled by their presence. As a charge was led into the box's crescent in front, they would be nestled firstly in the padded recesses on the box's front end, and secondly, in between the padded half-crescent openings which hinged inside, opening halfway in and allowing the charge to feel their padded comfort to either side, secured on either side of their abdomen by the openings themselves, all secured at the back by latches on the inside of the box's front end. Above an identical design was what awaited in the box's ornate lid, the result, as it was closed, being for a charge's rear not only to be secured, but presented out of an oval recess, for the room and its occupants.

'Secured and presented' was to be taken a stage further inside, though, for inside of the box, just behind the front's oval recess, a velvet ramp for the resting of the charge's front led diagonally down to the box's floor – the whole inside of the box, including the ramp, covered in sumptuous red velvet different from the box's tanned base. Like the outside of the base, the inside had four more leather buckles waiting for charge's arms, their black leather straps two in line, midway ahead, and two further forward set for forearms and wrists. To either side and in front of the ramp, they were matched by the ramp's own leather holding strap, three inches wide, to ensure the charge could not wriggle and hurt themselves, and ensuring their ass stayed quite still and presented. Wrapped from left to right over the charge's mid back, its thick soft leather fed into a waiting buckle beneath the ramp, the charge left with the comfort of not having a buckle on their side or back, and with the obvious understanding that even if they could get their arms free, there was no way to reach it. Complete restraint was necessary if a charge had to be taken to the box. With this in mind, one further addition was employed for those charges who needed that extra bit of attention over their wayward nature. Having had their collars already secured and padlocked, the box – between its two furthest buckles for the wrists – had a chrome steel half-ring protruding from the floor. With the appropriate collar, the snap attachment could be linked firstly to the collar, and then finally to the ring, holding a slave's head down with their face forced to velvet in submission.

On each side of the box, in line with the wrist cuffs and steel buckle, there were five small slits in the mahogany sides, covered by velvet grills inside and obscuring any light from entering, but providing ventilation and air. Due to their being so close to the slave's head, one could use them to listen to moans, and for learning of the corrections given, and verbal directions. Useful while administering appropriate corrections, they meant the lid could remain sealed, and with the slave able to answer back… if not gagged. Finally, the thought of lighting was brought in…the weak twenty-four volts in four bulbs recessed into each corner on the underside of the lid ensuring that there was no danger of fire or excessive heat when locked. The lid then finally brought down, the charge would be bathed in a gentle soft red, complementing their velvet surroundings. Locking the box was an ornate affair; details mattering to the Mistress, her insistence had been on antique-looking hinges, golden but worn, complementing the fine mahogany by blending to its style. On top of the lid, they ran sideways, either side folding over the edge to waiting receivers underneath. Golden and worn-looking, too, they topped each side's wall over the edge from the lid, neatly hiding padlocks away, safe from the users. Both could crest the box front with no danger of striking padlocks held out to either side, and unnecessary for holding the occupant. The strapping did that, and so the padlocks were excessive, only rarely used but for in parties at times. Their function, of course, was to secure the slave from escaping, no pitying attendee or wayward charge able to grant release without the Mistress's keys. With the charge now strapped and secured, and the lid covering even their back strap within, only their firm wanton ass was now presented outside, ready for the correction to come that they most surely deserved…..

As Jennifer now lay inside, surrounded by her red velvet walls, she tried in vain to understand her resistances. Again, she'd pulled away, the Mistress opening the box right in front of her, seeming not angry but tired, tired out by her wantonness.

She listened intently to another phone call, listened as her ass sat in the air protruding from the box's oval opening, its black leather surrounds holding her firm inside, the strap tight over her back, underwear already removed, her punishment to come in just a matter of time.

Who was the Mistress talking to? They were going where?…. For what time? Really hoped she could help her with what? It was a strange call; it wasn't work, but something else, something she'd never heard of before, and Jennifer became worried – had she really upset her Mistress badly this time? Was something really wrong? Was the Mistress thinking of ending their.... Suddenly, Jennifer felt the blunt rubber end of the Mistress's strap-on on her anus; lost in her worries, she hadn't heard her quietly come up behind her and now she lost her breath as she felt the tight walls of her asshole forced aside, the Mistress entering her firmly. There was mood in her entry, frustration and anger, Jennifer feeling it as the Mistress's advance made her try to pull up, but her collar snap held her head firmly to the floor ring. She gasped, letting out a groan as the Mistress pushed almost forcefully inside her already-lubricated anus, her usual tenderness missing as Jennifer felt her mood through her behavior. Groaning more, Jennifer wasn't gagged, feeling she wanted to say 'sorry' to her Mistress, but knew she shouldn't, as the Mistress would only hear her muffled words and become annoyed at her pleading. No, it was called a punishment box for a reason, and as the Mistress listened to the muffled struggles from inside the box, her strap-on bore down, herself half-smiling at Jennifer's acceptance, and her understanding of her wrong doing; perhaps it would be okay after all, as time would tell....

Chapter 2

The Journey

What had she meant? She'd cried when she told her, cried when she heard she'd spoken with someone else about their problems. Jennifer thought their little secret world was their own, free from outside interference. She didn't want the world to know, and wasn't confident enough for that; she'd balled out about the house, the Mistress's reasoning doing nothing as she'd cried in the hallways, the betrayal cutting deep.

Lost in her feelings, with hurt and with anger, she'd screamed back at the Mistress who'd finally lost it, shouting down her protests. Shouting and raging till Jennifer was sniveling in a corner, just the latest display of her bad behavior on show.

"It was this or nothing!" the Mistress shrieked, years of having her hard work thrown back in her face causing the statement, and it was Jennifer's fault it had happened, not hers. If Jennifer could stop being so selfish and stop crying, she would see the Mistress was trying to save their relationship, not ruin it, trying to put things right and not betray her… but she couldn't.

She bawled all afternoon, the Mistress leaving her to it, separate and alone at one end of the house with her feelings and woes. Even when she was controlled enough to sit sniveling, just the thought of it, that it might be over, caused her to well up and bawl again.

At five o'clock, despite her still shaken state, the Mistress had become determined, half helping her get dressed. Jennifer's reaches for tenderness were brushed aside, the Mistress grown tired of her sorrows.

She'd told her what the phone call had been, a call to a learning institution, and Jennifer had burst into tears when she'd told her what it involved. The Mistress had been discussing, for weeks, their personal problems and secret life with some woman, some woman who she was now being driven to see.

Tears ran down Jennifer's cheek, a half sob leaking out as she thought of what had been done to her. In a short while, she was going to be standing in front of some stranger in an office – someone she didn't know, but who knew everything about her and her private life. Again, the tears welled up when she struggled to understand how her Mistress could have done this to her, the Mistress driving at her side, cold, seeming to have given up on her sobbing.

It had seemed like hours, and probably was, must have been, with her lost in her anguish; Jennifer only came to when they left the highway, the soft gravel under the tires lifting her eyes to see the sun trying to peer through the trees all around them. The road wound down to the right, deeper into the woods, it growing quite dark and threatening, winding still further, and Jennifer voiced concern, only to be told quietly not to worry, that they were almost there… almost where she thought what was this place?

Chapter 3

Au Revoir

The road had continued down into the forest, really frightening Jennifer before levelling out and swinging to the left, and after a time it, arced a little to the right, all the time flanked by huge trees, the sun's piercing attempts held at bay by their foliage until finally the road arced left and began to climb. With the gentle sound of soft gravel escorting them, one final swing to their left brought a huge private home into view, the sun meeting them in the clearing as the car came to rest under the mansion's ivory splendor.

Exiting the car, Jennifer nervously followed her Mistress, her hand on her waist, and Jennifer's questioning was quieted by the appearance of a beautiful leather-clad figure on the house's front stairs.

And what a house; a Manor in fact, its front entrance of eight curving stairs lifting up to its huge pillared entrance, its roof held aloft by their imposing soft strength, the entranceway being ivory of color, the building strong but inviting. The warm feel married to the impression as its two large side wings rose up with the entrance till they both gave way to the chateaux-styled upper floor rising off the mid-section, its colonial roof tapering off, weathered, and melding perfectly with the forest surrounding it.

Approaching her, Jennifer gawped in awe, forgetting her Mistress's hand and simply following her to the dark haired beauty looking down from overhead. Hair short, just touching her shoulders, and she was dressed in thigh-high suspended stockings, a look of elegance gazing out from a black corset fitted perfectly. Elegant embossing on its front in black designs not understood tapered down to her waist where black panties were wedded. Adorning the clothing from above, a tanned beauty looked down with her gorgeous Venezuelan complexion with dark eyes, looking on warmly. A slight smile from her lips caught Jennifer off-guard, her feelings of attraction immediately written over her face before she caught notice of the beauty's waist below the corset. Gorgeous lace talons flowed from garter-belt tightness, stockings held fast with small pouches to either side. From between the small pouches, their neatness hiding the corset's imposing strength, strange implements hung between them, free around her waist – some obvious to Jennifer – her attraction stiffening off as she recognized a black cane, a leather strap, and something else… something she'd never seen before.

Rising up the final stairs, Jennifer felt herself swallow the true beauty of this woman, now devastating, close up. A short exchange of pleasantries sent feelings tingling up spines, Hispanic words washing around them like silk in the air….

"If you would follow me, the Mistress will see you now," informed their escort effortlessly, turning her gorgeous ass for all to see as she led a stunned Jennifer forward… into the Manor.

Led through the huge beckoning doorway, a large circular hallway greeted them, and Jennifer was finally able to pry her eyes off of the Venezuelan beauty in front of her, the black knee-length leather boots tapping their heels sharply off the ivory marble tile, moving over the floor in time with her beckoning tanned rear, shifting from side to side in her panties as she walked.

To the left and right, marbled floors led down opposing wings with ornate skirting, this giving way to ivory walls with French-dressed cornicing atop them at the ceiling. Eyes looked down either corridor at huge doorways, closed and ten feet apart to either side, their mahogany stark against the ivory.

A commotion took Jennifer's attention from the left wing to the right, seeing for a moment before they passed what looked like two more of their escorts, struggling mid-way up the passage with a naked figure on the floor. Dressed the same as their escort, Jennifer was shocked at them as they seemed to wrestle with the naked woman, dragging her reluctant figure on all fours through a doorway on the left… was that a leash?!

The image quickly disappeared as the sharp clicking grew more pronounced, the Venezuelan perfection shifting, cheek to cheek, up the huge marble staircase in front, with Jennifer transfixed as they left the hallway for the first floor, high above and beyond where they were. Entering to the right onto plush red carpeting, their escort's tapping gave way to soft booted footfalls. The carpet's rich ruby color met more ornate skirting, a strong varnished mahogany brown with walls of soft cream continuing as it had below; down the smaller upper wing, its length was flanked by doorways with an office feel, their varnished mahogany surrounds blending in with the skirting below. Following the soft booted footfalls in front, the closed doorways watched over their new arrival passing under their towering strength as an even more impressive doorway loomed large at the end of the wing, still mahogany, but more ornate; obviously, something important lay inside. Stopping just in front of it, Jennifer and her Mistress's quick glance at each other was broken as their escort, after seeming to pause in respect, knocked on the door with a similarly respective careful fashion.

A moment of silence, the world seeming to pause as they stood there beside one another, their escort in front and as still as the hallway; then the sound of the doorway opening forward to whatever lay within.

The large door fell away, their booted escort moving in with her heels tapping again on wooden floors, the carpet left behind as they entered after her. Jennifer watched as she peeled away to the right, her hand gesturing the two to continue straight to a point she chosen on the floor, a large commanding desk just in front of that.

All three came to a stop at the same time, Jennifer bewildered at the scene of the door closing behind them with another booted black-laced beauty like their escort sealing them in. Remaining by the door, another two stood like soldiers, neatly spaced apart on the room's left side, motionless and almost standing to attention with their eyes fixed on Jennifer. Two windows between them let in the dropping sun, making it work to peer its way in to the strange scene they now stood in. Through old-style wooden slatted blinds, its entry was hindered, giving a staggered hue and a mysterious look to the room, it having the same soft cream walls with ornate cornicing, but mahogany skirtings now met varnished mahogany flooring, itself matching the huge business desk's imposing panels as it sat strongly at the back of the room. Again on the front panels, Jennifer saw symbols like those on the black corsets, things she didn’t understand, but knew from their look that they were important. They hid the lower half of the figure sitting behind the desk, her dark hair beautifully straight and her black business-like suit soft but imposing, leaving Jennifer in no doubt that she was in charge as she penned a piece of paper, seeming to ignore all those around her.

“Appointment 17:30 to see you, Mistress,” their Venezuelan escort opened gently from her position on the right of the desk, now standing like the two opposite her on the other side of the room.

The woman at the desk seemed to ignore the announcement, continuing to pen the paper, an awkward silence ensuing with Jennifer and her Mistress beginning to look around, but not the others in the room, all of whom continued to stand like the proverbial military, motionless and respectful to the sound of the pen moving, easily heard. The pen stopped, placed to one side, the sound as it touched the table and the slide of the paper to the corner of the desk making both new arrivals turn their attention to eyes of blue with a green tint awaiting, staring out from a perfect mane. The dark hair glided like a silk wave as it crested the shoulders and continued to her breasts, solid and ample; they seemed to fill the pastel black blouse under her business suit and command the attention off the physically impressive black corsets around them. Not dressed in mouth-wateringly fine garmentry or showing ample parts of her anatomy, somehow she was still able to effortlessly draw their attention squarely onto her; it was as if she had something else, something more… power.

“So, you’re right on time.” The woman spoke, her

soft but commanding voice seeming to fill the room with a whispering tone. “That’s much more than I can say for some that come through these doors.” The voice continued unnerving Jennifer – it was velvety but strained, as if… as if trying to disguise itself…. “That’s a good beginning.” A similarly disguised smile unnerved Jennifer more.

“What’s going on?” Jennifer heard herself ask aloud, drawing the woman’s gaze immediately to her. Her eyes seemed to look at her in amusement, as if half-surprised that she’d dared to speak, and then back to her Mistress as if for an answer to this perceived insolence.

“Ah, I see,” the eyes came back to Jennifer. “She doesn’t know.” They moved back to her Mistress approvingly. “I find that in most cases that’s best.” They fell back onto Jennifer, amusement now competing with malice. “The results are far better if they’re not prepared.”

The two women seemed to ignore Jennifer for a time as they spoke, Jennifer slowly gathering what was going on…

“This is not a cruel thing you’re doing,” she continued. “Your relationship has gone as far as you can take it, and yet these problems still persist; if anything, this shows that you really do care for her or you wouldn’t be going to all this trouble – it would be far easier just ending it.”

“What..!?” Jennifer exclaimed, listening to the woman, a demeaning smile and dismissing look from her making Jennifer feel less than as if she was….

“How are they?…. I mean, they aren’t really hurt in terms of…” Jennifer heard her Mistress talk, but almost in a business tone about her, like she wasn’t even there, and with the woman behind the desk interrupting….

"Think about it: most people simply move on when things get tough; they don't have the patience or time to deal with the hassle, and neither do you, yet you are trying and finding the time to try and salvage this relationship." The woman looked squarely at Jennifer, her sudden powerful look stopping Jennifer immediately before she spoke. "It's obvious to me that you love this woman, that she is the one you want in your life; you've shown that by bringing her here – it's up to her whether she wants to show you that she loves you, too…."

'How dare she,' Jennifer thought, the look of anguish spreading across her face as this woman questioned her feelings for her Mistress; who was she to question her and their relationship? It was none of her business, so who did she think she was? Jennifer thought as she felt the weight of her gaze on her… but still, she said nothing; it was strange, as if her gaze had her held.

A short time later, the woman and her booted laced escorts left the room, Jennifer now far from impressed, searing feelings of hurt and anguish starting to pour out as she demanded to know what was going on, and what was this place? Who was that woman, and why were they talking about her like she was a piece of meat? What was going on?!

Her Mistress tried to reason with her, talked to her about the end of her tether, that their relationship couldn't go on like this, that she needed change….

"What?!" Jennifer exclaimed at what she was hearing, her world being pulled out from under her and tears beginning to flow – what did she mean they couldn't go on? Why was she doing this to her? She cried outwardly as she remonstrated with her Mistress, the whole world she'd come to know over the years falling apart right in front of her. She'd become used to this lifestyle of servitude and closeness, used to being cared for and cosseted from the outside world, her Mistress's money shielding them from a normal life and allowing them to live as they pleased, and as she started bawling and shrieking Jennifer could feel it slipping away from her with or without her protestations as she grew louder, reason giving way to emotion… to hurt.

"And what about me, what about what I want?" her Mistress retorted. "So you can be happy and fulfilled, but I have to just forget about my needs?"

"But I do fulfill them," Jennifer almost screamed, "I give you everything you ask, I…."

"Really!" her mistress cut her off. "Really! So that's not me that has to spend hours dealing with you at home! Hours I don't have when we should be spending them together! How selfish are you, when I come home and all I want is to be with you…."

"Selfish!" Jennifer screamed, hurt at the claim.

"Yes, selfish!" her Mistress shouted back. "You want the life you've got but you don't care about my needs! I work my ass off for us and every night is a struggle! Every night, I have to deal with you again and again, moaning and whining about 'I don't want to do this' and 'I'm too tired to do that'! What about me – what about my needs?!"

Jennifer bawled out, her Mistress becoming cold, her crying doing nothing anymore but angering her, turning her harsh like that business woman Jennifer already hated since meeting her. Talking to Jennifer like she was in her office, like some client she didn't know or care about; Jennifer railed as she heard what was going on. This place was an etiquette academy, a place where devoted women learned to be life slaves for their partners. In front of them was a contract left by the woman on the desk; it detailed all manner of consents for whoever signed it. Consent for Instruction, Consent for Correction, Consent for Restraint… all manner of permissions and sub-permissions detailing what the signer had agreed to. Jennifer's tears were blurring the words as she argued with her Mistress, her anger giving way to rage as she threw the contract on the desk, ending up sobbing in the corner.

After a time, her Mistress came down to her, her attempts to console her shrugged off, Jennifer's feelings of hurt and betrayal racking through her as she felt her world coming to an end. Her Mistress spoke about how she cared for her, how she loved her, how she wanted them to go on but none of it worked, Jennifer there just sobbing and shaking with hurt.

Eventually, the professional side of her Mistress came back, taking over care and turning to anger, Jennifer's emotions crushed and pressured, the charge pushed into the corner like she was a stranger, ending up on the other side of the room, crying and shaking.

The quiet lasted a long time, her Mistress lighting a cigarette, the soft exhales from the other side of the room almost soothing as Jennifer thought about what was going on. Her world was falling apart in front of her. Did she love her Mistress? Yes. Did she love her? Why was she doing this to her? Was she right? Was she selfish? What would she do in the world without her?

What kind of life would she have? The questions went round and round, Jennifer feeling sick with hurt, soft exhales still soothing her with the birds outside, their last songs of the evening before sundown, their last songs together before anything more, before tomorrow.....

She stood there in front of the desk, looking down at the contract; the tears had run out now, her Mistress standing by her side as she held the pen, all the questions still there. One thing she'd become certain of, though – if she didn't sign it, that was it: they'd be finished, and she didn't want that. How bad could it be, after all? She was a love slave by her own admission, and the people here would teach her professionally; it might improve their relationship, as her Mistress had said, and their world could go on together.

Nervously, she signed her name....

When the woman returned, flanked by her escorts, Jennifer's Mistress had already signed the contract as well. Soon, the woman's signature also adorned the paper and the two lace-covered beauties to the right of the desk had signed the page, too, Jennifer feeling slightly irritated by the thought.

Who were they to be involved in her life? Standing there in their knee-length leather boots with raised fancy edging around the trim, their faces emotionless like two lace-covered soldiers, exactly in the position they had been in before they'd left. The woman behind her guarding the door, and their escort from the main entrance, were back where they'd been, too, like some army, Jennifer feeling more annoyed at them than ever as the woman behind the desk surveyed the signatures on the page beneath her.

What Jennifer didn't realize was what she'd just signed; the two lace-covered women were actually lawyers, their signatures witnessed on the page. Unknown to her, too, was that the woman behind the desk was a registered medical psychiatrist operating a practice that took women into its care. The Manor was a government-registered medical facility, an asylum – Jennifer had just been committed!

"You're doing the right thing," the woman assured her Mistress, catching her questioning look as she stared down at the contract. "And so are you," the woman assured Jennifer, her tone soft and almost caring, but with the eyes of a scientist looking out at a lab mouse.

Chapter 4

First Day

That first day in house was surprisingly lenient after what the Mistress had described. After a short tour, showing the rest of the areas where a slave may wander in house, the women were split up into four groups. This was done to reduce their confidence, by reducing the group size of forty women down to ten a piece, and therefore enabling training to be employed more thoroughly, as imposed on less confident minds around the house.

Worryingly, at first, the women were stripped of their clothing, all belongings and attire taken away, the women left only with their underwear as they were assured that, as for the intendants around them, a house uniform would be provided for the guests at the end of the day. They weren't lying to them, and one was… their underwear was removed at the end of the day, leaving them in the uniform of the Manor for all slaves under its care…..

Before this, though, some were taken outside to the grounds behind the house, the sun low on the horizon now, while others were taken to one of two rooms, either the Library – where Jennifer found herself – or the Academy.

Even with splitting up the group into four smaller ones and keeping them separated in areas around the house so that they couldn't influence each other, the training didn't go well. For this most basic of beginnings, the women found their very walks being re-taught. From their gates to their stances to the way their heads were forced to be held high, it quickly became exhausting. In each area, the women found themselves walking up and down to the disapproving looks of their intendants, four of whom were assigned to each group, leaving a more imposing presence as the day wore on. Jennifer saw a familiar face in her four intendants: the woman from the stairs, their Latin escort…. She was their group leader, ultimately responsible for their group's behavior. As well as the four directly responsible for each group of ten, there were twenty-four other intendants in various shifts, and tasked with responsibilities around the house, available to be called on for extra assistance at a moment's notice. The women not realizing yet just how trapped they were…they would soon learn the guise. The guise of free movement…with the Manor so huge and giving an airy feel, with huge wide staircases and massive ornate rectangular-framed windows looking out to huge grounds beyond, the women felt free; the Manor's main doors between the pillars only ever closed at night adding to this feeling …but free they weren't….

Books were used, balanced on their heads in order that the right stance and balance would be married with each step, each time a book fell off leading to the intendants becoming more visibly frustrated. Eventually, Jennifer began to notice the strain on their expressions, but not as directed at their failure to manage what was being taught – instead, it became apparent to all that they seemed frustrated they could not meet out their direction as they wanted. As time went on, some were seen reaching their hands to the implements round their belts, only to pull them quickly back, frustration growing in their faces.

After a long afternoon, the women were all brought inside the main ballroom situated behind the main staircase of the entrance, a seemingly trivial doorway in the center of the wall leading to a room arranged in an oval, as the Mistress flanked by two intendants waited for them in the center of the room. Filled with a late evening light from the huge rectangular windows set in the back bay wall, the grounds outside and the trees beyond could easily be viewed from left to right as the glass followed the curve of the oval. The women all stared on nervously; as they were arranged in a circle, an intendant behind and to the left of each one as the women looked at the object preventing the Mistress from occupying the very center of the room, a large leather box….

Its dull black perfectly polished leather lay before them, its wrist straps at the far lower end and its ankle straps at its higher end, sitting menacingly in front of them.

"So," the Mistress began calmly. "We have gotten through our first day together." She cast her eye around the women. "From what I hear, though, despite the best efforts of my intendants, the results of today's lessons were not picked up well." She cast her eye around the scantily clad women, her eye coming to rest on Jennifer. "Is that because they did not deliver training in a sufficient manner?" She questioned, with Jennifer unsure of whether she was directly questioning her. "Well?" she lowered her tone. Looking into Jennifer's eyes, her raising eyebrows clearing any confusion.

"No, Mistress," Jennifer answered, slightly embarrassed among the group.

"No," repeated the Mistress, her eyebrows raising again, prompting Jennifer to answer.

"No, Mistress," Jennifer repeated.

Jennifer couldn't understand the anger that she was seeing as she spoke, not realizing she was breaking one of the Manor's highest forbidden rules; slaves were never aloud to utter the word "No." In the Academy, they'd soon be taught these lessons, that slaves were able to shake their heads or gesticulate their refusals, but to never actually aloud use this word, and they would soon stop trying to.

"So, we are in agreement, then, that the fault in the training does not lie with the intendants?" The Mistress questioned again.

"No, Mistress," Jennifer admitted for the group.

"No," the Mistress forced a fake smile, frustration showing quickly and turning to anger. "No!" She screamed, Jennifer starting to shake throughout her body, this caused by the scream that had almost caused her to stumble. "The fault lies entirely with the slaves, then!" the Mistress decreed. "When I told you your first day would be an easy beginning, that did not mean you shouldn't try! After all the money spent on you by your owners getting you here, and all the patience of the intendants today, this is how you show gratitude!" she continued screaming, glaring at Jennifer. "Well," her voice dropped, still glaring at her, "I think what's needed is an example of what happens when someone in this house is found wanting." Her voice rose as she spoke. "Bring her!" She so ordered, and Jennifer's arms were immediately grabbed by the intendants behind her, their powerful physiques easily carrying her to the middle of the oval in front of the box.

The room fell silent, each woman shocked by the Mistress's screaming, and Jennifer not knowing where to look as her flimsy upper underwear was quickly removed by intendants, her arms raised to remove it over her head before her remaining lower underwear was quickly taken down as the intendants dropped to the floor, squatting to either side of her. A quick fumbling and her underwear was free from under her feet, leaving her completely naked in front of thirty-nine other worried pairs of eyes, and the intendants behind them. Naked Jennifer froze with embarrassment, a stern look from the Mistress worrying her further as, below her, the sound of steel belting being opened signaled what was to happen next.

Almost as if rehearsed, after securing her ankles, the intendants rose, lifting their arms, their training having shown them just where to push Jennifer so that she was flopping over between them, over the box, almost glad something was happening and no longer feeling so silly, standing there naked, but in an instant feeling utterly on view. Totally embarrassed, she felt how high her ass was exposed as it was forced up for all to see by the high end of the box displaying it for everyone in the room as her wrists were expertly shackled at the other end, her head coming to rest at the low end and her ass pushed still higher by the box's drooped design. Her embarrassment almost reduced her to tears as she felt her ankles straining on the shackles behind her, the sound of belting coming together around her wrists belying the cool touch of the leather strapping that was now holding her completely immobile, only shock stopping her from crying.

Shock gave way to fear as Jennifer followed the

hard booted steps of one of the intendants who had strapped her down, on to the two intendants flanking the Mistress, the other having moved off to her right, now standing guard for her correction. Watching, Jennifer saw a cane being offered to the arriving intendant by one of the other two, the Mistress's gaze lost to her as she watched her return with it, its long black menacing form held taught as the intendant disappeared behind her, the sharp booted steps coming to a stop abruptly. A moment of calm, when feelings of all kinds ran through Jennifer's polarized mind as she heard the intendant behind her menacingly swing the cane in practice, its sharp swish through the air finally bringing home to her what was about to happen, and fear, nerves, and embarrassment all converging, feelings of.....

"Well," the Mistress's voice took over, all eyes turning to her. "Since you've all shown that if leniency is allowed you cannot be trusted, you will now learn what happens when slaves of this house are found wanting," her voice trailed off, her eyes falling to the waiting intendant, the room falling silent as she gently cocked her head – the intendant needing no further instruction.

The sharp crack was like fire! Jennifer's scream shocked even her, as she'd thought maybe she could be dignified in that... another crack brought more pain, her head jerking back as her eyes widened, her scream echoing off the oval walls and the next crack seeing her pull involuntarily hard on her restraints, her legs trying to run, but held fast like her wrists.... She screamed, then crying as the forth snap of the cane brought the first deep red line across her ass, the women behind her shocked and trying to turn away, intendants quickly shoving them back in line with sharp cracks breaking out as more minor canings began among the circle, the intendants keeping order. These were unheard by Jennifer, though, her feelings delivering her into shock, as she didn't know which way to turn; utterly embarrassed at her ass up for all to see, she screamed as the fifth snap brought agony, fear, and embarrassment, all joining her screams and taking her through strike number six, her heart thundering as she pulled hard on her restraints. Strike seven brought still more of her screams, taking her further into embarrassment as she realized there was no way to go through it with dignity, no way to handle it well as strike number eight snapped her into a new realm of pain, another line exposed across her ass for all to see, tears streaming through strike nine and her screams taking her through ten, eleven, and twelve; the snaps echoing around the room with her shrieks, her crying in between, suddenly changing on strike thirteen as, after the feeling of sharp fire across her cheeks, she caught sight of an intendant behind the slave directly in front of her, a look of satisfaction on her face making Jennifer angry, raging inside as she felt snap fourteen and the anger was gone, replaced by pain, her crying embarrassment back as fifteen brought fear, her heart thundering, her breathing erratic between shocked crying, her body trying desperately to pull away from the restraints by itself, and sixteen sending out a scream that she didn't recognize, snaps seventeen and eighteen echoing around the walls with her pain, her feelings immaterial, now left behind with her dignity as she resigned herself to hopelessness in the discipline of the intendants, nineteen and twenty bringing forth screams, but with her learning her first true lesson of the house, that a slave has no dignity and, if it becomes necessary for her to be punished, it is not for her to decide how she will take it, but rather for her to simply accept it.

The room fell silent again, Jennifer's final humiliation over the box that of all, to hear her pathetic crying and her whimpering as she was slowly unbuckled, the stripes across her cheeks there for all to see, tears streaming down her cheeks as she was carried back into line by stony-faced intendants, not an ounce of sympathy from them as they held Jennifer's limp form between them, her crying tolerated over this first day.

"Well," the Mistress began, every woman in the room now giving her their full attention. "I hope it has been made clear today that, in this house, a slave will do her utmost or she will be made to do her utmost." Her eyes moved around the shocked faces of the circle around her. "And just in case any of you are hard of learning," she paused, a small smile appearing at the corner of her mouth, "We'll have Samantha next."

Suddenly, the fear descended on the whole group, Samantha pulled forward by intendants like Jennifer before her, it becoming clear that it was not just to be one slave punished in this meeting. In fact, the process was repeated for a further two after Samantha that day, the house staff wise and trained in the art of subduing groups. They knew that if each and every slave was put through the punishment, they would all know and have gotten through the pain, and the deterrent effect would be lost. Far greater was the effect for those who did not go through it, the terror of being possibly next bringing an air among the new slaves of obedience through fear, this something that would have been lost in a mass punishment.

Chapter 5

Sleep Tight

The day had finally come to an end – with her ass still stinging, Jennifer was led along the east wing from the main hallway, to a room at the end of the east wing where she and others had been taken to. This, they learned, was the house's main medical facility, an actual infirmary – not a play room – where the needs of the women were tended to; in Jennifer's case, a hydration cream was applied to her rear.

For now, the day was over, and led by two intendants, Jennifer followed the three women in front of her, two more intendants following behind her: a procession of shocked and tired looking women with confused expressions, all naked and heading down the main stairway, hidden behind its grand ascending front as one entered the main hallway. As bare feet followed clicking heels, nerves started to fray as the light began to fade almost immediately, no one knowing what waited below them.

Arriving at the first lower level from the staircase above, they saw that the building followed the design overhead, stretching out to the left and right, two wings with four doors each – two on each side of the hallway, facing one another – with an additional door at the end of each wing. The lovely colors and French warmth of the Manor above gave way to a dark grey world, stark and cold, a feeling of prison immediate, this being a feeling the intendants wanted as they walked the women under cold dull lights mounted on the ceiling, the square plastic coverings over the dull bulbs reminiscent of a factory. Dark grey walls ran the length of the wings, the walls skirted with a wood painted dull white and the doors surrounded by the same, their facings like cells, the ceiling devoid of cornicing, sharp-angled grey walls meeting the roof as the dull grey paint closed in around them.

A procession of nerves followed down the west wing, the intendants splitting the four, each woman led through one of the four doorways, their final destination for the night becoming clear.

Entering into the second of the paired doorways on the left, Jennifer was surprised as the dull grey gave way to soft light, the room's mysteries revealed: dorms. Each of the four doors on the west wing, save for the fifth door at the end, was identical inside, the sleeping quarters of the women arranged in dorms, the rooms each having four beds on each side of the rectangular rooms, with two at the top and facing the door as you entered. The floors were polished maple, the walls a lovely cream, the Manor wrapping its occupants in comfort all over again, the skirting clean and white – the roof, though, was devoid of cornicing, leaving the cell-like feeling still hanging in the air. The light came from opposite ends of the back wall, two up-lighters in the floor blocked by purposefully built square surrounds, meaning that the bulbs could not be seen from any angle, their soft light funneling up over the back wall and accentuating the cream comfort, giving an oriental style feeling as the women were led to their beds.

Jennifer was led to the fourth bed on the left, passing the three already occupied, the intendants directing her with soft hands, a rare caring gesture that the women would learn was not common. The sound of muffled mattresses compressing could be heard as the women were laid on soft sheets, no covers for them, the rooms controlled at a constant twenty-two degrees. Other sounds sharply broke the calm, the clanking of steel and chains; the women panicked, as suddenly their left hands were taken up by the closest intendant, the sharp snapping sound of handcuffs emerging. Soon, all the women found their left hands cuffed to the top left side of their beds on their headrests, the soft mattresses and cream walls losing their calming effect as they noticed the steel barred head and foot rests cradling them in on the beds, leaving them feeling like prisoners… like slaves.

Everyone secure, the women watched as the intendants made their way out, their customary uncaring stances returning, no one even looking at them as they closed the door behind them, their tasks complete. There were eyes looking though, and this first night they would miss nothing, the women didn't talk, each having received sharp punishments throughout the day and quickly learning that, in house, one only spoke when spoken to. Cream walls and soft comfort were soon joined by another guest in the room as eyes slowly realized its presence, the sudden dimming of the lights very low to allow sleep revealing the guest's little red eye looking down. A little braver now, the women picked out the small camera in the left corner above the door, its thermal eye watching all as they lay.

They would learn, in time, what the fifth door at the end of their west wing was for….

For watching them….

Through this night and every night, another small four intendant team was shifted to look over them all from inside. Watching every dorm, they checked for any behavior unacceptable in house: telling, talking, or… touching.

From the fifth room, which was a control room, four screens showed each dorm, and sound, too, was pumped in, the intendants able to hear the slightest whisper, setting off a chain reaction, their black leather chairs left behind as they dealt with any broken house rules, with the women soon learning what lay in the east wing of that level.

Learning, as for Julie, the first to suffer the rules of the dorm: after she'd quietly whispered to the woman on her right, the lights had suddenly risen up in the room. The light bathing the room in cream was a signal that intendants were on their way, the calm soon broken as they sharply opened the door, a trundling gurney brought with them. The woman to her right could only watch wide-eyed, glad she had not replied as Julie was uncuffed and roughly hoisted up to a sitting position, her panicked look wasted on the intendants as two corseted beauties lifted a straight jacket from the gurney, forcing Julie inside. Her slight struggles met stronger hands, the ties on the jacket pulled tight over her back and making it clear who was in charge as, soon, the rest of the women got to watch her hoisted forward and placed face-down on the gurney. All eyes watching wide in panic as she was trundled past, intendants pushing her out the door, the gurney starting its journey down the corridor to the east wing just beyond….

Julie could see the dim lights glint off the bars of the gurney as, face-down, she passed under them, and for a second she thought she saw the stairs leading up to the main hallway pass on her left, the lights stopping for a moment, the darkness broken again with more lights signaling she had entered the east wing.

Trundling forward, she could feel her heart beating faster, the first set of opposing doorways approaching caught out of the corner of her eye as she lay there, hands tied behind her back as they continued toward them, panic beginning as they slowed to the left.

For a moment, Julie saw the rear end of one of her captors, the black-laced cheeks passing as the sound of a door handle took over, a rush of air soon following as, with an intendant at the front and one at the rear, Julie was wheeled in, almost squealing as she went.

The doorway passed around her, the room almost as dark as the corridor, no nice comfortable surrounds here; instead, an empty room with dark grey tiled floors, walls painted to match, a thin dank skirting separating the two, Julie noticed for a moment, before the ominous sound of sharp heels on tiles took her attention to them.

The room size mirrored the rooms the women were dormed in, but there were no beds here – just Julie on her gurney, pushed to the left of the room, a single weak light in the middle of the ceiling, out of sight, but revealing her fate in its center.

Able to see to the side, Julie looked to her right at a black wooden, leather clad horse, illuminated as if by torch, the rest of the room in semi-darkness, the horse arranged length-ways toward the door behind it and the wall in front. Bolted to the ground, it sat menacingly, commanding all the attention in the room with its long torturous wooden main beam, and all the ties and buckles necessary on its four black leather clad legs, to secure anyone who needed disciplining.

The sharp clicking heels suddenly stopped; looking to the wall in front of the horse, Julie was unable to see much at first, but as her eyes adjusted, the wall seemed to be adorned with items across it, dark shiny long items that the intendant perused, taking her time to choose. The quiet in the room was maddening, Julie hearing her own breath, almost forgetting there was an intendant right behind her in the darkness, the sound of hands running over and between implements easily discernable as her other captor made the right choice.

Soon, a different sound, as one was lifted from the wall, lifted and held as the intendant turned and made her way back, her sharp booted heels and gorgeous black lingerie almost enticing before the implement swinging in her right hand came into view… a long rectangular paddle.

Julie panicked, letting out a feeble moan as the intendant came to the top of the gurney, the paddle swinging freely in the air in front of her; it being obvious now what was going to happen next. As the gurney started moving, Julie felt helpless, the power of the intendants' hands on the bars felt alien as she was turned toward the horse, pitifully moaning, but ignored as she went. Gurney stopping at the top of the horse, she felt one more brush of moving air as the intendant in front of her joined the one at the back, their hands taking a grip of her jacket, Julie waiting to be unbuckled – but she wasn't.

Instead, she was turned around to her front before being lifted to a sitting position and then half dragged from the gurney to the horse, turned almost immediately, and pushed down over its length, the intendants having no intension of taking her jacket off. A loud panicked moan ensued as Julie let out involuntarily the realization that she was being left in the jacket, it frightening her more as she felt her ankles being trapped in leather straps, buckling securing her to the cold leather of the horse's legs, her own now held apart. Sharp boots came from either side, and with her ankles secure and Julie feeling the wooden beam on her midriff, she was glad she had not been saddled over it, its smoothed hard wooden edge pushing into her stomach now, the leather of the legs almost teasing her with comfort. Through the buckles below, on the other side of the legs, Julie got to see the intendants attach long black ties and raise them up to her, attaching them to the numerous hanging fabric buckles of the straight jacket, it being obvious they'd done this many times, her anguish totally ignored.

The intendants standing up, Julie's moaning increased as she felt how tightly secured over the horse she was, not able to rock back and forth now that the ties on the jacket were holding her down. With her ass facing the door behind her, she could see it closed through her legs, her lower half totally exposed now as, out from under her jacket, she could feel the cold of the room over her skin, her cheeks presented for the two intendants to either side of her.

The first strike made her squeal, the second coming even harder, as if to tell her to be quiet, and she bit her lip, feeling her ass raised between them as soft leather snapped across her cheeks for a third time. The cold air of the room was now unfelt by her cheeks, warming already as the intendants continued their work.... They never spoke.

She felt an arm reach across her back, resting on top of her, the hand curving around, taking her right hip, the feeling of silk lingerie and warm skin pushing against her on the left side and down her thigh, the intendant taking hold of her, the next landings of the paddle solid and controlled, and Julie letting out firm yelps as the intendant slowly chose exactly where to strike. Behind her, the other torturer stood back, watching the other intendant work, her glee at Julie's struggles across her face and Julie able to see her through her legs in the darkness. Her attention lost for a second, she became angry at her enjoyment, the next landing of the paddle catching her off guard and bringing forth an uncontrolled and solid scream, an almost immediate second landing of the paddle even harder across her cheeks, it becoming obvious that her screams annoyed her current corrector.

Julie's attention now focused on her as the next two sharp drops of the paddle, one on each cheek, quickly after each other, were slightly less forceful, as if testing her, Julie yelping lower with the first and then again loudly on the second, an instant and solid landing across both her cheeks bringing forth a huge scream, and then a pause. Two sharp snaps, again less powerful, Julie this time yelping, but trying to hold the yelps down, each time bringing a pause, the same again bringing another as if appreciating Julie's attempts... she was learning.

Learning without being spoken to, led by the intendants' discipline, their strikes continuing over her ass with Julie learning to hold back her yelps as much possible, learning to take it as any good slave should without complaint or undue noise.

She learned as the time went on, as her cheeks became increasingly sore, that restraint of pain and the controlling of noise made the intendants happy. They seemed pleased, and Julie could almost feel their reward in their paddling, for the paddling became such that it was landed strongly, but almost sensually, almost rewarding her efforts, the striking fading away but for the occasional time when her yelps were too loud, but she felt their tolerance with her efforts, and, almost… respect.

But dominance had to be maintained, and soon Julie felt all of her perceived respect with the intendants taken away as, after taking turns on her for a long time, she heard the sharp booted steps move around her, one on each side as they both headed for the wall out in front of her – the wall with the implements.

Julie didn't dare try to look after them, that decision made easier by the ties on her jacket holding her fast, and with her exhaustion, the bright light in a circle around her making her feel exposed, as in an interrogation, her ass still bared high for all to see her exposed cheeks, stinging and reddened as she breathed out, holding back moans. In front of her, she heard them again, heard them talking, and then a laugh; she was stunned! For the first time, they seemed human, and it was as if, if she behaved how they wanted her to and she did what they expected her to, they relaxed, as if pleased, it making them seem more like women and not jailers – less threatening, but it was much more than that.

The intendants were not just masters of implements and torture, they had been trained in how to dominate… to take control of an individual, not just with force on the body, but to control with the ultimate in domination, the controlling of the mind.

They knew that, by giving great fear and pain and then seeming to reward good behavior, by seeming to offer a way out, the distressed mind would seize that opportunity, would focus on that escape route to lessen its suffering. That focus, unknown to Julie who had already fallen into the trap, was centered on their happiness. By their maintaining that progression, Julie had perceived a way of lessening her pain, but this meant she was focusing on their happiness and not focusing on hers. By focusing on keeping them happy and being concerned always with how they felt, she had already forgotten about herself, the human mind only having so much processing power, and with that all tied up in fear and focusing on their mood, her brain simply didn't have time to think that, perhaps, there was a better strategy, a strategy that focused on how she was feeling instead of them…. Julie had already given away her control to them.

But this control could only be kept up by maintaining fear, the fear that, at any moment, the intendants could turn on her, therefore keeping the mind busy on avoiding this, and thus failing to find any other way out… a control that Julie now heard being attached around the intendants' waists.

Lifting implements from the wall, the intendants were busy attaching Julie's final torture of the night as she hung there, helpless in her cold lit circle, awaiting her fate as they chatted, seemingly oblivious to her struggles behind them.

Ideas of respect, and even friendship with these lace-booted torturers, quickly vanished as their sharp heeled taps approached from in front of her, their quiet chatting stopping as they rounded the horse on each side, Julie tightening in fear as she caught sight of the long black lengths attached to their fronts. Feeling vulnerable as the two moved in and around her, a silken hand taking her left thigh high up as the first intendant got into position behind her; this would have felt good in another setting, but here, it brought terror, Julie biting her lip and panicking as she felt herself tighten up as the first rounded-edged length began to push in from behind on femininity, her lips slowly forced apart, a squeal of disapproval met with a sharp spank on her right cheek. More involuntary squealing came forth as she felt the length push slowly inside her, Julie agonizing as she tensed around it, unable to stop it pushing deeper in, the lengths already oiled at the wall, out of sight and unstoppable. Involuntary squealing almost tolerated, her scream as the length went fully inside was met with a sharp angry spank on her right cheek, the intendant having none of it. Trying to hold her panicked groans, Julie received yet more spanks as the intendant slowly began to work her, Julie able to watch her muscular thighs tense as they rhythmically increased the thrusting of the huge length now inside of her. Warm hands on her ass took her cheeks, the intendant working her like some sort of dough on a table. Held fast, Julie’s spanked screams gave way to controlled groans, the louder bringing spanks and the lower seemingly encouraging the intendant, seemingly made to rhythm, with the groans sounding almost approving of her thrusting.

Again, Julie felt some sort of perceived reward, empathizing with the intendants' feelings instead of her own as she was fucked firmly, her groans echoing around the room, her panic abating at one stage, almost enjoying the punishment, before a sharp spank refocused her attention. The intendant seemed to realize the enjoyment, the feeling of silken thighs banging off of her helpless ass, the punishing thick length bringing moans of pleasure for a second as her lips began to tighten around it in approval, this quickly dealt with by the intendant spanking hard and thrusting deeper, bringing the sound she wanted more… the sound of punishment. Fear came again for a second time as the intendant worked Julie harder for a time before relaxing, but Julie couldn't help it, her enjoyment creeping in around her as she got used to this new house treatment. Her nerves abating, Julie felt the hard spank of disapproval as she let out her pleasure, the intendant working hard to maintain her dominance. Soon, she quickly learned to try and hide pleasure, to make her moans seem emotionless, but she couldn't; she wasn't trained well enough… that would change, though… starting tonight.

Tonight, as she felt her length retract, retracting slowly and carefully, the intendant's hands gently cupping her ass, she seemed to show care, respect, Julie was sure of it this time, and she was right. The intendants, too, had feelings and, despite how well trained they were to maintain distance, and hence control with the women, they couldn't hide it all; Julie groaned like one would as a lover exited, the feeling of the silken hand gently stroking her cheek instead of spanking, letting her know it was heard.

But heard, too, by the second intendant, her hands rough and disapproving; her length, though, meeting less resistance was not appreciated as it pushed inside, Julie groaning in her own disapproval, sharp harsh spanks doing little to change her tone as she let out her feelings, disrespect that would soon be dealt with thoroughly.

Her groaning disapproval brought hard fucking, hard deep fucking and hard spanks as the intendant rode her roughly, forcing her to sound out, as she wished no pleasure to be had as she fucked her like an animal. Julie wrenched and groaned against her restraints, a feeling of resistance coming up at the perceived ill treatment after the pleasure before, but there would be no mercy. The intendant knew what Julie was up to, and she would be shown this room was for punishment, not pleasure, and for all her resistance and growling, Julie eventually dropped her head, exhausted and breathless, her groaning returning to a controlled rhythm as she took her intendant's lead and gave her what she wanted.

Eventually satisfied with Julie's submission, the intendant slowed her performance, her rhythm dropping as an exhausted Julie groaned emotionlessly, not in pleasure but in exhaustion, the intendant's retraction lab-like, cold and uncaring when compared to her former.

Soon, though, there was caring, Julie's eyes widening as she felt the first come back with her length, her hands caring and finding no resistance, with Julie smiling out to the other intendant as the plan on her worked, the other unseen and smiling back, shaking her head as Julie moaned for her.

Again, Julie had fallen for another trap, perceiving that the first of them was caring for her, making her act up and perform well under her. In reality, none of the intendants cared much at all at this stage for them, and their objective was just to tire her, and if they could use mind games to have her follow them as they led her to exhaustion, all the better… correction being much easier to employ if the slave is willing.

The former now returned, and again there was to be no caring, no feelings of shared respect, just sharp spanks and deeper thrusting, meeting all of Julie's complaints; at one point, she even used a word, the sharp discipline this brought discouraging anymore. Taking turns, it seemed all her groaning and suffering was simply ignored, her body used like some piece of prized meat; Julie's howls echoing around the room, she was reminded she was here because she'd broken the rules, and "To be quiet and take her learning!"

The intendants even talked over her, talked as she struggled, about matter of fact issues in their daily lives, as if she wasn't even there. Talked over her, not to her, a tactic designed to make her feel less than, a tactic they'd all come to learn was the way of the Manor, a tactic that worked.

Eventually, with Julie almost catatonic with exhaustion, the wheels of the gurney could be heard trundling up the east wing, trundling past the stairs and on to the west, the women in Julie's room treated to a fearful sight as they all froze when she rolled in.

No resistance and only slight moaning could be

heard as she was lifted almost caringly by her intendants, their respect quickly hidden as they realized it showed, and they used the leather straps still attached from the horse to secure Julie face-down to her bed, the ties wrapped round her steel headrest and tied over on themselves.

Exiting the room again, the intendants didn't look back, closing the door behind them, but the rest of the women did. Looked on wide-eyed at Julie, the woman lying face down, exhausted and almost asleep already. Emerging from under her straight jacket, all different shades of punishment covered her ass, each of the women being shown what talking got you as the lights were left on all the longer so that they could see. Lights finally dropping, not a sound was heard that night or many others, Julie's learning teaching them that the dorm rules would be obeyed.

Over the weeks in the Manor, the change in the women could be seen clearly as words uttered during corrections became a thing of the past, no reply ever given verbally. Instead, these wayward protestations were simply met with sharper spanks or heavier drops, the women made to feel less than, made to feel beneath the intendants…. The feeling soon becoming part of daily life… soon becoming reality….

Submission becoming real….

Chapter 6

Miss Goodspank

"Miss Goodspank! Again," she instructed from the front of the room.

"Yes, Miss Goodspank." The reply came back from all the women sitting chained to their desks.

The morning had gone well, the routine over the last four days becoming familiar already. It began at seven each morning, the women gently woken by music filtered softly to their rooms, already having been instructed by the intendants what was expected and to be enforced.

At seven, they were expected to rise and stay quiet; no talking was permitted, most women finding this difficult and unnatural, but helped to obey by the nightly examples of this rule-breaking still being present in the morning and restrained to their beds. Left restrained as, at five past seven, an intendant would arrive sharply, the women to remain still as she walked the line, her sharp booted footsteps broken by pauses at each bed. The sound of gentle steel being uncuffed heralded the freeing of each woman, their nightly jewelry carried off with the intendant as she left. On her leaving, the women rose, with glancing smiles and darting eyes watched over carefully by the intendants, their behavior monitored from the room at the end of their wing. Monitored for signs of friendship, signs of camaraderie between slaves, notes made and quickly written down, filed into reports for the Mistress to see later.

This, of course, was part of a larger strategy for achieving the best results from each woman, for the Manor itself was not just some dungeon that used force to achieve what was desired. No – any fool could affect change by using brute force and fear, but that result would be found temporary, the slaves' natural wills returning, their behavior following their desire once this pressure was removed.

The slaves brought here were expected to return with much more than this amateur effect, the Manor's reputation outstanding in this area and justifying the high price paid by their owners.

How, then, was this achieved? Step one was, of course, dominance shown to the women over the first few days, the skill of pressure and release of guidance and escape bringing submission and acceptance, but this was only the beginning. The human mind eventually becomes used to any pressure, and as such, with the pressure handled, then begins to have free time to think and find interests, desires for the future, and so there lie's the key… desire.

Just as in any modern society, the people are controlled by having the majority of their energy taken from them by toil. By this labor, they tire, and any questioning of its importance or their happiness is sporadic, the daily weight on their backs from the pressures of life keeping any these thoughts at a minimum. The slave is not pushed too hard, so it does not drop the weight from its back, this holding it down over eight hours, the human mind only capable of so much processing. So involved with the toil and with no more processing power left, the happiness of the soul, or work's effect on its life, is not considered over time, the mind being involved with the weight on its back.

Unnoticed by most, as they do not realize that they spend most of their waking life at their work, and if they therefore hate their work, then they spend most of their life hating their life!

This, though, changes at the end of said day, the weight lifted from their backs, the slaves returning home, heralding a very dangerous time for society – their minds able to think with that time. This time, then, must be taken away, but not by force, for resistance would surely result, but by stealth from within, the slave believing that they made the choices themselves. Choices to use their free time in the manner that THEY chose and in the manner that fulfilled THEIR DESIRES.

Desires provided by televisions, radios, magazines, and cell phones, the Masters and Mistresses of this world having their will pumped directly into the homes and hands of their slaves, their choices – though their own – based on the options provided by their jailers, their prison unseen all around them.

So, too, the Manor operated with such sophistication; with authority accepted, the women were then monitored, their secret looks at each other recorded, reports made and analyzed over the course of each day. Unnoticed behind the scenes, the intendants devised strategies based on requests made by owners and the personalities of each slave. For a single rigid procedure would not work for all, as some were naturally more submissive, some wayward, and still others unsure. With each strategy, progress reports on successes or failures were submitted regularly to the Mistress, her will and direction ever present in the

Manor and reaching down from her office unseen behind the curtains.

Each morning, hands were left alone as the women were uncuffed, each having learned to quickly make their beds, this procedure getting quicker. Trimming the covers with their fingers and stepping back, facing the wall, their last step going down on all fours at the right side of their footrests. Hands palms down felt cold morning floors, nipples waking too, heads bowed to boards while asses were up behind them and presented like their beds.

Eventually, their group of four intendants would arrive after watching the efforts from the monitoring room at the end of the wing. The multiple booted footsteps felt more menacing than the first, seeming to move in unison and aloud, the women's perspective now in line and their heads bowed to the floor, leaving their ears low to the heels.

They struck toward them, a threatening feeling as if a gang of punishment was moving in the sharp tap of the last heels stopping at their beds, leaving the women feeling vulnerable as they stayed bent over naked beneath them. They could only hope fault was not found, the intendants inspecting their efforts closely each morning, looking for the slightest crease or misattention, this taken extremely seriously.

Serious, as it was believed that perfect form started from the moment a slave rose. If this form was not found in their efforts of personal house keeping, then who knew how bad it would get as the day wore on, these haphazard and truly unacceptable virtues of laziness not to be tolerated.

Indeed, it was for the slaves' own good that these

seemingly harsh levels of strictness were imposed, for without them, the cascading negative effects on their behavior could bring all sorts of lacking in attention throughout the day, and in this house, that simply wouldn't do.

With this in mind, the women tried, but knew that someone would be chosen. Only days into it, they knew the routine, and they knew no matter how well the beds were made, the intendants always seemed to find something, almost as if the least best was chosen, even though they were all just as good as each other. To be chosen meant punishment, or as the house staff called it, correction. It meant all the women now stood up and turned around, getting to watch. Looking on from the foot of their beds, watching as two intendants knelt down with the slave still bent on all fours, not risen like the others. As each intendant took hold of a wrist with their outer hands, they knelt down, facing the wall, their inner hands going under the slave's arm from behind, following up and toward their head, wrapping around the back of her neck and holding her down. The slave herself had the instant feeling of being trapped, the silken stockings of the intendants brushing up against her sides, doing nothing to excite her, but moreover just to frighten her. Watching, the room bore witness to the third intendant bending to a kneeling position at her midriff, securing her with her left thigh pushed underneath her stomach, the intendant facing back into the center of the room, her right leg kneeling on the floor and facing back. Her left hand completed the securing, passing over the back, wrapping around the waist while her other naturally took the remaining side, the slave squeezed firmly and feeling further trapped underneath them.

Presented, though, she was, her ass hoisted still further into the air with the third intendant's thigh underneath, making sure of it as she was held open for all to see. Secured and embarrassed, the slave got to listen as her final humiliation moved in behind her, the sharp booted footfalls of the fourth intendant bringing with her the long black strap-on secured to her front.

It was almost a relief when the intendant knelt down behind her, the shame of her ass displayed for the room's viewing briefly hidden, but only to be replaced with more as she felt the blunt rubber firmly push her resistance aside, the women getting to listen to her struggles as she was dealt with on the floor.

Listening on, the room watched in silence, the pre-lubed strap leaving silken walls, the slave's resistance now all but useless, her groans echoing around the audience. Watching, they bore witness to the gorgeous thighs and ass of the fourth intendant clenching hard, the thrusting starting to quicken, forcing deep inside with purpose.

Shock filled the room at the perceived violence, the women, though free of any restraint, held firmly by what they were watching, the sounds of struggle filling the air as the thrusting continued on, a scene of gorgeous corseted restraint and powerful stockinged thighs struggling to hold their captive as they administered their morning's correction.

Her yelping and increased struggles only tightened the intendants' grip, her complaint giving way to groaning as the inevitable began to happen. Silken stockings stroking her sides with mouth-watering thighs under and around her, the commanding hands becoming welcome as her moistening became apparent.

Soon, too, wetness around the room as the women began to arouse, shock giving way to want as jealousy began to take hold. Watching on, some bit their lips as thighs clenched down in front, giving out at what they were seeing, giving her what they now wanted.

A sharp spank rang out, the third intendant holding her ass up with her thigh and securing her with her left hand, suddenly striking with her free right, it returning gently to her waist, the groan let out signaling she was heard and her instruction sharply followed. For enjoyment was not the prize, nor wanted by intendants here who were carefully monitoring for this behavior, the slave's groans brought back to struggle now. Thrusting harder, she cried out under them, her learners smiling, the women watching, lush beneath with what they witnessed, moistening further as they learned with her.

With the third's spanks and the fourth's now punishing thrusting, the slave was held exactly where they wanted her, in punished ecstasy, the slave unsure of what to do as that feeling began to well up inside her, her moans becoming involuntary, bringing spanks and thrusting as she let out her screaming struggles, her body wrenching among the intendants as they gave her what she needed! The sound of the orgasm shattered the room, the women stunned by the noise as the fourth kept thrusting, the screaming echoing off the walls as the third had to help hold down the slave, not able to spank with the violence of her body's lurching. Screaming not giving way, and the body's shocked convulsing didn't stop the fourth's thrusting lesson being driven home, the slave letting out pitiful noises, her submission total and the sounds signaling the lesson learned, the fourth beginning to slowly curb her harshness. Screaming giving way to groaning, the slave's shocked body seemed to regulate her noises, the women wide-eyed as they watched the punishment slowly wind down, the smell of good learning filling the room, unnoticed before.

With the thrusting now rhythmic and down to a gentle tempo, the slave's body offered little resistance, willingly accepting the length going in and out as the third relaxed her grip, still holding her up on her thigh but beginning to stroke her ass, a smile breaking out on her face, seemingly happy with the performance below her.

For the first time, the women bore witness to the intendants' stony trained looks relaxing, the third looking up at the fourth, still thrusting, a gentle smile being exchanged, both pleased by what they were seeing beneath them.

Soon, retraction, and a groan let out which filled the room, an honest groan, a groan of exhaustion but pleasure, the women feeling jealous as the slave continued to kneel, the first two intendants holding her arms and now bearing her full weight as she relaxed into them, her body happily shattered by the experience. As the fourth stood up, her black strap glistened with the slave's good learning, the women salivating as they watched it paraded through them, the third still crouched, reaching around to the left of her own waist, to the pouches on her garter belt.

Throughout the days, slaves would see intendants reach for these pouches, much like police, and these pouches – sometimes two or three on either side – held accessories, things ready to hand to deal with unruly slaves. From the black-heeled boots to the powerful stockinged thighs, the black garter held a length of black leather strap on the left side and a black cane on the right, and sat tight round the waist over black panties underneath. Around the waist, its small pouches almost hidden under the corsets, it went almost unnoticed next to the black leather embossed splendor that constituted the house uniform. Their contents, though, always made the slaves nervous whenever a hand started to reach back for them, as what was produced was never a certainty, ever, different intendants having different beliefs on procedure, their experiences dictating their treatments given.

This time, the third produced a silver collar and, as she retracted her left thigh from underneath her charge, the first and second tightened their grips, a wave of nervousness passing through the slave. Nervous, as she felt the third move in on her, now completely kneeled and over her back, swiveling around and over top of her. Watching from behind, the women viewed the gorgeous Latin ass cheeks of the intendant pushing up toward them, straining her panties as she leaned forward to fix the collar.

The collar opened around the nervous charge, her worried struggle easily held down by her captors, the third bringing her confinement expertly forth. Finishing with ease, a small silver padlock was effortlessly reached for from the same garter pouch, the practice obvious as it was snapped into place and left dangling from the slave's neck like some jewelry swinging below. Still held down, curious eyes watched more as the third bent over, holding the collar with her left hand

and reaching around her own waist with her right, the women's eyes drawn across her gorgeous curved cheeks as they pushed back toward them. Again, the black panties strained to hold in powerful toned muscle within, the intendant reaching for her garter belt, her hand reaching into a pouch on the right side this time. Salivating at the sight, the women almost missed it as a rolled black leash with a silver holding snap was produced and taken toward the slave's neck, the room easily hearing the metal snap through the awed silence. Still watching the kneeling powerful stockinged thighs in front, they clenched back with the left leg raising. A black-heeled boot connected sharply with the floor in front, the right leg still kneeling and leaving her ass now fully curved out toward them. Black panties straining at their limits, the first and second released their grip now, the third rising to her feet in front of them, choreographed grace shown to eyes behind. Slave secure and in her hand now, leashed by the neck, she daren't move.

It was now that the first, second, and third intendants moved in unison, the first and second moving to the front of the room near the door, ordering the slaves to form one single line behind them, the third bringing the leashed slave half-way up the right of the line on her knees. Behind them, still at the end of the line, the fourth intendant bearing the glistening black strap-on finished the procession, the nervous women acutely aware of what could happen if discipline was not maintained. When all was ready, the first opened the door before moving through, the rest following, the whole line moving up through the second level west corridor, the leashed slave kept half-way up on their right and forced to crawl on her hands and knees, her shame displayed for all to see, leashed up the staircase with them to the main hallway above.

Continuing through the main hallway, the women moved in line down the west wing of the ground floor, passing doors and the occasional intendant coming the other way before following the first through the large double doorway at the very end of the wing to what was the main house's dining area. This was a large room that followed a circular curve, jutting out into the grounds at this end of the manor that could be seen through their large bay windows, wall to wall at the back of the room. Seen but not accessed, for there was no way through them, the windows unable to be opened and with no doorways to the outside, leaving the feeling of imprisonment in the room, though following the ornate French feel of the ground and first levels, and clearly secure. Inside the room, four sets of ten wooden chairs were arranged, five against each other to either side of four huge rectangular tables, greeting them horizontally as they entered so that those seated would face one another, and were in a rectangular formation, two sets bolted to the ground nearer the windows from left to right, and two sets nearer the doorway, only the seating able to move. There was no arrangement of which group of ten women would arrive first; instead, this depended on the level of punishment each group's morning's example would receive after their inspection, and how long it took her to receive it. This process was never rushed, and the women, at times, watching from the feet of their beds each morning, may sometimes have wished it was them being dealt with, but there were other times when they certainly didn't.

It was the range of punishments employed, and truly all slaves might enjoy the morning's attention from one of the mouth-watering intendants, but a strapping? Being held down over an intendant's knee, each strike of the strap snapping off the silent walls while the other women watched you struggle? To be then led on your knees, collared and leashed, not only alongside your own group, but through the hallways, your striped ass paraded for all passing to see, and on into the main dining area where other groups were sometimes seated before you, and would watch as you were led in on all fours. It didn't end there, for in the center of the room, at the top of the first set of two tables and at the bottom of the second set of two tables, there lay four steel half circle securing mounts jutting out from the floor. As each group of slaves was seated, one seat in that group's table of ten would remain empty, and that group's morning example would be led, leashed on her knees, and head down if she knew what was good for her. Secured by her neck collar by way of a padlocked fastening to the steel circle in the floor, she was finally ball-gagged by her intendant, another implement of black and leather which was carried by all house intendants in those garter pouches around their waists.

By this time, the morning routine was known well, and after the snap of the fastening and gagging, there was the point of the intendant's finger to the floor in front of them, meaning "Head down and remain still;" though now unnecessary, it was still given, routine making for good learning. The only saving grace for any example was for their group to arrive first, it being slightly less embarrassing to be led and secured down in a room with only their group present, rather than three tables worth of unfamiliar audience watching you be led in and humiliated. The last to arrive, obviously, was the most disobedient, her punishment having taken the longest, and usually displayed on her cheeks, all the women able to see and encouraged to do so.

When finally the room was at rest, all four examples secured on their knees by the neck with their hands bound behind them and ankles secured with leather short ties, the intendants would leave. The intendants in the room having secured the morning's discipline would leave to plan the day ahead, the final two staying on each side of the main door as they did so, keeping watch as still more of their corseted sisters were sent for, for breakfast. Sent with the morning meal, a breakfast of all house fair including cereal, eggs, cheese, meats, toast, and a selection of milk, water, and fruit juices, very like that served in a hotel, all brought in on four separate wheeled breakfast trolleys. Rectangular in form and dressed with fine white table cloths, with stainless steel platters and fine crockery on top, they were wheeled in to the outside of each table, the intendants serving and deciding who got what. A strange condition for the women, to see the intendants work, but it was necessary; no guests under their care ever seeing any other type of person in the Manor but the Mistress, the intendants, and slaves… it was to normalize it in them.

The policy also allowed, although the women would never guess it, for the strict monitoring and control of protein intake, a lesson from cults around the world who kept protein intake to a minimum. This had a deteriorating effect on the human brain, which began to function poorly without protein, thoughts able to be led and behavior controlled more easily in this condition. Although not dangerous if controlled properly, protein monitoring was questionable, so the intendants were sworn to secrecy regarding that and many other house procedures. Deciding, too, for the examples, their group of four fastened down alongside each other, arranged like the tables now surrounding them, facing inwards to the center of the room. The women, starving as the smell of food came, could feel pity for the four below served last…but made to wait.

Their final humiliation of the morning was to have their breakfasts mixed together and served to them in stainless steel bowls placed in front of their heads, as if they were animals, their gagged mouths salivating uncontrollably over the leather balls gagging their mouths preventing them from eating their meals just below…they were to eat last once all else had finished.

With breakfast served, the intendants retreated, no one daring to eat until all four trolleys had exited and the last two intendants guarding the inside of the door announced they may begin, and had thirty minutes to finish, before exiting, the double doors closing behind them, the sound of heavy locking sealing them in.

Freedom! The women all smiled, taking cutlery and greeting ravenously the food and each other. They had realized over the days that, although in house, silence was the rule, there were certain places and times where these restrictions were lifted. At breakfast and showers, and at evening meals and in medical settings, talking seemed to be permitted; so, too, in the grounds, though this was more to do with their not being able to be monitored well electronically, but it did, though, make the women love being taken outside.

It was, of course, monitored by the all-seeing cameras in the corners of most of the rooms, the women aware of that with looking up, but unaware of cameras they didn't see hidden in this place and that. They were never told of these permissions, instead left to figure it out, this done to foster an air of mystery in the house around them, to allow the natural female mind with its inquisitive nature to have rise to use these abilities. The restrictive nature of the house in regard to verbal communication was not simply brought in with barbaric form, but instead used to give good training and form, etiquette needed by slaves in futures when they would leave the Manor, it proceeding thusly…

: With the slaves knowing they were watched at most times, they would learn not to speak for fear of reprisals.

: To avoid this punishment, they would learn obedient censorship.

(Only speaking when spoken to)

This in-house constant monitoring was not done to give rise to paranoia, but was felt and seen in years of house training, to learn and bring forth the best in slave behavior. Indeed, those who knew of the house's existence commented favorably and heaped praise by mail, thanking the Manor's staff for their own slave's good turn-around upon their release back to them. Others, by way of conversation between Mistresses, passed praise on their slaves at the gatherings each year, their general impression of such good behavior by their slaves quickly generating the Manor's reputation as the premier learning institution for women. At the gatherings, it was clear that slaves that had been through the Manor's program were vastly superior in form and behavior to those who hadn't.

The house, though, was not a dungeon that brutalized women; they didn't want psychologically damaged women leaving them, as this would not be good for the Manor's reputation, nor good slave-keeping in general. True domination, it was believed, was only achieved if a slave wished to be dominated, therefore truly giving themselves forward. With this in mind, it would not do to restrict the women from communicating completely in-house, as this would indeed harm them, so restriction was employed to teach discipline, obedience to rules, and of course… waiting.

Waiting was an essential element for any slave to learn; many times in their lives, they would be secured or gagged, left immobile for long periods of time, and they would have to learn to patiently wait… waiting.

To facilitate this learning, it was necessary to learn the women waiting as a learned form, a state of being that they should pride themselves in being able to carry out, to show anyone observing just how good a slave they could be, and how well trained they were. One surefire method of learning this holding technique, or waiting, to a slave was to restrict speech.

There did, though, have to be times when the house slaves were allowed to talk, this promoting good psychological well-being and group strength for the purposes of house training, and allowing the ever-watching intendants to watch the house gossip on cameras, not only for amusement but to continue the women's programs in the correct directions wanted by their owners.

The enforced treatment of the morning examples also added discipline to the women, and eventually over the coming weeks, the women got used to the humiliations, and truly didn't mind them, growing confident as slaves, but what they did mind was not being able to talk during these confinements. With there only being very limited points throughout each day where they could converse with other women, the removal of these times was dreaded. Therefore, it promoted hard work by each slave not to be the one singled out like the four unfortunate souls on the dining room floor, and so ensured a constant attempt to do their utmost in-house. It led to a competitive atmosphere against each other, good behavior competing with good behavior, therefore bringing out the best form in all. In effect, it was similar to how western women in the modern world maintain control over younger men. By there only being a select number of physical companions for them, the women can demand standards of behavior, dress, and form, and for those failing to come up to those standards, they would be denied what they truly wanted, just like the women on the floor, and therefore would compete hard, believing their battles were against each other, too busy trying to attain their desires to see who was truly the source of their suffering.

Conversation flowed freely, Jennifer meeting Samantha and talking about her now infamous introduction to the house, over the box, and Andrea, who she'd been dying to ask a question.

"Oh, you mean my Jewelry?" laughed Andrea, Jennifer frowning with a smile at her laughter over it. "That's part of my Mistress's insistence," she explained. "She believes the only reason my little emerald should leave my ass is if her love is replacing it," she giggled.

Jennifer smiled on with the others as they laughed over the talk, all having wondered why this bubbly little Irish woman was allowed her anal jewelry, it evident and protruding from her ass in the mornings. A small stainless steel butt plug, not over-large to allow comfort, she had it always unless the intendants removed it on occasion, as they needed to in learning her. It was beautiful, having an emerald finish on its rounded bulb end, which sat beautifully deep between Andrea's cheeks, visible to any directly behind her. At times, Mistresses, on delivering their beloveds to the Manor, would have certain conditions and requests for their charges to enroll with them, and as long as they didn't interfere with the Manor's program, these would be honored throughout their treatment.

Smiling on, the women laughed, getting to know one another, the jewelry question now answered among them.

A loud sound of heavy keys in the double door locks brought conversation instantly to an end, all cutlery being placed down in front of them, bringing the women to look straight ahead at each other before the doors swung open upon them. The first two intendants entering pushed the doors gently and all the way to the wall before taking their places, standing one in front of each of them, their hands clasped behind their backs and their legs slightly open, their gorgeous corseted forms looking straight into the room. One at a time, the four intendant groups responsible for each dorm would enter the room, proceeding two along two, their four women box connecting its heels sharply and in time as they crossed the floor. At the foot of their group's table, in the middle of the room, two would stop while the other two moved on and up, one stopping half-way while the other proceeded to the head of the table, all ending facing the women still seated.

"Rise," was all they had to say, the women immediately obeying and moving down, with the intendants forming a single line facing the bottom of the room, to the door the intendants had entered through. Line established, the bottom two intendants turned in calm control to face the double doors while the outside intendant turned to do the same, the last at the rear already facing that way before the whole group, almost in unison, followed the leading two intendants, their feet lifting almost at the same time as their boots. And so it went on, each group retrieved by their dorm leaders and taken out, two at a time, the two remaining having to wait as the other two were escorted to one of the two rooms on the left of the west corridor, which were the shower rooms. Inside both doors, the two rooms were identical, and on entry the women were brought to a halt in line, the rooms having a long rectangular chamber, each split by a central wall in the middle. On the left and right sides of the center wall, large beech-colored modern wooden lockers covered the walls from floor to ceiling, one on top the other, their rectangular doors following the wall from the doorway to the left and right, along the entry walls for ten feet or so, and then up both sides of the room another thirty feet before turning inwards toward the central dividing wall, for two more lockers' length. This then left two entrances to the main shower room, which had the same rectangular form with beech-colored square floor tiles throughout, like the first now covering the walls, as well, with shower heads on the back side of the center wall in front of them, flanked by thirty feet of shower heads running the length of the room on both sides, on to the end walls' left and right, their own length of shower heads; completing the room, a small push-operated gel dispenser below each one for the women's convenience. On entry through the left and right doorways, the women met each other freely, seeing as the rooms were connected at the back passage to each locker room, and they became aware of other openings in the left wall and the right, its same wrap-around floor to ceiling beech tiles leading to other smaller rectangular spaces running the length of the shower chamber on both sides, along and behind its walls about half the size of the shower room on each side, and housing individual cubicles, their polished white doorways housing their brilliant white porcelain necessities within, and matching the white ceilings above throughout. Each day, when the lines were stopped in front of the center wall, the lead two intendants would move through the left and right entrances, checking the facilities before taking position back at the head of the lockers on each side of the dividing wall. Once order was good and the groups were still, one of the intendants at the front of the first group who'd entered would raise her arms, palm out, in a gesture toward the showers, and announce firmly "Twenty minutes." Calmly, the women would file in obediently, the water running as the intendants left them alone with their second chance to talk.

From here, again, the women had a short span of free time, able to move and talk quietly and do what they must while exchanging stories and pleasantries, not just within their own group, but with whoever of the other three groups happened to be showering with them that morning, each group seeming, though not enforced, to stay on their side of the shower room.

During this time, the intendants where not idle, the other two groups having been brought clear of the dining room and waiting silently in line, under guard in the wing. As they waited for their turns in the showers, the free intendants had moved to the dining room behind them, leaving the doors open so that they could listen as they waited for the showers, listening to the correction inside. Further pressure was necessary, as it was intentional to make sure they understood the price of waywardness when considering house keeping each morning, when they rose from their beds. As if to convince them of the necessity of this fine undertaking, they were treated to the final indignities of the examples still held within. Still secured to the floor, they stayed as still as they could be, obediently on all fours and aware from previous times what happened if they did not. Like before, and each morning, each groups' intendants who were not dealing with showers took a special interest in their own group's example while other free intendants filled in for any of their own group not there… all intendants being interchangeable, and accountable to do anything necessary. The lead intendants would again kneel at each example's head, taking her wrists with their outer hands and passing their other hands in behind her arms, around and up over her shoulders to the back of the neck, where they'd clasp firmly. Another intendant would then take a position on her left or right thigh, depending on what side of the group of four she was on, passing under the slacker's stomach and holding her ass up. Her hands, though, this time did not wrap firmly around her waist, but wrapped further around and under taking the slave's upper thighs keeping them firmly in their grasp, the slave's ass now pitifully exposed to the fourth intendant standing behind them… a warning.

After all was ready, the fourth intendant would step forward and busy themselves with removing the ball gags from each slave, the rush of fresh air to their mouths short-lived, as with the fourth taking position standing behind them again, the first two immediately pushed the slaves' heads down into the bowls. Made to eat like an animal, she obeyed, obeyed the directions forced on her head by the first two's hands on her neck, they deciding where and when from each area of the bowl she would eat, as behind her, the fourth stood guard, the reason for the women's obedience. They had learned by now that, as she put away the ball gag in her garter pouch, she would immediately then take the black strap of leather from her left hip, carried there as with all intendants, and be standing ready to deal with the slightest sign of insolence. This was, of course, extremely humiliating, many women openly crying at the first and even second times they were put through this, bringing the strap behind them to come firmly across their buttocks, their yelping scream snuffing out anymore resistance and making sure none of the others did the same.

It was harsh, even cruel, but it brought results; the bed covers in each dorm were always made perfect and the Manor was all about results…..

This humiliation ended with harsh words after breakfast, the four examples then split to two and taken to the showers by the arms of the first intendants who had fed them. Roughly pushed inside the entrances to either side of the dividing wall, the intendants would inform them, menacingly pointing and shouting, “Ten minutes!” The four women would meet in the shower room, sometimes still crying from their ordeal.

Cruel? Yes. Effective? Yes, as no one wanted to be them the next morning, and each woman worked hard to avoid it. With the women in the shower room now knowing they had ten minutes, they did their best to support one another, later coming to vow as the day went on not to be back the next morning….

“Time!” the authority-laden Latino voice resonated through the shower room, the women already having left the showers and dried from the towels in the lockers, forming into two lines as the intendants entered to take them back to their groups. And so each group was taken, one at a time, their four intendants moving with two at the front, one at the side, and one following at the rear, leading them up the west wing to the main hallway before passing behind the main staircase and on into the main ballroom. Inside, they were arranged in their quarter of the circle that was formed by all house slaves each morning in front of the intendants, who stood lightly behind them, themselves arranged evenly around their circle. The large presence of leather corsets being the full house compliment, but for the medical staff, gave a feeling of unrest, their captors able to reach out with their enforcement quickly if required.

Soon, the Mistress would enter, flanked by two intendants, one to each side of her, Jennifer recognizing the two of them from her office when she'd first arrived, sweeping into the room with an air of total command. Taking her position in the center of the room, the Mistress ignored all around her as she conferred quietly with the two around her, each discussing and advising, some occasionally producing pieces of paper, the Mistress's eyes widening at times with what she was hearing.

A short time later, the Mistress would share her feelings over the progress, or lack of it, on certain subjects, with no slaves being referred to by name, but displeasure would occasionally be directed at certain groups within the four. This then was a warning, and a chance, the only one the offending group would get to improve on whatever area the Mistress believed was lacking before outright punishments would begin. She seemed heavily focused on house cleaning; in her own belief, if slaves were lacking in their attention to that, they could hardly impress an owner outside of the Manor, and of course their lack of diligence and hard work in this area would look bad for the Manor's training, reputation, and ultimately the Mistress herself… this wouldn't do.

In line with this, and if warnings were not heeded, a lacking continuing, there were mornings when they arrived second in the ballroom, a guest arriving before them and never welcome in their eyes… the box. Its black leather torture waited for the Mistress, each slave of the offending group knowing full well that any one of them could soon feel the soft leather restraints tying them over it, their screams around the room serving to warn all that laziness would not be tolerated.

Sometimes, it wasn't even the offending one in the group who was chosen, innocent hard working members sometimes chosen instead, this of course done to instill fear in the group, and to ensure that even the group members not found lacking would work hard to try and encourage the others throughout the day, for fear of being chosen in the morning. The screams from the box, of an innocent, were always worse; the women could hear the feeling of injustice in their anguish, most crying quickly for the undeserving punishment. They were taught that it was the cruelest thing of all for a slave to be simply punished without being given a reason, for there was no basis for the slave to think against, no understanding or reasoning throughout the procedure, and certainly no feeling of deserving or fairness. If, then, that was the cruelest thing, then being punished for something you hadn't done had to come second, the uncontrollable crying when removed from the box after this leaving no doubt of that. Each time it happened, the women were left appalled, their comfortable rhythm emerging in house life shattered as they were reminded of their place by the whimpering forms, half carried from the box by intendants from their groups, and struck further in line if their protestations were too loud – a certain level of decorum in suffering now expected, the days of first arrival leniency now gone.

After each time this horror was witnessed, all slaves unsurprisingly worked extremely hard, but this would always tail off in laziness, an unfortunate characteristic of women, or so they were taught. In the

Academy, they were learned that the high levels of estrogen and the tendency for reliance on their advance communication abilities to get through life promoted this unfortunate circumstance, and was why discipline was necessary for slaves.

Outside these terror-filled mornings, most mornings' attendances in the ballroom passed without incident, the day's assignments to each group announced and any special conditions revealed, along with the occasional decree… which would be obeyed.

This particular morning, Jennifer's group had been assigned to the Academy again, where slaves were taught learning and etiquette, which was actually quite fun as compared to their first time in class. That time, they had been left aware of their legal obligations, and in no uncertain terms shown their actual legal contracts, under which they now were conscripted, having signed them on entry.

That had been a hard and boring morning, and at times quite shocking, when after being shackled to their desks by their left ankles, with the same nightly jewelry they were held in at dark, they were left by their intendants to the care of Miss Goodspank.

Miss Goodspank, as she insisted on being addressed, was an ex-lawyer from Canada who taught the class. Miss Goodspank had a soft caring face, and a similar demeanor to her soft voice, being in her forties with a long middle-aged teacher's haircut, which flowed dark blond to just beneath her shoulders. After introducing herself and instructing the class in how to address her, the two amply spaced rows of ten desks spread horizontally across the room, five behind five, got to view her shapely form hinted at from under her teacher's-style tan knee-length skirt and white blouse, showing that forty was no obstacle to a shapely figure. Her soft perfume, mixed with the fabric of her clothes, passed with her light blue soft silk neck scarf as she moved between each row of the two desks, one behind the other, as she placed a five page copy of a document neatly in the center of each desk, her practiced legal hand a shadow from her past. On completion, her soft low-heeled tan shoes made sounds far softer on the laminate floor than the intendants' sharp-booted footfalls as she made her way to her commanding large desk, of a wooden and aptly maple. At the front of the class, its four sturdy legs housing a broad top with a drawer at the rear, but leaving a clear view underneath to the seated Miss Goodspank, who sat affront a large clear white board. Behind her, it meant her head was just in the middle and at the bottom of it, the women having to attempt to look through her when reading their instructions in class. Around the room, the now familiar cream walls and ornate cornicing persisted, and looked lovely in the streaming sunlight as it entered from the left through the four large windows, the rear grounds outside in view.

In soft Canadian assertiveness, Miss Goodspank seated a pair of neat reading glasses upon her nose and instructed that the document in front of them was a copy of what they had signed on entry, or been tricked into signing in her case, Jennifer thought. Miss Goodspank explained that it was in fact a legal contract witnessed by two lawyers, their signatures there, and one doctor, the Mistress, which in effect meant that they had been judged mentally unfit and had been legally committed or sectioned under the mental health act to the care of the Manor.

It left the readers scared, laying down in no uncertain terms that they were in fact confined. What was more alarming was that they would continue to be confined until judged well by the facility's staff, and that their care had been entrusted to them.

On reading this, the feeling of their cool steel ankle chains securing them to their desks no longer had any sexual connotation to them, and felt more and more threatening as Miss Goodspank read through the contract with them. On page three, the chains felt even tighter as the contract confirmed in legal terms that they had agreed to the facility's behavioral therapies, and that the house staff were in fact exempt from any responsibility for the implementation and results of said therapies; in effect, the intendants could do what they wanted!

As the reading continued, eyes widened as the gravity of their situation sunk in, audible gasps being heard at times in the room as the pages were turned, occasionally drawing Miss Goodspank's eye. As she continued, line by line, her legal training seemed to kick in, her eye soon noticing a lack of attention in one of the women, this being offensive to her legal persona, as she gave her time to address this before suddenly calling, "Linda!" The shriek was sudden, the women all sitting bolt upright with the word, their attention caught on what a second ago had been a calm soft little woman and who was now a glaring source of anger behind her glasses. "Would you like to tell me what I've just said?"

No answer.

"Linda….." the voice growled.

Linda looked around, a little embarrassed at being singled out, a small smile appearing and quickly disappearing as she realized its offering wouldn't do any good.

"Right!" the voice was curt, Miss Goodspank rising quickly and opening her desk drawer behind her, and coming around the left side of it with a pair of silver handcuffs, and a set of matching keys, her stony face now shrewd. Marching straight over to Linda at the back right desk nearest the window, she didn't even look at her as she came around her desk, between her and the window, taking her left hand behind her. The women watched as she roughly grabbed her other arm by the bicep, slipping her hand down its length to the wrist, the sharp sound of snapping handcuffs leaving the women's impressions of a soft docile lady in tatters.

"Well," she uttered as she began kneeling down to Linda's ankle chain with the set of keys she'd brought. "It seems someone isn't paying attention and I am not going through this contract twice," she assured them, unlocking Linda. "Come this way," she instructed, grabbing Linda by her secured cuffed left arm and maneuvering her as a doorman would move a troublemaker. For Linda's part, she was embarrassed and surprised, the two emotions etched on her face as they all watched this previously nice and warm teacher push Linda across the class in front of them before spinning her around to have her standing against the right side of her desk, facing the window. An embarrassed Linda sent a look across the faces in front of her, now her audience, before turning away sheepishly as Miss Goodspank brought her hand back from her desk drawer with lengths of leather cord in her hand… short ties.

“Spread your legs,” she ordered from behind Linda as she bent down, her teacher’s skirt straining to hold her curves as she balanced on her heels. “Spread them!” A sharp slap to the back of Linda’s calf bringing a shuffling as she spread them apart. Her audience watched as Miss Goodspank effortlessly secured both her ankles, one to each leg of the desk with the leather ties, before rising and firmly pushing Linda, still handcuffed, over the desk.

“Stay still!” She ordered, her voice obviously irritated as she reached into her desk drawer once more for a black rectangular paddle, produced in front of Linda’s widening eyes. “Face forward!” she ordered with a sharp spank on Linda’s ass encouraging this as shock now descended on the class. “When I speak, you listen!” She shouted, the first snap of the paddle landing across Linda’s buttocks.

“Yes, Mistress!” A shocked Linda shouted out.

“Silence!!!” A resounding snap echoed around the class as it seared across both Linda’s cheeks. “In this class, you do not speak unless asked for an answer!” Miss Goodspank half-shrieked, clearly appalled at such insolence. “And my name is Miss Goodspank; what is my name?” She demanded as another searing sting landed across Linda’s cheeks, interrupting her answer.

“What!!!?” Miss Goodspank demanded, having only gotten half an answer.

“Miss Goodspank!!!” Linda forced out completely as the leather stung her ass, making her scream as she caught her breath and involuntarily tried to rise up off the desk.

“Down!” Miss Goodspank roughly pushed Linda

back down, interrupting her paddling for a moment, though not for long. A shocked audience got to watch a soft calming woman turn into an angry rage in front of them, a screaming Linda's ass beginning to redden, the paddling relentless, snap by snap bringing Linda to call out louder and louder, the strikes expert and painful. Stopping only for an instant, Miss Goodspank began to aim and strike down and sideways, just catching the skin with the paddle as it passed each cheek, making the sting that much more painful, Linda growing louder with each strike, her cheeks reddening before the class.

"Such noise!!!" exclaimed Miss Goodspank at Linda's struggles. "That simply won't do in class!" She exclaimed, removing her light scarf from around her neck and bending over Linda, stuffing it into her mouth! Gagging, Linda half-shrieked through the cotton.

"Don't you dare spit that out!!!" Miss Goodspank shrieked from behind her, still bent over her and forcing it further into her panicked mouth. Satisfied she was muffled, she straightened, and they watched her rise up and continue to paddle Linda, who was groaning through the silk, biting down, not daring to spit it out. Groaning continuing, a shocked Linda had her ass reddened all the more, a lesson for the rest of the class that in these lessons the teacher would have respect!

After what could only be described as a sound punishment, a tearful Linda was left tied to the desk, bent over and gagged as Miss GoodSpank retook her seat, Linda spread face-down over her desk in front of her. Taking the contract back up, all eyes gave her their full attention as Miss Goodspank cleared her throat, a crying groan from Linda drawing her teacher's attention.

"Linda..." Miss Goodspank growled through gritted teeth, her eyes dropping to the helpless form beneath her for a second. Silence ensued, the class getting to watch the tears running down the cheeks of a shaking Linda as she held back the sound of her crying, biting into the scarf instead.

And so the learning continued, the women instructed completely on their confinement. There were, as Miss Goodspank instructed, only two ways out of the Manor. One: the house management had to agree their behavior had been cured and that they were mentally fit to leave, this conclusion having to be signed off on by at least two doctors, there being only the Mistress and two others. The other two doctors were to be found in the medical section of the Manor, in the east wing of the ground level, one in the infirmary and one in the psychiatrist office, both medically qualified and able to sign off in this manner. The second way known in the Manor as "The way home" came in the procedure of the slave herself making a request to the in-house psychiatrist to consider her for release on the grounds she was no longer fit to continue. The psychiatrist had to consider after evaluation that the psychological well-being of the patient was being put at risk by continuing her treatment. It seemed medically sound, and the women did in fact feel some relief on hearing that there was someone watching over their mental health, but what they couldn't know and what became clear in the coming weeks was that the in-house psychiatrist was informed on patients' states by none other than the intendants, and very rarely was allowed to visit them in person. In such times as it was legally necessary for the in-house psychiatrist to do her regular checks on patient welfare, the intendants would choose the time and ready them, making them calm and relaxed, and delaying them as long as was necessary to achieve this. In other times, when they were brought to the psychiatrist's office because she herself had become concerned as she did her rounds throughout the day, watching over the activities, the patient would be escorted by two intendants. Throughout the visit, they would then remain in the office under the guise of security for the psychiatrist, making any reporting by the patient against the intendants simply a bad idea. In short, the intendants would have their way!

The contract was thoroughly gone through, the women left in shock with the realization that they were trapped sinking in, the golden sun wafting through the windows no longer as calming.

"Okay, class dismissed," announced Miss Goodspank, the intendants having already arrived and unshackled them. "Linda won't be joining you," she addressed the questioning looks as they filed past her, out the door, watching her open the desk drawer and produce a wooden ruler, Linda's eyes widening, the scarf still stuffed in her mouth. "Now…" Miss GoodSpank addressed her, having risen to her feet. "We're going to do something about that noise in class," she assured Linda, the door closing on the scene behind them.

Chapter 7

Splendor Of The Grounds

Lunch was a quick affair; Jennifer was retrieved from the dining area with the rest of her group and marched along the west wing, past the slaves on house cleaning duty who were busily dusting the hallways' cornicing and skirting under the eye of their group intendants, all except one, who was busy, too… being strapped.

The strap was a punishment they'd all come to fear – it was a strange punishment, as the strap was a short piece of light leather, very flexible, almost like a ribbon, but that belied its ferocity when used correctly. For the strap, all of ten inches long at full stroke, was just long enough to fall across both cheeks, but most often was concentrated on one at a time, bringing the unfortunate receiver's complete attention to her handler with every drop.

Best employed with the slave bent over, the intendants seemed to relish the challenge of holding the slave down for the punishment, their bodies jerking involuntarily and violently, trying to rise from the intendant's knee. All the while, other intendants nearby would let slip their appreciation at such skilled handling, letting out small smiles from the corners of their mouths as they cast their eyes from their duties to their sister and back again.

Intendants had their own styles, but most, like now, had the slave bent over between their legs, forcing the slave down, their stomach resting on the intendant's left thigh as she sat on a chair against the wall or, in this case, on a standing stool. The standing stool was one of many tools carried with house cleaning crews, and used to allow the slaves to reach up and dust the house's cornicing, something this slave obviously hadn't done very well.

As Jennifer passed the spectacle with her group, she saw the helpless slave lurch violently upwards, forcing the intendant slightly backwards against the wall, but there was no escape. As well as being bent over the left thigh with the intendant's left hand gripping high on her right arm to prevent her rising, her entrapment was completed by the intendant's right leg. This was lifted over the back of the slave's quivering thighs, the inside of the intendant's own gorgeous tanned muscular thigh clamping down across both of them, and bending at the knee, bringing an equally toned and clamping calf down under and in front of the slave's right thigh, leaving no chance of escape, her ass pushed high into the air. This then left the right hand of the intendant free to flail the lash as harshly as she chose, and this time, it seemed she was in no mood for leniency.

A favorite way of controlling the cleaning crews, the strap was witnessed almost daily by women. With one of the four groups always on cleaning, the other three groups would always pass them at some point throughout the day, and if not directly passing them, they would hear the howls from the wings, sharp snapping of the strap echoing down their lengths from some level or another. For there was no getting used to the lash – that was its horror, as a resistance to most punishments could be built up, and was encouraged and appreciated, it being seen as professional and good learning, but the lash was different. True, it not having the shear fire or fear of the bullwhip, but it could be deployed faster, and anywhere. Any gritting of teeth or controlling of breathing could easily be brushed aside by the simple expedient of a harder drop or a shorter gap. A bullwhip had to be drawn back, its throw controlled, its landing chosen at all times, time given to a slave to prepare, to resist… but not so with the strap. After multiple drops, it became almost as painful, and could be dropped repeatedly and with speed, reaching any part of a deserving charge and having them scream uncontrollably, regular reduction to tears not uncommon with the embarrassment of losing control the cause… but not this time.

Jennifer caught the look and couldn't understand…she'd smiled, just for an instant as she'd sent her eyes quickly to the right, seeing the full group passing her, watching her ass held high in the air for all to see, so that the embarrassment with her screams must have been total…but she smiled.

Soon passing, Jennifer didn't dare look back as the screams followed them… but groans, too. Not every drop of the strap was followed by a scream; the sharp snaps didn't lessen, but sometimes with a short rest between groups of drops, a singular and what seemed like a longer drop would ring out… and a groan followed. Not knowing whether or not the longer gap between groups of drops was just the intendant resting her arms before the next group, or if the long singular drop between groups was just her finding her aim or strategy, Jennifer's questions would soon be answered. She'd find out, too, how it felt to be held down in front of a passing group, to be the center of attention, and something else that the hapless slave smiling and groaning behind them now knew well… how wet the panties of the intendants got as they dropped the strap.

Soon, the howling faded behind them as they left the west wing to move into the main entrance hallway, and passed by the right of the marble staircase and through the hidden door into the ballroom behind, the women worried for a moment before the wooden facade door was opened in front of them, summer flooding in. The breeze almost carried them out, as still in line, they descended down the stone steps across the small half circular patio lip, and onto the grass beyond. Nature meeting their feet with tickling warmth brought smiles as they looked out across the huge expanse of grounds out back. Seemingly wild, a feeling of nature flooded in, the warm caressing sunlight bathing their skin in afternoon glory. Grounds stretched off in front to trees and thickening forest, hiding walls of twenty feet, unseen in the foliage behind. Witnessed only on their escape, at either side of nature's grasp, they gently curled back on both sides, a hundred yards from the manor's rear, their outward distance and meandering path giving no feeling of entrapment, their meeting with the house's wings carefully hidden as they curled gently outwards to meet the wall's edges, no sharp angles to alert the senses to their presence. But present they were, twenty feet, at that distance not looking high, the curving connection with the manor's rear walls not giving alarm under bathing sunlight and nature's glory, the women breathing deeply with their new senses of freedom… but they weren't free….

Naked but for smiles, stern looks from intendants

subdued them all, their line quickly splitting toward their waiting fitness aides, ten plastic aerobic steps waiting in two horizontal lines of five, and the women now standing one behind each, their asses now to the ballroom windows, a picture for anyone looking out.

In front of them, one of the intendants from their group's rear guard took a position directly ahead with a plastic step of her own and faced them all, the women's eyes on her gorgeous lines… Carly. With the sun shining from behind them, her gorgeous Floridian figure was drenched in afternoon sunshine, tanned and toned, her figure straining her leather corset to its limits. With black stockings, too, her garter fought to hold her powerful physique as her implements hung free, waving gently in the summer breeze, her cane hanging from the left and her lash hanging from the right, the gentle bulge of her garter pouches signaling more discipline within.

As they waited, Carly scanned the faces of her attentive group, watching to ensure they gave her their fullest attention while the sound of the other three intendants who had moved off to the right to two sheds strained the curiosity of the women. Unnoticed with the splendor of the grounds, they were almost hidden among a small group of fir trees like little forest islands; there were two groups of these in the grounds, one just behind and over to their right by about twenty yards, just far away but close enough for them to still make out the sounds of intendants laughing, seeming to enjoy themselves. Another little island was again just to their left, about the same distance away but a little further back toward the Manor. But it was the island on their right that they were curious about because only it had these two wooden huts side by side, their walls resting against each other, and only the barest hints of their presence visible through and above the foliage. The firs masked them almost completely with the tips of their two sloping roofs poking out among their tree tops, giving a picture postcard setting, belying what the huts were really for.

Each hut housed a sparse solid pine table, its four legs bolted to the ground, its rectangular shape facing the wall at the back of the hut. With nothing else in the huts, the Velcro ankle restraints at the base of the tables' legs immediately showed what the huts were for. Atop the front end of the tables' nearest the doors, black triangular foam pads rose above the tables' edges, their cushioning curls around the tables' lips with restraining harnesses fixed to each top, a foot wide and running two feet down on each table, from their high ass-lifting foam padded edges with two eight inch thick wide black Velcro restraining straps leading out, one from each side of the fixed harness, and lying loosely open on the tables' tops… waiting.

Velcro was not common in-house, staff preferring to make sure that fine quality solid leather restraints were used, in part to ensure the slaves knew there was no chance of escape, and in part to ensure the sumptuous thick soft leather did not injure their charges when extended corrections were necessary. This, by now, was known by the patients in the Manor, and so as each one began to be brought through the fir trees that evening, their eyes immediately told them what the restraints were for… speed.

Still laughing, the three intendants had now retrieved a small bag and had come out from one of the hut doorways which were kept open, both facing the right side of the two lines of five with the intendants emerging from the firs, their foliage brushing against their stockinged forms as they walked back behind the standing groups, Carly making sure they faced the front all the time.

The women's mouths salivated at the standard intendant uniform in front of them, almost forgetting their fear before realizing the other three intendants marshalling their group that day had now taken up positions, one to either side and one directly behind the back line of five. Some risked quick glancing looks from the corners of their eyes, becoming suddenly aware that the three had strapped on long black solid dildos, rubber strap now protruding from their fronts, secure and glistening, already lubed and threatening.

"Ahem." Carly cleared her throat sarcastically, hardly having to fight for their attention, her figure easily devouring them all. "Well, let's get started," her soft southern tone drawled out among them.

Soon, thighs were lifting as steps were climbed, Carly's implements swishing to the sound of pop music provided from a small IPad assembly brought forward from the huts by one of the three intendants now behind them on the grass, staying there as the rhythm flowed.

Fun for a while, but Carly didn't stop; soon sweat ran down her thighs and the women panted in front of her, having no match for her brutal speed of exercise as she showed them why she was their group's designated fitness coordinator. It was she that took fitness for their group and showed no sign of slowing as she forced them on, the women beginning to gasp. Missteps grew more noticeable, muscles started failing, groans became audible, and soon the first victim was hauled off, taken from her step. Grabbed from behind by the intendant on the left, she was dragged away still panting and unsure of what was happening. As she gasped over the grass, the occasional accidental bash of the pre-glistened strap bumping off of her thighs and ass gave her a hint of what lay in store. As the intendant firmly pushed her the short distance across the grass to the right, through the fir trees to the hut on the left, its doorway open showed the table waiting inside, its restraints soon being wrapped around the panting victim.

Pushed through the doorway by the intendant, her grip high on her left arm, more lube was spread across the backs of her thighs, the intendant bumping up against her as she pushed her against the edge of the table and down over the restraining harness. Seconds later, with her free arms spreading across the table's empty expanse, a still panting slave felt the fear as two eight inch restraining straps came around and up both her sides, across her back, instantly securing her in their fabric grip. With the harness locking her down, on the foam's high end, her ass pushed high was presented for the intendant already bent down and reaching for her ankles. Helpless already, her ankles were gripped, the intendant's hands wrapping one and then the other, both secured against the table's legs, holding thighs ajar, the whole process taking seconds, and without delay, her correction beginning.

It was in keeping with what they were doing, really… fitness training. With the exertions such as squats, crunches, aerobics, etc., it was only fitting that punishments would be delivered fast, and with only two correction huts, it was necessary that the women's lack of effort be dealt with quickly. Even wrists were left untied, the eight inch restraining straps of the foam harness easily able to hold them down while their hands flailed uselessly across the table's top, the intendants having no time for mercy… they didn't want a queue developing.

There would be no queue to hurry this first one, though, and with all the anxiety of a first time, she felt the intendant relish the occasion, hearing her audibly groaning in excitement as she pushed her pre-glistened strap deep inside her helpless femininity. Her first gasp of panic was overtaken by her long drawn-out moan, which followed the length of the glistening thickness travelling up inside her victim. Powerful muscular thighs easily pushed unsure lips apart, and moved on inside, the intendant allowing herself to fall over the back of the slave, at first with a groaning want as she enjoyed her helplessness before taking hold of both sides of her, rotating her hips around from behind and making sure her length filled her insides completely!

Panicked groans now fought for breath, arms flailing uselessly with fingers grabbing at the table's smooth surface, a sharp spank ringing out, the intendant unable to contain her excitement anymore as she started powerfully fucking her charge. Powering her length into her slave, the smell of pine, sweat, and leather filled their nostrils, her groaning charge secured beneath her.

It was brutal… brutal and merciless, hammering hard and deeply inside, their panicked cries completely ignored all through the afternoon, the intendants eventually losing their excitement and initial want, now settling in and having to work as hard as Carly! For, the more she wore the group out on the aerobic steps, all the more slaves had to be taken for correction, and the harder and faster the intendants had to work. Eventually, the huts were never empty, two slaves secured over the respective tables and feeling the pounding vibrations of the intendant in the adjoining hut slamming her weight against the slave’s ass next door. As correction after correction was hammered out on the slaves, their cries across the grounds echoed out for all to hear, the group cleaning the library on the first floor above jealously eyeing the spectacle below.

Bizarrely, the punishments did have a useful effect, with the women suddenly in shock at the speed of their corrections, the increased adrenalin produced by their body actually helping them in fitness training!

Chapter 8

Melting Ice

Jennifer awoke to another morning her previous days exertions giving a deep and thorough sleep in the dorm. Still sore inside, she stiffened as her cuffs were removed, making sure her bed was dressed perfectly after release and not wanting to be the mornings example. After breakfast and showers, she waited in line for the new day's struggles, and she didn't have to wait long.

Leaving the main dining area at the end of the west wing, her group was quickly turned toward the first of the two doors on the right, these directly opposite the showers; finally, their curiosity was partly answered as to what at least one of these rooms held… mops.

Not only mops, but dusters long and short, and soon they were laden with all sorts of cloths and buckets, some carrying the standing stools they had seen the intendants using in the corridors for correction. A long room with the same corniced flair as the hallway, the same ivory wall coloring and marble tiles throughout, but with shelving and more shelving as far as the eye could see on both sides from floor to ceiling. Five levels of white shelves in all, with every cleaning implement and potion you could imagine. In front of the shelves on the left wall, small portable vacuums lined up like soldiers complementing the women as their line straddled the center of the room, the light from outside gently filtering through the two large ornate windows at the farthest wall… they didn't open.

With the two intendants behind them keeping watch, the ones at the side and front continued moving back and forth, loading the women for their day's work ahead… and work they would. Soon weighted down with every cloth and duster, every stool and vacuum, they were turned around with plastic hoses, and clanking mops and brushes of all sizes, as the whole cleaning phalanx was marched out of the room and up the west wing to the main staircase, their ascension to servitude beginning for the day.

Having only briefly glimpsed the first floor on her arrival, Jennifer – like the others – was curious as to what it held, its obvious luxury apparent as they cleared the top of the marble staircase. For the first time in days, the women's feet fell on luxury, the plush thick carpet with its deep red pile soothing away the days of hard cold tile, the relief immediate and the feeling almost welcoming.

With only the briefest of glances to the right, there was the Mistress's office door which stared back in mahogany menace, and the women were turned left to the wing which none had seen before, their senses heightening. Soft carpet followed their senses down the west wing of the upper floor, four mahogany doors – two on either side – passing by, their soft welcome underfoot fading away to mahogany hardness with their entry into the large rectangular room at the wing's end.

The library… floors of real hardwood mahogany matching the skirtings and door surrounds, conveying strength, the hallway giving way to wall-to-wall book cases, the earlier cream softness gone as these reached higher and higher up walls that towered above the hallway and the Mistress's office behind it. Ornate cornicing was white like the ceiling where three huge chandeliers along its center looked down, watching the women as they were marched directly under them. All inline and spaced evenly across the center of the room towards four huge ornate windows forming the whole wall on the right. Practically a wall of glass, barely a brick between them, separating their largess as a balcony ran mid-way up and across them. Running wall-to-wall, its ornate iron blackness was accessed by a stairway of mahogany and matched a quaint design kept on by the Manor even after its renovations. Running wall-to-wall, this balcony gave access for cleaning the glass while a shorter bookcase beneath it offered more work for the women not yet aware of the boredom ahead. The library housed two huge rectangular tables arranged length-ways towards the door, one to either side of their group and running the full length of the room, boxing them in as they were brought to a halt.

With their group's two rear guard intendants now blocking their retreat, their left and front intendants met ahead of them, scanning down the line for any eyes that would not face front… they didn't have to wait long for an example.

With their clearly looking to make a show of someone, it was Diane who inadvertently offered to teach the group. Trying to look forward like the others, her eyes were nevertheless drawn by the room. Drawn away to the luxurious looking dark mahogany chairs with soft leather padding, twenty at each side of the mahogany tables and one at each end. Drawn up and away to the back of the room behind the intendants, where a wall-to-wall library stretched from floor to ceiling, higher than the book cases to either side, and yet two more behind either side of the doors. With huge lawyer-like volumes of green and tanned backings, they gave the feel of a university or legal institution, and her eyes were drawn still higher to the chandeliers above them. With gold and crystal splendor, they glinted in the light cast through the large clear windows, these completing the wall on the right. Morning sun peered in from the grounds out back as small panels halfway up the ornate frames lay slightly open, allowing in a breeze and sounds from exercise below.

"Diane!"

The sudden mention of her name brought her eyes down on their group's front intendants looking questioningly at her.

"Do you think we brought you up here for a tour of the Manor?" one asked shrilly, but not in an unkind fashion. It was obvious to the women that a victim had been sought, the pretense becoming routine in these matters. So well rehearsed were these displays, the women knew by now that at certain times, the group would be shown what would happen if instructions weren't followed. The tone of the voices in these displays left a certain comfort for the victim, as they knew they were being made an example of, but the sound of the voice was not angry or disappointed; instead it was rehearsed: the women knew this and the intendants knew they knew it. They'd learned that, by playing along and submitting willingly, the example would not be harsh; instead it was light and, at times, even pleasurable. Resistance, though, brought a different story, as very quickly hands would turn rough – they'd pull and yank, and anger would be felt.

Intendants were prepared to play the game with their charges, but only on their terms; dominance was theirs.

And so, as the head of their group drew a chair from the end of the left table and positioned herself sitting at the front of their line, Diane offered no resistance when Urst came down to collect her. Separated from the center of the line, she was brought straight to Nadia's Venezuelan justice. With a practiced look of irritation, she pulled her down from Urst's grasp, over her left knee, locking her in with her right leg brought over and down against the back of Diane's thighs. Taking her shoulder with her left hand, and satisfied that she was secure, she turned to Urst with a still practiced look of irritation and cocked her head commandingly toward the group before settling down to her pressing business.

"Welcome to the library," Urst's commanding Icelandic tone took over as the first sounds of spanks began behind her…

Diane was down for a long time, as Nadia seemed to be enjoying it, almost as if she was practicing; Diane herself played well, only beginning to yelp halfway into her correction when it became harder… she'd learned fast.

Because of this obvious learning, she was spared the strap, Nadia's stronger corrections remaining firmly attached to her garter and gently waving as she worked. The women had begun to realize that the lessons they were being taught in the Academy under Miss Goodspank were true, that better standards of play, or in this case correction, were rewarded. Not in a sense of increased favoritism or the sparing of discipline, but in the discipline itself – the intendants being professionals and, like with any professionals, admiration for good workmanship in their field was respected when observed. For Diane, the proof of this was welcome as she lay beneath Nadia, holding back what she could as her discipline continued. She could feel Nadia taking her time, choosing where to strike her, her hand sometimes coming up and Diane's cheeks rising in cooperation, Nadia's hand sometimes coming down and finding rhythm with the ass before her.

Locking in to this rhythm was the key to good play, as if not it was just straight punishment, which felt harsh and impersonal; yet, the feeling of being guided through correction left a connection between the two women. For the intendants themselves, they had to be seen to be in command, the respect and fear from the women necessary, but enjoyment between actors could not be hidden from one another. Any sign of pleasurable moaning or lustful looks was quickly dealt with through harsher strikes, the rhythm dropping away to straight and increased pain, even implements brought in to voice the intendant's displeasure at the performance. But, get it right, keep the pleasure hidden, and a silent understanding would emerge between the two; rhythms could be felt, and rhythms would grow… just like feelings.

For the rest of the women, though, the only thing growing was boredom. Instructed by their three remaining intendants, some were on their knees dusting skirting, others mopping around them, seeing their reflections in an already spotless floor. With longer dusters, others were atop their standing stools, trawling hard to reach the cornicing while more dealt with furniture and bookshelves already spotless, the slaves' efforts from the day before having left the room immaculate all around them.

House cleaning was utterly boring, their being not allowed to talk to anyone as they simply dusted and cleaned like they were… slaves. Endless tedium of dusting perfectly clean furniture, but instructed to dust it all the same, utter boredom as all the while cries could be heard from other areas of the Manor, echoing up through the hallways and from outside on the grounds. Meanwhile, their boredom, save for Diane, continued. Would it not have been better to be the one doing the screaming, to be tortured by intendants? The trouble was that, after a while, they realized they were being tortured! Forced into this endless boredom, this was torture alright, and Jennifer couldn't think of anything worse. This effect, unknown to the women, was partly the intent of the intendants; by having them utterly bored and wanton throughout the day, the tortures that were to come would seem almost a release, just as they themselves had already begun to suspect this as they dusted.

On and on, Jennifer had been up atop stools and down on her knees, and seen enough books to last a lifetime, and with the intendants now sitting casually at the right table – chatting, ignoring all the scrubbing around them – she was annoyed. Their four group intendants – Nadia the leader, Urst the professional, Carly the fitness fanatic, and Valerie the brute. Valerie, a Bolivian powerhouse, was the enforcer of the group, her massive thighs and powerfully built waistline honed by years of South American wrestling before her life in the Manor, and these could be brought to bear over wayward behavior as necessary in their group. Right now, though, the four visions of corseted lethality sat idly chatting, laughing aloud as the women suffered around them. Like the rest of the women, Jennifer knew this was pointless; hours had gone by, hours, and still they were there… made worse for her now as she saw the scene in the garden below her.

The same scene she had been a part of the day before, playing out below, the shattered women not knowing how lucky they were to be dragged away, tired, to the correction huts, their yelps and groans only torturing in Jennifer's boredom. Soon, she had a look of positive irritation on her face as she dusted the windows in an outwardly sloppy fashion; soon she was…

"Jennifer!"

She whirled around to see an angry Urst glaring up at her from the table, Jennifer's leisurely look gone and her learned subservient expression instantly back… but it was too late.

Urst angrily pointed back to the window as if there were dust somewhere to be cleaned, and Jennifer turned back with hesitation caused by fear of her look simply enraging Urst more.

Maybe it was the hesitation, or maybe the look, but almost at once, Urst was up, and soon a fearful Jennifer was dragged off her standing stool and away with it behind a raging intendant, straight out of the library and into the corridor beyond. Their journey continued only as far as the wall between the two mahogany doors on the left side of the wing, the standing stool forced angrily down. Almost immediately, Jennifer was pulled down over Urst's waiting knee, trapped in seconds by her other leg, her head forced down by an angry left hand before it grabbed her shoulder, holding her tight.

Trapped and fearful, Jennifer quickly realized what was to come, the events she'd witnessed in the west wing corridor the day before about to be replayed as she felt Urst's right hand reach up for her hip, the sound of unbuckling signaling her worst fears coming true.

For the first time, Jennifer felt the strap, straight across both cheeks; Urst's opening salvo had her cry out! The second saw her scream, her body lurching for an escape from Urst's powerful grip, but there was none.

"Quiet!" Urst demanded.

Jennifer was shaking, her breath quick, the shaking seeming to please Urst as she paused, Jennifer able to gather herself for what lay ahead as Urst was showing her a path.

By following her lead, Urst seemed to relax, administering Jennifer's correction in a more manageable way. Her first savage strikes had simply been meant to show dominance, to answer in her mind just who was in charge.

In the Academy, they were taught that this was done with unruly slaves who had forgotten themselves, the sharp and sometimes savage pain being only temporary and used to snap the slave back to her senses, and if this was shown by submission, the slave might expect better treatment as the correction went forward. For the second time that day, they were shown proof; at least, Jennifer was, that what they were learning in the Academy was true, and with Urst's powerful gym-bodied physique now commanding her, she was glad of that.

She wasn't down as long as Diane; long enough, though, to see her group leave the library without her.

Long enough for two passing intendants to come up the main stairway and witness her struggles. Not feeling the connection they'd heard Diane experience with Nadia earlier, Jennifer was annoyed as the two intendants walked past, laughing at her obvious discomfort, and she couldn't help trying to look after them as they passed, anger welling up in her…. STRAP!!!

She screamed out! Urst was enraged at her behavior, the full length of the leather coming down across both her cheeks. By looking after the other intendants as they'd passed, she had insulted Urst in front of them. She'd essentially shown them that Urst had lost control of her, or to put it another way, that Urst couldn't do her job properly… but she there was no fear that she would now.

Soon, Jennifer was up, Urst actually grabbing her by the scruff of the neck and glaring into her eyes before she took her… and there were no words. Marched by her side with one hand holding her by the back of the neck, Urst took her straight down the marble staircase and up the east wing. Only ever having being down to the west of the ground level, Jennifer worried as she remembered the first day, as she'd come in and seen a woman on her knees at the end of the east wing… leashed. Urst's boots were forceful, angry, the loud clicking of her heels on the tiles like thunder full of malice as Jennifer was half dragged up the east wing, hoping she might be headed for the infirmary at the end… but she wasn't. Her hope dashed, she was whirled around through one of the first sets of opposing doors… the set on the left.

Still being held forcibly by Urst through the doorway, she witnessed an alarmed intendant sitting on the right in full intendant uniform, but wearing a lab coat, as she looked up from a stainless steel desk set hard against the wall. With neat paperwork in front of her showing columns with names of slaves and what looked like minutes next to them, she asked Urst what was the problem in a concerned tone, blue eyes sharp against her brunette hair, shoulder-length and just cresting her lab coat.

“She dared to question my competence in front of others!” Urst hissed, her exotic Icelandic tone having none of the attraction Jennifer used to feel for it.

The lab coat shook her head. “We’re getting a lot of this,” she informed them. “I don’t know about these groups the Mistress has brought in this time; it’s been two weeks and we’re still seeing mistakes like this – I don’t think there’ll be many left at the end.”

‘Many left!’ Jennifer thought, still panicked; many left after what? At the end of what?

Soon, though, her mind was on other things with the lab coat rising from her white leather chair, its stainless steel legs grinding over the tiles as the room’s brilliant white walls stunned Jennifer for the first time. A small claustrophobic room, cold and rectangular and only six foot wide from the doorway, and ten feet in length, with the table at the near end and nothing at the other, the tiles from the hallway the same beneath their feet. The reason it was only six foot wide had Jennifer concerned, as she saw what it contained. Immediately across from the doorway lay a huge door, seven feet tall and four feet wide, with a stainless steel handle midway up on its left side. With a brilliant white finish, small digital red numbers on a panel five feet up on the left side of the door left Jennifer in no doubt as to what she was looking at.

0 degrees! Jennifer's mouth tightened as she read it, Urst unconcerned as she took leather wrist restraints from her garter pouches and bound Jennifer's hands… in front of her. With the restraints fastened, Urst padlocked them through their stainless steel rings, small padlocks flailing loose like jewelry at their side.

"Excuse me," the lab coat said in an almost matter-of-fact way as she moved for the door, Urst pulling Jennifer back with her into the clear part of the room. The clank of the steel handle faded away, to be replaced by the gentle sound of cracking ice, the huge door pulling back with a blast of cold air, the sound of loud whirring fans greeting them with its opening.

Almost immediately, wailing women could be heard competing with the fans, Jennifer stiffening as she heard them and Urst having trouble forcing her through to the horror waiting inside! Within the long rectangular room, the freeze was immediate, dimly lit with a yellow bulb above the door they'd just come through; Jennifer could see a huge box-like structure hanging from the roof at the end of the room, four fans spinning in their mountings. But it was the other mounts that immediately took her breath away. Eight securing mounts hung from the two lines of four, lengthways away from them down the freezer room, each mount having its own independent pulley system with a hand crank, four on the left wall and four on the right.

Legs! Dangling from the first pair of mounts to the left and right, and another behind those on the left of the second pair, and women screamed out, their naked forms gyrating with their legs kicking the air as if trying to climb some invisible staircase, their bodies writhing and twisting from left to right under pained expressions. They screamed openly, Jennifer realized… they screamed and didn't seem to care about the intendants inside, Urst not six feet from them. Ordinarily, the women would have been silent, their learned practiced expressions of submission in place, and not a sound from them, but here they were openly screaming, letting out howls as they twisted helplessly, Jennifer quickly realizing they couldn't help it and that soon neither would she be able to! Pushing inside, Urst forced her past them on the right before turning left toward the empty hanging attachment of the fourth pulley above them. Brought to a halt underneath it, Jennifer watched it sway, the constant icy blast never ceasing and the lab coat displaying cold indifference to the women's tortures, and proceeding to the second hand crank on the right wall. With some effort at first, counterclockwise, she began cranking the icy handle, the mounting above Urst and Jennifer coming slowly down on its chain Urst pulling Jennifer's hands up to meet it, their eyes meeting through their raised arms. Jennifer had fear in her, real fear, and Urst could see it, but her own expression was cold, strong, and only a slight resistance from Jennifer was felt, Urst's eyes doing the rest. A quick snapping of the securing mount through both the rings on Jennifer's restraints was then sealed by the mount's larger padlock, hanging open in its locking ring and now sealed over Jennifer's wrists, Urst finally letting her go. Taking one step back, she kept her eyes locked to Jennifer's, hoping Jennifer saw her satisfaction in them and watching her fear jump in her own eyes as the sound of ratchetting began beside her. Her arms lifted to their full length, Jennifer tiptoeing in trying to find still more height, trying to rise with the pulley before gasping in fear as she ran out of length and her feet were hoisted from the floor, a final cry releasing from her lips, Urst's glare no longer able to hold it inside her. Another cry as she spun slightly, her full weight causing pain in her shoulders, and her legs writhed by themselves as if trying to climb stairs that weren't there, Jennifer shrieking as she felt totally vulnerable, naked and fearful of what Urst was about to do….

And then it stopped; with a final turn, the pulley clunked to a stop, Jennifer now two feet clear of the ground and with her legs writhing with the other three slaves, now all crying out together. With some relief, Urst and the lab coat stopped staring at her, instead now totally ignoring her and the others, making their way out down the opposite side from Jennifer, her ears just able to pick up over the fans the lab coat asking, "How long for this one?"

"Twenty minutes should do her," Urst replied nonchalantly as they closed the door behind them upon their exit.

Fortunately, the light stayed on, Jennifer's first reaction being to call out to the others struggling beside her, but repeated attempts only finally brought a shriek from one of them: "Shut up or they'll keep us here longer!"

While legs dangled in the dim yellow torture, shoulders brought pain and shrieking cries, the cold biting at nipples and toes. The weight caught her by surprise; it was her own, and on her shoulders, her feet starting to gyrate like the others as soon as she'd left the ground and her body trying to climb the invisible staircase to get away from the pain, but the chain held her fast. Quickly, she began to struggle, her body starting to realize there was no escape, the pain starting to mount in her shoulders with her screams, and the wind that never stopped biting.

The icy blast kept coming all around, and mid-scream, Jennifer tried to turn her back on it, but it just wrapped around her, directly onto her freezing nipples. Searing cold had her kick off the invisible staircase into the icy torture, her howls joining the others as it let go of her nipples, only to wrap around the rest of her, her naked torso engulfed in icy breath. Her nether regions, too, now felt its searing grip, the cold having no shame in reaching down to her poor vulnerability, her lips nipping underneath her femininity which was shown no mercy. More screams again as the strain on her shoulders from her poor gyrating body forced her to turn, searching for some comfort, only to bring her nipples straight back to the icy wind. Not a man, so her upper body strength was predictably poor, and what little she had was now gone, her shoulders aching from the dead weight now, pulling on them underneath her body, kicking helplessly as she gyrated on the chain. The pain was excruciating and constant; there was no relief, kicks and screams and twists and howls just bringing more of the same in a different position, their chorus of pain writhing on with the fans in the dim yellow light around them.

Outside, a careful watch was kept by the lab coat, this one of the more extreme disciplining methods employed at the Manor. It was shock therapy designed to produce fast results, and due to its obvious danger, a careful watch on time was kept; Jennifer lucky, most women not hearing how long they were to be kept in the room, and so having no basis to work from. Most were simply kept for twenty minutes, but without any idea of the passage of time and with the constant whirring of the fans, this could feel like an hour. The lab coat, like all intendants on this wing, though not a doctor, had a medical background and was well-versed in the dangers of hypothermia. Unknown to the unfortunate guests of the freezer room, there was also a hidden camera where intendants kept a second watch, complete with their own set of time sheets to make sure no accidents occurred. Urst now had the satisfaction of sitting in the control room on the first lower level beside the dorms, having walked there to their monitors, joining the staff as they smirked, watching and listening to the women freezing inside.

"How dare she!" Urst thought as she watched Jennifer writhe in the room, having no mercy whatsoever as she thought of how she'd insulted her.

Kicking and screaming she'd been, but now Urst looked on assuredly at the monitor, ignoring the other three women kicking beside her as she watched her correction play out, Jennifer screaming in front of her.

Jennifer, unsurprisingly, was the last to leave, her final five minutes truly frightening as she was left alone to writhe in pain as she screamed out in the yellow light, her legs still trying to climb the staircase and her arms now totally strengthless. When the door finally opened, she was truly glad to see the lab coat, but her head just dipped as Urst came through behind her. Lowered down, every agonizing click of the ratchet brought her pain as the vibration through her shoulders brought her agony, making her to yelp… it was the final humiliation.

She cried when Urst took her in her arms; it was necessary because she couldn't stand up. After some check-ups from the doctor over the next ten minutes, she was released to Urst's care. She'd stopped crying, and she felt strange when Urst explained why it had had to be done as they walked calmly back to the dorm, the Manor silent but for Urst's boot steps. It didn't feel like she was under threat from her as they walked beside each other in silence…. Jennifer was in shock.

It felt like she was chatting to some friend – she couldn't understand why she didn't feel threatened by Urst anymore, but the staff did understand as they watched her carefully on the monitors, and would be spending a great time watching Jennifer as she slept that night in her dorm. On route and sensing it, too, Urst began to talk openly to her as they walked, knowing that after this kind of shock therapy, patients became suggestible, vulnerable for a time and easily led… now was a good time to further her learning… before the tears. Encouraging her to answer, it was difficult at first for Jennifer, who was unsure, as throughout the day, talking would bring punishment, but Urst persisted, continuing to coax her, Jennifer's nervousness persisting. Urst saw the look in her eyes and tried to reason with her, explaining that that's just how it worked here, that the intendants had to show they were in control or they'd be replaced, that her reputation, her standing in the Manor, was at stake by Jennifer not obeying her direction while under her care. At one point, Jennifer kept it hidden, but thought 'what about me?' before quickly remembering she was a slave, and it wasn't about her: it was about her Mistress and her wishes for her new behavior – that's why she was sent here. This place was starting to frighten her, though, as every day it got scarier, with new rooms and more treatments, more rumors of fresh horror after the women chatted at breakfast… at least the ones not having faced the horrors did while others sat quietly… disturbed.

As they passed the Manor's two huge entrance doors, open during the day to the grounds out in front, they looked back from their sealed state, their huge panels offering no escape as Jennifer thought about running the next day….

What she couldn't understand was why they left them open all day… she'd learn later that the doors were never closed, as a statement of professionalism. True domination was given from those submitting, this not an easy art to master, but a skill. To attain this willing gift from charges, great expertise learned over years was brought to them, the proof of this in the women's willingness to stay. To just savagely beat a person down physically, or threaten them repeatedly, would have brought a false submission fostered through fear, this only remaining as long as the fear was present. In this case, it would have been wise to close the doors, for when left alone with the fear lifted, the women might very well try to run. The Manor was a professional operation honed for learning true submission within its guests, which was given by them as a gift over their care, and their remaining quite willingly spoke of the intendants' levels of skill in this practice… to lock the doors would have been an admission of their failure in this art.

Instead, the Manor's doors were only closed at night and for security reasons – the intendants, though staffing at night being in a much reduced number, their eyes – though monitoring over the cameras were not able to be everywhere at once. With the women immobile, shackled to their beds, it was felt prudent to seal the doors at night this meaning the women were held secure within the Manor, safe… locked inside with the intendants….

"You don't have to be afraid," Urst assured her, turning to her and taking hold of her slightly as she saw her looking at the doors. "Obey the rules and you have nothing to fear," she assured. "Think of it as your way to control your fate, like your breathing in correction."

It wasn't the words – it was the eyes, the ice queen's brilliant blue eyes showing concern for the first time. Although quickly hidden when she realized Jennifer saw it, Urst didn't try to correct her even though she'd seen her see it.

Didn't try to correct this minor insolence because Urst's time in the Manor had taught her well how to manage slaves around her, and she knew what had just happened…

a connection… just one of a different kind.

Chapter 9

Power And Control

Waking that morning was different – Jennifer was frightened again. For the past couple of weeks she'd gotten used to the house rhythms like the others, but after last night, she didn't feel the same; not relaxed anymore, she was in shock.

Timid, she couldn't help but tense up as the intendants uncuffed her, couldn't help but pull back, her timidness noticeable. Her covers were stiff, stiff and cold when she'd finished, just as she had been lying in her bed that night, unable to sleep and desperately trying to curl into a ball for warmth, the cold staying with her most of the night, staying in her bones, but now gone… replaced by fear.

There was no sign of guilt from Urst; she barely even glanced at her as they were marched in good order to breakfast, the morning's example crawling beside them. Of course, there wasn't… the intendants were trained to show dominance to command and order, Urst actually feeling relieved at Jennifer's condition, her reticence proving to the other intendants that Urst still had what it took, her reputation secure… but there was guilt under the ice.

At breakfast, their table chatted, Jennifer finding it hard to join in and sitting quietly aware that the cameras were watching her behavior, or lack of it, the subject of conversation in the control room below them being that Urst was congratulated at the results, some telling her not to worry, that Jennifer had asked for it.

It was here that the ice queen could show her sympathy, slightly worried by Jennifer's obvious timidness, the house psychologist from then on paying more attention to Jennifer's condition upon receiving the report. Her scathing eye at Urst that morning did nothing to alleviate the mounting guilt Urst felt, even Nadia obviously irritated at her over the strength of her response on Jennifer, thinking it too much at such an early stage. Ironically, Jennifer was fine; in fact, her behavior from then on improved dramatically – it was Urst who really needed the house psychologist's attention… which she got, just not the helpful kind, instead being her anger at what she saw as Urst's overreaction on such a new slave, obvious in her face, but Jennifer would know none of this.

What she did come to know was that something had changed; the intendants treated her differently from then on, and she couldn't figure it out at first: she thought they were lighter on her, softer; guilt maybe, she thought for a while before finally realizing what it was… respect.

Her struggles had not gone unnoticed, and although they were never told directly by the intendants who tried to remain cold and uncaring, there was no way to hide these feelings of appreciation and affection for what amounted to favorites emerging within groups… those feelings not just limited to the intendants' side.

"Have you heard about the freezer room?" Andrea asked, wide-eyed and shocked, telling them about the rumor she'd heard. "Samantha in the second group told me about this place where they hang you up like meat, but I think she was just spreading rumors," she comforted herself, telling the women about what she'd heard between two of the groups.

Sitting at the head of their table's ten chairs – at the bottom left, the examples on the floor just to her side, with the doors twenty feet behind her – Jennifer listened to Andrea directly across from her, almost joining in when one of the helpless women chained to the floor down to her left groaned, moving slightly, her predicament convincing her to stay quiet and leaving Andrea chirping on.

She was very attractive, and such a nice little person that it was obvious why her mistress, whoever she was, was trying to hang on to her. Bright and bubbly, her Irish charm cheered everyone up each morning, just her presence enough to lift the mood around the table. To Andrea's right, Heather listened intently and Julie, directly across from Heather on Jennifer's right, sat wide-eyed at the news, herself no stranger to the intendants' personal attentions, although she had much improved from her short stay already.

"Oh, I don't know, it sounds a bit far-fetched to me." Heather's American southern Virginia drawl responded finally to Andrea's wide-eyed claims. Another gorgeous slave competing in looks, Jennifer thought, her auburn hair sultry and still, her demeanor calm and placid-looking. With brown eyes and a calming voice, she gave the impression that, of all the slaves, she truly didn't mind the predicament she was in. It was true, Heather having found early on in life that the lifestyle, as she'd learned, was truly her path to follow, and was not just comfortable, but truly happy for her, in its ways.

"I don't know, Heather, I heard something, too, not too far from this," Julie added from her side of the table, Jennifer remaining quiet as Heather turned to face Julie's claims.

Jennifer listened to them chat, almost squabbling about the validity of the rumor, and almost joining in at one point, but the camera preyed on her timidness, holding her down until finally, with almost annoyance, she blurted out, "They're not stories!"

The other three looked at her… the sudden entry for the first time leaving her noticeable, like the marks on her wrists from the hanging restraints she showed them, backing up her story as she broke down halfway through crying out what she'd been through the night before. Sympathy welled up in Andrea's eyes as she reached out across the table, taking Jennifer's wrists, sympathy coming, too, from other tables' slaves overhearing and bearing witness to Jennifer crying. Sympathy, too, for three others in the dining area that morning, the three others with marked wrists like Jennifer's now similarly broken down.

There was no sympathy at all, though, from the house psychologist after she reviewed the footage from the dining area that morning; after watching the near nervous breakdown of four slaves so early on, she railed against the four intendants in her office that day, her rage shattering their emotions as she played back the women crying out in front of them.

The Mistress, though, was very supportive; she believed she had witnessed good management, and despite the anger of the house psychologist in her report, with recommendations for intendant sanctions, she would have none of it. Legally needing the support of the house doctors and lawyer team to have her recommendations brought forward, the psychologist didn't get it, the Mistress's word holding sway over all of them, their positions in house directly under her discretion. Against such control, all the house psychologist could do was monitor the slaves' conditions, being legally allowed to discharge them if she thought their mental conditions were under too much strain, but other than that, there was nothing more she could do.

Doors slammed open, and mouths slammed shut as the intendants arrived to collect them. They were well used to corrections by now, but still feared them, quiet descending instantly over the dining area and proving they were being given their learning correctly.

Jennifer went through the motions that day, but she felt timid and afraid… she was in shock. Despite what appeared to be gentle persuasion from Urst, she couldn't come round. Instead, she stayed rigid, obedient, jumping at the slightest command, the intendants worrying.

Their worries were shown in their treatment of her… or lack of it, as they knew what a slave exhibiting these behaviors meant… they were on the edge of cracking, their next course likely to be to the in house psychiatrist questions then asked of the intendants in charge of them.

Unlike most treatment centers, the Manor was not in the business of brutalizing women; far from it. Instead, their focus was on learning and good correction. Yes, the discipline in-house could at times seem harsh, but its purpose was not to break the woman, but to guide her. She was not some new arrival who needed saddling, but a consenting adult who wished to walk this path in life and needed guidance from her intendants to let her do it. It was their job to provide this path and keep her safe on it, and sometimes this required strength in steering her correctly, but over do it, and she'd turn away from them, never to return.

This did happen.... Sometimes, a slave left because they were not strong enough to receive their direction, and instead proceeded down the way home. This was a procedure in-house which had been shown to them in their first days at the Academy, which provided slight reassurance to them and legal protection for the Manor.

It involved consultation with the house psychiatrist, who they were aware was always monitoring them, but after their initial meeting with them on their first day, never saw again unless they asked for a meeting. This procedure, even though consent forms had been signed, had to be there for legal reasons. Legally, the house psychiatrist had to remain apart from the in-house activities from day to day due to the danger of her becoming involved with what was going on and possibly biased over time. Instead, she had to provide an independent protective arm for the patients' vulnerable inside.

Legally, the intendants were duty-bound to provide such a meeting immediately upon request, as there were no safety words or other methods for the women to ask for help.

This, then, posed a problem for the intendants' abilities to instruct and provide direction, and so they actively discouraged any requests through a mixture of guilt, fear, and other methods while spreading rumors and lies. A favorite was to pose the question of what their own Mistress outside the manor would think of them if they returned to them a failure, after the mistress had spent so much money on them. To purposely spread the fear of their Mistresses disposing of them if they returned to them in less of a condition than they wanted. Also, there was embarrassment by failure: "What kind of slave are you if you can't handle what your sisters can?" And then of course, there was group punishment, ruthlessly witnessed in the first days of the Manor, as sometimes the rest of the group or groups were punished for another slave's failures, leading to their individually feeling the rest of the group's anger toward them in showers and at breakfast.

As well as guilt, they would also use their own strength and correction in usual ways, along with another powerful weapon… pleasure.

Over the weeks when dominance was accepted, power understood, and submission duly given, the situation in house calmed down the steely cold unfeelingness of the intendants' act, at times weakening emotions showing through with feelings for certain women, favorites emerging among them. It was natural, after a time, that intendants would develop feelings for their charges, it becoming noticeable to the others that some were treated better and less harshly, and with more caring. At times, the shattering screaming of pleasure that echoed down the halls was followed by hungry lustful looks, and obvious deep connection, this not only making favorites work harder for intendants, but providing one further weapon that was taken full advantage of… envy.

For every check and balance, intendants had a sly way to work around it, encouraged by the Mistress, she holding the ultimate power and intendants allowed to wield it only through her discretion.

So, through carrot and stick, rumor and lie, the slaves were held in check successfully for the most part; indeed, if a slave did leave, it was assumed to be her group intendants' fault. They themselves, after all, had control of their group's activities, and so they would answer to the Mistress when things went wrong, their professionalism called into question in front of the other intendants, though never in front of the slaves. Any disciplinary hearings of this nature were always held out of sight on the upper level of the Manor, slaves never allowed to see or even know it was going on. At these times, the slaves were all secured below, bearing no witness to these in-house power struggles and thereby insuring a united front against them.

There were sanctions, reprimands, and even demotion, as well as possible dismissal from the house. With this in mind, it was not in the intendants' interests to break the slaves, their own professional reputation and standing in the Manor being at stake, but the slaves were to hear none of this. It could not be that they had the slightest chance to gain a foothold and manipulate any situation, as in order to complete their behavioral changes, the house staff had to be seen to be all-powerful under the watchful eye of the Mistress.

In line with this, Jennifer did seem to detect some friction between Urst and Nadia that day… they all did. Nadia obviously concerned for her own reputation when one of her intendants seemed to have gone overboard in a fit of anger with one of her charges the night before, and she seemed to have made it clear to Urst to fix this. This seemed obvious as Urst continued uncharacteristically that day to try to coax Jennifer round, instead of using her usual ruthless cold attention for what amounted to her as work. When this seemed to fail to bring Jennifer out of her understandable shock, Nadia herself began to take up the challenge that afternoon, this actually worrying Jennifer further, what with Nadia's reputation for special learning.

Luckily for Jennifer, Nadia's infamous hands had a more caring touch throughout the day, it being obvious to all that Jennifer was under her wing as, several times during the day, in fitness and at other points when Jennifer like the others would have been disciplined strongly, she was overlooked, left protected under Nadia's hand.

Nadia showed such patience with her that eventually, late into that afternoon, she did feel better, at one point even smiling, Nadia giving her a pretend scowl before smiling herself, pleased she was alright and coming around.

She got to listen to the slaves around her being taken to and from the correction huts, Carly providing a constant stream of those in need of discipline, the sweat running down her gorgeous thighs in the falling evening sun. With it obvious to all now that the intendants were taking favorites, Jennifer found herself musing about how it would feel to be Carly's, but it wasn't to be, as other smoldering eyes already had designs on her.

Spared from discipline all day, Jennifer did feel better when she was secured to her bed that night with the others; better, but not right.

That night they came twice, Jennifer cringing both times as the door opened and the intendants came in to take their victims. Unlike during the day, these night visitors were not restricted to their intendant group, any and all seeming to do as they pleased. Twice, the boots had approached and passed her bed; they didn't speak, everything being carried out very quietly, a slave or two being uncuffed and led away to whatever lay in wait. Without words, it was all in the eyes, the looks… the smiles. Sometimes, some slaves seemed to be happy with what they could see in these eyes, following away cooperatively while others went reluctantly, realizing it wasn't to be fun for them. Indeed, the intendants had become so brazen over the weeks that the women now felt like pieces of meat, taken by them whenever they pleased.

Luckily for Jennifer, they hadn't come for her; indeed, in her present emotional state, she simply couldn't have taken it, she thought, as she huddled in on herself, naked in the dim calming light, its gentle cream glow funneling up over dorm walls from the hidden bulbs below. But finally, the door opened one more time, and a single set of sharp booted foot falls tacked their heels on the polished floor… and Jennifer knew. Knew as they came down between the beds in the dorm, knew by the sound of their careful approach, that this person was aware of a slave's fragile state… she knew they were for her. Already turned away from the door, she closed her eyes, not daring to look, but she knew, even before they stopped at the foot of her bed….

And there she was… in all her shattering Venezuelan splendor, the same stunning vision that had greeted her on arrival at the Manor now standing at the foot of her bed, Jennifer hearing her own breathing as she looked up at devastating Latin beauty.

She wasn't frightened, and followed Nadia completely as she uncuffed her and brought her to her feet, but so close that Jennifer's nerves began to show in her breath audibly heightening as Nadia ran a hand up and over the side of Jennifer's hip, her intentions clear. Jennifer was left in no doubt as her smoldering Latin passion stared lustfully at her, the smallest of smiles appearing as she tried to comfort her. The woman pulling her closer, Jennifer's nerves only heightened when Nadia produced a blindfold from her garter, the two womens' skins meeting at the waist, Jennifer's nerves unbearable now, when suddenly Nadia did something no one had seen before… she kissed Jennifer. Long and slow, Jennifer feeling her nerves rise then fall, and then rise again as she felt hands pull her in at the waist, the other women in the room shocked at the display of affection in the dorm. Releasing her lips, Nadia again looked lustfully into her eyes with the care of a lover gently cocking her head, her lips opening slightly, but with no words as Jennifer wondered what to do. With a pleasing smile, Nadia again cocked her head slightly, as if asking for a return, Jennifer carefully giving back what she thought she wanted, and Nadia smiling more in approval before raising her left hand up from Jennifer's hip, stroking her side, still holding the blindfold, its silk felt by Jennifer as it came up, almost having her look at it as it rose, but Nadia easily held her stare. Stroking the blindfold gently off her side, she brought it between them and looked down at it, Jennifer following her gaze before Nadia looked back up at her, cocking her head as if asking for permission with Jennifer mesmerized by her lead.

Soon her breath quickened again, but she didn't panic, her world falling black, Nadia taking her hand

and leading her blindly out… willingly, the other women left open-mouthed as they watched from behind her.

Jennifer followed, nervous but wanton; she was turned on, for the first time in weeks; she was really lustful and all she could think of was the corseted beauty leading her forward. She felt herself lusting after every sharp-booted boot-fall as Nadia guided her, naked and blindfolded, through the Manor. First up the west wing, then to the staircase and up to the ground level, Jennifer able to picture where she was led, around the staircase and up again, cold tile replaced by lush carpet as she realized she was heading to the first level, high above, where by now they knew the intendants were quartered, their bedrooms overhead. Lust followed boots as they left the staircase to the right, a short distance till soon Jennifer heard the solid sound of one of the large doorways opening and felt the atmosphere change as she was led inside, left aware that she was in a smaller place now. The strength of solid wood closing behind her was followed by the loud sound of a locking key. Nervous, she heard Nadia's soft booted footfalls on the carpet approach her, the feeling of silk hands taking hold around her waist and gently coaxing her forward before lips came to hers over her short breath and fears.

She focused totally on the sound of Nadia's breathing, her senses heightened and responsive to every coax and pull, obedient in a way she hadn't been since arriving – she wanted her. Drawn forward, she heard Nadia sigh willfully, their lips parting as her hands began to explore her, Nadia able to let her guard down and enjoy it, no one watching her performance or work now. Guided forward, soon Jennifer felt the cool sheets of Nadia's bed come to meet her, their fine touch just enticing, brought down over her captor's lair, her scent flowing all around her. Turned on her back, lying still and open, responsive to any touch and having to fight not to smile, she knew Nadia was half-knelt over her body, feeling the weight through the bed, the heat as she approached. Every sound ruled her world as she waited for Nadia's direction, waiting for her will on her. The sound of unzipping and leather buckling sent shudders through her mind as she realized her captor was removing her boots… and then her corset. Feeling the vibrations through the bed, she heard the sound of leather sliding off Nadia's legs, imagining how it felt as the sound of fabric slipping down the back of her thighs came next. Biting her lip, Jennifer felt the bed depress next to her thigh from her intendant's knee, then next to her head as Nadia's hand came up to support her, the woman moving in over top of her prey now.

Letting out a sigh of nerves, Jennifer shook at Nadia's first touch, her palm stroking up Jennifer's outer thigh and on up her side as a powerful muscular silken thigh followed up between hers. Wanton breath was suddenly trapped under Latin lips, the gentle capture followed by gorgeous weight, Nadia letting her full body push down on Jennifer beneath her. Hands with the touch of a lover wrapped around her, the care bringing instant submission from her willing subject and Jennifer risking her want, gently cupping Nadia's waist, pulling her down on her. The risk brought Nadia's response, squeezing tighter, Jennifer's heart beating hard against hers as she took her offering. Sighs now came from Nadia, too, Jennifer letting out more of hers as their bodies began to talk, Nadia's first grind up against her bringing Jennifer bucking up instantly from beneath her. With her want rushing forward, she pulled Nadia down, her squeeze becoming tighter as she grinded Jennifer deep into the bed covers beneath them. Starting to lose it, Jennifer became clawy, noisier, even pulling tighter as she let out her… SPANK!!!… The sharp feel of Nadia's hand against the side of her hip steadied her, for a moment slightly freezing as she held her breath before following Nadia's groan of appreciation as the intendant maintained control over her, working her how she wanted.

Grinding her down into the sheets, and Jennifer let out her want, groaning as she felt powerful Venezuelan silk push up against her, over and over, the occasional spanks bringing her round to her attentions, bringing her behavior to what she wanted.

Soon, she felt Nadia's appreciation, too, with the wanton following of her direction as Nadia could feel her submission and the totality of it. She could feel her searing desire responding fully to every touch, following her totally in any direction, smiling, kissing her as she felt the devotion. Hands moved slowly up Nadia's sides from her captive below her, Jennifer's timid touch encouraged as she tried to please her while the woman ground her down. Jennifer's world still black, her mouth watering for the scene around her, able to feel the room's silken luxury, her mind racing, guessing at what scarlet mystery was there – the room imagined like the ruby red carpets outside in the hallway.

Under gentle uplit walls, their want continued, scarlet passion watching over as hands dropped down lower. Pulses quickened as hands searched below, thighs tightening as sighs escaped, moaning encouragement as she reached between them… and nervous groaning as she finally found her. Her world invaded by Latin passions, her silken cage was forced aside, resistance falling as flooding came moaning out to the lovers' want.

Moaning, too, Nadia ground her into the sheets, her passions high as she felt her silken warmth against hers below. Jennifer's body flicked between fight and flight, Nadia feeling it, seizing her, chasing her shattered nerves inside her, grinding her dominance into her chosen favorite as Jennifer lurched, her moans unhindered and Nadia's spanks only heightening her tension, groaning out under panicked entrapment.

Soon she couldn't hide it, gushing forth, her body giving what trapped words could not. No one there to hold back her passions, Jennifer becoming fearful as Nadia's powerful gym-sculpted body gripped harder and harder, beginning to surge hungrily against her again and again. Latin groaning filled the air as Spanish lips stroked silken white below, Jennifer hearing a deep groaning she'd never heard before in Nadia as she thrashed herself against her demanding satisfaction. Holding on, Jennifer groaned out, fearful as gushing came with violent seizes, Spanish screams soaking out below with a frightening grip, Jennifer crying out from underneath. Nadia pulled her in completely, her fear only serving her want, chasing it, pulling her close as she showered her in dominance! Groaning turned to screams, passions running down Jennifer's thighs, tanned fury grinding with gripping nails competing over fear as Jennifer screamed from beneath her, pulled in completely to her dominance, completely to her world…..

Screaming turned to moaning, bodies grinding on, searching out the last of shuddering feelings and ravenously devouring them as their heavy kissing filled the room. Jennifer let go totally, following Nadia's every direction with no resistance or thought of else, only Nadia's will important as the night surged on and on….

Surrounded by her scent, only Nadia was important, their gushing screams and ripping bodies, their words as yet unspoken, only direction followed utterly, both tiring but holding on. One more hunger, though… one more hunger was to come, Nadia pulling Jennifer up to an obedient kneel, sitting displayed in front of her, no more nerves now as she showed herself utterly to her, given completely to her now… and Nadia knowing it.

Caring hands reached for her blindfold – a lover's touch, no way of hiding – the gentle slip of tying silk brought a ruby rush to meet her. A lair of passion, scarlet want, her denial lifted with her blindfold, her ruby prison red around her, questions answered by her captor. There was much more, though, more as she stared into her eyes, the emotion staring back, Jennifer seeing what she wanted, Nadia's stare having a look of confusion, both feeling something deeper….

Kneeling face to face, their world was theirs, time standing still for them, words not needed, their eyes saying all after weeks of dominance, forced submission replaced tonight by something different; she was hers… gifted and complete.

Nadia smiled… looking into Jennifer's eyes with

so many emotions – want, lust – but there was something else, something Jennifer felt, something both of them knew was there. Still with no words, Nadia stroked a hand up the outside of Jennifer's thigh, her lover's touch gently taking hold of her waist before deep brown eyes and the wanton smile pulled her close, her domination coming with the gentlest of kisses, Jennifer letting her eyes fall closed – sensitive to every tiny groan from Nadia as they kissed, silk touches stroking.

Small moans and gasps followed hands and lips, Jennifer growing louder as she felt Nadia move up, gently forcing her legs apart and leaving her knees inside Jennifer's, thighs held open, silk touches now working. Flowing down toward her submission, the touches came as she trembled outwardly. Lower and lower, pulling at times, Nadia's breath quickening and unable to resist, gripping her charge as she worked her way down, Jennifer gasping out at hands around her waist, one dropping to her thighs. Her attention focused on Nadia, she held on, eyes closed, feeling her hand work up and down, back and forth, stroking along the length of her thigh, each time getting closer, each time her breath heightening. Nadia gripped her tighter by the waist with her securing hand, holding her thighs apart, her own firmly between them moving closer each time, her hand sensing warmth below, Jennifer's vulnerability waiting as a prisoner in her grasp. Nervous moans from a shifting body saw Nadia chase her dominating side, rising and securing Jennifer with a vice-like grip, escape impossible, her hunger demanding. No chance of escape, Jennifer flooded below, her begging femininity wanton for touch, her breathing becoming moaning, her passions groaning out as she felt Nadia's hunger stroke her lips below. No punishment could stop her groaning out loudly, forward, Nadia kissing her instead, forcing passion up against her, Jennifer's hand drawn down through her thighs between them, Latin flooding and flowing out, joining hers below them. Uncontrollable lust surged through Jennifer's head as she stroked Nadia's silken lips below, her groaning following hers as the two women's hands worked feverishly between them, the first circular touch on Jennifer's clitoris forcing her to groan, fully surging against Nadia's kiss, gripping her captor with her other hand as she tried to close her legs with nerves, but couldn't, Nadia powerful thighs holding them open. Nadia's wanton fury began to surge forward loudly with Jennifer's struggle against her will, feeling her try to close her legs under the pleasure making her grip her helpless captive stronger. Her hand below became faster and faster, circling around as she felt Jennifer struggle. The pleasure unbearable, she broke from her kiss, screaming aloud, Nadia seizing her lips again, screams through their kissing from circling below, body surging with pleasure as the tightening began. Panicked and thrashing, and Nadia tightened all around her, fear of being trapped surging forward with want, desire surging up from tightening below as she screamed uncontrollably, her body lurching inside her. Screaming out with Nadia, both women flooded below, screaming in agony, orgasms tearing them asunder. Female want and circling fingers showered in flooding, screaming together, bodies seizing and holding. Jennifer strained to close her legs, but Nadia held them open, her fingers circling harder, her screaming for mercy ignored, her orgasm tearing her up as she was forced to endure Nadia's will – savage screaming surging out as she was ripped from inside. Screaming in agony under Nadia's hand, the woman forced her on through it still, never ceasing below. Panicked and thrashing, Jennifer screamed at the ceiling, screamed for her mercy, but was forced on regardless, Nadia enraptured by her entrapment as she screamed in her grasp. Tears flooded down Jennifer as she started to cry, unable to take it, pleasure surging inside her with no choice but to suffer as Nadia circled on harder, reaching deeper inside her, bringing agony forward. Suddenly, more screams, the room flooded with trapped femininity and Nadia surging below brought on by Jennifer's total collapse, her nature to seize the vulnerability. Collapsing forward on top of her, Jennifer felt Nadia's full wanton weight, her entrapment complete, the circling stopping, bringing shock shuddering on as she cried, Nadia wanting to hear it aloud. Squeezing her tight, all etiquette fell as she knew she'd just fallen for her, and knew she was hers…

Nadia could feel it, and she wanted it; she cared for Jennifer that night, had let go of any minor infringements, didn't punish when she should, Jennifer hers now, that becoming obvious. What wasn't obvious was the reverse psychology Nadia had used, this happenstance having come many times before. Always in control and never falling herself, she knew this time was different as she pushed it away in her mind. Jennifer's cries had woken something inside her and, with all the complications that would bring for her training, she denied it, brushed it aside, tried to lie to herself as they groaned there. This night, it didn't matter; this night was theirs to be had, one knowing she had fallen and the other denying it as they fell.

Lying there, finally talking, their embrace never stopped, Jennifer embarrassed but sure of it, sure of what she was feeling and making sure Nadia knew it, opening up completely in front of her. Wanting her to know, so they spent hours talking, talking and touching, holding each other close and again breathing their passions, engulfed by their feelings, the room filled with their want and watching them fall.

It couldn't last – Jennifer wanted it to go on forever, and Nadia too, but she had to take her back, and Jennifer was offended at first as Nadia's controlling look came on before being purposefully subdued as she saw the hurt in Jennifer's eyes. She explained that these things did happen, but that it wouldn't be easy, structures and controls in-house meaning loving tenderness could not be shown, that both of them would end up being brought before the Mistress, Nadia lucky if she would be kept on as an intendant and Jennifer certainly to be thrown out. Relationships between intendants and slaves were strictly forbidden in the Manor, it having a reputation as a house of training and etiquette, not some lowly lust factory for enjoyment. Professionalism was paramount in order that business and money kept rolling in, and the Manor's reputation was what maintained that.

She explained that intendants often had a favorite, and sometimes felt even more for them; she smiled. The other intendants knew this and knew to keep quiet for their own sake, their own forbidden intrigues at risk, too. It was the power struggles through them, as well, though, blackmail and scheming for position in house rife, so they would have to keep quiet. Nadia spoke softly, Jennifer agreeing.

An hour more, and Jennifer had to go, Nadia's practiced expression of dominance returning as she dressed somewhat haphazardly in her intendant's uniform, the passion of the night softening her. Taking Jennifer by the arm and straightening her up as she stood in front of her, she drew the blindfold, Jennifer understanding from their conversations that she'd have to be an intendant now. In public, she'd still have to punish her hard and Jennifer would have to accept it – she was, after all, her intendant; she'd smiled as they'd kissed, Jennifer giggling, smiling through the affection as Nadia playfully spanked her ass. Already, though, the first signs of what would be a strain for them emerged, Jennifer almost offended by Nadia's coldness as she'd pulled her forward, straightening her up to her, Jennifer pulling back slightly, an immediate slap on her ass and strong look of disapproval from Nadia making her start, her hurt look immediate. Nadia's practiced cold expression broke at seeing it – she didn't like seeing her upset already. Dropping her eyes, she took Jennifer in her arms, her gorgeous brown eyes flicking up to hers as she spoke, "We have to do this if we want to be together; think of it as an act… okay?" she smiled, squeezing Jennifer reassuringly.

Jennifer eventually smiled back after thinking. "Yes, Mistress," she whispered, the two immediately breaking into a smile, Nadia kissing her passionately before playfully spanking her thigh and looking into her eyes for understanding.

"Intendant," she answered Jennifer's questioning look. "We have to keep up the act," Nadia repeated, raising the blindfold in front of her, Nadia's smile the last thing she saw before accepting her darkness.

Led through the Manor, it was five in the morning, and not a sound could be heard as Jennifer followed Nadia's direction, the plush carpet leading to the stairs and bringing the sudden sound of Nadia's boots on the tiled floor, signaling their arrival on the ground level. Parading her naked charge around the main hallway staircase, Nadia stopped briefly behind it, knowing the cameras couldn't see them. Gripping Jennifer's hand tighter in the darkness, she drew a finger over her smile, her gentle objection duly obeyed. Jennifer took the smile away, having forgotten in her excitement a slave's position, her learned look of submission awaiting, direction returning. This proper etiquette to be observed at all times, proper behavior a plain face until instructed otherwise.

"Etiquette," she whispered in her ear. "Don't leave me looking like I can't perform my duties," her tone was quietly hard, but full of warmth and emotion. "Remember what Urst did when you left her like that."

Jennifer recoiled, hurt again, like in the room.

Nadia saw it, feeling her disappointment. "Don't make me have to punish you," she whispered deliciously in her ear, a playful warmth in her tone, Jennifer having to fight hard not to smile as Nadia placed a hand on her stomach, pulling her back against her corset. Held in her grasp, Nadia's playful spank didn't help, Nadia watching her struggle with trying to hold on and control herself.

She reveled in her nakedness, proud to be being led up the wing by someone as incredible as Nadia, wanting people to see her and wanting to be seen, but there was no one, Nadia gently whispering reassurance. Jennifer responded to her request for control, taking care to shield herself from the cameras as she spoke, feeling Jennifer stiffen outside her dorm, applying her etiquette as she was asked.

Leading her inside, she knew the other women were all asleep, Jennifer again denied being the spectacle she wanted to be. Conscious of the camera watching their every move, she obeyed completely, taking care to have an expression of submission and even fear as Nadia cuffed her to her bed, her eyes just for a second flashing into hers as she turned away, powerful and strong, the camera seeing only a professional intendant marching out after dealing with an unruly slave.

Behind her, though, wanton eyes followed her sharp boots, powerful Venezuelan thighs drawing her attention to them as her ass lurched from side to side as if in triumph, her garter unmanaged on the left, her suspender hanging loose underneath.

Jennifer slept better than she'd ever slept that morning; she wasn't frightened and had no intention of leaving…. Nadia had fixed her.

Chapter 10

Dark Questions

When the boots came in that morning, the sound made one slave wet. Memories from the night before had to be hidden, easier as Urst and Valerie uncuffed her, harder as Latin passion marched to breakfast just beside her.

Hidden well behind a face of plainness, her instructions followed, doors sealed on breakfast… and her interrogation.

Andrea pounced almost immediately from the other side of the table, her bubbly Irish charm leaping out as an unlikely inquisitor, but surrounded by back-up, all eyes on Jennifer.

"So!" Andrea burst out, hardly able to contain herself. "Did you scream or squeal!?" She demanded, her smile beaming out as the whole table burst into laughter, Jennifer reddening as she dropped her head, no longer wishing to be the center of attention as she had the night before.

"I…" she stammered, her smile leaking out. "I learned," was all she could manage, trying to remind herself about the camera above.

"You must have learned well," Suzanna quipped from the bottom of the table. "You were gone most of the night," she smiled, laughter breaking out around the table and Jennifer reddening further.

"I thought you were all asleep," Jennifer stammered with her head down, trying to defend herself.

"What, show yourself awake with Nadia coming into the room?" Heather smiled from across the table. "The Mistress of pain herself," she continued, Jennifer looking up. "I'll stay away from those hands, thank you very much," she continued, smiling, eyeing Jennifer closely as the table laughed, all acutely aware of Nadia's reputation for being able to administer the harshest of learning with her hands if required. "But you were in them all night," Heather continued accusingly, looking directly into Jennifer's eyes, the whole table focusing on her squirming. "And there's not a mark on you," she smiled suggestively, Jennifer looking down again, her embarrassed smile setting off the table's laughter and the other three tables looking on in bemused curiosity.

"Oh, leave her alone," Diane pretended to defend her. "She has about as much bruising on her as you do when Carly's finished with you." The table burst into laughter, Heather now reddened herself in trying not to drop her head too much in admission.

The table laughed on, the women truly beginning to bond with each other now as shared struggles and hard learnings had brought them closer over the weeks, another unseen strategy of the Manor. Much like in the army, new recruits were pitted against the intendants, their support for each other against their seemingly cruel whims fostering strength inside them, stronger women emerging.

Heather, though, didn't feel the group's strength, more its jovial sarcasm now, as it was her turn to face its teasing, her special relationship with Carly common knowledge by now. Undeniably Carly's favorite, Heather seemed to have been singled out by her at first, far more attention on her and harder punishments given, the women watching what they thought was malice sent in her direction. It was a southern thing, Heather had explained – the group didn't get it. Something to do with the southern states of America, Carly being Floridian, and Heather Virginian, that seeming to make her an almost immediate target for Carly as she'd pushed her hard, almost forcing her will on her, Heather resisting hard back, but eventually, willingly, she'd seemed to submit…

After this, Carly had relented, and hers now, she treated her well, the other women watching through the day as little looks and smiles fleeted between them, and at night there was more evidence of their southern bond. Carly would come for her frequently after dark, the other intendants never taking her, leaving her alone, it now being understood who she belonged to. When Carly didn't come for her, she got a good night's sleep, and when she did… well… she got a good night's sleep… eventually.

Becoming someone's favorite in house, although openly hidden, had huge advantages, these being apparent to those who weren't in this position; try as the intendants might to pretend to treat them the same as the rest of the group, they were frequently spared harsher punishments, enjoying the unofficial protection of their intendants. This protection, though, did not extend to the accusations from their sisters, this being the reason Heather's face now competed with Jennifer's for the scarlet prize.

Around the table, accusatory looks now focused on the left-hand side of the table, starting with Jennifer as, head bowed, she faced the beaming Andrea across the table from her, and then clockwise to the right, Heather's head similarly bowed, the woman doing her best to stop her smile getting any bigger, to Julie, Amandine, and Diane. Crossing back over to Jennifer's side of the table, Suzanna at the far end led to Monique, and Linda, then an empty place and back to Jennifer, this seating position uniformed now, simply where they had all sat on the first day and continued to.

The empty place was, of course, Vanessa's, who now listened intently as she was knelt on all fours, shackled to the floor by the neck with the other three morning's examples.

"Well, at least you don't have to worry about who's going to take you next," bemoaned Julie, not a favorite yet and frequently taken by many.

"You'd hate being taken by only one," laughed Linda across from her. "You'd miss being a hussy!"

The whole table erupted with laughter, Julie pursing her lips and half-pretending to glare at Linda as she joined the reddening faces.

"At least I'm not the teacher's pet!" she returned, the table bursting with laughter again at Linda, now a regular victim of Miss Goodspank, something continued on from day one in the Academy.

Linda joined the scarlet club now, trying to think of a return, but coming up with nothing under the pressure, instead trying to shift the attention to the intendants. "It's probably just another strategy anyway," she shifted. "To get us to do what they want, they must have countless slaves going through here; they can't have favorites all the time."

"Who said you were Miss Goodspank's favorite? I think she hates you," Suzanna drew the table's laughter straight back to Linda, not letting her escape, her reddening continuing as she gave her a sarcastic look before breaking into a smile and dropping her head.

Linda's claim, though, did hit home all around the table, Jennifer suddenly suspicious like the other women, but hoping it wasn't true; were they just being manipulated?

Suspicion, too, was suddenly abound above, two intendants in the control room now focused squarely on Linda, squinting at her and then each other after what she'd just said. The intendants did use such tactics and many others, but these were strictly to remain their business, and it was absolutely forbidden for any of the house methods to be discussed with slaves. They were to remain completely oblivious to the manipulation and pressures used against them, this done to ensure there was no way they could feel any kind of understanding as to what they were going through, no way to guess what was coming. It had been found, over the years, that ensuring ignorance left the slaves vulnerable and on edge, never being able to guess any direction or course, leaving them nervous and fearful, a much easier state to manage them in. Any slave who knew what was coming could ready themselves against it, even employing their own strategies for getting through it, this breeding confidence and even insolence, a condition that would not foster good learning. Any attempt by slaves to try and predict what was coming was known as incitement, and brought the most sever punishments on those involved. The main concern was for the intendants – had one of them broken ranks and told Linda of their methods? If so, house rules had been broken, and severe consequences would follow, the intendant likely dismissed; it was the intendants' duty to find out… and Linda would tell them. Fear was necessary, as without fear, slaves would not obey completely; it was fear that had them try hard to avoid harsher treatment, fear that snapped them to attention when an intendant arrived in a room or corridor, and right now, Linda didn't sound fearful… but that would change.

Outside again, glistening sweat and the savage work-out filled their time on the steps, but one mind among them couldn't quite concentrate. Distant, she kept thinking about what Linda had said; was it just a tactic, was her night with Nadia an illusion with nothing there, just a well-rehearsed play on her feelings? She couldn't believe that – she'd seen the look in Nadia's eyes, felt her heaving desire in her bed, and why had she whispered at the dorm room door, why would she care if the cameras heard if it was all an illusion… unless that was all part of it, to convince her it was real. She couldn't concentrate, Carly's instructions in front barely heard as her mind wrestled with the 'what ifs' and… SNAP! Jennifer's mind was suddenly jolted to attention as the feeling of warm soft leather licked up across her cheeks from behind, turning her head to see a coy smile from Nadia as she was reattaching her strap to her hip as she moved off down the line, her eyes widening as she nodded toward Carly, directing Jennifer to focus on her… an order that was duly obeyed.

The look was what Jennifer needed – it was warm, caring, and there was no way she could be faking that, and her strike, warm and playful, the lightest strap she'd ever witnessed, Jennifer was sure, and started concentrating… too late, though, as Carly had seen her.

Not once, not once did Jennifer enter the correction huts, not even with Nadia – it had to be her will, it made her more sure, and hopefully soon they'd get to talk, and maybe she could ask her, have her sooth her worries and clear her mind; the training was ending now anyway, and there were no cameras outside, but it wasn't to be.

Clearing away the steps and materials, the women were formed into line exhausted and panting, two gorgeous corseted forms in front, one on the left while Carly took the rear, completing the standard marching order. About to move off, Jennifer suddenly felt a hand take her arm; it was Carly coming in on her from behind.

"And where do you think you're going?" Carly's voice almost purred as she tightened her grip slightly, her devastating blond hair adorning her staggering body which was dripping from her exertions, but she wasn't tired. "I'm afraid this one hasn't quite put the work in like the others," she announced. "And I don't think that's quite fair, do you?" She questioned Jennifer in front of the others, raising her eyebrows and playfully cocking her head. "No answer," Carly announced, Jennifer unsure of what to say. "She must be tired – well, if she can't answer with her mouth, then we'll just have to find some other use for it." She declared as she pulled her gently out of line, the other women smiling to themselves, happy at the chastisement, it having been noticed and resented that Jennifer had not been savaged in the correction huts like the rest of them.

Jennifer suddenly felt a strange feeling, as she didn't want to go with Carly, it written all over her face as she confirmed it, Carly noticing her looking down the left to the Latin corset that faced away from her.

"Valerie, could you come and help me with this one? I want to make sure she's in peak performance like the rest," Carly announced, seeing Jennifer's discomfort and seeming to enjoy it.

Another Latin corset duly appeared, built stronger and more powerfully than the one she wanted, her smile, too, seemed to come from getting off on Jennifer's obvious pain.

And she watched them leave, ordered by Urst, and Nadia never said a word, the group moving off with Nadia not looking back… if she cared, she was hiding it well.

"Awww, don't worry," Carly gloated over Jennifer's obvious feelings. "We'll give you back, once we're finished with you," her expression changed, all smiles leaving as she took on a more threatening stance. "Straighten up!" she ordered, Jennifer startled by her scream, it being such a shock from Carly's usual soft composure.

"Do you think I'm different? Soft?" demanded Carly, glaring into Jennifer's eyes. "Do you think you can afford to disrespect me in front of the others?" Her eyes were piercing, Jennifer quite shocked, having never seen her angry, shaking her head in response as she felt the intendant's grip tighten on her arm to the point of pain.

Valerie looked on smiling, quite enjoying the sideshow, her powerful presence doing nothing to calm Jennifer as she suddenly realized she was all alone, and outside with two powerful intendants… she began to feel afraid.

"I think you have to learn that having the eye of someone in here doesn't mean you can take liberties; I think you have to be reminded of your place." Carly's angry look changed to a sour stare.

And suddenly they were off, moving toward the correction huts as Carly kept her strong hold on her, pulling her firmly toward the group of trees hiding the huts, the same trees that would hide her when the two of them had her in there… alone.

To her surprise, they moved past them; passing by, they turned behind the group of trees now shielding them from view from any prying eyes in the Manor. Turning, Carly's mean look couldn't hold, as being the soft one of the group, she seemed determined that Jennifer wouldn't see her that way, but her mischievous smile wasn't threatening like the others. Passing her to Valerie, Jennifer felt her powerful strong grip, definitely threatening, but she hardly had time to worry as Carly suddenly got down on all fours in front of her, a smile taking hold as she went. Jennifer was stunned as Carly's black panties strained to hold in her powerful aerobic cheeks – drenched in evening sunlight, sweat ran down her gorgeous thighs, dripping to the grass below. Mouth open, Jennifer stared in awe as Carly reached back and eased her panties over her cheeks to her thighs below.

Mouth open was exactly what they wanted as Valerie took hold of the back of Jennifer's hair, easing her down to her knees and more as her own knees found the grass, kneeling beside the two as she was pushed further down toward her correction.

"Get that tongue out," Valerie instructed in her strong Latin tone, Carly smiling underneath as Jennifer was made to oblige. Hearing her own breath as she was forced between the cheeks, Jennifer felt the heat of Carly's body before she was smothered in her ass. Carly's groan vibrated through her body straight into Jennifer's face as her tongue fell deep into the hot wet crevice, the taste of Carly taking over her senses, her body flooded with her scent.

"Deeper," instructed Valerie, pushing firmly from behind, Jennifer breathing through her nose, the heat and smell filling her inside, her own crevice soaking just like Carly's. "Deeper!" a spank rang out, Valerie determined on her will, Carly's groan confirming her instruction as Jennifer found depth in Carly's ass. Pushing down inside, she fought for breath as Carly groaned, Jennifer's tongue squeezing down between her walls, her ass her total focus.

Giggling through her groans, Carly shuddered underneath her, feelings tickling up her spine as she squeezed on Jennifer's tongue. Gasping up for air, Jennifer breathed as Valerie released her for a moment, only to push her back down deep, Carly's ass all she could taste, Jennifer's groans making Carly smile, feeling her struggle in behind her as she punished her with glee. Jennifer was rhythmic now, her world Carly's ass, her tongue trapped and squeezed, her… parp!

It was a shock, Jennifer's tongue immediately pulling back in her mouth as she gagged on noxious fumes.

Holding her through her struggles, Valerie flexed above in laughter, Carly, too, laughing out as Jennifer was pushed back down toward her ass… but she pulled back again.

She couldn't help it, the smell still in the air, and another push brought more refusal… she pulled back a second time!

All laughing suddenly stopped as a truly angry Carly turned around to meet her as she reeled back into Valerie's powerful grip behind her.

Carly came straight up into her face, Valerie peering over her shoulder, trapped between real anger; now for the first time, she feared her group's aerobist.

"How dare you?" hissed Carly, seething in rage at the refusal and taking hold of Jennifer's neck and pulling her forward. "That's the second time you've disrespected me today," she glared into her. "Oh, you're going to learn!" she assured her.

As Jennifer was marched back across the grass, Valerie followed behind, Carly leading the way, Jennifer's arm clasped in her grip; no longer acting, she was truly angry, but not the Urst powerful and emotionless anger, not the Nadia authoritative and commanding style… it was something else… scorn! Her nails digging into Jennifer's arm, the charge wanted it to stop, but didn't dare say a word, the look on her face enough to keep her quiet and the Manor looming large over their approach, cast in shadow with the sun now passed behind it.

Straight up the steps and into the ballroom, Carly's grip never ceased, entering an empty room kind to Jennifer's plight, but there was just embarrassment ahead as curious-faced intendants and slaves watched the spectacle pass, Jennifer half-dragged through the hallway. It was obvious to everyone from the look on Carly's face that Jennifer was about to be dealt with, the thundering crack crack crack of her intendants' boots rammed into the tiles as she pulled her the short distance to the rear of the main stairway, all of it clearing up any doubt.

Embarrassed, Jennifer's arm ached as Carly pulled her down the stairs, her world immediately falling dark as Valerie followed, sealing any chance of escape. They arrived only briefly on the first lower level, its grey prison-like atmosphere menacing as Jennifer became fearful, Carly raging in front of her, the fear suddenly climbing as she was whirled around again to the left and straight down the adjoining staircase to the second lower level....

Her dark world became even darker, the walls changing from grey to black, only the dimmest bulbs in factory-square lighting cases above, one to either side on the roof over the landing as they arrived. Freezing... it was freezing, much colder than the wings above, a tactic subtle and unseen, left in the background and unspoken. A psychological trick learned over years, it left slaves unwanting for the corridors, the wing's coldness uncomfortable and making for slight relief in the warmer rooms. The coldness brought fear with its discomfort, making the managing of slaves along the wings slightly easier, their timidness accentuated by the temperature, the realization of their trouble heightening as they went. This realization brought complicity, the slaves fearing angering the intendants further and so behaving better as they were taken, resistance rare and unwise.

Jennifer couldn't make anything out, only Carly's hair as she was pulled up the right wing, the cold suddenly engulfing her body as she trembled in the darkness, not daring to resist. Two sets of sharp boots echoing off the walls in the darkness, one in front and one behind, told Jennifer she was trapped, as if she hadn‘t already realized it. Her cold feet followed on the tiles, almost invisible below as a door passed on the left, its opposite almost missed on the right as they passed under another bulb, barely on. Brought to halt, Jennifer shivered out her breath, her nerves, through the roof her exhale clearly being audible.

"Silence!!!" Carly screamed in the darkness, still raging at her earlier refusal. "Hold her…" she hissed, pushing her back into Valerie's grasp, Jennifer's body trembling to her delight. As her eyes adjusted, Jennifer heard Carly fumbling in her garter pockets, hearing the sound of keys emerging in the dark as her eyes picked up two doors in front of them, Carly beginning to unlock the one on the right. Out of the corner of her eye, Jennifer picked up the faintest outline of a dark door at the end of the wing, but it was the door directly behind her that made her start as a muffled scream made her turn, Valerie instantly spanking her from behind. Carly spun around at the insolence just as the door opened in front of her, calming light like that in their dorms flooding out and revealing a raging look as she reached forward, grabbing hold of Jennifer, the slave's fear making her resist….

"In!!!" was all Carly could get out as she raged at the insolence, Jennifer giving yet another example of it as she was roughly dragged through the door and spun around, face to face. "Are you trying to make me hurt you?" she glared into her as the sound of the door closed behind them, sealing them in. It wasn't that Jennifer remembered she couldn't say the word 'no' – it was true fear at Carly's rage and mounting terror at where she was that left her only able to shake her head, her nerves shattered and unsure if it was safe to cry.

Carly looked at her for a moment, pursing her lips slightly as she realized the fear in her face; Jennifer was ashen white, frightened, this seeming to soften Carly, but she was still angry.

"Take a look around." Her voice had dropped but was still strong. "You're going to be here for a while," she assured her. "This is a different classroom from upstairs… down here, no one's allowed to fail… down here, everybody learns."

Frightened, Jennifer timidly looked around, seeing that the room was calm, warm, having the same cream-colored walls as their dorms, the same uplighters, one at each corner of the square room, its ten foot by ten foot dimensions feeling tight, the roof only just over six feet high and making it tighter. Hidden in their purpose, built square surrounds on the uplighters in the light oak wooden floor funneled their calming light up the walls to the same cream roof above. The scene was still till Jennifer's breathing suddenly lifted her eyes, starting at the device hanging from the ceiling in the middle of the room.

"Well." Carly smiled as she watched Jennifer's eyes widen at what she was seeing. "Let me introduce you to the ball."

Hanging from the roof behind a visibly amused Carly was a perspex ball. Four feet in circumference, its top-most part passed into the ceiling above. Jennifer looked bemused as she surveyed a hole in the curve nearest her, facing the door behind her, its edge having a cream padded collar all around it, giving a clue as to what was to come.

"Don't worry." Carly smiled, her voice menacingly sarcastic. "You'll soon know what it's for," she assured her as she passed her back to Valerie.

Jennifer watched as Carly turned away, her attention drawn to her garter, the sound of keys beside her gorgeous curves, the light accentuating her intendant's uniform as it strained to keep her in. Her stockings straining to the sound of leather corseting, Carly's arms reaching up to the left of the ball, the sound of a key finding its lock followed by the heavy plastic unfastening of a bracket, unhinging back out from the left of the ball as it opened.

Jennifer hardly had time to worry before Valerie pushed her forward, her feet unsure as they clumsily grasped the floor beneath them, Valerie almost pushing through her as she moved her by the arm to the right of the opened ball. Its shape lay there menacing, beckoning its victim; opened on a heavy plastic hinge in the ball's right, a three-quarter moon section sat curved and open in the room, the remainder of the ball held fast in the roof above Jennifer, who was able to see up inside as she was moved to the open section. Roughly pushed on through her nerves, and Valerie turned her toward the circular hole in the open section, Jennifer's look back at her answered by a spank, her head spinning back to her front to meet Carly as she moved to the other side of the open perspex, their eyes meeting through the hole. Jennifer felt Valerie's free hand take the back of her hair, her head secured forward as she was pushed into the collared hole, the sound of boot heels tacking at the floor having her nerves explode as she was trapped between two corsets, their leather grasp gripping her between them.

“Enough!” Carly screamed at the slight sound on her exhale, the scream directly in her face, freezing Jennifer for a second as her head passed through the hole, Carly’s hands beneath her chin immediately tightening a strap at the base of the collar, Jennifer feeling its hold tightening around her neck.

Nerves unabating, she waited for Carly to scream again as her breathing grew louder, the feeling of entrapment growing strong with her neck being squeezed all around. The sound of soft leather buckling below her chin drew a slight sound in her breath, Carly’s eyes flicking scornfully before falling back to their chore as the cushioned collar tightened still further.

The trapped tension in the room bore witness as a trembling slave was secured in its center, a final look from an angry intendant’s eyes the last thing she saw before tacking heels and trapping hands now moved behind her, lifting her arms out to the side, her neck held fast by the collar strapped around her.

Fearful, her eyes saw calming cream, the wall plain out in front before her arms were suddenly released, left alone in the air, and then the feeling.

Feeling of tightening by the neck, her head pulled forward as intendants pushed behind on the ball’s open section, Jennifer’s entrapment now too real. Calming cream was suddenly glazed as the three-quarter hinged section carried a trapped slave by the neck to her circular sealed prison, its perspex surround now becoming her world. A sudden sound from Jennifer’s nerves shocked her as it bounced around the ball, the spank felt but also heard strangely, as the sound came from outside and behind. Her left hand roughly pushed aside, Jennifer saw Carly's hands work up the ball's left to the perspex hinged lock, sealing it in on the ball's shape, neatly clamping it into a dip in the plastic prison, its surface now smooth.

Carly's sly look for a second through the perspex was the last thing Jennifer saw before the muffled sound of heavy boots leaving her behind was more felt than heard, like the closing door and heavy locking, Jennifer left trapped on her own.

Still worried about making noise, she fretted as she heard herself breathing aloud inside the ball. A few seconds later and she calmed, realizing no one could hear her, and then she fretted again as an attempt to shift her weight met immediate resistance by the neck. Instinctively, she lifted her hands to the ball's smooth surface outside, its domed shape preventing them getting in to her head. Panicked, she instinctively tried to pull her head out, but feet uselessly slipped on the smooth floor below, her weight instantly transferring uncomfortably to her neck as the ball held her fast, her hands unable to assist as they slid uselessly on its smooth surface, nothing to grip on the outside. After a few more seconds of useless fumbling, Jennifer realized it was hopeless, her hands finding no grip on smooth perspex, their search in vain as they came to rest at either side of the ball, her neck now in pain as she finally submitted to her prison. To avoid the neck strain, she brought her feet together to stop the slipping on the slick floor below, her posture now straight and submissive, her hands rested on the ball, her ass still stinging from her correction before. A lone figure secured by the neck in the center of the room with the calming light on cream walls doing nothing for her as she breathed heavily, waiting for whatever was going to come into the room to get her. Her gaze, though, finally saw the opening, unseen before due to the dark roof of the ball buried into the ceiling above, and unreached by the light from her room below, and she suddenly realized it had a hole in it. Three feet diagonally above her… she made out a hole about a foot in circumference, oval in shape and angled directly at her face, her neck restraint presenting her to it. Still fearful and bewildered by the new treatment, she suddenly became aware of the pain across her cheeks from her correction before. Unable to help it, she reached back to her discomfort, hoping no one could see her, her soothing strokes on her warm cheeks short-lived as a muffled noise to her left brought her hands quickly back to the ball's surface, fearing more punishment.

She quickly realized it was footsteps, travelling upstairs to her left on the other side of the wall, and she surmised that the first of the two doors on the left must lead upstairs above her, the door on the right that she'd come through leaving her under these ascending boots. Listening, she could hear more than two sets of boots; soon they ascended above her, the noise becoming different as boots to her left came through wall and perspex, becoming boots overhead, heavy and menacing, clearer as the sound came through the open hole above her… the hole.

Almost forgotten about in her struggles, and she suddenly realized it was open above; her mind quickly guessed, then guessed again, her nerves matching as she looked around the inside of the perspex ball and back to the open hole three feet diagonally above… no, she thought. The realization made her try and pull back again, but the ball's grip hadn't loosened, her nerves reaching higher as her body finally realized it was truly trapped. Breathing becoming heavier, she heard the sounds washed around her in the ball before muffled voices came down through the hole. Looking up, she could only guess at the horror as she became silent and fearful, still pulling uncontrollably at her neck restraint, her nerves trying to flee.

With her hands trying to grip the smooth perspex outside, her hopeless position dawned more and more as new sounds filtered down from the darkness above. She could make out three voices and Valerie laughing, then boots, and then sharp clutter; was that crockery? A few seconds later, and she determined it was, then rolling, the rolling of wheels heavy… and toward her. Suddenly silence… Jennifer looked at the hole above her, nerves reaching new heights as she froze, holding her breath and realizing something was about to happen….

A commotion above the sound of sliding overhead as something suddenly pushed through the hole, her body freezing to the spot… an ass!

Gorgeous perfect cheeks, voluptuous and toned, sat tanned above her, Jennifer stunned and not knowing at first what to think till suddenly the sounds above made frightening sense… cutlery. Sealing the hole completely, and just three feet diagonally above her, and she looked timidly to her left at the plastic of her cage, her hands flexing uselessly against its outside, held tight by the neck as it dawned on her the reality of what was to happen. Confirmed almost at once, she heard the sound of plates setting down and murmured voices above. The sound of running wheels before a catering trolley, she imagined food being wheeled in above her… she was right.

Sitting above her, suspended in mid-air, beautiful tanned cheeks sat poised, the uninterrupted view of the bare femininity between them stunning Jennifer as she was forced by the neck to observe the sight. Lowered into her perspex prison from the darkness above, the calming light from her room below bathed the tanned cheeks in a warming glow. Not Carly or Valerie, nor Nadia, she didn't recognize the intendant, only the gorgeous South American Latin tan, Jennifer realizing that now another group would know her plight, one of their intendants drafted in to punish her. She wondered why it wasn't Carly, a strange curiosity coming over her at the question, sharply pulled away as the clatter of crockery above signaled something beginning. Tightening up, Jennifer steeled herself to what was about to happen… but nothing did. Instead, she was treated to quiet observation of this voluptuous beauty above, the contemplation interrupted occasionally by cutlery finding crockery and the murmur of voices. Soon, the smell of food drifted into the ball around her, Jennifer realizing what was happening above. It becoming obvious what was to come, Jennifer's mind wanted to run, but flight wasn't to be, the embrace around her neck a tight reminder of that. Instead, her nerve-shot body breathed heavily around her, held to attention in the room, her arms resting helplessly outside as she faced her beautiful punishment within… beauty not to last.

After a time, she calmed, quiet acceptance almost there; her body, though worried, becoming still and restful, the sound of cutlery above almost rhythmic and pleasant. It was almost as if the calming atmosphere experienced overhead was filtering down to their charge held below. Filtering down, too, was the smell of fine food – once over her initial nerves, strangely, Jennifer thought she found herself actually becoming hungry, her predicament seeming to lessen in its immediacy. After the initial shock and worry, Jennifer's emotions began to calm, overridden by hunger as her mind began to wander. Still forced to survey directly the full cheeks just overhead, her mind had her vision as she began to muse about Nadia. Questions still to be answered, she wondered… why had she just walked off? Perhaps she couldn't be seen to care openly, the other intendants teasing and obviously showing that, at least in their group, their open secret was not open. And then there was breakfast; was Linda right? Was it all a strategy? How could she find out? And then, of course, there was… PAAARRP!

The blast of air hit her directly, the sound startling her to attention, her mind clearing, and then the smell!!! Her gasp sucked in more as she gagged instantly on fowl air! Coughing brought more breathing, more foulness as she pulled by the neck, her hands straining against the perspex outside. Coughing now to spluttering, her palms banging uselessly against the ball, her head not able to pull out as intendants laughed overhead, the assailant feeling the struggles beneath through her pelvis, Jennifer's plight bringing mirth all round above her. Choking now on the fowl stench, her throat rasped at the air, her feet sliding out from beneath her, her palms banging hard against the ball, her neck held fast as PAAARP!!! Another blast and choking tears, screams as she panicked, the air thick and disgusting, her body struggling, straining to escape, meaning muscles needed air, held breath needed to inhale, the taste surging down her throat as again the ass opened up to her screams underneath! Screams to coughing to choking tears to pulling hands as a new sound surged into the ball, Jennifer throwing up everywhere, her panicked shrieks matching her banging palms as she struggled against the ball, terror engulfing her as she choked within the horror. Screaming out in terror, she threw up again, choking at the neck, each breath bringing the fowl stench and choking, her screams shattering inside the ball, her mind totally oblivious to the intendants entering the room behind her.

Shrieks of terror jumped even higher as hands seized her from behind, her arms secured as, panicked and choking, she tried to wrestle from their grip. Screaming, she almost threw up again as a sudden click and pull backwards brought a blast of air surging all around, the shock and backwards movement emptying the rest of Jennifer's stomach to the floor. Crying tears rolled as she saw Carly out in front while Valerie's vice-like grip around her arms left her hanging uselessly by the neck from the ball's open door. Like some poor farmyard animal, she cried in shock under the merciless grip of her tormentors.

"Enough!!!" screamed Carly, glaring into her face as Valerie's grip moved to her waist.

"Be quiet," growled Valerie, her Latin tone menacing from behind, Jennifer's shock sniveling to a whimper, but with a still audible SPANK! "Be Quiet!!!" screamed Valerie, her voice filling the room and Jennifer freezing, shaking in her grip as Carly continued glaring at her from in front.

Held between the two, Jennifer shook, Carly's still glare and frightening posture from in front matched by Valerie's grip and tightening anger from behind.

Carly moved closer, almost nose to nose with a quivering Jennifer. "Shut…your…mouth," she slowly growled, glaring into her eyes, no mercy at all.

Still shaking, Jennifer watched her turn away, nothing attractive about her now as she watched her bring forth new implements, unseen before with her struggles… a mop, bucket, and cloth.

With Carly glaring at her one more time, as if disgusted, Jennifer watched as Carly mopped up the floor, ignoring her obvious suffering before dipping the cloth into pine-smelling liquid in the bucket and moving to the ball. Still shaking, Jennifer stood quietly as Carly cleaned inside the ball, repeatedly dipping into the bucket and ringing the cloth, dripping water for her efforts echoing in the small confined room. Finishing the ball, she ran the cloth over the still-present ass, cleaning away Jennifer's efforts before turning to her face with the same cloth, the gentle smell of disinfectant a relief as it removed the smell from around her nose. Whimpering, Jennifer felt ridiculous and panicked, and still held in the open ball, she felt the pressure between the two angers of the intendants, the room's silence making her start. SPANK!!! Carly's free hand found the side of her ass as she glared at her, the jolt keeping her controlled as she paused for a moment, looking into her eyes with no sign of her anger dropping. Satisfied that Jennifer was controlled, she dropped the cloth to the floor, her hands falling to the restraint under Jennifer's neck as she sighed, clearly disappointed in her. Jennifer felt ashamed and wanted to cry, but she didn't; she also felt relief as she felt Carly struggle with the restraint, seemingly having difficulty loosening it, Jennifer feeling it tighten at first before… suddenly, Carly's hands fell away, the restraint left tighter as a push from behind sent her back to the ball! Jennifer screamed in panic as the view of Carly disappeared and she swung round into the closing ball, the ass waiting for her inside! Screaming, she thrashed her hands in fright as they were roughly grabbed and pulled aside, the feeling of Valerie's corset ramming up against her from behind forcing her forward as Carly sealed the ball from the side. With the hinged lock sealed again, Valerie let go, the sudden release having her panic, screams and thrashing loud as she slammed her palms against the ball again! A harsh spank did nothing but have her scream out as she pulled back against her neck restraint, clearly frightened and distressed, the next sudden lash of strap across her cheeks having her howl once, twice, and a third time, too!!!

Her screams almost deafened her in the ball as savage hands seized her cheeks, a leather corset ramming up against her from behind, pulling tight. "SHUT UP!!!!!" came Carly's voice. "If you don't start behaving, I'm going to lose my temper with you," she assured her, Jennifer shaking her in her grasp.

Still shaking, Jennifer was quiet and quivering as she felt the hands leave her ass and pass around her waist, pulling her tighter, Jennifer's body feeling totally vulnerable to Carly outside the ball. But nothing happened – Carly just held her… tight, a common tactic when dealing with a panicked slave, as it reassured them, let them know they were being attended to, cared for, and sometimes reassuring words would also be used, but not this time, as Carly too angry for that. After a time, she felt Jennifer calm, her breathing slow and pulse lessening. Strangely, it shot back up when she let her go, Jennifer fighting back a squeal as she listened to the boots leaving the room and the door locking behind them.

The procedure began again… to the same result… and then again. This time, though, Jennifer was calmer; the fear had lessened because she knew what was coming… she thought, and then Carly unbuckled her neck restraint. Pulled free, she breathed heavy, it being obvious that she was relieved.

"On your knees," instructed Carly inches from her face, a menacing raise from her eyebrows over her tone convincing Jennifer to drop immediately, head down and on all fours. Carly squinted down at her as if deciding whether or not to punish the hesitancy, Jennifer feeling it above her before Carly's inherent good nature saved her from the pain, and she instead produced a collar and leash, Jennifer duly attached, head remaining down at all times.

And then they were off, Jennifer walked by Valerie who had been given the leash from Carly as Jennifer crawled behind her, head down, the sound of heels echoing off the walls in the warm light of the cramped room. Led out of the door to the dark corridor outside, the sound of boots lessened as they sent their crisp sounds down the dark empty lengths to either side of them, Jennifer shivering as she was forced to crawl in this dark foreboding cold space under the Manor. The eerie quiet pervaded the corridor, a maddeningly still atmosphere, Jennifer forced to endure it as she was halted, the only sound that of Valerie closing the door behind them, leaving her vulnerable and alone, the dark stillness keeping her fearful and unsure of where they were. Expecting to be led up the hallway, instead she felt her leash being pulled straight across the corridor to the door on the opposite side, Jennifer feeling Valerie jar her leash in anticipation of her nerves as they shot up again, Carly opening the heavy door in front… and screams greeting them!

Momentarily stunned, Jennifer almost forgot her own predicament as her eyes fell on a table at the back of the room, an outstretched form spread-eagle, her hands tied to the top of the tables' corners nearest them while her ankles at the other end revealed a dark scene that froze Jennifer as she heard the buzzing sound of an electrical wand pass over the shrieking victim… Linda!

The room dark but for gentle amber coming in, uplit from corners beyond the table, out of sight and from behind, and to Jennifer's right, the dimmest of glows brought the dark browns and blacks of the dungeon into view. The table where Linda was held was a dark rack sitting atop a platform, two steps leading up to it at the back left of the room, not eight feet from her. Jennifer was able to make out two intendants in their black uniforms, one standing over a shrieking Linda and another squatting near her head, mouthing fear as Jennifer watched her hands convulse and grasp from within their wrist restraints. The rack itself was gorgeously cared for, its black wooden holdings offset with sumptuous leather trim along its edges, and struts making its three feet stance off the floor look an almost comfortable place to be, if not for the screaming telling otherwise.

Jennifer became aware as her eyes adjusted to a large space to her left, barely lit with amber glow, betraying another table strewn with countless implements, neatly placed, and on the wall behind it, the same, the room having everything needed to bring whatever change in behavior the intendants desired in them.... Carly moved to the right.

Jennifer almost gasped as three gorgeous forms came into view in front of them, the hard black of floor tile giving way to purpose-built leather matting the whole right side of the room just beyond the doorway, a sumptuous soft firmness. Leather matting dull in the amber glow led to three forms bent over a black rectangular box, leather-clad and built into the floor, six foot wide and with restraint holds at its base on the floor, both at its head and its foot.

Like an altar, its purpose was obvious, any slave able to be either bent over and secured with head down and ass displayed for their correction, or on their back and spread eagle, their screams not able to penetrate the heavy door behind them as what would seem like hours passed.

The three forms, though, were not secured; they waited patiently, heads resting toward the back wall, their powerfully built physiques instantly recognizable as intendants, only their panties removed but their remaining uniforms answering any doubt as a shaken Jennifer was led toward the one on the left. Amid the shrieking torture and buzzing wand, Jennifer was leashed toward her first encounter, the powerful muscular cheeks open and waiting for an already over-worked tongue. The sight of three stunning rears would have been a turn-on if not for the fear that permeated the room, Jennifer unsure of what was to happen. Led forward, she felt suddenly trapped as Carly came down on her left side, kneeling and taking her by the back of the hair, Valerie's silky thighs now pressing against the back of hers as she knelt behind her, completing her securement, soft leather corseting pushing against her naked ass.

Then she saw it! Jennifer almost reeling back, Carly at once seized her by the back of the hair, the grip violent and intense, her eyes meeting hers as she looked up into their angry glare, Jennifer freezing and obeying. Amid the gorgeous crevice in front of her, a dark wet line stood out between the cheeks, wet and glistening, its brown freshness waiting for her tongue, Carly determined Jennifer would learn as her head was forced into the warm cheeks in front of her. Ready to gag, Jennifer's body tightened, forced toward the horror, leaving her about to shriek when suddenly she was met by a scent… chocolate!

Absolutely banned in house, no slave was permitted this pleasure, women forced to kneel obediently at dinner tables and in the library as they watched the intendants enjoy this delicacy, their salivating another enjoyed torture. Here, though, suddenly Jennifer was forced to have it, her mouth suddenly erupting in salivation as she remembered the gorgeous scent, her tongue almost immediately coming out as she was forced into the warm crevice, the silky cheeks stroking her face as she was gently buried in the ass.

Mouth suddenly erupting in taste, the chocolate flooded her mouth and covered her tongue, the scent of gorgeous pussy and intendant mixed with silky chocolate and sweat. Behind her, captors gently squeezed, amused by the sudden rush of feelings throughout their charge, smiling on as a familiar happenstance of the treatment began. Carly tried not to laugh as Valerie gently nodded her head in confirmation as she felt Jennifer's pussy flood beneath her against her trapping thigh, the stimulation and shock of the scene making Jennifer lose control, her emotions everywhere.

Amid the sounds of continuing torture to their left, her head was lifted out to a smiling Carly, unable to hold in her enjoyment of the scene as they gently took her to the next silky crevice and pushed her down again to her second cheeked prison. Another rush of gorgeous chocolate, and Valerie's thigh now ran with Jennifer's gratitude, her emotions surging as, amid the screams and begging for mercy, she was treated to unbelievable pleasure. The scene drove her wild, her feelings surging as the smell of fear from a shrieking slave mixed with her own selfish gorging of forbidden silk… she didn't care.

To their left, atop the raised platform, Linda shrieked as the wand was drawn down her outstretched front, her body convulsing before it was lifted, allowing the shortest of breaths before coming down again. Screams followed her tightening body as it pulled hard, involuntarily, at her padlocked restraints trying to run, but to no avail, her torturer drawing suggestively closer each time to her femininity below. Held open and vulnerable, Linda tried to close her legs, but they were flayed open by the ankle restraints, panic wracking her senses as she begged for mercy, the wand lowering each time.

All the while, the intendant squatting at her head at the top of the rack whispered suggestions to her each time the wand was lifted from her. She pleaded with her to tell them the truth, trying to convince her to help them, that she was on her side, begging Linda to let it stop if only she would let them help her, Linda's shrieking confirming she was giving them nothing.

Soon, the voice in her ear changed, becoming menacing, describing how the electricity would be increased so that soon she'd lose her chance to have it stop, that if she didn't tell, the intendant couldn't help her after that, that Linda would be left alone with the one who tortured her, under the Manor and out of sight.

The voice in her ear wasn't helping, and far from it, had no intention of helping her – instead, it was a carefully rehearsed play, learned and used many times by the intendants, their skill so good at its administration that they could actually predict at which point a slave would break. They could predict at what point she would tell, if there was anything to tell, and if there wasn't, it made no difference, fear put back into slaves taken down to this point being something the intendants had decided was necessary for Linda, her smart-assed attitude noticed in house, and to be removed, replaced by an attitudinal state they preferred… fear.

The intendants' gorgeous curved ass strained her black panties as she squatted at Linda's ear, playing good cop to the bad cop electrifying her above. Through Linda's screams and jarring body, the soft voice drawled on at her side, Jennifer overhearing as she tongued.

"I want to help you, Linda, I want to make it stop, but you have to help me…" electric current snapped and crackled, Linda's screams filling the room as they followed the wand's direction.

"Help me, Linda," the pretend drawl came again. "Help me make it stop… tell me who told you… tell me her name…"

"No one told me anything!!!" Linda shrieked. "No one told me… aaaaaarrrrghgh!!!!!" Screams replaced words as the wand finally slid under her, the intendant above not believing a word of it as she brought Linda's punishment down between her legs while, on the floor, Jennifer's pussy slid down Valerie's silky thigh behind her, soaking an already moistened skin. As Linda's torture continued, Jennifer sank her tongue into the third waiting crevice, engulfed in ass-chocolate and torture, her own senses electrified as she found herself truly turned on with her pussy soaking as cheeks and thighs rubbed up all around her while Linda begged for mercy overhead. With her senses exploding at the scene around her, Jennifer's mind became alive, it obvious from what she was hearing that there was some sort of ploy going on, poor Linda inadvertently finding it at breakfast and having to suffer for it now.

No suffering for her, though, as Carly pulled her back, smiling as she watched her lick her lips before she was leashed out on her knees again, leaving the screaming Linda behind, Jennifer only able to feel sympathy for a while before her captors led her back into the room to the ball, her learning not yet over.

The procedure repeated itself, Jennifer losing control, crying and then gaining composure before crying again. But she strengthened each time she was led from the ball to the dungeon and forced to gorge on creviced delight; she grew stronger and more able to handle the unpleasant side of ass. Indeed, in the future when presented with the opportunity of pleasuring ass, the little accidents that occurred at times simply glanced off of her as she remembered the ball, and strangely but with obvious reason, she salivated when it happened, her body thinking of the creviced delight that would follow, a link made and learned well, Carly teaching her firmly that day.

A long day, and with the last trip to the dungeon, she was left alone, the heavy door sealed behind her, fear of what might be only temporary, as, too tired to resist anymore, she surveyed the empty quiet. The intendants were gone, Jennifer's belly full of their contribution to her learning that day, and poor Linda gone, too, the rack's restraints lying open and limp, like Linda somewhere in the Manor above. After a time, Jennifer became curious, the smell of torture and sweat still present in the room. Surveying the implements to her left, she didn't want to approach them, nor the box on the black matting, now empty, but open with fearful restraints. The platform, though, had her curiosity; the rack. Having listened throughout the day to poor Linda's screaming, she now couldn't help but approach it, mounting the stairs to its menace as Linda must have been made to do, the fear she must have felt making Jennifer shiver as she surveyed it.

She wondered how the intendants could do such things when it was clear the slaves were really scared, and wondered how they could be so cruel – didn't they feel anything?

The door opened behind her, making her start and

spin around as almost immediately it was closed again behind a strong-looking Carly, eyeing her as Urst had done when she'd come to get her from the freezer room. It was the same look, the look she'd had to stare into as she was lowered down to her from the pulley, shaking and in tears.

Jennifer didn't know what to do, their eyes staring across the room before the boots made their approach, the sound intimidating in the silence as Jennifer felt weak and embarrassed, powerless and ashamed. Throughout the day, she'd grown to fear Carly, the lovely Floridian gentile of the intendants; she had to fight not to pull away as she approached, fear of what would happen if she did helping her steady. On the platform above, she steeled herself, looking down at the deck submissively as Carly came up the steps; she didn't want her near. With nerves fraying, she easily dropped her head further, Carly making her feel uncomfortable and unpleasant as her boots mounted the stairs to get her.

Carly took her in her arms, Jennifer having to fight hard not to resist, her body wanting to pull away, her head dropping as she was wedged between Carly and the rack's edge, powerful silken thighs pinning Jennifer between them and the rack's leather. No feelings of desire, though; only awful entrapment, her body wanting to leave, her eyes not knowing where to look as Carly's leather corset pushed against her fighting body, silken leather sealing her fast.

"Heh," said Carly, Jennifer looking up timidly. "Look at me," she instructed Jennifer, obeying but still timid. "Don't you ever do that to me again," Carly's warm soft southern tone began to re-emerge. "I let you get away with ignoring my instructions on the step, then I give you the pleasure of me, and you resist…" She looked accusingly at Jennifer who was blinking, trying hard not to look away. "I didn't like seeing you frightened down here, but I'm not going to apologize. You could have really embarrassed me today, but luckily it was just our group that was out. You better start respecting me like the others, do you understand?" her tone softened further.

"Yes, intendant," Jennifer almost whispered, trying to respect her in her grip.

"Heh," Carly's eyes widened as she surveyed Jennifer's timidness continuing. "I said 'respect me'; don't fear me; you don't have to fear me if you respect me, just don't take liberties with me, do you understand?" She asked, clearly feeling guilty about what she'd put her through.

"Yes, intendant," Jennifer answered honestly.

"You learn well." Carly wrapped her in her gorgeous southern tone. "I can see why you have someone's eye," she drawled coyly, smiling as Jennifer's eyes lit up. "Are you ready to be given back to her?" she smiled more as Jennifer lost control, a smile leaking out and quickly pulled away, fear returning as she realized it, dropping her head. "Heh." Carly lifted her chin with her finger. "Don't worry, you can't be blamed for falling in love." She smiled, enjoying Jennifer's struggle as she half-smiled, not knowing where to look, Carly smiling more as she watched her face redden and clench, her taking her hand not helping. "Come on," she beamed, the delicious sound of her corset untacking itself from her as she pulled back and took her across the platform, down the stairs to the door. "Now remember," Carly stood her straight to her, just before she reached for the handle. "When we go through this door, you respect me in front of the others, right?" She questioned, widening her eyes.

"Yes, intendant," Jennifer answered, taking on her practiced plain expression, bowing her head slightly.

"Good." Carly smiled as if congratulating he. "Come on," she beamed, a friendly squeeze from her hand signaling she was pleased with her, the southern softness returning, and Jennifer feeling better around her now, a feeling that would continue.

Chapter 11

Jealous Falling

"You refused one of us? After being offered our pleasure....?" Nadia looked at Jennifer with wide-eyed amusement as she held her by the arms at the side of the correction huts. Out of sight of the Manor, the rest of the group filing away, they had a short time before they'd be missed, Jennifer wanting to ask questions but stinging from Nadia's efforts, now feeling submissive and unsure. No longer seeming to be spared from Nadia's ire, Nadia had corrected her just as much as the others, and more, seeming to punish her harder, as if trying to prove some point. Now alone with her after being shouted down in front of everyone yet again, Jennifer was left quiet and alone, Linda's fate in her mind, but Linda's question even more.

"You're lucky it was Carly..." Nadia's eyes narrowed, breaking into a coy smile and shaking her head, Jennifer loosing a small hint of the same at the corner of her mouth. "Heah," exclaimed Nadia, tightening her grip, Jennifer controlling herself and dropping her head. "Heah," Nadia pulled her gently up in and toward herself. "That's not what I meant," she assured her, seeming to try to coax Jennifer on.

Timidly, Jennifer slowly looked up out of submission, still unsure of the effect and relieved to see a smiling Nadia beaming back, but left confused and out of sorts... another ploy maybe?

"What's the matter?" Nadia asked, reading Jennifer's changing expressions.

"Nothing, Mistress," Jennifer spoke for the first time in hours.

"Mistress!" Nadia almost laughed, bringing more confusion over Jennifer's face. "I had to," Nadia assured her, trying to explain her day's efforts. "I can't not deal with you because of us – the word would get out."

Jennifer passed a confused look to their retreating group in the distance, three well-trained and more than aware sets of boots pushing the herd.

"The groups are tight," Nadia explained, answering Jennifer's questions. "My secrets are their secrets, and theirs mine; it's the windows I'm worried about," she cocked her head toward the rear of the Manor, blocked by the clump of trees and correction huts. "We have to fight for each other in here, I've told you before, any word of this and the other intendants will use it."

Jennifer looked up into gorgeous brown eyes, the Latin voice running up and down her spine, almost opening her mouth, but her training getting in the way.

"For goodness sake, we don't have much time," Nadia encouraged, seemingly yearning to talk with her and squeezing her like a lover.

"I don't know what's going on," Jennifer blurted out, her emotions taking over after what she'd been through the past two days.

"What do you mean?" Nadia looked concerned, her thoughts immediately turning toward what must have happened the day before underneath the Manor.

"Do you know what happened yesterday?" Jennifer asked incredulously.

"When they took you down…" Nadia said, her face turning to regret, "I didn't want them to do it," she assured her, looking troubled.

"You didn't even look back." Jennifer lost her train of thought as Nadia made her think of the moment.

"I couldn't," replied Nadia mournfully. "The windows were right above us, even the high offices and rooms," she referred to the Mistress's office and the intendants' quarters. "If anyone up there had seen me looking concerned…."

Jennifer's emotions started to well up at what she was hearing. "Do you even know what they did to Linda down there? What they did to me!" she blurted out, tears starting to appear in her eyes.

"I didn…" Nadia trailed off as Jennifer's tears ran. "I…"

"They tortured her for asking if what you're doing to me is a ploy!" Jennifer cried out, unable to find an easy way to say it. "They had her screaming on a table because she suggested it at breakfast!" Jennifer raged, remembering Linda's screams in the darkness.

"She asked about us?" Nadia looked horrified, wide-eyed at the thought.

"No, not us!" Jennifer almost screamed back. "She suggested it to the others, why the intendants keep taking them, that it's some sort of trick to make us all do what you want." Jennifer's hurt verged on rage because Nadia had thought about herself while she was weeping.

"Look," Nadia tried to steady Jennifer. "That's not true, at least not from me, but you have to…"

"Oh, what a lot of crap!" Jennifer let go, forgetting herself. "You let them stick me down there and then you beat me here all day; do you really think we're that stupid!?" She shrugged out of Nadia's grip, turning away, full of pained anger…

"Stop right where you are!!!!!" A raging Venezuelan tone rooted Jennifer to the spot, her mind snapped back to reality over what she'd just done! "Is that what you really believe?" Nadia almost hissed, coming to rest just off of her shoulder, Jennifer wanting to curl up from the anger, but too fearful to move. "Have you any idea, the risk 'm taking for you? For us!" Nadia raged, "Well!" She finally grabbed her by the arm like Carly had the day before spinning her around, almost shaking her in temper. "Answer me!" She glared into her trembling charge.

"I don't know what to think," Jennifer sobbed. "Every day, we're beaten and punished and forced and told! Told what to do, what to think, and laughed at by you…. What are we supposed to think?! You're always playing games with us and pushing us down!" She sobbed, dropping her head and half falling as Nadia took hold of her again, Jennifer's sobbing real.

Hurt eyes looked down, anger trying to leave as she felt Jennifer sobbing in her arms. "Have you ever heard me laughing at you?" her voice was still strong, Jennifer cowering…. "Well?" she asked again, trying to be as gentle as she could.

Jennifer shook her head, too hurt to answer.

"I'm not playing games with you," Nadia tried to reason with her, feeling a struggle beginning to surge in her grasp, Jennifer uncomfortable being held by her, and then bringing a sudden and frightening tone into her voice as she seized her in tight, Jennifer freezing as she went, "The fact I haven't done anything to you for your utter disrespect should make that clear to you!" Nadia suddenly raged, clearly angry at Jennifer's display, but it was hurt at her trying to pull away that was triggering her anger.

Jennifer almost squealed as she was whirled round, Nadia seizing her timid form, her arms trapped in an instant and now held under rage. “Now, you listen to me!” She shook her, “Listen to me!!! It was supposed to be a strategy, okay?! It was supposed to be!!!” Nadia glared at a frightened Jennifer in her grip. “You were supposed to be fixed and none the wiser,” Nadia raged on. “Supposed to be stopped from leaving the Manor to believe I had feelings for you, to keep you from leaving!!!” She suddenly ejected Jennifer from her grip, the grass coming up to meet her as she sprawled on the ground, her intendant’s rage being paced off for a moment before she came back, now towering over her. “I wasn’t supposed to end up like this; you weren’t supposed to do this to me!!!” Nadia raged over her, looking like she was about to attack her for a moment before she whirled off to the side of the huts, Jennifer bemused at the rage and unsure of what to do next.

Moments passed by with Nadia’s back to her, Jennifer not daring to move before she heard something amazing… crying! It was Nadia! Crying!

Eventually, Jennifer stood up, and Nadia didn’t turn, not even aware Jennifer had moved. Standing closer, Jennifer inched forward with no intension of reaching out, but the sound drawing her nearer; it was real… it was real and Jennifer knew it… no one could fake the hurt she was seeing….

Nadia rubbed her arm over her face, composing herself for a moment; she could sense that Jennifer was there. Slowly turning, Jennifer saw the same look she had had, the same tears, the same hurt… but she couldn't help asking….

"Why did you let them take me down there?" she questioned, her hurt showing.

"I told you I couldn't stop it," Nadia answered truthfully, the honesty ringing in her voice. "But I didn't want them to," she breathed heavily, looking away.

"Then why did you treat me so hard today? Why did you treat me so cruelly?"

"Because I like you…" Nadia stammered, not able to look her in the eye, Jennifer realizing it was jealousy she'd felt all day, Nadia's anger at her being with them.

"But you're with other women all day," Jennifer uttered, confused at what she was saying.

"Oh really!" Nadia growled, making her jump as she finally looked into her eyes. "And just how deep in Carly's ass did you have your tongue?!" she demanded angrily, Jennifer seeing her point as she dropped her head.

Both women breathed heavy for a moment, the heat from their bodies just felt inches apart, Nadia the one finally to break the deadlock, taking Jennifer once again.

"If we want this, we have to deal with all of it," Nadia declared. " I have to train you and you have to be trained; that's just what happens here… I'll try not to enjoy it too much, and you better not!" She eyed her jealously, Jennifer fumbling inside and unsure of what to say back… "Unless it's me doing the training," Nadia finally said coolly, the wrong sound coming out as she wrestled down her emotions.

Jennifer smirked a little at Nadia's struggling with her feelings, an immediate seized and angry look changing her expression as the two women froze in each other's stares again. Nadia the first to start smirking, Jennifer falling soon after… 'falling' being the right word… she hoped.

Chapter 12

Professional

Jennifer slept well that night the best sleep she'd had in days. Feeling her questions were answered, her mind had mused on about where things were going, a certain intendant the last thing she thought of as she slipped away.

Awakening to the sound of their dorm door opening, the first thing she grasped was the sound of the boots on the laminate floor, her mind quickly distinguishing the pair that meant the most to her as they fell with the others, making their way toward her.

Fighting with all she had, she tried not to smile as the Venezuelan beauty eyed her from overhead, the control in her eyes better than hers, but softer than usual, Latin passion betraying her. Almost at once, though, whispered concern unsettled Jennifer's morning muses.

"You've been chosen," Nadia whispered as she made long the unshackling of her favorite. "You're to be taken for worship; don't worry, just be professional," she whispered her concern.

Worship, a common occurrence, the women talking at length over meal times about this strange procedure. Taken in selections of four, one from each group, the women found that each week another poor example was to be led with the others, naked, to the upper level and made to bow to the Mistress.

In her office with the other three, they had to stay on their knees in a bow. Heads down, arms stretched out, palms on the floor, this odd procedure having a purpose. The Mistress, genuinely uninterested in their attempts, would be involved in whatever paperwork happened to be occupying her at that time. For hours, she would work while the groups' offerings on the floor in front of her desk had to remain still and silent, her usual guards just to the left, standing watch in front of the windows.

Spaced evenly on the floor, a half circle of trained slavery would remain docile and obedient, arms outstretched toward the great desk where their fate was decided on a daily basis.

This most humiliating of procedures was not simply for the Mistress's amusement, but had a real purpose, being a test, an example to the Mistress. Unable to cast her eye everywhere at once, she had to rely on her intendants, had to rely on their reports, her attention needed elsewhere, her following of training progress mostly viewed through filed reports.

Responsibility to owners and clients would not be satisfied by this alone, however, as indeed the Mistress had to review and had to justify owners' investments, had to assure all was going well, and that time constraints for returns were being followed.

With the Manor's reputation as the premier facility for behavioral adjustment at stake, it would not do for a slave's return to be devoid of the desired changes, nor for any delay in said adjustment. Progress review, then, was essential, the pressure on slave and intendant maintained in this way.

As the four nervous souls were united in their nakedness, they were marched along first the lower level in standard single file, an intendant from each group making up their escort. Etched on their faces, the seriousness of this day's event was picked up by their charges as they felt the pressure of the meeting to come as feet began the ascent up the stairs to the main hallway above. As they arrived, the serious nature continued, passing intendants who usually would have been sending obligatory smiles and pleasantries did not. Instead, they seemed to move fast, giving a wide berth to the precession as it went. This alarmed the charges even more as they left the cool tiles of the marbled hallway below, and began the ascent to the first level, high above, warm carpeting not a comfort but a worry, lush depth feeling like trepidation underfoot.

Mounting the last stairs to the landing, the transition saw a jump in nerves raising even further, the procession turning right, the intendants stony-faced in their official stances, becoming solid like the doorways passing by either side.

The doorway at the end, though, held focus more, a solid wooden glare, and the group was stopped before it. All still, the intendant leading their group waited before knocking, the obligatory pause a sign of respect and house rules.

There was no answer or signal to enter; instead, the lead intendant – after counting the correct time of waiting – took the handle and pushed the huge weight inside. Perfectly balanced, the door moved effortlessly with the intendant's entry, their group following in silence, the slaves' fear heightening as the Mistress came into view behind her desk at the back of the room.

Under a midday sun held off by slatted wooden blinds, the atmosphere was tight, the Mistress's two corseted guards standing in front of the windows to the left with their hands behind their backs, attentively watching the procession. So quiet inside, the sound of the Mistress's pen could be heard as it ran back and forth across her papers, the women being arranged in front of her desk as if entering a lion's cage and not wishing to wake it.

All silent, and the Mistress was busy with pen, barely even lifting her head from her work, as if not noticing the four naked forms brought trembling before her.... but she had.

Attention, though, was being paid more to her intendants, sharp ears and eyes monitoring their instruction to the women as they were brought to order on the floor in front of the Mistress.

Particular attention was being paid to neatness and presentation, not only their own immaculate dress, but to how the charges were laid out and left in bows.

A stickler for presentation, the Mistress would notice the slightest maladjustment of arm or leg, the women's elbows and knees prodded and pushed, their positions managed and set as the midday sun fought its way into the room. Through the half-closed wooden slats over the windows, the French style of the room felt warm and welcoming, but was fought down and held by the power of the furnishings around them. As if a template for the house, the room felt strong and secure, large and surrounding, its tans and browns leaving an atmosphere of strength over its bowing captives, held small in its midst. Shoulders were taken by intendants in front as they knelt, and directed, positioned and set. Learned eyes gazed down backs, the women's postures perfected, form left precise before the intendants were rising themselves, their order departing, quiet and calm, the door closing behind them on the stress left within.

Almost immediately, the silence was crushing, the slaves left alone on the floor; their fate was their own as they tried desperately to stay still, to hold the position they'd been left in. A maddening sound now tortured the four as they knelt. Overhead on the desk, the pen ran back and forth, ensuring no comfort could be found, no muse or daze, its quiet moving keeping attention fixed squarely on the Mistress, the slaves kept aware at all times that pain was just overhead, sitting in front of them.

Hands outstretched in a semi-circle of worship, the four knelt in unison, palms down for the Mistress, her two corseted intendants to the left providing more pressure, just in reach. For two hours, in silence, with the Mistress who worked overhead while they remained still under corseted watch, not daring to move. The two guards affront the windows guarded stillness with perfect form, their trained poise and seeming calm-covered desires just within.

Over the hours inside the office, the occasional shifting of weight from tired bodies at times threatened to bring forth the Mistress's ire, but she forewent any reprisals for these small infringements from three of the slaves beneath her. They were, after all, new and learning, the Mistress pleased overall with the progress.

The fourth slave was different, though, the Mistress had noted, giving not a sound – a perfect performance and a real credit to the intendants of her group, the Mistress truly impressed at her display: she seemed… professional.

Chapter 13

Night Out

Led out the door, the office closed behind them, the relief instant in slave and intendant alike: cramped and exhausted, the women were only too happy to be led to wherever the intendants desired.

The rest of the day passed by fine, more pointless cleaning in the library seeing an uneventful last half of Jennifer's own time, she being more than happy with that.

At dinner, she felt strange, almost at peace with the others laughing at her group's table, laughing and talking. She found herself laughing also, smiling and involved; for the first time in days, her head was clear and she felt like part of things again, like her group was one big happy family.

There was one who wasn't laughing, though: she hadn't smiled in days, was quiet, withdrawn, Jennifer recognizing what she was feeling – it was the same as what she'd felt after the night in the freezer room.

Linda was suffering, picking at her dinner, and she looked right on the edge, the intendants pushing her to the point of quitting. 'Damn them', Jennifer thought, 'how could they do this to people?' Linda's lovely personality was gone, and Jennifer even tried to speak to her, but the bubbly little person of days before just politely nodded, looking down at her plate, her heart broken inside.

That night, the intendants went too far, Jennifer watching from her bed unable to believe it when four of them came for Linda! Almost in tears as she was led out and away, her poor emotions were written across her face, Jennifer wondering what was to become of her, but then to her surprise, two intendants stopped at her own bed.... She was to find out.

Led through the Manor, she thought of Nadia and whether she knew about this.... she didn't. Unaware that her favorite was distressed, Nadia herself was somewhat busy: busy but not distressed.

The situation was not to improve; taken up their west wing, they passed the main staircase and moved on to the east where, in the distance for a moment, the sound of laughter and merry voices quickly faded from the end on the right as a doorway quickly closed. Moving down the dark dim corridor, cold tile under foot, they approached the same doorway, the sound of rhythmic beating betraying a party going on inside; a party they were invited to!

Door opening, a cheer stunned the women who were pushed forward by their intendants, more greeting them inside, the two feeling truly naked as drinking corsets whooped like animals, clearly drunk and in their element, the setting jarring, with neon all around. A real nightclub, deep red in color with small black tables against every wall, and matching leather sofas with small stools dotted around the room. For a moment, the two victims took it in as cackling voices fought with music, the sounds all pervasive and overwhelming, intendants bending low to ears on sofas, laughing to each other, eyeing the nervous charges. The club's bar covered the room's center, a square design for a traditional piece: the last thing in the room, that was. Its neon blazing filled the room as a gantry shimmered in its center, reaching high and adorned with bottles, the scene quite elegant save for the music.

Through the bottles, though, something else, not traditional nor elegant, a black form hiding behind the bar, intendants whooping as they noticed their fearing charges' eyes on it.

"Don't worry – you'll find out soon!" came a drunken voice from within the club, looks for its owner a waste of time, the writhing melay laughing back.

Only the top of the thing was seen, recessed in a pit in the club's floor, a circular hole behind the bar on the left surrounded by leather cushion and matting.

"They look like they're in a hurry." The women heard the laughing voice from somewhere t their left.

"Well, I'm not; I need a drink," a reply came, some intendants moving for the bar across the floor. Sharp boots sounded over music as three passed them, barely even looking on at them, tongues dry from a hard day's work as they occupied the area in front of the bar. Still left alone, the women became accustomed to their surroundings, their senses getting used to the din around them as more of the club became evident now. Red walls matched, lowered to black sofas, dark laminate flooring aside from the pit at the back, strobeing lights and a dance floor on the left with quiet seating, dark and hidden to their right. About ten intendants sat on their left, some quite merry and some quite loud, some merrier still, then more in darkness to their right, like preying wolves looking out across at them.

They were left there, left like ornaments, intendants passing from left to right and others eyeing them from the bar, all laughing and drawing them looks at times, then going back to their own conversations, the women ignored for minutes in between as if they were invisible. The two watched as people had fun; some danced on the floor to the left and others passed behind the bar – still others went back to the dark seating area on the right, coming back after a time, strangely more animated and involved.

They watched as there were drinks for everyone, but none for them; seating for all, but not for them. Watched as the intendants grew louder and more aggressive… more hormonal. Watched as the dancing got closer, as the passers by grew bolder, and they grew timid as they sensed them all closing in on them, only a matter of time now before the first hand brushed their thighs as it passed, hormones fueled by their night club excesses, the women shuddering as the whole club seemed to close in around them.

Then it happened, brushing hands now seizing wrists amid whooping cries, two frightened souls pulled forward into the heaving club by wild-eyed assailants, their hormones demanding. Pulled through a throng of leather gyrating bodies and wandering hands sliding where they pleased, lusting where they wished. Any protest useless, their hands not their own, as any chance of escape was sealed off with the pack rising from their seats to the left and right, following the smell of fear in the air… the women truly worried by the large number of intendants around them. A leather wall of flesh and want now sealed them in to the back of the room, whoops and cries, heaving and screaming to follow as they were led behind the bar to the sight of their doom.

And there it lay… its sight stunning the frightened women for a moment as they peered over the edge.

Below, in a pit four feet down, lay a black circle of restraint and fear. The women, used to the implements in house, took only seconds to realize its purpose below. A circle of wood coated black with a finish boasting leather restraints for four at a time. Like some demented bar bull, but minus the mount, four places lay arranged to hold calf, wrist, and waist. Eight sumptuous restraints of powerful leather lay open, waiting for calf and forearm and midriff alike. Sealed inside, bent-over victims would be restrained and held, across one of four mounts, their leather angled back and sloping up. Designed to keep the rear positioned up like the correction huts outside, so that each captive would see their opposite struggling right in front of them. The anguish on their faces, the struggles of their pain, adding to their own as the table turned and the screaming went on.

Approaching the pit, laminate had already given way to matting, red and soft as it flowed to the cushions at the edge, joining at the top before slipping over the side. Flowing down over the edge to the pit below, the circle descended to a ring of sumptuous red seating. Stitched and soft, the leather was meant to comfort those sitting inside over those long nights of lust.

Comfort not for the victims of The Table Of Woe, but for their assailants, abound now and determined to use it. Some, already having descended, sat inside, shouting and grasping up at the air, baying for blood. Nervous victims pushed onward toward the pit's near edge, they watched the table below, spun by hungry hands awaiting their descent. Amid whoops and cries, the table turned in front of them, a foot ahead of the sitting intendants' knees, their hands spinning it amid their excited screams.

Soon, more screams, the women pushed over the edge, crying out as they went, their feet sinking into seating below. Hands all over them, instantly seizing whatever they wished, making sure comfort was gone, screaming back in its place.

Still screaming, they were pulled in, escape now impossible as excess-fuelled hormones pulled them down into an orgy of fear. Almost at once, the comfort of the seating fell away to the cold ring of laminate in front of them, only for that to disappear as they were hoisted up and onto their knees, their instinctual lurch away over the wood seized and pulled back as, screaming and panicked, they felt the first cool leather restraints seal around the tops of their calves, their legs left dangling over the table's edge. For an instant, Linda had been pulled away, around the other side of the table; lost in the leather, she suddenly reappeared, facing Jennifer's screams, the two directly across from one another and united in fear. Sharp spanking broke out, meant to heal and calm, but the stings of their corrections did nothing for their nerves, the women witnessing each other's anguish, terror in their eyes. Panicked still further, they screamed, struggling under the corsets and feeling the second of the straps now wrapping round their waists, intendants unfeeling and reveling in the squeals of their victims as they sealed them to their mounts, asses angled and trapped…. They were going nowhere.

Soon, more whoops and torment joined atop the table, more intendants drawn in, helping seal and trap, the revelry of fear irresistible to them. Some grasped them underneath, some took hold behind, and still others squeezed, intendants laughing on as tongues of their sisters licked up faces of fear. Whoops of joy as the table was spun right by those seated, the women's hands now taken down, wrists sealed to the deck. Hands behind them explored their creviced fear, and underneath to their trembling submission, the last of their escape now taken away, strapping around their forearms and just below the elbow, their fate sealed as they spun in fear.

Final whoops of lust and hands of want now retreated back with the approval of two lonely souls now gently spinning in front, their slow-circling fear and embarrassment the focus below.

The two women shook, Linda crying with nerves, her tears running down her face as Jennifer was forced to watch. Forced by the straps, the two were face–to-face and bent over the mounts, vulnerable and frightened as the whoops and the screams spun with the beating of the club blaring, reds and neon's splicing with corsets and leather.

More now arrived as they spun, their voices growing louder, the pit getting fuller, groups fumbling with leather attachments, black and large under the neon red. Soon the table was stopped by ankles grabbed from behind, whoops and screams shooting up, the first silky thighs sliding between calves, hands cupping cheeks as they came, the women panicking in the midst of it all.

Jennifer groaned first as she felt the blunt rubber find her lips, pushing them apart, the slow but firm and determined thrust continuing to push up against her until her resistance was opened fully by the thick oiled shaft, her walls filled, larger than usual, Jennifer straining against her wrist restraints as she was opened for the crowd.

Her groans set off a cheer as the powerful thighs behind her contracted, the hands squeezing her cheeks and pulling her waist back onto the member, making her gasp for air as the leather corset of her assailant gently pushed up against both of her cheeks as she was filled to bursting. Groaning out, she felt her captor rotate her hips, her powerfully built ass cheeks contracting under her corset, the crowd whooping aloud as they watched the style, Jennifer filled completely – her groaning confirming it. Slowly, and to the crowd's pleasure, the huge black length was slowly retracted, Jennifer's hips seized by her captor as she worked her for the crowd, forcing her to moan as she wanted her to sing for her pleasure.

Worked slowly and firmly, the length was moved in and out, the hands squeezing and pulling, walls filling and emptying, groans growing and deepening, Jennifer's mind already away, her eyes closed from the noise as she provided enjoyment for the audience.

All at once, though, a squeal brought her back, her eyes opening up on a distraught Linda being filled right in front of her. Forced to watch her struggles, she cried out as her resistance was broken, forced aside behind her, her anguish immediate as she cried out, ripping hopelessly at her restraints as she was opened up for the crowd, her panicked cries fuelling their laughter. Pulling hard at her restraints, she screamed in the neon din, face red under the club lights, her screams leaping out and escaping, but not for the rest of her, held down on the table, Jennifer forced to watch her anguish grow.

Screams of laughter filled the air, drowning

screams of torment down below, tears running down cheeks as hands seized and thrust a wailing Linda, torturing her on. Watching Jennifer saw her struggles begin to die, her hands stopping their pulling at restraints, her world collapsing with her tears, her eyes closing in defeat. Shaking as she cried, the laughter leaping as they were filled, groans and tears from either end of the tables assured them its name was duly earned.

Jennifer could hear her, hear her crying under the din, under the laughter and the music; she listened to Linda's heart break inside in front of her. Her eyes still closed as she cried, she listened as they thrust her down into a dark place inside herself, Jennifer maddened by what she was seeing, angry at what they were doing to her… and then it happened…

Jennifer's lips closed on hers! Almost immediately, Linda's eyes flicked open to see her dorm mate's closed eyes and sincere affection as she struggled to hold her disorientated lips. Panicked and out of sorts, Linda tried to back away but was held firm under her restraints, and pursued tightly by Jennifer's affections, she couldn't find escape, Jennifer determined to hold on. Slowly, panic gave way to confusion, struggles to curiosity, the pit falling suddenly silent under the music and the intendants looking on in disbelief, even the thrusting falling away. Linda, for a moment, passed her eyes round the corsets, suddenly aware of what they were doing and soon sure of what would happen, but Jennifer never stopped. Kissing her harder, she forced her tongue inside to Linda's, slight resistance soon overcome, her passion persistent and unrelenting and Linda's eyes soon gently closing.

As she felt Jennifer's wave of support slip silkily back and forward, all of a sudden, she found herself kissing back – unsure quite of why – but following her lead as another wave of cheering erupted from the pit.

A wave of cheering all around them, drunken mirth and supporting laughter as oiled shafts forced tightened walls, Linda's crying backing off. There was no escape from her restraints and no escape from Jennifer's support. Pursued by Jennifer's tongue, she calmed and soon relented, tears slowing as Jennifer guided her, tears stopping as Jennifer cared for her….

Chapter 14

Union

"Are you out of your mind?!" Nadia glared having heard about the night before from intendants that were there. Almost growling she whispered harshly when she pulled Jennifer aside at the correction huts the next day. "Have you any idea what they could have done to you in that pit if they hadn't thought you were just getting into it?" Her angry concern was evident as she chastised a bow-headed Jennifer, gripping her arm in the scornful way of a lover. "If they hadn't thought you two were just playing along, I might be talking to you in the infirmary right now!"

"They were crushing her; I just wanted to help her; I…" Jennifer was cut off.

"You haven't seen them crushing anybody yet!" Nadia growled, annoyed by Jennifer's naivety. "Luckily for you, they took it the way they did, and I'm sure you paid for that mistake." Nadia widened her eyes, motioning her gaze toward Jennifer's lower regions before shaking her head and sighing, Jennifer looking hurt. "Look, I don't want you getting harmed in here." Nadia took her in her arms, real concern flowing from her. "Do you understand?"

Jennifer nodded back, seeing the concern across her face.

"From now on, I'm not letting you out of my sight." Nadia pursed her lips, shaking her head, her face tightening. "You get into far too much trouble." She broke into a strained smile, Jennifer following, touched by the angry concern.

“Why did they take me?” Jennifer voiced timidly, looking up at Nadia and worried she might become angry as she felt how tightly she was gripping her. “I thought because I was with you that they….”

Nadia’s grip tightened, her face straining further, Jennifer stopping at the look….

“That’s been fixed,” Nadia assured her, an angry look drifting out over the grounds as she spoke, Jennifer relieved the strained look wasn’t directed at her. Jennifer listened as Nadia explained that she couldn’t be everywhere at once, that she had duties and sometimes had to be away… but Jennifer didn’t understand.

“But I thought the others listened to you in here; we thought you were…” Jennifer trailed off, Nadia gripping her hard and looking into her.

“Who thought?!” she demanded. “Who thought what…?” She cut to a low and sincere whisper.

“Our group,” Jennifer replied nervously, it having been obvious to the group over the weeks that the other intendants in-house seemed to respect Nadia, to treat her differently somehow, like she was senior or….

“Listen to me,” Nadia growled, pulling her close. “Don’t think… and don’t speak! Don’t speak any of those thoughts out loud: do you understand me? It’s not for a slave to think or question,” she instructed, echoing the teachings from Miss Goodspank’s classes. “It’s for a slave to obey.” She looked intently into Jennifer’s eyes, as if looking for confirmation, Jennifer slowly nodding dutifully. “If you’re heard trying to figure out the strategies of intendants in here, or worse, questioning the ways of this house, you will be severely punished," Nadia assured Jennifer, again looking hurt, as if she was threatening her. "No," Nadia shook her head, seeing the hurt. "Not by me," she assured her. "Eyes and ears are everywhere in here… look what happened to Linda because of her loose talk over breakfast." Nadia cocked her head as if wanting assurance that Jennifer understood.

Jennifer nodded timidly, looking up into serious Venezuelan eyes, their deep brown softening as they tried to reason with Nadia's charge. "I'm trying to keep you safe," Nadia assured her, "But you have to stop making mistakes like that; I can't be at your side all the time."

Jennifer continued nodding, relieved it was concern over anger that saw her gripped in Nadia's steely embrace. "What if they come for me again?" she asked, worried about the night.

"Don't worry about that; no one will be taking you again," Nadia almost growled, looking away over the grounds and trying to hide her look away from Jennifer, a pleasing feeling emerging inside the charge, it only tempered by the fear of the jealous strength she was seeing before her.

'Fixed?' Jennifer thought, and she didn't ask more, but believed it, the grip around her waist confirming a lover's jealous rage at what had happened. It wasn't the first time Nadia had "fixed" things in-house. There were other intendants in other groups who were just as strong as she was, but it was evident to all that Nadia was different, the other intendants acting differently around her, like she had some sort of sway they did not, some sort of power.

None of the women in Jennifer's group could

figure it out. Couldn't, but were happy she was head of their group, some of the other intendants in groups being real brutes, their work witnessed on slaves' bodies in showers, at times. Nadia's hands had a frightening reputation, but she could at least be reasoned with, when she hadn't lost her temper…

"And you have to promise me not to do anything like this again," Nadia demanded forcefully, her lover's tone gone, replaced by an intendant's control for the cameras overhead, Jennifer understanding the act as they walked through the ballroom from the grounds behind it.

"But they were killing her inside," Jennifer whined, remembering Linda's torment.

Nadia became outwardly angry as they approached the main hallway through the ballroom door behind the staircase, a group ahead in full cleaning detail, scrubbing the hallway ahead of them, Nadia unsure if the intendants ahead in charge of them had heard Jennifer's protestations.

"They had decided on a course of treatment for her, and it is not for a slave to question that." Nadia announced loudly, making sure she was heard, slightly embarrassed by Jennifer's brazen attitude toward her in front of the other intendants.

Jennifer didn't see it, though, caught up in her concern and feelings for Linda; she forgot herself, forgot her place. "But what they were doing to her was wrong; she couldn't take it: she was…"

Enraged at the insult against her authority in front of the others, Nadia suddenly seized Jennifer by the mouth. "Are you questioning the ways of this house!?!" Intendants, surprised at a slave's questioning, were immediately given the sight they expected after such insolence, Nadia violently pulling Jennifer to one side and knocking a cleaning slave away from her standing stool, taking it over and roughly pulling Jennifer immediately over her knee.

"It is not for you to question!!!" Her Venezuelan rage filled the hallway as Jennifer felt her legs being trapped behind her, Nadia's thigh coming down across the backs of hers, the first spank ringing out like a gunshot off the walls in the hallway, this followed by a dozen more! All cleaning stopped inside the hallway, even the intendants open-mouthed at the severity of the chastisement; they were witnessing Jennifer crying out, struggling, enraging an already embarrassed Nadia above. Shocked by Nadia's force, feelings of hurt and confusion saw Jennifer struggle instead of submitting, enraging Nadia as the room watched her refuse the first path of least resistance, angry fury now finding her cheeks below.

Crying out in agony, Jennifer grabbed Nadia's calf beneath her, the sudden feeling and screams for mercy finding sympathy in Nadia's rage and her hand seizing on her, rear punishment ceasing for a moment.

The room bore witness as a shocked slave whimpered from her pain, the hands holding her above gently squeezing now, clearly affected by her struggle. Gathering herself, Jennifer felt the unseen squeeze as a response now, and as immediately expected, her training in the academy kicking in, she realized she hadn't taken the first path, and that that was the reason for the severity.

With the pain and force ceasing, Jennifer was for a moment allowed to breathe, allowed to decide once more. Learned from the Academy, failure to take the shown path of intendant discipline brought harsh direction, the slave severely dealt with for such disrespect. However, after such strong treatment, the slave would be allowed a chance of redress, it being understood that momentary lapses in training under stressful situations could happen, and a second chance to follow a path was accepted, etiquette for intendants to follow.

A sign of respect and slave professionalism, minor infractions in order were sometimes tolerated, it being accepted that harsh discipline was sometimes hard to bare. But this wasn't respect: it was something much deeper, the intendants watching, looking at each other and back again as the unmistakable look of female anguish gushed from Nadia's eyes, the intendant clearly struggling with what she was having to do.

Gushing down upon the submissive form spread over her knee, her hand held back her body desperately, feeling for Jennifer's response, not wanting to chastise her further as eyes watched in stunned silence.

Gathering herself, Jennifer's shocked breathing calmed as she realized Nadia was waiting, the room itself collectively breathing a sigh of relief as they heard Jennifer's own submissive sigh signal that her pain was to lessen. Relaxing into her thighs as best she could, she signaled her submission, her body still shocked and finding it difficult to relax, but her head dropping all the same.

A wave of relief not only passed over Nadia, but the room itself – such had been the violence of the assault that shock had descended on those watching. With her rage dropping, Nadia became suddenly aware of what she had done, guilt competing with professionalism as she felt Jennifer timid and frightened beneath her. For a moment, she forgot herself, her hand gently stroking Jennifer's rear as if in apology at what she'd done, the effect on Jennifer profound as she felt her struggle with her direction.

As if accepting an apology, Jennifer again sighed even louder, catching Nadia off guard and making her aware again of her audience. Momentarily stunned, Nadia felt feelings rush through her as Jennifer relaxed into her thighs, her hands rapping around her calf and gently stroking as she ceased resistance, the room watching Jennifer's head truly drop, signaling her submission to her correction… and more.

Intendants working in-house over the years knew very well the difference between anger and correction, between fury and jealousy, and Nadia quickly tried to hide her feelings at Jennifer's sudden total submission, but it was too late. They watched Jennifer as she breathed in Nadia's scent, Nadia's hand coming down over her ass once more, Jennifer's acceptance making Nadia's attempts to hide what was going on impossible. Firm and dominating, Nadia's hand fell, trying to show command and professionalism, trying to hide it as Jennifer's groans followed her completely, betraying a pointless attempt to mask what was forbidden in-house between intendants and slaves.

Watching on, those present and bearing witness to the couple's final union could offer no reason why it shouldn't go ahead. With her cheeks reddening, Jennifer groaned on, squeezing Nadia's calf gently, holding to her with an expression of want, each spank bringing a moaning submission that Nadia couldn't tone down. Spanking firmer, she felt Jennifer's weight shift as she tried to direct her, shift not in an effort to escape, but to let her know she was suffering, suffering for her. Having to hide her own pleasure, Nadia fought a smile as she tried to quiet Jennifer's submission, spanking firmer, gripping tighter, trapping her shifting legs with her own as she suddenly became aware of her lover's passion, her wet lips finding the inside of her warm thigh behind her.

With spanks ringing out, her ass reddened further, Jennifer remembered the slave being punished in the hallway and the smile across her face as she'd passed her. She understood now why she had smiled; crying out in front of everyone, she wanted them to hear and wanted them to watch, watch her struggle with her lover, watch her groan with her pain.

Nadia hadn't meant it, but it was obvious to the intendants watching: they'd witnessed the hurt and confusion, the anger and the rage, and after that day, no one dared come near Jennifer, violent passion making it clear who she belonged to and what would happen if she were troubled.

Chapter 15

Unmasked

Lying on her bed, Jennifer smiled as she felt the gentle sting on her rear, shifting at times on her sheets as it wouldn't completely go away, and she didn't want it to. Lying naked in the glow of the uplighters, the calming cream of the dorm drifted with its silence, the occasional shifting of cuffed slaves on sheets making Jennifer smile. She was dying to talk to someone, anyone, about what was going on with her and Nadia, their group already buzzing with it, but she didn't dare talk under the cameras.

With Jennifer almost asleep, the now familiar night visitors arrived, their sharp heels raising those from their slumber who were not already asleep, but their learned ways keeping their pretense up, these women appearing to sleep like the others. Julie… almost a comedy now as she was taken again; it seemed she was just too fun for the nightshift to put her down….

The door closed on their departure, the silence drifting over them again, shifting on sheets, signaling relaxing, those left behind thankful and at rest… and then the door opened again.

Sharp heels, singular, driven by one intendant alone, the rhythm alerting someone familiar to their stride before her arrival at her bed.

Jennifer opened her eyes, fighting back a smile for the cameras as a devastating sight greeted her from the foot of her bed. Having to catch her breath, she gazed upon the corseted curves straining out from the leather and lace, Hispanic eyes devouring hers as she looked down to perfect knee-length boots, black reflecting the room's glow around them. Something else, though, new in her hand… beside the boots, it hung from her grip black and unclear, questions to be answered as she moved in toward her.

Coming to rest near her cuffs, the Latin scent engulfed a willing victim, her emotions straining inside as two forms fought their smiles, keys finding cuffs… and then…

"I didn't want this." Nadia's gentle whisper was hidden from the cameras and confused Jennifer as she made long the uncuffing. "I have to take you; this wasn't my choice." Keys taking far too long, Jennifer listened, staying quiet as her intendant instructed, "I'll be there with you, I'll keep you safe, you have to play along for me, whatever you feel you're being instructed to do, go along with it, don't resist. If it get's hard, don't reach for me; I'll reach for you, let you know I'm there. If you don't like what you're being made to do, remember me, remember you're doing it for me, not her – you're making me proud, showing how well you work for me, everything you do is for me; do you understand?" Nadia gripped Jennifer's arm in gentle questioning, her body on top of hers as she finally removed the cuffs, Jennifer's hand hidden under her corset and gently gripping at her thigh with silent answer.

Her eyes transfixed by Nadia's gaze, she searched for the emotion given out by her own, finding concern competing with it, confusion now entering her mind. Raised from her bed in front of her devastating assailant, Jennifer moved as the room listened in secret to the relationship they all wanted to know about, Jennifer catching for a moment what she was seeking, Nadia having to fight off a smile at the obvious willingness of her all too enthusiastic captive.

Jennifer's look faded, though, as Nadia raised her hand with the leather form, her other gently caressing her waist as it took her, doing little to ease her trepidation… a mask. Learned in the Academy, they knew of its frightening effects. Breakfast alive with tears from those who'd experienced it, and now Jennifer felt her breath quicken as Nadia looked deeply into her eyes, trying to convince her to calm and to follow. Tensing, Jennifer felt her free hand stroke her waist as she pulled her forward, opening its form in front of her, the first fear emerging as the black sealing mouthpiece appeared, its ball-like structure having a tube running through its center to the surface of the mask, providing the only air she'd have, a shiver passing through her at the thought. Gently holding her, Nadia cocked her head, Jennifer's nerves abound as she looked upon the sensory deprivation below her. Mouth sealed, it would then tightly cover her face, strain fueling fear as it wrapped around her head, ear pads finding hers and taking sound till finally it would seal completely around her head, her world locked inside. No way to get it off, buckled straps at the rear would be sealed with tiny padlocks, leaving a prisoner inside completely dependent on her captors. The breakfast tears filled her mind, some women already gone, nerves shattered by the experience, the fear now for her as she tensed in Nadia's grip.

"For me," Nadia's words whispered over her.

Looking up, Jennifer's eyes fell into hers as she

paused, swallowed, and then dropped her head, Nadia taking away her senses with leather wrapping her up, Jennifer now her dependent and needing her direction utterly.

The tiny padlocks snapping shut on the buckles behind her signaled that the bars were now closed, her prison complete. Still held in Nadia's grip, and with her head on her shoulder, it was immediately disorientating, the padlocks felt and not heard, only her breathing left inside. Nuzzling close to Nadia and not being able to smell her scent, she was confused and then suddenly frightened as she started up, Nadia seizing her as she struggled in her grasp! She tried to cry out, but only muffled moaning filled her ears as a huge attempted breath tasted rubbery from her mouthpiece, a panicked mind not able to get out. Ramming forward into Nadia, she panicked further in her prison, her instinctive reaching for the mask held by experience, pulling her close. Panicked and thrashing, she was held by Nadia now, waiting, listening to the moans, the fight for air through the mouthpiece as it restricted its charge. Expert in its use, Nadia knew to hold on, that soon the fight for air would leave her tired and more controlled in her arms. Monitoring her closely, Nadia felt the struggles die away, listening at the air, hearing the sucking growing louder. The restrictive nature of the mouthpiece soon told, thrashing falling away, only grabbing remaining, muscles growing tired, the draw through the mouthpiece not providing enough air to keep a fight up for long. Soon there was shaking, too, crying hidden under leather, her panicked breath being allowed to catch, Nadia taking her in her care. Body shaking on her shoulder, Nadia took the time to calm her, took time to hold her, gently running fingers down her back, comforting and stroking, not hurrying at all. Getting the treatment of a lover, Jennifer didn't know how lucky she was, the other women taken through it, left to scream on their knees.

Leashed, and worse, no one had heard them being pulled through the manor, many breaking down at breakfast, the intendants happy at spreading fear. But not for her, the stroking continuing, the caring working, her breathing shallowing, and held gently, she squeezed her guide, her shaking too falling off and away. Rubber breath and the sound of breathing, and Nadia's touch, were her only senses, her last link and her last guide through this new horror from the house.

Nadia's first gentle move brought panic, Jennifer instinctively squeezing down on her arm, fearing she'd be left alone in her cage as she latched on to her guide, her dependence immediately obvious. There was no need to worry, though, as instead of rough jarring and brutal coldness, a calming stroke along her frightened grip and a gentle pull saw her follow on. With her grip increasing, she moved in silence, the absence of intendant boots on the floor scaring her, she was so used to the Manor's soundtrack.

A small ways on, and they were turning right, the short pause to close the door giving Jennifer time to become aware of the sudden change in atmosphere. The hallway was colder, designed to make the passage subconsciously unpleasant; it gave Jennifer a new take on her now restricted world. Able to sense changes in temperature as they walked, her mind gave her pictures of where they were, the sound of her breathing following on. The tiles were as cold as always under foot, but maddeningly, there was no sound of boots beside her. Strange that she'd miss their sound, it usually bringing slaves fear, a signal they were being taken for treatment. Now, though, their absence brought a new fear – a panic as she held onto Nadia's arm, feeling totally dependent. Her senses began tuning, her body's reasoning heightening, reaching for anything it could grasp and any way of sensing the world around her. With her breath in her ears, she felt the tapping beside her, and then again… yes, the heels felt, but not heard, her feet occasionally picking up their impact through the tiles. The new sense frightened her again as it emphasized how trapped she was, her grip squeezing on Nadia's arm bringing them to a halt. Kindness, her free hand stroking gently around her waist and pulling her close brought a feeling of warmth and support, Nadia risking it under the cameras and Jennifer responding to her touch. The short show of support left Jennifer willing to go on, their starting to move again slowly and deliberately, Nadia guiding her gently on, helping her through.

The stairs… another short pause and Nadia's arm lifted hers, guiding her up to the first step in front. Slowly, Jennifer followed, deftly searching for the next one in front of her, holding her arm dependent on Nadia's direction. Almost immediately, her mind began counting; she'd never counted before, but her mind seemed determined to latch on to any control, any sense it could find. Guided up slowly, the air began to change, warmer in front and her nipples sensed the difference. Their being already erect from the cool wings below, it was a welcome feeling as they left the stairway behind them. Strangely, her mind suddenly became aware of how naked she was, as if not noticing before with the temperature down below. It made no sense to her, the hallway on the first lower level having been colder than the room, but she'd not noticed this there. Confused, she followed up the last steps, more aware as she felt the landing and Nadia's boots tacking beside her. A welcome second hand stroked her arm as it held the other, her breathing heavy again and Nadia able to hear it outside. A gentle pull forward and her feet found new tile, smoother and colder; her mind showed her the main hallway, her senses searching for answers as the naked feeling grew. Suddenly, she realized what she was feeling, space… strangely, whether by memory or temperature, she could feel the size of her environment. Different from the tight wings, she could sense the size of the main hallway, the space leaving her feeling vulnerable and open, her nakedness all too apparent. Again, a squeeze on Nadia's arm signaled a wish for support, her nerves shaken with this treatment and her mind trying to stay calm. Again, her love came, and it was love Jennifer could feel – she was sure of it. It was slow and caring, pondering and supportive: she'd seen slaves beaten and screamed at, whipped and tortured, but she'd never seen this, and that's why she was so sure of what it was.

The realization filled her with warmth, the sudden wave of emotion making her want to wrap around Nadia to pull close to her side, her hand squeezing again, but not from panic… with something else… and suddenly the wave inside her leapt further as she knew Nadia had felt it. Knew because suddenly she was close to Nadia, pulled by her now in closer, making her suddenly want to kiss her, this bringing her back down to reality as she realized how impossible that was now. Her yearning sounds in the mask, heard in her own head, suddenly met with nails on her arm, stopping her instantly in her tracks, only for the nails to release… a hidden stroking in their place, a further squeeze reassuring her. She realized Nadia could hear her easily through the mask, the realization calming her as she saw that there was a way to communicate from inside, a way to express panic if it became necessary. Moving on again, she gently stroked back, wanting to be sure Nadia knew her feelings, her response slight although felt enough with a gentle bite of nails afterward telling her 'careful', dutifully followed and understood.

A pause again, Jennifer's breathing calm as she felt her arm lifting, knowing the main stairway was now in front of them, guided by Nadia's hand, cold tile left for warm carpet and her second foot following gladly, now ascending on upward. Slowly, she followed the gentle pull of her guide's arm, her senses not able to smell her, but reveling in the body heat felt beside her. Soft velvet warmth consumed each foot fall as she raised one step at a time to whatever fate waited above her, their sudden cresting onto the landing bringing nerves as they turned right.

Her trepidation became obvious as she knew full well where they were going, Nadia having to coax her gently forward, her slowing walk betraying common knowledge among the house guests of what followed with the mask.

Breakfast stories told of savagings, masked terror and lack of breath, and tears and breakdowns in the mornings filled Jennifer's mind now with realization. Breathing became heavier still, louder with each footfall, the velvet hallway feeling threatening as she imagined the first doorways passing by, the intendants asleep to either side, some stirring as if aware. Then the second pair affront the office, their destination like before, that time blindfolded when they'd turned left, but now with Jennifer masked, they turned right....

Not for Nadia's room, not for pleasure, but to the Mistress's chambers now, lying in front, with no windows, no leaving, no mercy. Imagining the solid foreboding doorway just in front of them, she felt Nadia pause, but couldn't hear the knock. The correct time waited, Nadia began to move; she could sense her working the handle, opening the door, her breathing shallowing as she tried to be quiet. A slight pull forward followed before she was immediately stopped and then released, Nadia's final touch of fingertips instructing her to be still... and obeyed.

Silence... but for her gentle breathing her lungs trying to tease air in quietly, fearing what might come if she were loud. Still, absolutely still, she stood there not daring to move, maintaining the position Nadia had left her in, thinking of the office and the worship, and how she'd worked for her and her reputation that day. She didn't realize it, but it had been that attention to Nadia's instructions that had brought her this ill will. Impressed, the Mistress had become interested in her and had began paying attention to her training, subsequently discovering who was learning her and soon summoning this night time meeting. Jennifer could feel the atmosphere in front of her and behind, her sense of temperature attuned in her other's absence; she could feel the hallway to her rear and the warmer interior now in front. Still staying perfectly rigid, she began to almost sense the doorway she now stood in, the gentle sound of her breathing keeping her calm as she felt open and on display.

She was, as strong eyes conversating with her deliverer had begun assessing what stood before her, strong hands soon to follow, not gentle or caring, their malice immediate as the thud of the closing door signaled the beginning.

Dragged across a plush velvet pile, its warmth provided no comfort as she was roughly pulled across the room and stopped before being released.

Again, she didn't move, it now impossible to breathe quietly as her lungs had already begun to fight for air. Through the carpet, she could feel heavy steps around her like an animal stalking prey.

She knew she was being assessed, the Mistress exploring her body, inspecting the intendants' efforts with her, but that wasn't what she was most concerned about. She wanted to know Nadia was still in the room; not able to sense her, she felt vulnerable and alone. The steps slowed and then continued, Jennifer not able to sense even direction as she tried to work out if she was talking to someone, but couldn't… and then she was grabbed.

Suddenly from behind, the connection of the Mistress's body with hers made her breathe much heavier than she had done yet, the sound giving the Mistress great mirth, all apparent as she felt her laughing through her body, her hands exploring her aimlessly as if trying to prove a point…. She was at her mercy.

Strong arms matched a large physique powerfully commanding her, confidence total, and Jennifer felt it more than obvious as the Mistress worked her way around Jennifer’s body, leaving her timid and afraid. Laughing again, she bluntly explored more delicate areas, reveling as Jennifer’s breathing became strained with her fight to stay still and not resist, the penalty in her predicament unthinkable as she began to panic with the pressure the Mistress pushing on her more. Beginning to groan with the strain, she knew from the stairway how easily she could be heard, but couldn’t help it, the pressure becoming unbearable as she fought for air, a panicked cry bursting forth as her nerves reached a breaking point… and then silence.

The laughing stopped, and then the murmur of voice vibrating from the Mistress’s chest through her back, and then a pause, then the feeling of voice again, Jennifer suddenly realizing the Mistress was talking to someone as she sucked in air, sure of who it was. She may have been sure, but suddenly she was stinging, her sudden release followed by a savage hand across both her cheeks. She didn’t know what she’d done wrong – maybe it was her breathing, maybe it was too loud, but it couldn’t be helped. Left alone for a moment, she sensed the Mistress move off to her front left through the vibrations in the floor, only to come back toward her, her body tensing as hands took her waist…. They were Nadia’s!

She sucked in air, releasing a sigh of relief and quickly gaining Nadia’s nails in her back, discouraging any further signs of gratitude as she was pushed gently forward and right, and then to the left, her body starting a little as the front of her legs came against the unmistakable feeling of a bed… huge.

With Nadia’s hands still around her waist, others

suddenly clasped her hands from the front as she was pulled forward, her elbows meeting the silk sheets only to be pulled firmly forward, her face then finding the same as the Mistress left her in no doubt as to who was in charge. Face down, she felt huge powerful thighs crest the side of her face, their silken texture not felt through the mask, but only through her shoulder as they knelt beside her, the vibrations of words funneling through the mattress. The hands holding hers suddenly released, Jennifer waiting for them to arrive on her back, but they didn't. Instead, they seemed to remain above her, the sudden slide of silken thigh on hers from behind signaling a welcome visitor, Nadia guided onto the bed by the Mistress.

And so it went on, Jennifer feeling words exchanged through the mattress as she was… explored… used. All the while, her constant fight for air had her attention. At times, she was made to kneel at the end of what she came to realize was an enormous bed, feeling the unmistakable cavorting of two bodies in front of her through the mattress, leaving her feeling sad and used.

Again, suspicions of Linda's breakfast assertions of strategy and not interest crept into her mind as she felt the unmistakable feeling of uncontrolled thrashing through the mattress that could only mean one thing…. She hoped it wasn't Nadia.

Grabbed roughly again, she was pulled forward, the Mistress clearly enjoying herself as she spun her below her, lying her on her back as the Mistress pulled her by the waist, coming down lying on top of her. A familiar blunt feeling worn by the Mistress now began to push Jennifer's lips apart below, signaling that her latest fight for breath was about to begin. She entered slowly this time, seeming to enjoy Jennifer's struggle, as if her fight for breath was providing even more enjoyment than the act itself… and it was.

It was her personal turn-on, as she reveled in the panic of slaves, loved to cause them fear in her quarters, loved to listen to their panicked fight for breath. In her mind, their anguish was fun on the one hand, and a test of their commitment on the other. A test of their learning at this stage, but she made no attempt to hide her personal pleasure at their truly awful emotional suffering.

The Mistress was indeed a sadist – it didn't take a genius to work that out. What should have been the pleasure of mouth-watering silken thighs holding open her own was made to feel torturous and horrible by the Mistress's brutal way, Jennifer able to feel her laughing at her through her body as she struggled beneath her. As she pushed deeper inside Jennifer, she could feel her laughing at her struggles as they grew more desperate beneath her, the reaching for mercy simply palmed away, the vibrations of laughter increasing as a tear rolled down inside her mask. A sudden powerful lurch from the Mistress's waist saw her squeal as she filled her completely, straining her walls to breaking, the thrust bringing a sudden lurching of her own. Thrusting on above her, the Mistress laughed over her, straining for air and held tight under the mask, Jennifer's panicked reaching joined by muffled shrieks.

She couldn't breathe! She couldn't get enough air! Shrieking, she reached up but was palmed away, her hands thrashing over the bed and trying to pull away, unable to prevent herself as the powerful grip on her waist wouldn't let her go. Her head began to panic, thrashing back and forth with her arms, her screaming contained by the mask until finally hands descended on her shoulders… and the thrusting stopped.

Desperately fighting for air, tears rolling down her cheeks in her panicked world, she was unaware at first of the murmuring voices above her, crying in the mask with her body contorting, giving the tell-tail shaking of shocked distress to those outside. Humiliated, she was still filled by the Mistress, her grip unrelenting, the feeling inside awful and unwanted, the murmuring voices vibrating through the bed with her tears.

Then they grew louder… a lot louder, Jennifer almost able to hear what they were saying through her body before the Mistress suddenly savagely withdrew from her, the yelp sure to bring pain, but none came….

Instead, the feeling of two bodies jostling on the mattress, the vibrating sounds of anger further away, but still obvious to Jennifer as she felt two powerhouses screaming back and forth, their rage fighting it out with each other.

Her struggles subduing, Jennifer caught her breath, but the anger didn't cease. Like a thunderstorm around her, Jennifer felt its fury pushing back and forth between bodies on the bed above her, incensed and searing. For what seemed like ten minutes, Jennifer felt the rage. Good for her, she managed to recover her panic, dropping as she wondered what was happening, the voices lowering, Jennifer no longer able to feel them, her breathing shallow and her state quiet. Helpless, she lay there, frightened to move before finally someone came for her, rough hands pulling her up.

She didn't resist, incurring only minor slapping as she was roughly forced onto her knees over the bed, the powerful hips quickly finding her vulnerability, her femininity breached. Again, she began to fight for air, but as quick as the thrusting had started, it stopped… again, the vibrating feel of angry voices through the mattress came before thrusting resumed, but there was no laughing from the Mistress this time, and no saving hands.

Instead, the Mistress roughly but rhythmically seemed to be trying to prove a point, as if asserting her dominance, but that didn't make sense… she was dominant. Instead of the torturous pounding or humiliation of before, Jennifer found herself professionally dealt with, but not for enjoyment… she could feel that.

The way she was being fucked felt like an intendant at work, as if learning her; it was hard but not driven by cruelty… it was something else, something she'd felt before, something familiar. As murmuring vibrations signaled sharp words, Jennifer felt the tempo increase, as if the Mistress had been angered, her response seeming to be to take it out on her. It was as if Nadia had done something to annoy her; it felt like the way Nadia had fucked her the day after she'd been taken away and dealt with by Carly and Valerie when she had gotten…. It suddenly dawned on her what she was feeling…. Jealousy!

In an instant, it all made sense, the power in house, the respect of the other intendants, the nights she wasn't there and Nadia's ability to swing things her way…. Nadia was the Mistress's!!!

As Jennifer continued fighting for air, she realized

now why Nadia had been so shocked by Linda's breakfast strategy talk, realizing the danger she'd put her in, the suspicion that she'd brought on their group. A suspicion that must have had bases if Jennifer was right, because Nadia would know what the Mistress was thinking, and now the same suspicion was driving jealousy into her, the Mistress angry, sure that something was going on between them.

The pounding Jennifer received went on, but it was the last, as if the Mistress had lost interest. Made to kneel at the bottom of the bed again, it had seemed like hours, the murmuring voices subduing, the rhythm of laughter felt again, Jennifer sure of it and becoming quite adept at feeling voice. What she didn't like was feeling the laughter going further, sure this time that there were two different types of thrashing on the bed.

Eventually, she was pulled up the bed again, but this time between two obviously tired bodies. Listening to the murmuring, it sounded amorous and pleasant, like two lovers cavorting, and Jennifer definitely didn't like that. She could feel relief between them, the Mistress not seeming to be angry; she could only guess that Nadia had talked her around, convinced her it was strategy, Jennifer happy to play along. Hands ran over her, but carefree and unrestrained, especially on Nadia's side, Jennifer guessing the lights were out. Nadia squeezed her lower down, obviously trying to reassure her as best she could, but it was the touch that was the voice… the touch was caring and concerned – it was the touch of a lover.

Rested and grateful that it was over, she was used a little more, hands wandering over her, the two definitely laughing, but not as much as Jennifer inside her mask, glad it was hiding her smile!

Chapter 16

Fear

Breakfast, finally – Jennifer had lain awake long before the others, Nadia bringing her down and cuffing her in the early hours… it wouldn't do to see slaves regularly leaving the Mistress's chambers.

Managing to not be the morning's example wasn't just luck, as Nadia had no intension of burdening her with that after her night's extreme restriction, Jennifer really breathing a sigh of relief.

The doors closing, the chatter began, but slow, worrisome, even cross-chatter between the tables tender and quiet; something was wrong. Rumors of all sorts had begun, intendants happily starting some themselves, pretending to drop loose chatter while learning slaves throughout the day. Some were nonsense, just to spread fear and keep control as usual; others, though, seemed to have some basis in truth, the evidence stacking up.

"They were laughing about it last night," said Julie, referring to the cackling fun of the intendants when they'd had her on the Table Of Woe with some others in the club.

"What can it mean?" asked Suzanna quietly, all aware there were cameras in the room after Linda's experience, and of how they walked a fine line as they spoke.

"I don't know, but I haven't been punished heavily in days," Heather whispered.

"Are you missing it?" joked Suzanna from the

opposite side, a sarcastic glare coming her way in response.

"I've heard it, too," Amandine's beautiful French accent silked across the table. "They keep mentioning it like it's some sort of party."

"Are you talking about the open day?" a fellow worrier asked from the other table to their left.

"Yes," Andrea replied, sitting closest to her. "Have you heard anything?"

"We were outside yesterday and they were laughing about it in the correction huts," came a hushed whisper. "The strange thing is, hardly any of us were in the huts; we were just worked out on the steps."

Andrea didn't continue talking, thinking she'd risked enough – instead, she looked timidly over at Jennifer, as if looking for an answer, all aware of how close she was to Nadia.

"I haven't heard anything," responded Jennifer. "I couldn't hear anything at all last night," she answered honestly, her experience sending a shiver down her spine and the spines of a few others at the table who'd had the pleasure.

"Something's up," determined Julie. "They never go this easy on us unless something's wrong."

The paranoia was well founded, their not being allowed to know what waited for them or question much, Linda's example proof of that; the women could only infer from the sidelines, intendant behavior one of the few signals they had for what was coming in-house. All groups had noticed that before new trials or types of training, a period of grace seemed to emerge, a restful time where women seemed to be allowed to gain their strength.

Chance loose talk between the doctor and one of the intendants in the infirmary as they argued had let a patient hear there was nothing graceful about it. Lying there on the bed after being pushed too far by the intendant, she'd heard the doctor chastise her leather-clad assailant for not allowing her enough rest before her latest teaching, that her body hadn't been given enough time to heal since the last. It was, then, not a caring gesture for the women's wellbeing in house, but yet another callous calculation, simply to allow the healing of their bodies before the next sadistic push.

This, then, is what had all four groups in hushed tones… rested, healthy, and afraid… just how the intendants preferred them.

The doors opening on breakfast had them all start, their nervous order following dutifully to showers, the cameras not needed to secretly gather what the women were feeling, the intendants happily watching the nervous procession.

Marched on to the ballroom, timid forms maintained their place in the great circle, leather guards hardly needed behind them. Soon the doors opened and a perfect form of power and grace swept through into the circle, her two intendants trailing behind. The women were relieved that no dominant contraption was in the center of the hall, no screaming to be heard this morning, but again this fueled suspicion, their easy treatment worrying them as the Mistress took center stage in front :

"Alicia caned for 10 resistance!

Sylvia strapped for 20 disobedience!

Andrea spanked for 10 misattention!

Samantha caned for 10 insolence!

Maria whipped for 20 disobedience!

Kim whipped for 20 misattention!

Julie caned for 10 insolence!

Diana spanked for 20 disobedience!

Chloe spanked for 40 misattention!

Vanessa strapped for 20 insolence!"

The morning's list was read out, a familiar scene not just designed to embarrass those who were on it and left red-faced now, but for more subtle reasons. Yes, it did embarrass and make slaves try hard not to end up being held out in front of everyone each morning, but it also subtly justified the women's treatment. Unnoticed, it made for the normalization and acceptance of such harshness among them for, as example after example of women's chastisements was read out, the regular weights and amounts of said chastisement became commonplace. If another could take 20 of this and some other take 40 of that, then you have no reason to complain about taking 10 of that.

And so it went on, subtly, as was the way of the Manor, the gradual increasing of punishments, strengths and amounts unnoticed as time passed by… not that it would have made any difference if it was….

"And it has come to my attention that, yet again, a lack of effort in the library's cleaning has led to some severe restrictions for Lyvia's group." The Mistress growled, truly angry that this group led by Intendant Lyvia was not able to dust more of the invisible dust never present in the library to begin with. "I do wonder if the members of this group are actually wishing to starve," the Mistress's angry tone continued thundering off the walls in the ballroom. "If that is so, they may continue with this lack of effort, and I will ensure that they will!" She screamed, glaring at them as they stood, desperately hungry, their heads bowed in submission with Lyvia having placed them on rations, a group punishment reserved for severe disobedience and an attempt to bring pressure from the other members of the group onto the flagging members.

"I have also heard of chatter which is giving rise to rumor among groups." The Mistress growled, looking around all present in the circle. "This is bordering on incitement!" she suddenly bellowed, all slaves almost lifting their heads with the rage, but luckily managing to stay drooped and submissive in her presence. "If this continues, I assure you, I will become personally involved with each and every one of your punishments," she growled, looking accusingly around the room.

"YOURS IS NOT TO QUESTION; IT IS TO OBEY!!!"

The scream made those present start, the jolt through them all reinforcing their fear of the towering force in their midst… obedience assured.

This particular morning's ire, given generously by the Mistress, made an already fearful and worried house compliment even more so, a humorous result expected and witnessed by the staff… a lack of paperwork!

With such fear laid down, the slaves would become more dutiful and attentive for a time, their behavior markedly improving and making an easy management system even easier for the intendants – less breaches of rules to deal with and hence less reports to file. Of course, after a time, paperwork would start to rise again, behavior slipping, giving a signal to management that more fear had to be brought down… to keep everyone happy!

Cleaning was indeed improved, not one piece of the imaginary invisible dust escaping in the library under Lyvia's group as they starved throughout the day. Outside, a fully fed group not under rations fought hard on the steps to keep up with their intendants. Easily able to outpace them, their version of Carly was left annoyed at their efforts, feeling some sort of insolence was being committed and wanting to take various members to the correction huts, but it wasn't her decision, and none were taken… leaving suspicion growing.

Inside the Academy, it went well, the group even witnessing a caring gesture between Miss Goodspank and Linda, who'd been cared for by her after her horror at the hands of the intendants during interrogation. Far from the house psychologist, who herself for once was not immediately sympathetic and did believe Linda had brought it on herself with loose chatter, it was Miss Goodspank who had cared for Linda's distress, and the real reason Linda had not left. That and, of course, some added, rather risky support from Nadia's favorite sitting beside her. Unknown in the Academy as they served, one of the four groups was currently outside the front of the Manor! Yes, the front, a privilege forbidden to all, not just in terms of rules, but no window of the Manor, large as it was, opened to the front – only to the rear, and with the high walls around the grounds at the back, beginning far off the Manor's west and east wings, psychologically it wasn't immediately apparent to the patients that they were prisoners… but they were. That's why the guard with them was so enormous outside, over twenty intendants, some close and some further off, pretending to mill around and lark in the sun, but ready to chase down and seize any who tried to run, no walls out front to hold them. This had been an active choice by the management, not wanting owners who delivered their charges to feel they were placing their beloveds in any real struggles, or to be threatened by the Manor's largess, its facade of peaceful learning assured.

And the reason for such grace of slave movement this day? A delivery. As far as the delivery man knew, he'd offloaded four large pallets of food and party materials to a large manor house. The beautiful sweat suited woman who'd greeted him asking nicely to have the pallets left at the front of the house, as she'd be expecting help later, signed his sheet and wished him a nice day, her smile making him do the same as he'd left, unaware of her glaring after him, angry that she'd had to provide such an act.

True to her words, the sweet woman had her help, ten of them, naked and obedient under her stare, which certainly didn't match her sweet act.

With such large pallets, it took all afternoon to unload them inside. The plastic had to be stripped from them, the boxes opened, the contents sifted through, all under the direction of the intendants who escorted the women back and forth, sometimes in groups of two, sometimes five, but never lifting a finger to help. Of course not, as manual labor in-house was beneath them, and was in fact forbidden to them, ensuring slaves had their place.

If it was found by slaves that the intendants were working hard like them, it would foster an Esprit De Coeur between them, a feeling that they were equal, and this would not help their management. Instead, it was necessary to subtly ensure that they understood their lower order by taking away any ability to decide, any ability to choose, and to ensure hard work while the intendants blatantly stood by, doing nothing.

This, of course, showed without saying that there was a clear divide between them, immersion in this atmosphere over time becoming accepted with the application of good management. This was not just advanced learning techniques – as outlined in the Manor's description of punishments in literature provided for slave owners who were deciding whether or not to commit their beloveds after learning of their care: denial, or chastity, etc. – but the careful and professional application of well-rehearsed behavioral programs which were tested and known to achieve certain results. This, then, was the main reason for the constant in house monitoring of slaves on camera, the reports filed and thereof discussed and used by the intendants to tweak and tune their behavior modification program with different strategies, slave upon slave adjusted as necessary. Over years of management, it had been found that secrecy from slaves about modification and application was necessary to facilitate good adjustment in behavior, which was why the rule of incitement was applied so harshly, and absolutely no descent tolerated. In keeping with this, there was the hermetically sealed environment from the outside world – another euphemistic term from the Manor's literature, used to disguise the fact that the women in house where actually prisoners – which meant those in the Manor's care never came into contact with anyone from outside. There were no visitors or any other distractions, such that the women remained fully focused on their treatment and willingly committed to the intendants' advice and direction on them.

There were, of course, times when this advice was doubted and slaves had to be encouraged by intendants to see that their directions were… correct.

This was achieved with much faster results if slaves where unhindered by outside influences, their minds able to fully focus on their treatments because their world simply was their treatments.

This, of course, like the morning's role call, provided an environment that made for ease of acceptance of these treatments, the women hearing of harsher courses provided for this one or that. Knowledge of these harsher courses which had been provided for some meant that, when a course which was much less harsh became applied to themselves, acceptance was almost assured. What they couldn't see was that this acceptance at each step with the behavioral strategies and their intensity meant, over weeks, they were slowly and delicately increased by intendants, so that what may have been viewed as harsh on their arrival was quite common halfway through.

In view to keeping this charade of earned privilege, the intendants themselves had to earn their positions in-house, a lengthy and costly procedure taking years to work through, designed not just to ensure professional ability, but to find those who had a real appetite and determination for this lifestyle. Only then, the management believed, after years of trial and error would they have the staff with the professionalism and knowledge to justify such high claims and prices. All intendants, then, had to earn the award…

Freedom Of The House

A title all intendants held which was awarded ceremonially and held on the wall in the main dining area.

This did two things…

One, it provided a sense of authority and legality in the minds of the women under their care, as they were not just being savaged by some fool who'd learned to wield an implement.

Two, it meant that although the intendants were not present at breakfast each morning, their names were, and constantly being picked up by the women from the wall, their beautiful expensive-looking plaques with their gilded italics making for more justification of their authority over them.

Indeed, after some time in the Manor with unavoidable relationships forming, both professional and platonic, with more secretly developing between staff and slave, many women looked at the awards on the wall with pride at being under their care, and with some jealously, wishing they were under the care of another group's staff.

Today, though, there was no such pride in one group, however, the poor women tormented by its leader, forcing their tired bodies to strip down yet another of four pallets, its boxed materials to be brought in by the tired women as their huge intendant guard ambled around them in the sunshine, doing nothing.

They were tired and hungry, as the second of the pallets had been mostly of fine food, its scent wafting around them, leaving them starving as they'd been escorted down the east wing to the freezer room, the food checked and logged, a more normal logistic than sometimes was stored there. The third pallet seemed to be inspected heavily by the intendants, as if whatever was in the boxes was very important, but the fourth, which was comprised of one huge box, was a mystery, a mystery that remained unopened and took ten slaves to lift and carry it….

All afternoon, the pallets were stripped and emptied, carried and stored, the intendants luxuriating outside, their tans topped up under glistening sunshine and their leathers warmed as a fine afternoon was enjoyed by all… all of the staff anyway.

At dinner that evening, a tired group ate heartily at their table, not feeling totally in agreement with the other groups' paranoia that treatment had been so lenient recently. Another of the groups also did not feel totally sure that some of the women worrying around the tables had a case, they themselves just taken off rations by Lyvia, and allowed to gorge for the first time, the food surprisingly rich over the past week…

“I’m telling you something is up,” Suzanna whispered timidly under the camera’s eye.

“Up?” questioned Heather, similarly mindful of what was above them and monitoring from the corner.

“No one is being learned,” she determined.

“Whipped, you mean” Heather laughed at Suzanna’s acceptance of the Manor’s euphemisms, her training thorough.

Suzanna grimaced, a sarcastic glare breaking into an embarrassed smile before she continued with a serious note. “Hardly anyone is being taken at night, and those that are come back fine,” she worried on.

“Would you like to put a request in for intendants to come and get you?” Heather joked sarcastically, the table laughing with those from the adjacent table who overheard.

“Look, I’m serious, something’s wrong,” assured Suzanna.

“Well, it will be if you keep questioning,” Heather said, motioning up to the lens looking down on them, all the women speaking quietly and thinking their hushed tones would be missed by the camera, so high as it was. The microphones secretly built in to each table, though, made sure the intendants monitoring could hear every whisper as they carefully watched for any signs of incitement. This group fortunately, however, would not be burdened by any discipline as they seemed to have great control over themselves, having a constant reminder among them of what would happen if they didn't… Linda.

"Look, whatever's going to happen is going to happen; there's no sense fretting about it," quipped Julie between mouthfuls.

"Well, you'd be used to having that attitude the amount of times they come for you," replied Suzanna, irritated no one was entertaining her concerns.

"What's that supposed to mean?!" Julie retorted loudly, glaring down the table.

"Heah! Heah, heah…" Andrea jumped in quickly, trying to calm things under the camera. "She's just worried, that's all, a lot of us are; there's lots of stories going around."

"Yes, like our party delivery," Diane chirped up, referring to the word from the tired group at their side, almost asleep over their table. "And that kind of marries up with what Samantha heard," she continued, referring to a morsel of intendant speech picked up in-house by her group.

"What, about an open day?" Jennifer dared.

"You haven't heard anything?" Amandine asked, the group aware of Jennifer's closeness to authority.

"No, I… haven't thought about it really, what with what happened," she replied, being the latest recipient of the mask and still slightly shaken by the experience.

"Have you asked?" enquired Monique.

"I haven't thought to ask… she's been distant recently, and I thought she was just busy," replied Jennifer.

"They all seem to be busy," Suzanna assured her, staring hard at Heather, her message seeming to find traction and Heather starting to think instead of responding sarcastically.

The same worries passed around two of the four tables, the other two having things to occupy them, one exhausted from their day's work and the other ravenously enjoying their lifting of sanctions.

With dinner over, they were retired early, again rested, the house quiet and bringing a growing sense that something was wrong. Such ease was not granted for nothing in house, even the most placid among them beginning to feel the paranoia… pervasive and ever growing…

Four sets, strong powerful, tacking into the room, the heels seeming to assure those inside they meant business, offering no words, their arrival surely a result of Suzanna's questioning her efforts, now to be felt by those of her group. Stirring, Jennifer thought of who they'd take – not Julie, as she hadn't questioned, and not Heather as she'd stayed unconvinced, but Andrea… she hoped not, as she hadn't deserved it. Suzanna… surely, she had to be learned… then the boots stopped at her!

Jennifer looked up wide-eyed, four foreign groups' intendants looking back, professional, strong, without smiles… this was not for them, so it was no pleasure call.

With one stepping forward and leaning over to uncuff her, the feel of her corset's leather brushing over Jennifer's skin shocked her… didn't they know who she belonged to?! With the sounds of her cuffs coming off, Jennifer felt like demanding whether they did, but knew well not to question. Instead, she dutifully followed in silence, shocked that her protector wasn't there, that she could let this happen to her, the other group members similarly confused as they watched their privileged one being taken all the same.

Jennifer was relieved when the dull lighting continued under the square casing bulbs, the grim grey corridor of the first lower level continuing past the stairs; she didn't want to go down there. Instead, they continued on, passing the first set of opposing doors where Julie usually lived, and approaching the second, Jennifer able to feel the beating of the nightclub on the right – surely, she wasn't going to the table on her own!

Only a small sigh of relief was born inside her as they turned left, as this was a door she hadn't known yet, all the rumor and stories in house flooding her curiosity, half building an image in her mind, but being held back in check by fear, none of the intendants smiling. Inside, that changed as they moved in with the door closing behind them, Jennifer greeted by a lovely calming atmosphere.

A bar, not like the nightclub just across the way behind them, brash and loud, but instead like the upper level of the house, a rich ornate atmosphere, decadent, French and present all around. On entry, heels met with dark laminate, brown skirting leading to darkened black and brown art deco walls topped with ornate cornicing. The theme continued directly ahead, the quiet bar-front styled as the walls were, the design stretching across the rear by some ten feet as well, with glinting golden accoutrements and fonts, an intendant already behind the bar, pouring drinks and exchanging pleasant words with her sisters as they arrived, calming Jennifer enormously. Pausing nonchalantly at the bar, Jennifer allowed her gaze to drift right, such was the ease of the atmosphere, her eyes pleasantly surprised as their ten feet square arrival platform followed stairs down to a large seating area, the color scheme starkly different. Ten stairs down, with glinting brass banisters on each side, the same dark brown laminate floor continued, five booths on the left housing five small tables against the wall, cream leather seating on each side fit for four as the cream walls appeared again, art deco giving way to warmth and relaxing feeling, gentle jazz music meandering quietly in the background.

Jennifer breathed a sigh of relief as a smile almost escaped, and looking on, her gaze continued right; then she stopped….

Another device… her calming thoughts immediately left her as, in the remainder of the room, her eyes fell on a square box six feet by six feet, and only four feet high. White and surrounded on all sides by the same leather seating as the booths, they formed a square around it, there being one way into the square from the side nearest her, the flat backs of the square of seating the same color as the bar front and walls beside her. The way in, then, was obvious, the space only two feet wide and having the stark white of the box beyond it standing out in the space, flanked by the dark backs of the seating as they guarded the entrance. This, though, was not what had Jennifer's attention, as the seating only a foot from the box and all the way around had such a height that any occupier would have the box as a table, the entertainment becoming clear. As Jennifer realized it, her calm left her, noticing the hole directly in the center of the box's top was just big enough for someone's head to fit through.

"Like what you see?" a leather clad tormentor asked, having glided over unseen by Jennifer, taking her by the waist and enjoying her trepidation. “Well, if you like the look of it that much, why don’t we get you acquainted with it?” An evil smile brought rowdy applause from her three sisters behind her, the bar staff smiling, too.

Soon, sharp heels descended the stairs with nervous feet cold on the laminate floor as she was taken directly to the gap between the seating, three crowing corsets carrying drinks behind her, Jennifer realizing she was the night’s entertainment.

Laughing on, two held the drinks now, one holding Jennifer as she watched the remainder move to the left of the box, an elegant brass hinge and padlock atop it, unseen from the stairway, taken and unfastened, the box easily splitting open down a line across its top. With the front opening toward the gap in the seating, it hinged effortlessly forward on two huge brass hinges on its right. Perfectly balanced, its elegance struck Jennifer as she watched a section in the shape of a T swing out over the hinges, the bottom of the T swinging into the gap between the seating and the box, its left high side able to swing across the seating on the right, dangerously close to the leather. The elegance only held her attention so long as she now bore witness to what awaited inside. The hole in the box’s top was now halfed by the opening, it revealing four leather attachments hanging from fixed positions, two to either side of the hole, flanked by two more on either side of the box at ankle level. In front of them, at the box’s lower left corner, only a small cube of its front wall remained with the swinging off of the T-shape above and overhead of it, now lying open, hinged over the seating area on their right. Jennifer noticed what appeared to be another brass padlock and hinge on the front of the small cube to the left below, it holding closed a hatch which seemed to open upwards, allowing entry when the box was closed, her imagination feeding her with the horror of what was coming.

Not needing explanation, the intendants reveled in the expression on her face as the one holding her pushed her inside to the jeers of the others behind her as the box's opener in front reached forward for her, taking her right arm as she entered the square, seating now surrounding her.

Spun around now, she felt the pressure of the jeers as she watched their laughing faces, something she would endure in the hours to come, hands pushing on her shoulders and forcing her to squat as they nestled her neck into the back of the halfed hole, her hands taken to either side of her. Stretched fully, she felt her nerves rise as the gorgeous soft leather buckling was wrapped round her wrists, her arms fastened tightly under and against the box's top. With her palms facing down, her hands hung limp and useless to her now as yet more buckling was secured around the middle of her arms. With all four buckles tightly secured, Jennifer could do nothing as two corseted beauties pulled her legs apart beneath her, each securing an ankle to either side of the box. Hanging uselessly from her restraints, malevolent smiles rose to inspect her before pulling back, leaving her trapped within, the women proudly examining their work as they left.

To jeering excitement, the T was brought slowly back, Jennifer now sealed inside the half hole with it now brought back to completion as the box was carefully fitted back together, the snug fit of smoothed wood around her neck comfortable but tight, no way for her head to get down inside the box. As if trying to prove a point, the box's opener now resealed the brass padlock on the latch, her smile at Jennifer's entrapment making her feel scared as she moved off, taking a seat with the others.

Resting their drinks on the box in front of Jennifer, she felt trapped and stupid… it was humiliating and they were reveling in it.

"How do you feel, Jennifer?" one of them teased, Jennifer feeling already like she would cry, the pressure of four cackling women all powerful and surrounding her getting to her as she feared what they would do.

Pity, it looked like, but Jennifer knew different; after stroking her face and teasing her further, they seemed to leave her alone, instead chatting amongst themselves about various things, occasionally lifting their drinks from the box in front of her before returning them again, quite ignoring her plight.

Jennifer listened to their opinions on house matters, on the women, and what they thought had to be done with them. She listened as they laughed at certain treatments and their results, becoming slightly angry at the callous talk, but hiding it well, her training saving her from ire as she maintained a submissive face throughout the discomfort. It was made easier by her restraints, as they were indeed sumptuous, made of some of the softest leather she'd yet been imprisoned in. It left her more than comfortable as she hung under the box, able to support herself with her legs if she wished, or to hang all her weight from the buckling. It did dawn on her quickly, though, that this comfort meant she was to be held there for a long time, this shallowing her feeling.

"Oh, just wait till Friday!" one of the intendants' thoughts loosened with her drink. "You'll get her then and make sure she pays!!!" the whole four burst out laughing, Jennifer realizing they were talking about the big day that was being prepared, more rumor gleaned as one of the intendants caught her eye.

"Don't worry, sweetie," she demeaned, bringing the attention of the others back to her. "We haven't forgotten about you, and don't go telling the others what you're hearing; besides, you have enough to worry about tonight!" They all laughed on at Jennifer's stony worried expression, she trapped in front of them.

And so it went on, more laughter and more chatter, Jennifer trying to stay quiet, hoping not to be noticed as glasses were lifted and placed back around her… and then the lights dimmed.

"Whoooooow," came a drawling excited tone from the four intendants, smiling at a fearful Jennifer, showing they hadn't for an instant forgotten about her as blurred shapes appeared in the gloom behind them, descending the stairs further out. Four more intendants, leashing a slave by their side, hooded and obedient and dressed in corset and leather… dressed like…? For a moment, Jennifer was confused, as slaves were not allowed to be clothed, and then it dawned on her, that it wasn't a slave; it was an intendant….

Sometimes intendants were drafted in for games like this, games where they needed expertise delivered to a slave, expertise that another slave simply couldn't give. On the one hand, it meant no accidental over-excesses from hands that hadn't learned how to train, but on the other hand, it could mean very intentional over-excess from hands that had… hence the hood. It had been found over time that the intendants' nightly pursuits, though fun and quite normal for those privileged enough to have found their way so deep into the lifestyle, had at times complicated the very real training going on in-house, and this meant delays for the owners waiting for their slaves' coveted return. In an effort to prevent this, disguise was often employed, the women therefore not realizing just which of the houses intendants delivered the coup de grass on them; thereby, subsequent training delivered by the same intendant would not be adversely resisted due to ill feeling toward them. Over years, it had been found that this method did indeed prevent delays, the women never sure who had done what, and therefore more malleable and less resistant to the entire house compliment of staff as a whole.

As she was brought forward, Jennifer could only get the briefest of glimpses in the darkened room, a light above the table now the only real light in the room, bathing the table-top in brilliance, she now the center of attention for those seated around her… laughing.

The four intendants now filled her view, devastatingly beautiful as always, their corsets shining, leather glinting under the light as they leashed their sister, crawling beside them, out of view for Jennifer, her head locked and unable to view below the table-top.

With excited pleasantries exchanged, soon excited jeering began as Jennifer felt the vibration to her right, her body tensing as, unseen, at the box's lower left front, the small square hatch was now opened, allowing their sister to crawl in, Jennifer feeling they'd just let in a wild animal beneath her.

To the laughter of the seated compliment in front, a small commotion below was lifted and shaken in front of her, the keys to the padlock now closed and maddeningly placed on the table top just in front of her as she watched them laugh on at her worried expression, their sister now sealed inside with her.

Now, silence, and Jennifer felt the pressure of eight eager faces staring at her, watching her every twitch as she worried in front of them, vibrations below her signaling someone moving, her tensing breath amusing them, and then… she shrieked as suddenly nails seized her underneath, the shock having her scream to the audience's delight as she wrenched at her tight restraints uselessly as the animal beneath continued grasping at her flesh, her panicked screams useless as her head wrenched in the hole to the table's applause. To the laughter above, she screamed in panic before a sudden spank, loud enough for the intendants to hear from outside, shocked her to her senses, the nails abating as she was controlled from inside, her panicked body tensing and shaking, a further release of noise from her bringing the nails instantly back to her sides, her scream delighting those above before another thunderous spank brought her under control from beneath.

Staying silent this time, she realized she was being shown a path, but still shaking with nervous fear, she felt the hands come again, but with her silence, no nails. Instead, they explored, gently stroking her shivering body, and Jennifer felt them work around her, showing her who was in control and how she must behave. Her nerves building with their movement, she felt the intendant kneel between her legs, her hands stroking up between them as they were held helplessly apart for her, Jennifer's body beginning to shake excessively as they approached her… then a spank! Not vicious, it was a control, an objection to her excessive shaking, Jennifer trying to calm, to follow the path, as again the hands explored. Circling around behind her thighs underneath, the hands cupped her cheeks as she felt the face and hair of the intendant slightly stroke her vulnerability and thighs at either side, her mask removed, the woman seeming to inspect her lips, her jump forgiven and unpunished.

Above, though, was a different story; so focused on her instructor below her, expressions of fear and shock had begun giving way to pleasure and more, this only amusing the drinking audience for a moment before their natural sadism began to demand more.

Suddenly snapped back to her audience in front, Jennifer looked on as they jeered one of the intendants reaching into a bag she'd brought with her, her hand retracting from the black cloth revealing a snapper. A small electronic control designed to sharply instruct with electric shocks, not overly painful unless delivered to delicate areas like the ones held open and vulnerable for her assailant below.

Fearful, Jennifer for a second panicked, the intendant reaching forward toward her face, the audience laughing at her relief as she passed her hand behind her and then again at her shock as she realized what was being done.

Unnoticed before, a small white ring atop the box's back right was lifted by the intendant, an effortless tug taking away a circular plug and leaving a six inch hole.

Leading directly inside, and a wide-eyed Jennifer watched as the intendant mischievously grinned at her, now dangling the snapper above the hole, reveling in Jennifer's panicked look.

With the soft elegant jazz still playing quietly in the background, the audience fell quiet, the smiling intendant easily heard as she raised her eyebrows. "Enjoy," she crowed, dropping the snapper.

The audience burst with laughter at Jennifer's panic, the dull thud felt inside by her as the snapper hit the floor, only heightening her fear as she felt her assailant move for the prize dropped beside her. The audience able to sense what was going on below simply by following her eyes, they fell quiet as a nervous Jennifer started pulling at her restraints, her assailant nestling between her helpless femininity once again. At first, just the hands, Jennifer almost holding her breath, but then…

The first snap on her midriff saw Jennifer wrench upwards, screaming out to her delighted audience. Only a tiny charge, but the fear made it huge; she shrieked as another two found her abdomen, true panic beginning as she wrenched, screaming out from her restraints, the intendants howling with laughter as her panic turned to tears, the humiliation breaking her with the fear built from below.

To jeering laughter, her tears continued, the shocks stopping below and suddenly nails finding her sides, the pain bringing her back, fear replacing tears before panic saw her wrench at her restraints to the howling audience above before a huge spank suddenly found her rear. The jolt was savage, and then another, Jennifer's wrenching stopping, the demand for control from below dutifully followed, the soothing hands coming back as if rewarding her behavior.

And so it went on, intendants drinking and jeering, Jennifer humiliated and panicked – at times she'd relax, find her way on the path, but then the intendants would notice, reach for the bag, and drop some new nasty inside through the hole, the cycle beginning all over again.

Truly enjoying their entertainment, the main event was still to come; nervous and tiring, Jennifer began to fade away, the intendants noticing and, of course, then the bag was reached for….

A wheel, something Jennifer and the others had really come to fear, glinting as it passed by her head, and she realized the gravity of the situation as she felt the thud with it landing inside with her. Suddenly reacquainted with just how open her femininity was, she was catapulted back from her tiredness to her audience's delight in front of her. Her controller inside seemed to have mercy at first, her warm hands working gently over a fearful timid body, totally hers and at her whims, and then it came…

Its sharp jagged teeth of cold steel and merciless application seemed to be amplified by her entrapment; like the snapper, it was no worse than those regularly used on them, but with Jennifer held open and vulnerable, the fear made it the sharpest ever. Grimacing, Jennifer let out a squeal to the audience's delight, her body shaking violently in her restraints with every landing of the teeth. Hardly needing to touch her at all, it was as if she were being shocked by the landings, so much so that her controller beneath seemed to become irritated by the display, some sharp spanks and gentle digging of nails forcing her back to the path, a short rest seemingly granted.

Then the wheel came again, its sharp teeth wandering over a shaking Jennifer, unable to stop pulling uselessly at her restraints as, underneath her, arms were held open, her legs all the same, her vulnerability presented to her torturess below. The wheel lifted from her hip, Jennifer shaking to the pleasure of her audience, only to grimace and hold back a squeal as it came down on her again, down on a shaking stomach, her midriff vibrating as it went, its cold steel wandering up her body, lifting and coming back. As Jennifer held her squeals, to her audience's delight, she felt the teeth suggest a course, Jennifer beginning to nervously exhale as she realized her left breast would be first, the wheel coming down on her left side and beginning to rise.

The intendants reveled, their experience telling them Jennifer's strained look beginning to turn left was the signal from below at what was happening underneath. Drawing a deep breath, Jennifer felt the cold teeth gently climb onto her left breast, her pull on her restraints total as she gritted her teeth before the steel found her nipple, forcing a shriek to the waiting crowd in front, their laughter being her return.

With the crowd laughing on, she felt the sharp teeth circle round her nipple in a particular pattern, gently and rhythmically, as if the intendant beneath her was enjoying herself, having fun with her body. The feeling of a total lack of control pervaded her as the wheel continued around her nipple, its sharp teeth biting and nipping, the intendants laughing and drinking merrily as they looked down on her discomfort. All staring sadistically, they watched for the pain, smiling as they tracked it with the fear across her face. The march of her suffering matched the travel of the wheel wandering over her nipple, forcing expression up above. Suddenly, she squealed as nails plunged into her sides, the intendant beneath receiving a howling applause from the audience around her, their claps and jeering signaling their appreciation as Jennifer tried not to burst into tears under the pressure beneath and the humiliation above.

Another horrific night, Jennifer stunned and confused at why she'd been chosen, as she'd done nothing wrong. More than the way the humiliation left her feeling the next day, it was the abandonment that did the real damage. Left truly disturbed, she couldn't understand where Nadia had been… why had she left her? Why had she let this happen to her?

Outside the next day, Nadia was disturbed herself at the condition of her favorite, her explanations of the Mistress's suspicions about them driving her to order this doing nothing to help her.

"We have our programs to follow, but sometimes the Mistress insists on directions of her own; we've no choice but to carry them out or to let them be carried out," Nadia tried to reason with a stricken Jennifer.

"Let them…" Jennifer struggled, her eyes full of hurt as Nadia pulled her closer, her resistance and looking away tolerated only because it was her.

"I knew it was going to happen, but I couldn't stop them taking you, so all I could do was ensure they didn't go to far," she tried to reason.

"And what if they hadn't listened to you?" Jennifer uttered, still looking away, pushing her luck and gushing with pain. “What if they don’t listen next time when you’re not there again…” she held back tears, honestly hurt at Nadia’s abandonment.

“I Told you I wouldn’t let you out of my sight again,” Nadia purred, Jennifer squinting up, confused as she drew her finger up her left side before spinning it gently and rhythmically around her nipple in a particular pattern, in the exact same way Jennifer had felt in the box! The sudden realization hitting her at just who had been torturing her inside, the pairs strain breaking into smiling laughter!

Chapter 17

The Calm

The week had been strange – Monday, Lyvia's group had been worked all day, bringing tables from the room adjacent to the room containing all the cleaning materials on the ground level. The mystery as to what lay inside it was rather disappointingly answered, it being simply a store room for extra tables, chairs, and other oddities required at times around the house; not only was this disappointing, but also hard work. All afternoon, women moved back and forth, up the west wing to the ballroom and back, twenty tables moved in all, the reason guessed at as black rubber table cloths from the third pallet's boxes were revealed. Having to fit them over the tables took some effort, their huge thick rubber edges sealing tightly over the tables' own, making them smooth and neat as the rubber cloths continued eight inches below, this giving a firm fit which wouldn't come off easily. After their afternoon's efforts, the women were made to push the tables to the right of the ballroom, their understanding of the second pallet's huge compliment of food leaving them sure of the feast that was yet to come, a feast they were sure they wouldn't be involved in.

It was the way of the house, they were learned in the Academy, that the lifestyle was much more accepted by anyone participating if their surroundings were suggestive of the same. What that meant was that, with dingy cheap facilities, the same attire would not lead those involved to think much of the procedures or wish to be involved, but grandeur was different.

Grandeur like the soft power of empires which let their flags and symbols cast out across the world, giving a quiet suggestion to the human mind that this huge force – able to bring such massive resources – was to be respected. This respect is quite unconscious from the person, but is natural when faced with such largess, making the person feel small, humble and in awe, all traits that those in the Manor knew well how to use in order to train and manipulate a subject.

It is then logical, from this awareness, to ensure that surroundings are sumptuous, that clothing is the same, and that facilities are luxurious – the very presence of such amenities meaning less work for the intendants, the participants already feeling small and privileged to be a part of such attentions.

With this in mind, the long and seemingly oversized emphasis on preparations for such events as the one coming soon were not seen as abnormal by the women; on the contrary, this attention to detail was appreciated, even if the strangeness of this one provided them with worry.

It was the secrecy of it all, loose words and rumors dropped willingly by the intendants spreading fear and discomfort, but the one thing that had them all uncomfortable was the behavior exhibited by intendants as it grew nearer… leniency.

This was not their way, and aroused obvious suspicion as the women were rested, fed, and put down to bed earlier and earlier as the week went on. They quietly whispered amongst themselves at meal times, exchanging stories of their certainty that intendants wanted to deal with them each day for their small mistakes as usual, but were holding back.

Tuesday…

Everyone was kept outside as a huge meeting with the Mistress and the intendant staff went ahead in the ballroom. All morning, the women were kept out, but hardly pushed on the steps or scrutinized, as they were left in groups, sunning themselves on the grass and waiting for their turn at fitness.

Occasionally, loud voices and group laughter drifted out from the ballroom, having their intendant guard squint in disapproval as if worried some secret would get out.

Lunch came, and the day seemed almost over, the afternoon's excitement consisting of Lyvia's group being forced to remove the first and third pallets' debris from the ballroom and place it out front, where it might be picked up by some unsuspecting refuse collectors tending the Manor.

The third pallet's empty boxes held no mystery, their contents still stretched over the twenty tables on the right of the ballroom, but none had seen the first's, which now had all its boxes empty. As usual, there just happened to be an enormous intendant guard out front, sunning themselves in case any of Lyvia's group got ideas of liberty, the women hearing this and that discussed as they came maddeningly back and forth for the umpteenth time with empty boxes, plastic shrink-wrap, and pallets.

"Nothing really," Samantha answered Andrea across the table at dinner. "They just seemed to be talking about clothes, about how snugly they fitted;

they must have new corsets or something," she mused.

Suzanna looked hard at Heather, but didn't say anything, Heather having no sarcastic comments as the two became suspicious along the same lines.

"I just want to know," chirped Andrea. "I wish they'd just tell us… I hate all this secrecy."

"I don't think you'll have to wait long," Monique said dryly, her tone dwindling as she ate from another huge dinner plate, larger than yesterday's.

Evening came swiftly, just like their retirement, the sun still in the sky as they were taken down to their dorms earlier than ever. Truly bored, some among them were almost desperate for attention, even of a harsh kind, anything better than the dorms again… but no one came… save one.

Looks of true jealousy and almost anger came from her sisters as Jennifer was led away by her mouthwatering Hispanic captor, the sound of her boots driving them mad as they were left bored and chained… and awake.

Jennifer dutifully obeyed, so happy to see her that the placing of her finger gently over her lips brought tingles of excitement. She almost didn't notice how still the Manor was as she was glided naked through it by Nadia's hand. Ascending the staircase to the main hallway, and then on up to her quarters on the first level, Nadia seemed to pass hurriedly, as if she didn't want to be seen by anyone, even though the Manor seemed empty and as if no one was there.

With the door closing, Jennifer couldn't help but release a beaming smile, Nadia raising her eyebrows at the insolence before breaking into one of her own, the two women falling into one another's arms and then to bed, unable to hide their want.

There were few words, just groans and love – no professional touch or guided hands, just two lovers and their natural ways; one, though, still willfully and obviously obedient… no training required.

Thrashing… thrashing hard on the sheets, groans of ecstasy as two secret lovers released their pent-up lust, hidden for days as they'd passed each other and now passing down their thighs as they gushed forth, squeezing each other, groans filling the room as they let it all out.

Inseparable now, spent with lust, they lay moaning in each other's ears, entangled thighs moistened from running want, their bodies refusing to let each other go, simply waiting for breath to catch before releasing again….

Shaking and moaning contentedly, their lust abated for a time, still they couldn't let each other go, a long bout of deep kissing beginning as Nadia rolled on top of Jennifer, grinding her into the bed, the two giggling through wanton lips.

Calming, Nadia wouldn't let her go, gazing deeply into her eyes with Jennifer still pinned beneath her as she kissed gently, starting to stroke her like a lover, Jennifer's response the same, the two descending into after-play, the world stopped and theirs.

"How've you been?" Nadia's silken Spanish tones finally washed over them, past the moaning.

"Missing you," was all Jennifer could say, pinned and complete, their laughter and kissing competing with their arms for more of each other.

"Why so much? I've been around," teased Nadia, the two laughing at their secret passing of each other in the Manor, it being hard to bare.

And so it went on, two lovers gently fawning over each other, talking freely for the first time in days.

Eventually and inevitably, the conversation moved to the preparations, Nadia for the first time seizing up Jennifer easily, able to feel it through her, the full gorgeous weight of her body still firmly pressing down on her.

"I can't…" she tailed off, seemingly caught between love and loyalty. "I can't tell you what it is," she uttered in an unsure tone.

"Don't get into trouble over me; I'll be okay," Jennifer tried to support her, not wanting to trouble her love… but something went wrong.

An immediate seize through Nadia's body, and a look of guilt had her pull from Jennifer, their beautiful moment shattered as Nadia turned away to the pillow, her breath troubled.

Jennifer didn't ask; after a time, she just gently squeezed as if trying to support her and ask at the same time, a strong look coming back with a half-seizing grip, Jennifer looking frightened, the emotion picked up immediately by Nadia as she changed to caring.

Another guilty bout with the pillow, and finally Nadia came back to her, her touch caring and supportive. "Look… sometimes, training in the Manor is taken up a level," she chose her words carefully. "This is not us," she explained. "The Mistress judges when these times are right and we have to carry them out; it's why you're here, to be trained… that's why we're here – we have no choice."

Jennifer looked back, the riddle of her words confusing her, leaving her troubled, but it wasn't the words that had her troubled really; it was the touching, hands laden with sympathy Jennifer could feel, the guilty caress as Nadia seemed to be apologizing already for something still to come… and which Jennifer began to fear.

The rest of their night, Nadia tried to calm her, their enjoyment tainted by her sinister words, feeling Jennifer's worries inside her, but not willing to tell her further, as the guilt…. The guilt made her fearful.

Their walk back through the Manor that night was quiet, still… cuffing her back to her bed, Nadia wanted to kiss her, wanted to hold her tight to reassure her… but she couldn't. Jennifer could see it, though, worrying her further, their fleeting looks hidden from the cameras, bedding down for the night as Nadia motioned with her eyes for Jennifer to turn away to the pillow. Left on her side, naked and troubled, jealous eyes watched with hers as Hispanic perfection strained black panties, cheeks sliding from left to right under corset, her boot-falls leaving wet those watching from behind her.

Wednesday…

A strange day almost normal, groups were split into four and sent to normal training both in and out of the Manor, but something was missing… staff.

Hardly an intendant was seen all day by those on cleaning duties, and again that morning, there was no assemblance in the main ballroom, no role call of disciplining or embarrassing examples. Instead, a normal abnormal day for all: all the training, none of the discipline, more of the worry.

The intendants themselves were busy with the fourth pallet in the main ballroom, as sealed inside, they laughed casually as, with some effort, an enormous purpose-built black velvet curtain was revealed.

The huge drape took twenty to haul it out across the ballroom floor, twenty more to steam iron, it an activity bemoaned that was for the slaves in house and beneath them, but completed all the same.

All intendants present had work now as, with five sets of ladders, standing stools, and all the precision of an army, they hoisted the huge drape to the ballroom's middle pulley and line system, it being obvious this was not their first time doing this. With flawless rigor, the winches at the far end of the ballroom by the huge bay windows and the one on the opposite wall by the door were used to bring the massive black wall of velvet across the middle of the room and up, twenty tables now hidden from sight behind it on the right side.

Reports to the Mistress detailed how the new velvet drape did indeed look wonderful, another excellent decision by her to replace the older tawdry looking version, its experience and age having begun to show.

And so to dinner, the rumor mill flying as the house sensed something coming, fears and protestations, suspicion and mirth fleeting between the tables, all watched carefully from on high, any sign of incitement a sure indication that intendants had broken ranks.

None came, though, the intendants themselves knowing this was a time of great strain and watch; a test more for them by the Mistress to ensure order and separation between slave and intendant was being maintained, these monitoring times another way of controlling the house.

By the time dinner was over, the mirth had won over the suspicion, the pallets of food and the tablecloths sighted as conformation of the party ahead. One, though, definitely knew something was wrong as she sat quietly with her knowledge, worried and alone.

Thursday…

The strangest yet… all women were kept outside, sunned all day, games played on the grass with intendants laughing, and lunch brought outside for them!

They were all worried, as relaxed as the sun left them and as appreciative of the fun permitted, they could all feel it. The intendants, after days of holding back, couldn't hide their looks of malice upon them, like predators circling their prey.

Thoroughly run down outside all day, they began to realize the strategy as they were taken for showers before dinner time. All forty at once, two groups had to queue in the hallway, tired and ready for bed early, just how the intendants wanted them. Queuing in the hallway, it wasn't necessary to spread rumors as the smell of fine food, obviously superior to what they were used to, filled the hallways, the preparations for what lay ahead obviously having been going on inside all day.

Starving and ravenous from their hallway queuing, the second two groups had to suffer all the fine scents before the first two showering were taken to the dining hall, where a surprise lay in store.

The food… not expecting to have involvement in such luxury, it was a glorious surprise for all to find that a menu fit for royalty awaited them. So hungry, none questioned the announcement as their food was laid out, that it was in appreciation of them getting this far, Suzanna's cold worried look at Heather finding every sympathy as she returned one of her own. Jennifer, too, had her own worried look as she ate the finest meal she'd ever had in-house, Nadia's chilling words washing over her mind.

To bed early, the women only too happy to be taken, utterly tired and appreciative of the early night, the intendants strategy having worked to perfection, group management at its finest.

For one, though, rest would be short, and most of her group, save Suzanna and Heather, were already asleep when she came for her. They watched, beginning to worry further as they noticed how she quietly took her favorite away, not with lust and want, but with a face of concern, leaving them with the same.

Try as she might to calm Jennifer, Nadia couldn't hide her own worry, picked up easily by her favorite. She handled her with all the care in the world, fondling her and doting over her, stroking her and more, Jennifer falling asleep twice after the day's exertions, only to wake up again in her arms, as if she couldn't let her go… as if she didn't want to.

Finally, she had to take her down, Jennifer remaining silent as usual as they moved through the Manor, the perfect cover for someone hiding her worry… but Nadia couldn't. It was in how she took her, how she walked, slowly and hesitantly as if she didn't want to let her go. Worried, Jennifer sensed the same as she was cuffed; the fleeting loving smile, as her eyes flicked to tell her to roll to her pillow, barely disguising the strain on her face.

Nadia paused as she stood up – she'd never done that before under the camera, usually just operating professionally, but she couldn't help it. Looking down at the innocent form on her side, eyes closed on her pillow in obedience, Nadia was consumed with guilt already over what was about to happen. Realizing her stillness under watch from above, she snapped herself together and began to leave, her boot steps obviously more hurried than usual, determined no one would see the tears rolling down her face….

Chapter 18

Opening Day

Then it was morning, and strange… strange right from the start, as intendants arrived, but only two….

Carly and Valerie came, no hint as to why and no morning's example, none for any group, all thinking it odd as they were marched to breakfast, the groups getting in each other's way, all arriving together.

Doors closing, confused looks could give no answer to each other over the small breakfasts laid out before them, bringing more questions, each thinking their group had been rationed, what with the small size of the portions.

Time, inordinate… with such small portions, they'd expected the doors to fly open any minute… but they didn't. In fact, breakfast time passed and continued, the conversation initially curious and then becoming worried, then quiet… and then quieter.

Finally, when the doors did open, they were all in the state wanted above, confused, questioning… fearful.

Stony looks from the small intendant guard escorting them to the showers did nothing to help them, two long queues of ten slaves in each line, waiting at either side of the west wing as twenty more were preparing inside, no one talking with the guards still present. Then, twenty more did the morning wash as the first two groups now shivered outside, the morning chill on the marble tiles helped little by the sun at the end of the wing.

Still, there were no answers as sharp boots escorted forty worried souls, naked and fearful, up the west wing. Heels tacking, implements swaying, the guard said nothing, just giving off the sound of their boots as they were marched through the main hallway, the blast of sunlight welcomed by all before they were turned past the stairway and into the ballroom.

The door opened on a strange sight, trepidation obvious among them as strong looks forced the women inside. Quickly arranged into two lines of twenty, one behind the other, they all gawped at the huge black mass now in front of them… the curtain.

The huge black shape seemed menacing, seemed to have them pinned against the left side of the ballroom as it towered over them. For a moment, all attention stayed on the dark form before a sound they'd never heard before stunned them in the silence… locking!

Never before had the ballroom been locked, the entrance now being sealed by a huge key, with fearful eyes trying to look to the side as an intendant made sure no one could leave….

Worried eyes darted back and forth to the door, the curtain and the intendant guard now disappearing behind it, at either end, no way to see through the wall of fabric.

Silence… all hearts now pounding as the smell of fear could be sensed, the women like animals, knowing some awful disaster was about to befall them, wanting to move away from it, but there was nowhere to go… the room now sealed.

Quiet, oh so quiet… just one guard at either end standing by each winch, their stony looks beginning to break as they eyed each other across the room with evil smiles, the women now in real fear as they watched the intendants simultaneously reach up toward the winches, a sharp click shattering the silence!

Rumble followed click as the whole curtain came crashing down in front of them, the women pulling back in fear as suddenly the whole house compliment of intendants came into view on the other side. Screams!!! Like lions, the leather horde broke ranks, immediately surging forward on their terrified victims! The women instinctively pulled back, meeting the wall behind them and screaming out in panic as leather-clad lace surged over the fallen fabric in front. With arms reaching out from maddening eyes, they seized their targets and dragged them away, kicking and screaming, shrieking as they went; they were dragged by the horde to the room's other side!

The other side! The right side of the room where the tables of fine food were supposed to be had only twenty bare tables arranged and waiting, the first screaming victim slammed over a black cover, her thighs bouncing of its rubber edges as four intendants descended on her limbs!

Screaming out, her hands were sealed to the table legs, leather cuffs already mounted and buckled around her wrists, her ankles, too, in seconds, sealed, all four intendants now shifting to her ass behind! Others being ripped past them to other tables by intendants, and they heard the first scream of Opening Day as a huge strap-on found her ass, merciless hands holding open her cheeks as gym-sculpted lace-clad thighs clenched behind her, driving a blunt oiled rubber end, opening her up! Her panicked screams found the walls with the others, each one tightening in vain as determined assailants, lust-crazed and wild, whooped and screamed as the terror began.

Only twenty tables saw the rest being herded by the guard, too many to work on at once, the remainder pushed to the windows where they fell together in a corner, cowering in fear. Smiles and rants as their guards teased and threatened, focusing on some and telling others they'd be next as more screaming victims were hauled out again, some tables missed and soon to be filled.

Some froze, some shivered, some cried, some squealed… but all feared as they watched the tables' limbs buckled, cheeks grasped and held wide, merciless lust bringing screams, intendants opening all victims with no mercy from behind them. Above the screaming came another, Julie breaking from the corner, panicked by the horror; she ran for the door, a useless effort sure to be punished!

And sure it was, as unnoticed before, the Mistress was among them; dress attire as intendant, she'd been lost in the melay, but a savage scream saw all now find her as her shrieking anger shattered the room…"GET THAT ASS!!!"

The door handle moved, but the door stayed sealed, the shriek seeing Julie turn on four running corsets, leather-clad wolves descending on her screams, legs and arms grabbed away as she was hauled to the tables!

Running from intendants was an extreme insult and brought special attention, as poor Julie knew well, her panicked screams for mercy finding none as she was slammed over a table. The two intendants in front barely had time to buckle her wrists before her torturer from behind nestled a strap-on between her cheeks, her panicked legs kicking out and coming to nothing as they were seized and shackled, four intendants now intent on her special learning, their attentions all over her, Julie shrieking below. Julie screamed, pulling on her restraints as free hands found her cheeks, holding her steady over the table as a wild-eyed tormentor pushed her oiled learning deep into her ass!

Screaming echoed around the room as crying victims were dragged to the corner, others then pulled away, those left cowering under guard as they watched the full horror play out just in front of them, a horror they were all soon to be part of. Those still to be dragged away for the first time froze in terror at the scene, the intendants laughing with glee over their fear, the cries of

"Fresh Ass!"

"We Need Fresh Ass Here!!!

ringing out, bringing terror as they signaled another poor savaged soul being cut free from her table and replaced by another terrified slave, hauled up by the guard and fed over to the wolves.

With glee, the fresh victim's terror was ignored, her hands grabbed away and her involuntary squeals of panic met with laughter as she was lashed to the table, bent over and secured. Behind her, a sweating, powerfully built intendant, complete with lust in her eyes, took position on the form, her sisters holding the slave's cheeks. Utterly at her mercy, most victims squealed as they met the wet blunt end of the huge black strap-on nestling in their crevices, pushing up against their asses, the other intendants laughing aloud as they held a woman's cheeks apart. Their asses being tighter than they had ever been made no difference as huge experience coupled with huge thigh muscles meant one slow long convulsion that didn't stop pushing and saw the most determined victims shrieking to the room, signaling that they, too, had joined the ranks of the penetrated.

And soon it was her turn; being pulled from the corner by three familiar faces gave small mercy as Jennifer was lashed over a table, looking all the while for Nadia, for her help, for protection, only catching a fleeting glimpse of her at the back of the room, her back to her as if ignoring her plight.

Why wasn't she helping her?

Why wasn't she taking control like she had in the bar when she'd crawled in the box with her?

Then the reason crossed her vision, the Mistress, strutting among the tables like a General as she inspected the work, congratulations given to some intendants, encouragement to others, screaming audibly rising at each table she visited. Nadia couldn't take control because she wasn't in control.

"Oh, don't worry," Carly suddenly appeared, squatting down to her ear at the head of the table, clearly enjoying herself at Jennifer's plight as she followed her gaze to Nadia. "Aaaw, she still loves you," she teased maddeningly. "That's why she can't come over here… she can't open you." Jennifer's gaze turned, meeting Carly's wild eyes as she spoke. "That's why we have to do it for her," she hissed, her eyes lighting up with all the evil of a Mistress as Valerie took position behind her.

Jennifer breathed hard as she felt the blunt oiled end of Valerie's strap-on nestle in her crevice, Carly cupping her face and watching with glee as she saw it find its way down in her eyes, Jennifer groaning out to her pleasure as her ass was opened up. Not paid any attention like this since she'd arrived at the Manor, Jennifer was tight like the others and groaned out in strain as Valerie's huge Bolivian hips slowly convulsed, forcing open a super-tight ass. Carly squealed out with pleasure as Jennifer struggled in front of her, not able to resist grabbing her by the back of the hair as she watched the dildo descend being played out on her face, Jennifer crying out at the depth inside her. Huge thighs pulled back, Jennifer gasping for air as they then convulsed again, forcing her walls, Jennifer groaning out to Carly's screams, excited by her struggle as another intendant at the far end of the room tried to block it out, the sound of her favorite being dealt with killing her.

It wasn't over when Valerie had literally reamed her out. Mercifully, she had gone slow and strong, but she had opened her, her huge Bolivian thighs showing little mercy, though she had tried to make it easy on her, Jennifer feeling that. Next, though, it was Carly, and there would be nothing easy about her. After getting off looking into her eyes as she'd struggled through each opening, it was her turn to do her work. Taking position between Jennifer's legs, she fondled her ass cheeks, making sure Jennifer knew she was enjoying every second before Jennifer felt another warm oiled blunt member descend into her crevice. The gym instructor of the group now had her silken thighs meeting the backs of hers as she drove her member all the way inside, taking Jennifer's breath away as she clenched her ass cheeks, her hands signaling her full intent, that Jennifer was to feel it.

They might have made up after Jennifer's refusal with her tongue, but she hadn't forgotten the insult, and whereas Jennifer had refused to enter her, she had no such shared intentions now. All the gorgeous gym-sculpted muscles in Carly's mouth-watering thighs flexed from behind, pushing deep into Jennifer, who groaned beneath her as the intendant slowly and repeatedly filled her, working her how she liked, getting off on making sure Nadia heard her on the other side of the room.

She could feel Carly's enjoyment – she wasn't punishing her with her entries, but she was more than fucking her, and clearly enjoying it, Jennifer feeling that as she tried not to tense up, not to resist, not to cry.

Strangely, it was Urst to her rescue eventually, leaving Valerie at the front and taking over for Carly, Carly's resistance felt on withdrawal, as if unhappy at Urst's insistence.

Carly had had her fun long and hard, but not viciously, Jennifer knowing who she had to thank for that, and she groaned in relief with Carly's final retreat, falling limp over the table, thankful it was over, and Carly's final teasing was hardly even heard as she moved off, stroking across her back as she went.

Urst's entry was careful, slow, her management of her rhythmic and gentle, unnatural for Urst's punishing thighs, leaving Jennifer wondering if Nadia was behind this, leaving Urst to care for her… and she was.

As it went on, though, and with Carly's incessant teasing from the front, eventually she cried, cried long and hard, along with everyone else, the intendants certain they would keep pushing till they did.

It was clear from the screams around the room that some had never been opened before, and others hadn't been for a long time, Jennifer included.

No stranger to anal, it had, though, felt like the first time – it was the pressure, the fear. The fear of their predicament, the entrapment, the sheer number of intendants and their enthusiasm for their work. Many of the slaves, over their fear that day, noticed the wild looks in their eyes, as if they were not themselves, the same looks they had had in the house clubs at night.

Through all this, the mood seemed to normalize throughout the day, maddeningly, as if they got used to it, a strange calm emerging as the women's cries seemed to lessen… and then it happened.

Amid all the struggling cries, one started moaning as if enjoying it, as if having pleasure in their midst as they suffered around her, and how dare she?! How dare she betray them like this; who was this bitch?… Julie!

That horny little bitch, betraying them like this, most thought, but soon something strange happened – another started moaning, and then another, as if Julie had opened their permission to enjoy. Soon the women seemed to be compelled to cum, truly tired of their fear, and the relief seemed to sweep the room like a wave, shrieks of pleasure replacing pain, the intendants laughing, having seen the phenomenon of group hysteria many times before.

For some, though, it wasn't like that; truly disturbed by what they were going through, their shrieks continued to fill the room, barely disguised by the few who were enjoying it, and the rest that were accepting… they were soon to be discharged.

Eventually, though, they were all taken to that height of sensitivity inside where pleasure meets pain, forcing the body to pull hard on itself to pull hard on restraints. Inside, with the sensitivity becoming unbearable, the women screamed out, trying to pull away from the restraints, no escape from the thrusting bringing tears, forcing them to scream through their learning… domination assured.

Even Julie collapsed eventually, the little slut, although the intendants managing her that day had their work cut out for them; clearly shattered from the effort, she'd made them put in that same effort, bringing her respect in the hallways in the coming weeks ahead.

There was no such respect in the hallways on the way to the infirmary, though. Finally unshackled from the tables, intendants drunk on power jeered and laughed as tears and cries filled the hallways, some being dragged and some carried, their bodies destroyed and their spirits crumbled.

Afterwards, that night, nurses escorted by intendants did their rounds, all slaves still cuffed to recovery beds to prevent them from wandering off, their conditions in need of monitoring. Tenderness was delivered with lubrication, nurses' fingers easily slipping in and out of hugely dilated assholes, helping to sooth where they could, the women allowed to groan and cry into the night. Among them, the house psychiatrist tried to bring intendants under control, their wanton power lust sickeningly apparent as she viewed their efforts that day, appalled by their butchery. Some intendants weren't able to hide their pleasure at the women's discomfort, through occasional smirks breaking out among them and to each other before sharp spanks were delivered to the asses of those wailing just too much.

Order would be maintained!

Now they would see who really wanted to be slaven and who would leave; it was closing time on amateur night, and only professionals would walk out of the recovery rooms… all accept one who would run that night.

She arrived amid the others, but didn't whoop or jeer; instead, she tentatively approached a shattered form. Coming close to her bedside amid the melay around her, her reach brought a reaction that struck down her heart, Jennifer pulling away instinctively, not even able to look at her as she lay hurting inside. Unseen above her, another inside hurt, too, tears welling up in her eyes at her care's condition beneath her, turning away and raising her hand, hiding her grief from the others, but eventually running from the infirmary before she lost total control. While intendants all over the house partied into the night, one cried alone, curled up and sobbing, heart broken inside like her care far below her.

Chapter 19

Hearts Of Pain

Ten days, ten days of pain, recovery, and breakdowns. Each day, there were fewer sobbing women as broken slaves were led away to the house psychiatrist who mercifully discharged them, much to the Mistress's irritation.

After so much time and effort had been put into them, and as she saw their broken natures and wrecked minds as a real signal of progress being made, she was left at odds with the house psychiatrist… she saw things differently.

A proponent of the lifestyle herself, the psychiatrist's beliefs in the training in-house kept those under its care safe, to a degree. For her and those in house without the brutality and sadism of the Mistress and intendants like her, true slaves were not broken pitiful creatures who lived in fear and worry. They did not live cowering in corners, treated like animals, but were respected, educated, trained individuals who had found themselves and chosen a life path that truly made them happy.

For them, they had the privilege to follow the way, and unlike others who spent a lifetime in pursuit of material wealth because they were kept in permanent want due to financial pressures, they already knew, due to their places in society, that these things only gave happiness until they were normal in life, that not taking very long.

Therein, an individual would find themselves back

at their beginnings again, wondering what could fill this emptiness, this longing for fulfilment, these jealous wishes as they watched those around them in each other's arms, smiles of contentment ripping at their hearts. This deterministic material want, when one could have anything, soon showed that this treasure was an empty box when held alone at night. Surrounded by trinkets, their glittering emptiness provided no love or solace, the years wasted in coveting this wealth, bringing poverty in feeling and emotional unhappiness. After such discovery, that the material chest held no treasure, hearts were left to the ravages of time, theirs having been spent and lost, never to return as they watched those with less, in each other's arms with a wealth they could not themselves buy.

Some would find their way to alcohol, and others depression; some would leave this life early while a few, a precious few, through accident and otherwise, would find the way. A state of living that did not restrict or turn away from those internal longings, a way of being that did not hide or feel ashamed at desires of the heart, but sought to culture and control, to teach and provide a real way to fulfilment. This path did not seek wealth – far from it – but did seek to provide treasure, true submission and slavenship allowing one to be that treasure coveted by those who truly owned them, loved and taken care of in the deepest of ways.

To this end, their Mistress, too, would also have faced a journey, a road to find herself, one of hardship and sacrifice toward material wealth, one that would have provided no happiness at its end, this learning radically changing her beliefs in life.

Unlike myths and fantasies purported by those who

would sell these mirages to immature and imprisoned minds, leaving them unable to break free of their own insidious training by societies, countries, and religions, the way offered the truth of the human spirit itself, and a path to the fulfilment it needed.

Through the mind… that was the lifestyle's guiding hand, not the body. The body offered emotion and stress, hardship and pleasure against all that could be found in this world, all its lies and false paths, only the mind able to guide one to true happiness when individuals were ready for this journey. The disappointment these false paths provided was not a waste, but a preparation, a forcing of the individual to look inside themselves, to face their internal desires, their curiosities, and their fears. As this trepidation inside mounted over years, one would eventually face a choice as the sands of time ran out, either accepting the deep inward calls for personal discovery and fulfilment, or denying, as so many do, and having all of the decay that this would bring.

And what did it bring? Jennifer thought. Lying in the infirmary, she thought of her endless days of slavery before… her nine to five empty existence.

She thought of her attempts to break free each weekend, pointless late nights of booming music and deceptive smiles, of leaping heart strings seizing the hope of finally finding that one, only for them to be dashed each midweek,

"I'll give you a call….."

"I'll see you….."

Empty…pointless voids…and heartaches…

Then the party… she hadn't even wanted to go, one of fates little twists delivering her that night, her friends meeting wealth and dragging her along to the slaughter and then abandoning her for it, time telling on them as they received what they deserved from this abattoir of money.

But that was in time… for her, that night, sitting on that back lawn with the huge house behind her and the laughter and chatter of a class she didn't understand, there was only loneliness and pity.

Sipping champagne and fondling the glass, she had wondered why everyone seemed so happy in life, and why she wasn't to have it, wondered what she'd done wrong to have this empty road and why her heart was never held, and her dreams were never shared… and then she'd heard the voice….

"Are you okay, my dear…?"

Lost in her thoughts, Jennifer was suddenly pulled back to shock and stunned stammer, to a soothing southern drawl that wrapped her up in its care in an embrace she'd come to love.

Eyes falling on others ten years older, Jennifer smiled as she remembered getting wet, as such was the elegance of the stunning form before her. With a grace in motion so staggering she'd been lost for words from the start, the warming smile over the black dress had sealed her fate instantly.

That night on the lawn, eyes glittered over glasses to each other as the sweet sound of care and understanding washed over Jennifer for the first time. It was a sound she'd want to follow, a sound that would finally bring her the place she'd so longed for… it was the sound of her Mistress… the sound of the lifestyle….

Her journey had started right there, she being frightened at first, but with curiosity overpowering her and love guiding her as she learned from her hand. Learned as she provided for her, surrounding her in all the fulfilment she'd ever dreamt of, her eyes each night resting on hers.

Endless gatherings, secret places and discoveries, the people and the parties and the pleasure and the love, all under the hand of her Mistress, through doors she hadn't even known existed which were hidden in plain sight like the doors inside of her.

Her Mistress, though, was strong, strong and demanding, not in violent lashings of temper or fury, but in deep passionate assertions, always wanting to explore new roads, new directions and ways.

This same aptitude that had forged her business empire, the same burning embers inside her that had pushed her forward in life, had pushed them forward in love… pushed too hard for Jennifer's liking, and now she found herself here.

"You love her," the house psychiatrist assured her as she sat patiently at Jennifer's bedside, reassuring her on her rounds. "If you didn't, you wouldn't be here, wouldn't be going through this learning for you both."

Her words echoed Miss Goodspank's assertions from their learning in the Academy.

"And don't you think this is hard on her, too? How many nights has she spent without you, worried sick about what you're going through, our progress reports probably just making it worse."

Jennifer squinted as she listened.

"She's probably lying there at night, worried what you'll think of her for enrolling you here," the psychiatrist continued. "Frightened that you'll never go back to her after this," she went on, making Jennifer think of her out there, and what she was doing.

Thinking of each other was all they could do, strict rules enforced by the Manor and the contract now signed, barring all contact with those inside and out, the owners provided only progress reports, no contact at all with those enrolled.

"Getting this far proves your love and she knows it," the psychiatrist assured her. "And besides," she whispered lowly, "You just came over the most difficult trial," she smiled encouragingly. "It's all great from here," she finished, looking down at Jennifer with fondness, placing a hand gently on her midriff before rising to the next bed along the ward.

A strange look, Jennifer thought, but she felt praised and complimented by it, as if she'd done well, as if she'd succeeded. It was a look she'd see a lot coming her way over the next passing weeks, a look coming from intendants, themselves feeling respect for those who'd made it, those they now considered true slaves… a look that, just for a second, she was sure she saw even coming from the Mistress.

But another look was firmly fixed on her now, unseen Hispanic eyes looking down from the camera above, her own emotional turmoil sent soaring as she watched the psychiatrist bring Jennifer's mind to her love for her Mistress. Watching in agony, she saw the love spread over her face, with her own anger, guilt, and tears following her to her bed that night.

Chapter 20

Respect

Day ten and she walked out, back to the Manor, to the servitude that had brought her here… what an apt choice of feeling.

Something was different, though, as the Manor was calmer, emptier, resembling a spa now. Intendants passing in the hallways didn't seem to ignore or sneer at the women anymore; it felt like, well… respect.

It was…. Having passed through the house's greatest trial, and still staying on, the women seemed to be thought all the higher of. Seen in the eyes of the intendants, they looked at them as one would a professional in their field… but they were still slaven… still to serve…

House duties were suspended as they waited for all who would continue on to leave the infirmary; their number was now twenty-six.

In the coming weeks, with fewer of them around, the intendants seemed to relish them more when they had them under their charge. Not enough for all to go around… on the one hand, this was nice, as they received looks of praise and attention when they were delivered into various intendants' care, but on the other hand, it left some bored and rather too enthusiastic at disciplining them when they got the chance.

Still, the new breath that seemed to pervade the Manor eventually settled down to a professional feel, the women themselves seeming to be affected by it, this shown through their demeanor as their newly found status washed over them. Passing each other in hallways, the women would catch smiles, small grins as they began to feel truly slaven, no longer beaten and ordered, but directed and kept as one would a prized racehorse or breeding mare.

This new treatment found its way out in their behavior as, pleased by their acceptance as professionals by intendants, they began to play up to this respect, to perform to the best of their abilities, trying hard to show just how good they'd become.

That, though, was to come in the following weeks; right now, with duties suspended due to some still waiting to leave the infirmary, and due to most being able to walk but not completely bend, they had the chance to show acceptance of their continuing journey as they were made to give thanks.

Give thanks… a euphemism for pampering the intendants, the Mistress describing this procedure during an assemblance of all who had made it in the ballroom one morning. They were now privileged, as she put it, to be on a new level. To be real slaves, almost at a level the Manor would allow to carry its name when they left – no longer simple trainees without discipline or form.

It had been a long journey and they had been carried there by the intendants' hard work, the Mistress assured them from the center of the circle, her eyes looking at them with angry pride, as if having trouble bestowing praise over her natural dominance.

This training had taken an enormous toll on the intendants, she explained, leaving them tired and worn out after their latest huge effort to push them through to the next level, it having demanding such sacrifice on their time and energy that great thanks was now to be given to them to show respect for their efforts.

No mention of the women's efforts to get through that now infamous trial, or their recoveries thereafter, was given, and, of course, neither should it have been, as they were slaven, here to accept direction. What was undeniable, though, was the respect this had brought them through, their acceptance of that direction, there for all to see in the eyes of those who looked at them, in the intendants' care over the coming weeks when they had their chance to learn them.

And so, to thanks… essentially, what it meant was learning to be a masseuse and to pamper and serve all intendants' needs in the most intimate of fashions.

The justification for this was twofold :

1. A good slave would be expected to serve and cater in this fashion with trained excellence if a Mistress was to be satisfied with her.

2. They couldn't bend.

Still struggling with internal bruising, the women could not completely bend, thus preventing normal duties in training, so it made sense to allow them an easier time while they recovered… giving thanks.

Rooms were converted to sauna-style luxury white

cotton sheets on mattresses, and laid on desks, tables, and floors, soft warm towels, oils, and candles… all over the Manor, the calm appreciated by the recovering women. Even the Academy had two full spa tables brought in and arranged so that the intendants, two at a time, could be disrobed and attended to, for hours if necessary. Worked on by two slaves at a time, directed by two further intendants who installed the virtues of good muscle relaxant techniques and the art of patient pleasure-giving in the women… as they tried not to bend.

Jennifer, too, winced more than once as she spent hours in the Academy tending, and toning, hurting inside as she reached over again and again, the intendants teaching and occasionally warning her to be more astute, her attention waning over the afternoons with her pain. She even dreamed about it, those nights, like many others in the dorms, their heads filled with it, this being their only function as they recovered.

Nearly a week went by and the one person Jennifer had wanted, then feared would come, and then wanted again, never arrived… until day six.

Jennifer was stunned, losing her poise as she waited beside the nearest of two spa tables, put face to face with Nadia as she arrived in the same staggering beauty as the first time Jennifer had seen her on the Manor's stairs. Stopping as she came through the door with the other intendant, Jennifer forgot herself, staring too long….

"Slave!"

The scream was shattering, Jennifer's head going down immediately under the searing rebuke from one of the two intendant guards present. No longer needed to direct their efforts after days of learning how to please with their hands, the guard simply made sure of tight etiquette now, Jennifer failing under their watch… it was an insult.

Her failure was a reflection of their work… their reputation in house at stake, leaving them a choice now as they glared at Jennifer, deciding what to do.

To punish her meant Jennifer screaming, and other intendants would hear that, and after days of their direction, Jennifer's obvious loud failure and theirs would be announced to the house. Jennifer stayed perfectly still under their glare, her face lamenting her mistake as she looked at the floor submissively, showing she was waiting for their direction… and it worked.

Her submission strategies from the Academy were well-learned, the guard satisfied with her offering, but now watching her like hawks.

Jennifer was actually embarrassed in front of Nadia, as she'd never been rebuked in front of her before and truly didn't want to lift her head now for fear of catching her eye as she and the other intendant moved behind the tables.

Listening, Jennifer heard the unbuckling of uniforms, disrobing… slaves were not allowed to handle the in-house attire, as slaves were not allowed clothes at all… and then she appeared.

To her right, Nadia lay down, Jennifer forcing herself to turn to her needs as she'd learned under the intendants, their watch heightened over her now. Jennifer was momentarily stunned, her mouth wet and filling with saliva at Nadia's gorgeous form below her, not expecting it as she heard the guard stir, forcing her from her trance, her hands quickly lifting forward before slowing her reach… 'poise' she heard herself say in her mind as her hands came down on Latin beauty.

She stroked up silken perfection, feeling Nadia stir as she went, not knowing what it meant but knowing her own feelings as, suddenly, she was wet elsewhere, embarrassed as she realized the extent of it and glad she was hidden behind the table, and Nadia, below Jennifer's waist out of sight of the table opposite and the guards at the back of the room.

Pushing her fingers into Nadia's warm muscles, she heard her sigh slightly, more than once as she worked, and then again as she stroked down, following the contours of her spine, her exhale lifting to almost moaning… if she was trying to hide her feelings, she wasn't doing a very good job.

She didn't want to; Jennifer may have recovered, but all Nadia had thought about as she did so was how she couldn't look at her that night in the infirmary, her guilt at not being able to protect her more had consumed her, eating at her day after day as she'd waited to see her. Now, lying beneath her, she gently tried to let her know how she felt, to see if she felt the same.

Kneading her back, unsure of what Nadia felt or why she hadn't come to see her sooner, she heard her again, and then again…

It dawned on her as she worked… realizing Nadia was trying to talk to her as the guard looked on, and she tried to talk back to see if she was right. Pushing her fingers deeper, she almost tried to speak with them, offering Nadia as much pleasure as she could to see if she responded… and she did, Jennifer sure of it as she moved her hands, sweeping them slowly together and dragging them on Nadia's skin, almost smiling as she groaned out for her….

Catching the guards' expressions out of the corner of her eye, Jennifer kept her smile as Nadia groaned willfully, the guards like the other intendants aware of their union and disapproving of such an obvious show of emotion in public for a slave… but they could do nothing about it.

Instead, they focused their irritation on Jennifer, waiting for their chance to pounce, waiting for one wrong move to let them deal with this outrage.

But Jennifer was careful, her smile kept and her head lowered, her hands doing her talking. Nadia, though, was under no such restrictions, and utterly happy beneath Jennifer, feeling her touch showing her she didn't hate her after all, a wave of relief passing through her as she felt her attentions and determined to show her she still felt the same.

Again, the moaning was light but audible in the quiet room as Jennifer neared her waistline, her staggering Latin tan all Jennifer could focus on as her obvious interest moistened ever more, another light groan let out as her hands swept up over Nadia's gorgeous ass….

Cupping her cheeks, it was Jennifer who almost moaned, her lower regions flooding as she felt Nadia's warm cheeks push between her fingers, their solid toned strength and silky softness causing Jennifer to swallow as she felt her body beg for her….

She tended to Nadia more than ever with the touch of a lover now, her hands guided by want as she squeezed her cheeks longingly, Nadia's breathing announcing her pleasure as Jennifer ran her hands. Ran them together, one on the outside of Nadia's left cheek and one on the inside, dragging down over her skin toward her thighs, letting her fingers drop into her crevice as she went, an unmistakable appreciation audibly announced to the room. Passing her ass, Jennifer took the top of her left thigh between her hands and squeezed, dragging her hands together over the skin, the powerfully toned muscle slipping slowly through her hands and then releasing as she was reaching deep again. Deep on the outside, almost finding the thighs' front, and deep on the inside, her hands feeling the obvious warmth above as, just for a second, the top of her right hand crested Nadia's soaking femininity on the way in, and again on the way out, Nadia audibly appreciating the touch.

Finally, Jennifer's smile broke as she did so, the pressure of a lover's want unable to be masked anymore… exactly what they'd been waiting for!

With the guard seizing their chance, Jennifer let out a scream as rough hands seized her by the hair, forcing her to the wall, black uniforms smashing her with their elbows and rage, beginning to beat her, unable to discipline, they were so angry, instead beating her savagely as they….

Suddenly, another scream shattered the room, the first intendant's head clattering off the wall as an elbow smashed into the back of her head, hands seizing her by the hair and hurling her, screaming, to the floor. The second intendant had time to look as Nadia's left hand found her face, her right forearm coming crashing under her chin, choking her off Jennifer, her screaming cut as she was rammed against the wall, Nadia enraged as she seized her.

Jennifer could only look on as she watched an intendant being strangled, Nadia unable to stop as she forced her back into the wall, the sounds of struggle choking out, her eyes raging down on….

Grabbing her from behind, the other intendant had risen, trying to pull Nadia off, but instantly receiving her left elbow backwards into her face as she whirled around, rage seeing both her hands scything for her face, her right knee following to her stomach, Nadia airborne as she took them both crashing to the ground, her full weight on landing ending the intendant's efforts as she lost control, beating her from above!

Nadia's screaming shattered the room as she lost it, both intendants finished; only the arrival of two more, unseen by her, saving them as they entered, hauling her off, Nadia's rage streaming out in Hispanic anger as she kicked and raged at her entrapment between them.

Two more, still, arrived, tending to their beaten sisters and hauling them up as Nadia, still screaming, was wrestled to the back of the room, her final ordering in half-broken English, raging at her two subduing sisters, convincing them to let her go as they pulled back in front of her, Nadia's screaming seeing them off more than her shoving.

A volley of threats between bruised-faced intendants and an enraged lover shattered the room as the fresh intendants pulled a confused and frightened slave away from the other spa table, giving no thought to touching the other who was still up against the wall, no one daring to go near her, Nadia's final deafening screaming seeing all of them out, the door closing behind them.

Screams of "Who do you think you are!" and "The Mistress will hear of this!" were now gone, leaving silence, Nadia's shaking rage still filling the room. The threats were useless, and all the house staff knew it. They had been more angry at the lack of power, some feeling seething jealousy at Nadia's unofficial position in-house. For some, her advantage caused them to burn with jealousy, unable to handle her obvious pull over them. It hadn't been the first time over the years that this had boiled to the surface, but the result would be the same… nothing.

It was covered up – they all knew it was pointless to address the Mistress about her own, as she'd never chastise her, and more than likely would fall on them for their efforts. Instead, Nadia moved among the groups in-house that saw things her way, the others raging in jealousy, but no one would see the Mistress about her… no one needed that kind of trouble.

Before that, though, another battle played out, a battle of two hearts – one fearing and one raging, both shaking in the quiet room, alone now. Nadia didn't know what to do, and she stood shaking, realizing she couldn't stop herself, that her rage had been instinctual, and that…

She'd fallen in love with her….

It was Jennifer who broke the silence. "What's going to happen now…..?" she worried, Nadia's angry glare turning to her at the question. "The Mistress… what will she do?" she worried out loud.

Through a huge effort, Nadia calmed her,

convincing her not to worry, that nothing would change.

“How did you meet?” asked Jennifer, Nadia raising an eyebrow at the sudden question.

“At a party,” she answered finally, her training fighting her in the intention of not giving information to a slave.

“She taught you everything?” Jennifer asked quietly.

“.....she taught me professionalism,” Nadia answered after a long pause, not sure she liked talking about this or how much longer she would.

“Is she still teaching you now?” Jennifer asked.

Nadia suddenly sealed up inside, her eyes narrowing as she fixed all her instincts on an impertinent slave, her body about to lash out and punish severely for such impertinence, but she paused, Jennifer’s hurt look as she cowered away from the aggression making her realize she might be wrong. After a short time, she pulled back, realizing she was overreacting, Jennifer’s real fear at her sudden rising showing her that she hadn’t meant it, Nadia looking down, sorry she’d made her feel that way.

“You’re always learning from them,” she said finally, then suddenly looking up. “On the day you’re not, you’re not their slave anymore; you’re their equal… and that’s not slaven.”

The words were honest, true, running deep into Jennifer’s mind, but she didn’t get a chance to think on them long; her vulnerable feminine gentleness had aroused her intendant’s interest, her body now surging with testosterone after winning the fight… soon, she had other things to think about….

Chapter 21

Denial

Jennifer's body, the next day, felt like she had suffered a beating… a beating she had loved. One of two secret women drawing all attention during uncuffing, their feelings obvious for each other as those watching wished they had the same.

As Miss Goodspank brought the day's lesson forth in the Academy, Jennifer was lost in her own mind, her attention drifting to Latin yearning, Nadia's touch all she could think about, the footsteps coming up behind her missed as a hand fell on her shoulder…

"Jennifer," Miss Goodspank's soft authoritative tone brought her back. "What have I just been saying?"

Silence… a long pause, and Jennifer had no answer…

"Well," Miss Goodspank announced haughtily, lifting her hand away, "We have our first volunteer, and I think her attention is about to improve." She motioned an embarrassed Jennifer to the desk at the front of the class.

It was embarrassing, Jennifer having never been over the desk before, but bent over and secured by her wrists at one end, her ankles shackled to the wooden legs nearest the door, she kept her head down, avoiding the class watching on.

She heard the desk drawer being opened and the sound of the wooden ruler being lifted out, and then a teaching hand on the back of her head and a soft voice as she was turned to face the smiling class.

“Now Jennifer,” the soft voice made fun, “We can’t very well teach the class if they can’t look into your eyes as we go, can we?” Jennifer felt the ruler placed threateningly, length-ways on her back to encourage an answer… “Well…?”

“As you wish, Miss,” Jennifer answered, a small nervous smile appearing as she watched her group staring at her, some almost laughing at her predicament.

It was well meant, as the group’s taunting smiles were not disparaging, many themselves having already been over the desk and more in class; instead, the mood was good-natured, though Jennifer did feel the embarrassment as well as the support.

The Manor, from the outset, had taught that all women are bisexual, and those who say otherwise are in denial, unable to deal with their deep-seated natural instincts to be close to one another, to be close to their sisters.

The program had reached the stage where it was time to install that belief in all its patients, most not needing this lesson, but some still nervous and needing a final understanding built in that it was natural, that it was normal and it was good.

“It Is Natural!

It is Normal!

It Is Good!”

“Once again!” Ordered Miss Goodspank, the class

repeating aloud and smirking as they did, repeating along with the teacher, her own interest in the subject obvious and well-known.

"It Is Natural!

It is Normal!

It Is Good!"

"Now, we in the Academy do not tell lies," she repeated her mantra to her mischievously smiling audience, sitting cuffed by their left ankles to their desks and giving their full attention today, much to Jennifer's embarrassment as she fought not to smile back. "We at the Academy provide evidence so that our students are confident in their lessons and can leave class knowing their teaching is correct," she continued, placing a hand on Jennifer's bared ass, making her close her eyes momentarily as she reddened, the class laughing out at the pressure. Miss Goodspank, too, smiled with them, the style of teaching in the Academy being quite relaxed and a welcome break from the more punishing harshness of the intendants.

"Today, Jennifer has volunteered to prove this," Miss Goodspank announced, coming close to laughing with the rest of the class this time as she rose, Jennifer also laughing slightly with the pressure, her eyes momentarily closing again as her sisters laughed at her predicament.

Walking across the room, Miss Goodspank informed the class that the evidence of sisterly love would be provided to each of them and shown to all as they watched her go to the back of the two rows of five desks, to the one closest to the window… to her favorite.

Linda’s reddening at her approach now matched Jennifer’s as all eyes watched fleeting looks between teacher and student as her ankle cuff was unlocked, another reason Jennifer’s wayward mind on Nadia was so tolerated in class being that the was teacher well-known to share similar feelings for her sister.

A guiding hand now brought Linda to the front of the class, behind Jennifer, the wooden ruler still lying threateningly on her back, the class bursting with mischievous grins now as Jennifer closed her eyes in embarrassment, biting her lip with the pressure.

“Jennifer,” Miss Goodspank’s authoritative but warm tone rising in response to her eyelids closing, she brought them open immediately. “Do keep your eyes on your classmates as they must learn from your example. You don’t want me to lift that ruler, do you?”

“Ni… Understood, Miss,” Jennifer took her offer, but almost broke the Manor’s rules in the process with the pressure, no patient being allowed to utter the word “no” at any time. In the Manor, head shaking or other close forms meant the same and were insisted upon as replies, instead of using the word “no”… a rule severely punished if broken, even by Miss Goodspank.

“Careful!” she announced loudly, quite appreciating the class mood and not wishing to change it sharply by having to administer severe punishment. “Keep your mind on the rules,” she guided, her voice dropping to a caring tone as she led Jennifer.

“Yes, Miss,” Jennifer acknowledged, obviously

thankful Miss Goodspank had allowed her near miss to pass, where other intendants would not have done the same.

"Now," Miss Goodspank announced, the class brought to a more attentive state with her leadership as she placed a soft hand on Linda's shoulder, pressing gently, her ever-willing favorite dropping to her knees behind Jennifer's femininity.

It being obvious what was about to happen, all students inadvertently strained forward on their desks, biting their lips with Jennifer as Linda took her thighs in her hands and leaned forward into her warmth. Obeying her teacher's direction, Linda was engulfed in Jennifer's scent, her tongue finding her sister and beginning a long day's example, Jennifer soon moaning audibly to the class, the other women watching her embarrassed eyes turn to pleasure as they were given the day's lesson by her.

Smiling behind her, the class fell silent, shifting uncomfortably as they, too, became aroused, still cuffed to their desks as Jennifer, with Linda's help, proved almost immediately the last of the three announcements right in front of them.

"It Is Good!"

Moaning louder as Linda sucked tender points, she groaned wantonly with Linda's tongue sliding deep inside her…

"Jennifer," Miss Goodspank stroked her fingers down the ruler lying on her back, her next moaning tighter and controlled, responding to her threat. "Better," she announced, lifting her fingers.

With the class looking on, Miss Goodspank smiled with them as they listened to the obvious pleasure in front of them, the embarrassing feelings lifting as they got used to the display, their smiles changing from mischief to want as they were ordered to watch Jennifer's eyes.

The next moan to receive Miss Goodspank's disapproval was Linda's! Forgetting herself, she released her audible hunger as Jennifer's appreciation flowed over her tongue, her scent enrapturing her as she pulled on her thighs with her hands reaching deeper inside.

"Don't enjoy her too much, dear," Miss Goodspank looked down coyly at her favorite, her hand gently coming to her shoulder, Linda looking up sheepishly, still buried in Jennifer's femininity with the class bursting with laughter at the jealous display.

The tension had lifted, the class now enjoying themselves as they watched Miss Goodspank quite forget herself, taking her hand from Linda's shoulder and running it gently up her back in a manner of supportiveness now that Linda had accepted her disapproval at her longings.

For a minute or so longer, they listened to Jennifer moaning, to her tight controlled pleasure before, with one more placement of her hand on Linda's shoulder, Miss Goodspank left her favorite pleasuring on as she moved to release another from her desk.

Andrea…

Her smile beamed before the class, her face reddening as she was uncuffed. Risen by Miss Goodspank's hand, her eyes locked to Jennifer's, the class laughing as she almost burst with emotion. Taken before them and led toward Jennifer, she laughed out aloud, unable to contain herself any longer and not entirely unhappy with what she was about to be made to do.

Jennifer, for the first time, made a sudden connection to the obvious louder laughter in the room, and to all the mornings Andrea had tried to engage her in conversation at breakfast….

"Well," Miss Goodspank announced, the laughter brought into check as she, too, suddenly realized Andrea's hidden attraction, now more than obvious to the room. "Sometimes you get what you want in life," she announced, looking at Andrea, the whole class bursting with laughter.

"SSsshhhh Shh Sh Sh Sh Shhh Sh…" soft Canadian assertiveness quieted the class. "We can't hear Jennifer." More laughter quickly subdued by the teacher's hand as she raised Linda from her work, bringing quiet sniggering as she glared at her, in half feigned jealousy at what she'd been doing.

A sheepish look from Linda brought more mirth before suddenly Miss Goodspank ordered her to spread her legs, a look of real fear that she'd done something to offend her emerging before she took Andrea's hand and placed it gently between her femininity, smiling at her warmly, Linda smiling back.

"So, Andrea," she addressed a now stunned charge, first with her want of Jennifer announced and now having her hand on the teacher's favorite, leaving her not knowing quite where to look as all eyes were on her. "What do you feel between Linda's thighs?"

Andrea, stunned, didn't know what to say.

"Andrea?" Miss Goodspank pushed, her lawyer training coming forward.

"Yes, Miss," was all Andrea could say.

"Is Linda wet?" she helped her on.

"Yes, Miss," Andrea replied.

"Is Linda very wet?" Miss Goodspank enquired.

"Yes, Miss," replied Andrea, the tension building in the room.

"Is she?" Miss Goodspank asked rhetorically, a look of jealous irritation toward Linda only half-feigned as the class burst out laughing, Linda's sheepish guilt setting them off again and relieving the tension.

"Well, if Linda is VERY wet," Miss Goodspank gave another half-feigned look of irritation at her favorite, "That must mean it was good, don't you agree?"

"…Yes, Miss," Andrea stammeringly answered as Linda's femininity sat on her fingers, soaking them with her arousal while her want lay tied down and bared for her over the desk beside them, her nerves all over the place as their teacher saw the look.

"Well," Miss Goodspank announced haughtily, slightly irritated that she wasn't at Andrea's full focus. "You don't sound completely sure, and that won't do to convince the class… I suppose, then, we'll need another example… won't we?"

"Yes, Miss," Andrea answered, the class beginning to grin mischievously as Andrea now looked sheepish, Linda beginning to laugh as Miss Goodspank pointed to the spot she had been kneeling in before, and the class burst out laughing at Andrea's embarrassed desire, written all over her face.

"Now, now, that's no way to support your class member," she announced, feigning disapproval at her class mates. "A round of applause for your sister; this is difficult for her, opening her present!"

The class collapsed with laughter, clapping ringing out, intendants in neighboring rooms confused at the mirth and disapprovingly enquiring to the control room before being assured everything was in order.

Back in the Academy, Andrea's eyes lit up with desire, her heart pounding as Miss Goodspank allowed the cheering class to encourage their sister, burying her face in between Jennifer's cheeks, her tongue sinking instinctively inside her.

With a raise of her hand, the class was brought to silence following Miss Goodspank's direction as she played along, cocking her head to Jennifer as she desperately tried to hold back her moans, but soon lost control due to Andrea's unmistakable enthusiasm!

With the class laughing out, even the well-controlled Miss Goodspank's etiquette was shaken as she dropped her head, closing her eyes and trying not to lose it with her class in response to the obvious strain between the two actors, it all now playing out in front of them.

"I'm not quite sure what this example proves," she announced, raising her eyebrows at Andrea's obvious enthusiasm, pulling on Jennifer's thighs and trying to bury herself further inside, undoubtedly reaching places Linda hadn't!

With the class laughing, Miss Goodspank reached for Linda, both catching Andrea's beautiful emerald green anal jewelry shining between her cheeks as she bent forward on her knees, making the scene all the more mouth-watering.

"Nice," Miss Goodspank announced before casting her eye down at Linda's waist. "I think her owner has a great idea there." The class laughed on as Linda's look suddenly dropped slightly, Miss Goodspank more than serious.

Two weeks later, Linda would have a ruby red one of her own, insisted upon and declared as a form of punishment for misattention in class, but in reality an announcement to the house that she was taken, and to be treated with care.

Soon, groaning grew from Jennifer as she felt some of the most incredible attention she'd ever received on her femininity, guilt with her love for Nadia forcibly overridden by Andrea's attention as the class watched her brought to a shattering orgasm! Screaming out uncontrollably, Andrea heaved herself into her, pulling on her thighs and extending her tongue fully before sucking and forcing a screaming that shocked the class, Jennifer shaking in over-stimulation as Andrea wouldn't stop, ignoring her sensitivity and hungrily reaching inside her, her own desire unfulfilled and demanding more of her, her secret attraction now announced….

"I don't know if we need to see if that was good," Miss Goodspank announced, having brought Monique from her desk, the class bursting with laughter as she stood beside Andrea, now herself brought up from her knees and looking embarrassed, her legs made ajar for the class and her glistening desire for Jennifer obvious.

And so it went on, all women made to go through

the lesson, and all at its end having enjoyed and been encouraged to realize that, most definitely,

It Is Good!

It Is Natural!

It is Normal!

These lessons were harder to believe, and some could not accept them, and so, what Miss Goodspank had begun… the intendants would finish!

It was obvious to all what was being done to them. For some, this part of the Manor's training was more than appreciated, it already being their natural instincts, while for others, the encouragement pressed on them in-house over the coming days was harder to bare. It was, though, to be had, intendants determined, and over the next week, the women who were not of a natural persuasion for this learning would be made to feel the same, the Manor's name carried by them on leaving making it absolutely necessary. There would never be a time when this great house would be brought into disrepute by their hesitancy or refusal at any event, party, or otherwise, and instead their absolute enthusiasm for their own kind would be witnessed by any involved or watching them, the Manor's reputation assured….

The intendants would make certain of it!

Over the next week, the women were submerged in sisterly love. Forced to view some of the tenderest kinky liaisons on video in the Academy, they were then given to the intendants for afternoons of fantasy becoming reality, and slowly but surely, all resistance to their teaching crumbled as, more and more, they became ever more receptive to the touch of their sisters…

Confusion then began to develop near the end of the week as the women began to be heightened, and then punished if they neared orgasm. Confused, they looked to their intendants for answers, simply to receive harsh rebukes, but were still forcibly excited.

Over the last two days, the women were turned on, disciplined, and punished in more and more sexually exciting ways, but curiously, never allowed to orgasm – any who inadvertently did receiving kinky, but not painful, lashings over the intendants' knees with straps. Not severe at all, instead they were brought back to a state of arousal in front of any and all who would pass in the hallways, and then again not allowed to orgasm.

The women began to groan under this seemingly new form of intendant sadism, the intendants openly laughing at their frustration as they were "Edged".

Brought closer and closer to final release, they were then stopped from finishing.

Watching like hawks, the now massive over-staffing of the intendant guard, due to their smaller number, made this easily possible, the women intentionally made more aware of it, their every move being monitored, their even being escorted to the bathroom, no doors allowed to be closed on their privacy.

Obviously, the intendants were enjoying themselves and taking great pride in keeping them completely frustrated, but a few dared to finish themselves off in dark places, thinking they would get away with it… they wouldn't.

The canings over the box during assemblance for this outrage were savage, the Mistress enraged at their waywardness and insisting on increased severity, the screams frightening as she left them in no doubt not to try it again.

By the end of day two, the whole house was unbelievably horny, several slaves taken away that night and punished for trying to masturbate in desperation in their dorms, the smell of their sisters around them being too much. Their desperation earned them punishment, but no relief, and instead real fear was brought back, and secured in their dorms, they realized what they would face in assemblance the next morning.

They would not be disappointed; the rage of the Mistress was fearful, this day becoming the final time any would try it… but it was too late.

An obvious staged and controlled part of the Manor's training program, what was not staged was the Mistress's anger, all fearing what was going to happen next as she announced that the failure of individuals was the failure of them all, and hence,

"All would be punished!"

They didn't have to wait long for the latest sadistic

lesson from the house… chastity.

Chapter 22

The Torture

The several canings that morning were again savage. Real fear as the women watched, real tears as the victims were unshackled, their openly crying slumped forms carried back to the circle under the Mistress's glare.... She had no mercy.

Why should she?

She was responsible for the Manor's reputation. By this time, the women were not raw recruits but experienced slaves, and knew full well the consequences of their actions. The women were not shocked or surprised when it was announced in assemblance that there could be no guilt felt for their pain, as they were ultimately responsible, in the Mistress's own words...

They asked for it...

With the crying subsiding, the women were held in the great circle that morning for a longer time. Berated harshly by a truly disappointed Mistress who claimed she had not seen this many fall to waywardness at this stage before. She attributed it to the excellent training of her staff, who had indeed worked very hard to increase the women's desires. Her smile toward them in appreciation for their hard efforts quickly faded as she glared back to their slaves, held frightened among them after watching the morning's punishment, tears still running down the faces around them.

Watching on, the Mistress moved out slowly from the circle's center, her own unique house uniform still being sex-laden leather black, but styled over with gothic power, her corset more threatening as she brought it toward them. Ending at the waist like the intendants', her black panties beneath held her femininity strong. There were no garter pouches aside her belt, her close intendant guard forced to carry all implements she would need for her will. Thighs suspended like her intendants' in silk, their powerful toned strength seemed angry at the confinement, the black on black embossed symbology over her corset now understood by her captives as not just meant to be decorative, but to be a statement of truth. "Well," the Mistress sighed exhaustively, walking around the center of the circle and casting her eye over her fearful captives, themselves no longer feeling like proud slaves, but fearful first arrivals – such was the savagery of the assemblance's discipline. "After they've got you this far, this is how you think of repaying them?" she asked rhetorically, her huge brunette mane perfectly set following her stare as she moved slowly among them, her powerfully built waistline atop her gym-sculpted physique making her seem all the more threatening. "I am not going to allow you to waste their efforts," her voice raised from a hiss to a definite growl as her anger built over their misled behavior.

Turning slowly back to the center of the circle where the two torturesses still stood by the box, she extended her hand to the one on the right, now no longer responsible for strapping down as the other remained on guard to the left, cane still in hand, its black length glistening with sweat and fluids from the asses that had had to be punished.

From behind the box, the right intendant held out a black form, straps dangling from it, the Mistress taking it before turning back with a look of assuredness as she held out this unfamiliar implement before them.

Walking toward them, her look moved from anger to certainty as she explained what she would now have done – in light of their recent failure.

“Since you have shown that you cannot control yourselves,” the Mistress trailed off, anger fighting into her look… “Even at this late stage,” she growled, holding back real rage. “You will be given one more chance to show that you can walk the line… the line that you will be set on for the rest of your lives,” she assured them, casting her face along their standings, determination in her eyes. “This house is not without understanding,” she suddenly changed her tone, a softness unexpected and so stark a difference to her growl that the circle fixed on her words. “With such…” she trailed off again, looking admirably at her intendants’ corseted finery. “Stimulation… it is understood that certain slip-ups may happen from time to time. It may even be argued that it is inevitable that some will become wayward when surrounded by such… charm,” she eyed her intendants’ uniforms with a mix of appreciation and hunger. “What, then, to be done with this at this stage?” she asked, staring at Julie, the slave’s tears dried up while her cheeks still stung from the caned lines over her ass behind her. “What to be done with such obvious appreciation of this house’s complement?” She stared into Julie’s eyes, almost nose to nose with her, Julie having to fight hard not to pull back under this harsh test of etiquette, knowing full well that, if she did, the insult to the Mistress would mean any pain she now felt over her ass would be nothing compared to what she'd then be given….

The Mistress smiled at Julie's struggle, able to hear her strained breathing and understanding the effect she was having, seemingly pleased as the charge struggled before her, or as she saw it… struggled for her.

With her movement off the circle, the crowd bore witness to her seeming impressed reaction to Julie's efforts; her mood seemed to calm, as if Julie's compliment to her in etiquette did much to sooth the mornings ire.

"What to be done with you all…" she dropped her head, gently shaking it as her waist curved, her decision out in front of them. "I have watched over the months and been impressed," she unexpectedly complimented them. "And… horrified," she put them back down to the place they were used to being held at by her. "Impressed by your efforts… impressed by your learning… but not at your memory without our constant reminding." She paraded still, holding the unrecognized implement among them. "Like this morning," she broke into a smile of pure enjoyment over the thoughts of their screaming over the box, the women now throbbing around her. "You don't' seem to be able to fully hold your now more than learned behavior," she looked accusingly over them all. She sighed, raising her mane at them. "I have provided you with Academies… With treatment… With the best teachers that exist." She cast a warm look at her intendants around her. "And yet, still I must bring my hand to you in these mornings…"

she lamented, dropping her head.

They watched her turn back, crossing again in front of the box and back the other way, their eyes picking up the two torturesses still behind her, their minds suddenly fearful of where this was going as they had not dismounted, and the box's leather strapping was still open and seemingly waiting for them.

"What are we to do?" She stopped, the box directly behind her, maximizing their fear as they watched her make her decision. "I am someone who likes to tackle a problem head on," she moved her powerful hips away, terror sweeping the circle as she reached out, stroking the back of the box, its leather buckling and open straps running under the Mistress's hand as she caressed it lovingly. "I am someone who believes in discipline!!!" She suddenly roared, confirming their worst fears as she turned her head accusingly at them, her look determined as she glared along their shivering bodies.

"Bring her!!!" She shouted, her finger landing on Julie, the intendants behind her immediately forcing her forward into the circle and toward the waiting box!

Brought nose to nose with the Mistress, Julie's look of anguish was written all over her face, her eyes screaming with the unfairness but her mouth remaining quiet. The Mistress stared into her eyes for a moment, seeming to ignore their cry of unfairness, as if searching for challenge, searching for refusal of her decision… but none came.

The Mistress relaxed her head back, a small smile even appearing, Julie visibly relieved but still terrified of the box beside her.

"My instinct," the Mistress assured them, "is to meet waywardness…with fire." She stroked the box lovingly again, next to Julie, the pressure obviously rising in her face as the Mistress watched her fear grow. “But those who lead know that sometimes clemency for good behavior can be more effective.” She looked around her audience, all caught up with Julie’s fear and not knowing what was to become of her or who was to be next. “Sometimes,” the Mistress addressed them more loudly, assuring all could hear her. “A second chance… a chance given in respect, in good will, can achieve great results from those who would follow.”

A visible wave of relief passed through the group as the Mistress seemed to offer this olive branch in front of them, less so for Julie, just inches from the box and still confused and frightened.

A sudden look of care and emotion that always stunned the women whenever the Mistress displayed it…. “A chance to say sorry,” she looked into Julie’s eyes sympathetically. “A chance to show us you are listening, a way for us to build forward together,” she came close, sliding a hand around Julie’s waist, pulling her gently against her corset, looking longingly into her eyes. With the tone of a lover’s caring, Julie thought, like the others, that she was about to kiss her, and offered no resistance, a response the Mistress was testing for and pleased to have found within her. The Mistress smiled at Julie’s choice as if confirming she was safe, the room on a knife edge with Julie’s plight, all feeling the lifting tension that they might be safe.

“This, then, is how we will proceed.” She raised her free left hand, still holding Julie against her, looking caringly into her eyes, motioning for her to follow her onto the triangular implement now beside her. Obvious to Julie now what it was, as standing so close, she looked carefully back into the Mistress's eyes, the Mistress's ever so subtle lift of her eyebrows asking… and Julie gently nodding her head in acceptance of the Mistress's offer.

Chastity

Hardly surprising that the Mistress had targeted Julie with the offering, knowing full well her earned reputation as house slut, the slave beyond any embarrassment of it now, encouraged to be proud of her hunger in the Academy as long as her discipline matched it. There was, though, the suspicion developing that the Mistress had taken a keen interest in Julie of late… not something Julie or anyone else would have wanted, as it usually meant nights of masked desensitization at her pleasure…. strangely, though, that hadn't happened for a while.

Regardless, they were all grateful for the reprieve, all keen to avoid the box but all very aware that this was their last chance….

So, then, to that chance and to the implement all now recognized as, for the first time in countless months, an item which was in effect clothing was administered to them.

Their having been devoid of clothing for so long, the intendants laughed at the looks of confusion as the women felt its sumptuous leather curve around their forms, their memories of looking well flooding back as they bore witness to each other and how good they looked.

The house implement in question was the Manor's own uniquely manufactured chastity belt. Looking like another part of the intendant uniform, it was gorgeous. Black leather trim sumptuously took the inside lines of their thighs, curving up over their ass cheeks and encompassing them completely, much like the intendants panties, the women smiling with the intendants as two of them at a time sealed them in, laughing permitted as the intendants watched the appreciation at how good they felt.

What wasn't realized was that they were also laughing because, soon, the women certainly wouldn't be laughing, the intendants' fun unseen amongst them as they knew the torture in front of them. With sumptuous leather edging fitted around them, the women laughed out before etiquette held them to. It couldn't hold their smiles, though, as one intendant in front and one behind tightened their belt buckles, smiling back at their enjoyment of cool leather resting against their skin, but not touching their femininity within. Smiled more as, still holding them between them, they buckled their belts closed at one side, their femininity now prisoner away from them, unrealized as beautiful little golden padlocks were produced from garters, sealing them in, shutting at the right side, and curiously, once more at the front. With the inaudible tiny snapping complete, the tiny golden jailers were allowed to drop against the women's hips, that felt, but the one at the front not so, their smiling encouraged as they viewed their little golden jewelry with instinctual enjoyment, only some few slaves sensing the malevolence of the intendants' fake grace.

Shining bright against their black confinement, the tiny padlocks glinted on the women's hips and fronts, causing them to smile as they looked upon them, unknowing of how they'd hate them hours later. The design felt immediately strange, outside on the front a bulbous hard plastic black triangle covered over with leather moving gently down from their waist, lifting imperceptively out, encompassing their whole lower waist and obvious female regions and curving beautifully underneath them, the bulge strangely comfortable for the women's thighs to rest against. Continuing back and under them, the bulge flattened out but continued up their rears, opening out to mirror the shape of the front again. Ending at their waists, the leather encompassed them from behind also, but the hard plastic shell was beautifully covered over by the leather and stopped well short of being half-way up their asses, the leather only continuing up from there.

The intendants continued smiling at the women's admiration for their truly beautifully designed clothing, only a few more sensing the intendants' smiles were more than for their enjoyment. The women were allowed to amble around for a time, the intendants laughing in small groups, the ballroom having an airy feel as, following their lead, the women talked, even laughter being permitted!

Very quickly, the women realized the strangeness of their implements… they could not feel anything.

The leather edging almost a centimeter think with sumptuous layers of softer leather behind and inside it left a truly tight but comfortable fit, the skin breathing freely through the front and back of the leathered plastic, through curious perforations. Like five little strikes at a time, these paired groups of small holes ran up the outside of the seams to either side next to their thighs at front and back, allowing air to pass freely in and out along the belts, ensuring no extra heating was felt inside. After a time, the women barely felt them on their figures… from the inside.

From the outside, they ran their fingers over the gorgeous leather, smiling at its softness as they admired how good each one of them looked, only some finding it uncomfortable that, underneath, they could feel nothing.

The bulbous V-shape designed front and back gently lifting from the waist, down both sides and then pushing out inches in front and to the rear as it dropped two inches below their bodies. The belts ensured, as both sides met underneath, that not only was it impossible for their femininity to touch the front or bottom of the belt, but even their assholes and most of their lower crevices also had no way of coming into contact with the belt.

The most sensitive parts of their lower female anatomy had, in effect, been isolated, with only a few of the women beginning to worry about it.

The hard leather-covered plastic faded only a quarter ways up their rears, ensuring that, although covered by leather after that, their ass cheeks could more than adequately be accessed by striking implements through the leather, the belt then only serving to hold in their pain at the rear. Some of the more astute slaves, normally learned in this way, quickly realized this, intendants' laughing as they saw it on their faces as they ran their fingers over their rears, realizing implements could deliver pain, but fingers could not sooth in the same way, the leather thick enough to prevent that.

"So, then!" The Mistress suddenly addressed all

the meandering groups, the intendants walking purposefully toward their respective charges as the great circle formed quickly around the Mistress again. "May today learn you all that we only have your best interests at heart," she smiled warmly, but was unable to hide the dark undercurrent everyone could see beneath.

Split up after assemblance, the women were taken to strange tasks; there was no fitness, there being little point to it as they could not perform on the steps outside with their new clothing, and nor could they be punished in the usual manner in the correction huts without removing it.

Forced to stand in the Academy, they were still cuffed to their desks, the mischievous smile from Miss Goodspank doing little to calm their growing suspicions as they realized they could really only stand or lie down with these curious purpose-built belts.

In class, the first of many tortures that day was begun, live sex performed by intendants over the now familiar desk, allowing Miss Goodspank to point out and teach methods while increasing the desire in them all… the desire that had been growing in them for days.

More in the library, a small guard keeping watch over the cleaning as a larger group of intendants showed how erotic sisterly action could really be, some dropping implements with their jaws as their groaning filled the room. The slaves barely able to perform their tasks, the guard did not stop them from viewing half leather-clad intendants, their uniforms hanging everywhere as they savaged each other, truly loving their work.

Relief from it all came early that day… too early.

Taken down to the dorms, all groups together were surprised, first at meeting everyone on the first lower level, and then at how strange the scene looked, all slaves having their sensual leather chastity in place, but surprised mostly at the time… it being just three o'clock…in the day!

Intentionally held together, packed like sardines, the women could barely move in the corridor, the scent of their sisters around them driving them mad as they were encased in a pheromone orgy. An intentional ploy to ensure more suffering, the intendants smirked at one another as they watched the frustration on the women's faces around them. Taking only a few at a time from the front of the lines and securing them in their dorms, the women were forced to queue for what was soon to be one of the longest nights of their lives… once they'd suffered through the rest of the day.

Pushed together so tightly as they waited for confinement, inevitably, the frustrated women felt the hands of their sisters fall not entirely by accident between their legs, excitement at the promise of an ease of their yearning dashed as they felt for the first time how effective the belts where.

Inside, beneath the leather, burning frustration begged for their sisters' fingers, soaking want only inches away, left in agony as nothing of any relief could be delivered. As the realization creeped in, more and more women began to learn how trapped their needs were, making the hunger well up inside them, worse than ever as they waited their turn to be shackled.

Inside the dorms, the intendants were like factory workers. With so many women to shackle down, they were like leather clad emotionless machines, women uncaringly pushed down on their beds with their fear ignored as two emotionless powerhouses roughly shackled them fully.

The shackles were new, frightening, as it was obvious what they were; they were medical restraints, their dull light brown seen in films; they were utterly effective and meant to be worn for a long time without discomfort, it becoming obvious just how long they were to be confined.

Outside, as they waited in the lines, the women could hear the shackling and at times occasional slaps as intendants got tired, lashing out at the women for waywardness as they saw it, their work hard enough without the women having their legs in the wrong place or resisting. It wasn't the slaps, though, that had the women worried – it was the occasional wail or, more accurately, the occasional wail that was being snuffed out… they were being gagged!

Looking around, all worried as they were not able to see the extent of the confinement, their minds racing as they realized it was extensive, and soon to be theirs. Very soon for Jennifer as she neared the head of the corridor's queue, her worries about what was coming about to be answered!

Taken by strong hands, it wasn't her group confining her… no Nadia, no Urst – it was unfamiliar intendants, an intentional move to ensure there would be no favoritism or easing of suffering, as the women were all to suffer equally.

Jennifer froze as she bore witness to her dorm, the few women in front of her shackled and lying on their backs completely spread eagle, medical ankle restraints six inches long, mauve-colored and wrapped around their ankles and secured to each side of the bed!

In the beds' centers, the new fear continued as a waist strap bound tight the midriff to the bed, no way to wriggle or lift the body, the intendants determined no way would be found to rub any femininity against the inside of the belts. Above the waist strap, frightened faces looked up at Jennifer as she passed, roughly marched through the dorm by two tired and unsympathetic intendants. Jennifer feared more as she saw the reason the few cries had been snuffed out, the gags employed being made not of a soft leather ball, but of white silk length scarves, the women left biting down… more evidence they were to remain here at length.

They all knew, intimately by now, the scarf gag of silk or cotton, when employed, was to be used to allow gagging at length. No danger of suffocating on growing saliva in the throat, a torturess trait of the ball gag… the scarf gag meant sufferers could be left on their backs unattended without fear of suffocation and without the constant need of monitoring…. it meant they were to be left for a long time!

Soon Jennifer was pushed down to her bed, the hands rough and uncaring, no connection to her group and soon employing her ankle restraints. Jennifer breathed heavily out as her nerves came forth, garnering a sharp look from her captors as they secured her ankles to either side of the bed below, convincing an already well-behaved slave to maintain her etiquette. Still offering no trouble, Jennifer watched as the intendant on the left drew up a waist strap from the floor the dorm, it being astrewn with countless restraints as the intendants sweated on, ensuring all would be secured. Their passing it across the bed in front of her, and Jennifer shivered inside as they brought it down across her waist, another glare at her breathing holding her down as quickly, with practiced hands, they secured it to either side, tightening it down, Jennifer wanting for the first time to squeal.

She felt trapped! Looking down at her secured belt, and with her legs held apart, the medical restraints had her frightened, seeming to menace more than their shackles as they seemed to assure there was something coming, Jennifer for the first time trying to move and feeling just how tightly she was held… she couldn't move!

Breathing out, she began to lose it, fear welling up as etiquette fell away, and opening her mouth, she…. and it was in….

As if sensing she was about to lose her control, the intendants brought forth her gag, managing to pull it across her opening mouth as out came a small squeal, snuffed out with their efforts, leaving them smiling down at her, pleased they had caught it. Hoisted up to a seated position between them, Jennifer's panicked hands found their waists to either side of her, tolerated as they smiled to one another over her panic, her gag wrapped around her head and secured over her nerves….

With their lying her back down, she instinctively squeezed their waists for comfort, but received none, only menacing smiles thrilled at her fear, her teeth biting hard on the scarf and the intendants gleefully watching as they took her arms finally behind her.

Behind and over her head, they laughed as Jennifer screamed into the gag under the pressure, its job done –

only muffled panic ensuing, her cry a prisoner, too, shackled inside with the rest of her.

Calming slightly, it being obvious that screaming was pointless, she breathed heavily as she watched them secure her left arm with a six inch mauve restraint meant to hold down mental patients in secure wards, this now employed on patients who were perfectly sane… for now.

Sane, but wayward, as Jennifer watched them take it back to the top left hand corner of her bed, securing it like her ankles, now spread eagle like the rest, feeling the strain of her confinement and its determined tightness… their will….

And with a final laugh at her discomfort, they were off. On to the next slave, her screaming more than Jennifer's, light slapping calming her down before gagging and confinement saw her scream horribly into her gag…. Andrea hated confinement.

Jennifer waited, struggles and muffled screaming around her, but they didn't come back. She daren't move her free arm for fear they might get angry, angry at forgetting to secure it…but they hadn't.

As Andrea struggled beside her, Jennifer gently passed her gaze around the room, noticing that all who were tied down had their right arms free. It made no difference, of course, the medical ankle and wrist restraints being complete with padlocks, and even the waist strap was padlocked twice under the bed, but why had they left their arms free?

With a final desperate screaming into her gag, and a jarring of trapped legs, Andrea finally exhausted the patience of the intendants, her slaps becoming painful as she screamed in agony… but it was too late. The intendants had decided a beating was needed to bring her around, her screams of anguish finally quieting as she cried into her gag, ceasing struggling confirming to the intendants that they were right as they left, showing no regret.

And so it began….

Boredom

The women were left, things quieting down, their dorm doors sealed on those who'd started crying after being dealt with by the staff.

Soon, though, even that petered out, the dorms quiet and the women more than aware that the cameras were watching.

Confused at their early confinement, some began to stir, the tight hold they were in becoming harder to bear as they muffled out moans through their gags, each expecting intendants to burst through the doors at any second… but none came.

After a time, some even dared to move their free arms, certain that this would do it, that soon beatings would ring out around them, but it didn't.

Above, in the control room, intendants indeed were watching, but all smiling, laughing, having seen it all before. Many eyes watched Julie, sure she'd be the first to reach… but it was Linda, and eyebrows raised, the intendants surprised they had been wrong.

Reaching delicately between her legs, Linda ran her fingers uselessly over her leather-caged need. Her face one of frustration, the intendants watched on as she fumbled with one of the two golden jailers padlocking her torture below.

"Don't worry, Linda"….a voice aimlessly drifted over the dark control room, all the intendants in house now present. "You'll find out tomorrow!" Laughter erupted as encouraging smiles from leather-clad mischief-makers sought out the source of the mirth, certain she was right.

They watched as Linda was soon joined by the others, their moans becoming more audible, the intendants raising eyebrows and beginning to consider their hands, too, as the etiquette weakened below them.

Considered, but held off, as they watched the women explore the fronts of their belts, the intendants smiling down at their curiosity below them as they felt the fine lines of the small hatches held tightly shut by their golden jewelry. It wasn't long before expressions told of their obvious realization, fingers following the lines of the leather hatch as it circled underneath them, an obvious way in to their suffering for any lucky enough to hold the key… but none did.

Instead, the intendants watched as, within minutes, groans had become more audible, louder, the women smelling their sisters trapped around them, all now in investigation between their legs, their free hand exploring the small hatch but their yearning, needing, feeling nothing trapped below.

Intendants reveled as they watched the desperation grow with the fingers, some noticeably trying to push hard against the belts, obviously trying to push up against them from inside, but the waist restraints holding them firm, frustration beginning to appear on their faces as they cried out, their sisters crying out with them, setting off a gagged desperation, an orgy of suffering beginning in the rooms.

Twenty minutes, half an hour, an hour… it wasn't even five o'clock, the women fully awake and hornier than ever, Julie suffering more than most as she started half–screaming, pulling at her restraints with the rest… but there would be no relief!

Laughing aloud, the intendants watched the suffering below, each dorm the same, the hand left free doing nothing but increasing their suffering, the intendants laughing as the slaves desperately tried to find a way to use it, to find a way past their chastity… but there was none!

All it did was hammer home to their minds that there was no way to alleviate their pain, their screaming need from inside as they lay completely awake, utterly bored and sure of countless hours still to come. Realization of what this was dawned on them all, as open screaming into gags began, forced from the hunger needing inside.

The dorms were noisier than they'd ever been, screams of agonizing frustration allowed to bawl out through the gags, the intendants enthralled by their efforts as the misery played out below them.

Soon, women started openly challenging the camera, desperate for anything other than this, for even the release of some torture… but none came… of course not… they were already getting it!

But for toilet breaks every few hours and the slaps of annoyed intendants having this task, made more difficult by their desperate pleas on being secured back down, the women were made to suffer in anguish, this new form of torture absolutely abhorrent to them, their now being super-sexed individuals left to look down at their chastity in frustrated agony.

The screams raised to an unacceptable level through the gags, these only able to do so much after seven hours with no release, it being only ten o'clock and with the whole night still to go, looks from the intendant guard left on nightshift signaled what had to be done as they viewed the near anarchy developing in the dorms below.

The doors swung open as raging intendants appeared, the loudest they had witnessed immediately chosen as the lashing cat came down on their midriff, a two-intendant whipping that shocked those looking on! Only one voice screaming now as they stood over her, raging scything strikes coming down on her as the others froze, looking on, her screams filling the room through her gag. Savagely, it didn't stop! Going way longer than any normal correction… it was a warning!

A warning to them all as the door sealed after the intendants' rage, the women left with the sobbing individual reaching uncontrollably for her pain, left to cry among them, her front reddened and suffering, ensuring the night's coming wailing would be muted from then on.

They suffered on, no one sleeping, and tears ran down every face, every cheek by morning, the women desperate, suffering, and tired… but there was no rest.

Watched like hawks at breakfast and during showers, a few desperate individuals tried to touch themselves, but got caught… and the wings echoed with their screams!

All through the day, cheeks set on fire by strappings couldn't be tended to, fingers allowed to uselessly claw at the fine leather, the fire held inside underneath the belts now adding to the contained frustration… the women were miserable.

Breakdowns started happening all over the Manor, intendants seeming to exhibit care after a time as they were taken away one by one… but the women were wrong.

Those who broke first were simply the first to be taken back to the dorms, their screams of anguish unheard as they were secured even before one o'clock, the rest of their sisters' anguish to join them soon as another term of horror was scheduled.

By three o'clock, gagged screaming filled the dorms once again, more women fed well and not realizing their drinks had been laced with huge doses of extra caffeine; there was no respite, no release, their gags more than ever having difficulty with their screaming.

At only half past three that afternoon, the doors flew open, and this time with a huge contingent of intendants, it still being early during the day and the whole house more than active as the women braced themselves for all the same whippings they'd seen the night before… but none came.

Instead, fear was abound as large boxed machinery was trundled in on trollies. These sitting in the center of each dorm, eyes widened as electric dials flicked to life, red LEDs and menacing numbers rising in the boxed machines, one atop the other, as wires were attached and led to the foot of each bed.

In utter horror, the women squealed, the intendants paying no notice as they readied the latest nightmare for them, their anguish ignored as, two by two, after securing their right hands atop their beds like their lefts, they moved to their waists.

Screams of fear were gagged down as keys took away the front golden padlocks, the women made to see a small oval shaped device brought forth from intendants' garters and attached solidly to the wires over the foot of their beds.

Completely sealed and sheathed over with plastic, the wires were made water-tight by fittings on the receiving device now atop them, the women themselves unaware that the large machines were transformers, the power brought down to six volts to doubly ensure no accidents could happen to them. They, though, didn't know this as they put two and two together, feeling the rush of cool air as the intendants pulled open the triangular access hatches on their chastity belts, revealing their glistening femininity inside, leaving them squealing in fear and now fully tied down to their beds.

Struggling below them, the women feared more as intendants seemed to ignore them, operating more like scientists on a lab mouse, intent on their mad experiments as they brought the device to their femininity, the women shrieking as they pushed it inside them!

Still ignoring their screams, even the heaviest strugglers among them received no beating; instead, they felt them gently below, pushing the device inside them with their fingers, seeming to want it positioned just so far in, the women agonizing as they worked on them.

Soon, fingers retracted from femininities, the touching that would have been begged for hours earlier now welcomed in its leaving, the women feeling the closing of their belts' hatches, the padlocks repositioned as the intendants rose away from them.

Things calmed some, though still with crying and small slaps of legs bringing order as the intendants tidied away material, but never released their right arms, the women now totally confined.

No smiles, no mischief… just an orderly withdrawal, the women left with their worries as two fine wires led from their belts, across their legs and down to the floor, finding their way with the others to the machines left on and menacing them with their dials from the centers of the rooms.

And so it began…the second early afternoon, all now over their fear and, like the machines in their dorms, left horribly turned on.

In desperation, some tried to bring the attention of the intendants, anything better than this anguish, trying to scream through their gags so that some, even harsh treatment, would come to them… but none came. Slowly, it became obvious to all as groans became squeals of frustration, gagged torture wailing out as the women tied down realized there'd be no relief through what was going to be the longest night of their lives!

In the control room, it was a different story, with only eight intendants inside the room, it being sealed to avoid over-indulgent staff losing control.

Instead, the intendants sat beside one another two by two with their own monitor to watch their own dorm… to torture.

One of the most delicious games which all intendants craved in-house, it was their job to ensure maximum frustration throughout the night.

"Careful, don't set her off," she laughed beside her. "Keep her suffering." Her sister said, the two crowding together and viewing the monitor, their mouths watering, silken thighs touching as they watched the anguish below.

The groaning had given way to screaming in the rooms, but there would be no intendants sent. The women, utterly horny, had received the first of many tiny vibrations from their little oval torturers inside them, the intendants above them deciding which one to turn on and for how long before turning it off from upstairs, the delicate art of edging by electrics beginning.

It was a delicate task indeed, needing great practice and skill, one having to accurately judge the facial expressions to assess the suffering and the point of arousal to ensure the correct amount of vibration to administer in order to keep the subject fully aroused, but not enjoying, instead held in full frustration and never allowed to finish.

This was aided by the sound of their suffering, noises through their gags difficult to distinguish when the women were all calling out in anguish together, but a useful guide, along with certain other pointers that the intendants knew well to look for.

Smiling together, the eight intendants above reached for camera angles and set off buttons, inadvertently crossing each other's as they giggled in the dark control room, excited over their much sought-after task.

Inevitably, hands occasionally fell on each other, and not long before they had only one in use, the other welcomely between each other's thighs.

It was encouraged… although the room was sealed after years of over–staffing, slip-ups teaching that this was the best way to work this procedure as it was accepted that there was no way to watch this fun all night without release… it was the slaves that were to be tortured, not the intendants!

The first one to cum at her post was heralded by the others as she slumped over the desk, reddening in the darkness with her guilt before kissing her partner and shortly bringing her, too.

The heralding slowed as the night went on, orgasms becoming common, and replaced with smiles and close looks, the intendants working on throughout the night and listening to each other's fun in the dark control room. As panties soaked through, they were dropped to ankles, eventually removed for easy access. It was necessary and an accepted part of the procedure, the lust caused by viewing having to be relieved by their sisters around them. This cleared their heads and gave much greater concentration to the truly necessary job running beneath them, their clear thoughts coming with their bodies' relief, ensuring there would be none for those suffering in shackled frustration below.

Chapter 23

Sisters

And so the third night's torture began at one o'clock that day!

Women openly cried as they were taken down to the first lower level's wings and made to wait in line again as those ahead of them were shackled in their dorms, the women's hearts breaking inside.

The intendants didn't correct or punish because, with so many in the wings crowded together, they couldn't reach them anyway… they didn't have to. The suffering caused by their crying was infectious, more and more beginning to wail as, inside, their desires were still burning, sealed below in confinement as they, too, were soon to join them through another night of frustrated hell.

Looking on in crying anguish, some dared in desperation to let their looks linger on intendant faces, only arrogant mirth looking back and signaling there was to be no mercy as another group in front was taken away, sobbing to their dorms.

Wailing on for much longer than the previous nights, the queues took an age to go down. Jennifer herself cried at one point, more in support for her sisters, the weaker among them beginning to truly break down. Taken by the wrists, some wailed at intendants, desperation overtaking them, sharp slaps to their thighs delivered as they were taken to confinement.

With two perfectly sealed chastity belts in front of her, Jennifer stood next to Andrea, tears quietly running down her face as she suffered beside her, the gorgeous forms of four intendants appearing from their dorm and taking their group of four inside, the wailing quieting as it was left behind in the wing… and, shock!

All four were stunned as their eyes fell on the scene inside… their chastity belts were off! Not just off, but the women were sealed together, two to a bed, the one on the left having her left hand shackled over her head to the headrest above, the other one on the right having her right hand shackled over her to the same. This made sure the women had to lie on their sides, facing each other, their legs left free and their faces wearing what had the four women shocked… smiles!

Smiles were abound as some of them had even tentatively begun to stroke each other's sides with their free hands, the intendants not intervening as they continued busily sealing the rest in.

Still staggered, Jennifer was stunned as she looked at Andrea, a small smile appearing on her face through her still-running tears as the chastity belts in front of them were worked on by intendants, and suddenly slid down the women's legs and to the floor. Almost immediately, Andrea's smile increased as the intendants, squatting, moved back to them, their hands on their waists, taking hold of their golden jailers and soon granting release as the rush of cool air and freedom flooded their femininity below.

With the sudden turn of events, Jennifer was shaken once more as an all too familiar face, not seen for days, emerged from the throng of intendants before taking her wrist while another took Andrea's and guided them to Jennifer's bed on the left. Without words, and with Andrea almost bursting with embarrassed emotion at being sealed with Jennifer, they were shackled together, Andrea on the left and Jennifer on the right. As the shackles snapped shut, Andrea finally slipped out a laugh in nervous tension, no correction coming as their tenders laughed, too, both more than aware of Andrea's attraction from the Academy reports and it being no accident she was being sealed with her prize. As if to hammer home the tension, Nadia bent down, kissing Jennifer passionately in full view of the other intendants before glaring in half feigned jealousy at Andrea, the slave's smile fading instantly under the power. Message clear, Andrea was released from Nadia's ire, only half real, as she centered her glare on Jennifer, now a small smile appearing with her practiced jealousy, Jennifer fumbling under the power, too, both women weakly smiling back. Now having given her warning, Nadia sighed, giving a last squint at the pair shackled below her as she shook her head, turning away, her gorgeous Latin figure only adding to their want. With her cheeks shifting powerfully from side to side in black panties beneath her corset, her exit was burned into Jennifer's mind as she watched her go, the sound of her boots heavily tacking the floor as she went being a final turn-on as she left them to it… left them to each other.

With the door's sealing, it began almost immediately, horny giggles and begging relief seeing the women laughing on as cuffed orgies broke out among them.

The Academy's lessons now proven completely, the women gave in to themselves, their resistance gone as they begged for each other's company. Those who had been reserved about being with other women had no such hang-ups now as fingers ranged and kisses flew, feminine flooding drowning out groaning want. Watching from above, the smell of feminine lust overpowering all below had a similar effect in the control room overhead, the Manor's walls straining to contain the simmering passion throughout the wings that night.

As it became clear that intendants wouldn't be coming to stop them, it was obvious to all what had been done to them over the days, but with fingers stroking and wanton groaning, no one cared as passion took over among them. The ravenous women were simply encouraged by each other's wanton groaning, joining in writhing ecstasy with each other as three days' torment came to an end, their lips together and their hands below as they moaned in ecstasy, pulling together as they wanted relentlessly. The smell of sex in the rooms the next day was almost overpowering, the intendants returning to witness the Academy's teachings proven in full, the women from that day on being true believers and looking at each other differently. That forced change under the intendants' learning would see an unbelievable improvement in wanton cooperation for their attentions in disciplining, and otherwise proving it was indeed good for everyone involved.

That, though, would come the next day, long after the wanton craving for each other across the dorms. That night, the scent of female want and groaning ecstasy would expand the women's desires far beyond their partners beside them and on to their hidden attractions. The crushes they had on each other, once hidden, were now exposed, indulged as shame was banished, left behind under the Manor's teaching. Group pressure saw them give in to natural desires throughout the night, screaming, groaning, and scented flooding learning all to accept themselves and each other, to have their natural want, their want… of their sisters.

Chapter 24

Sports Day

An incredible sleep, and waking in each other's arms, the excitement that morning was etched on the faces of these new women, truly turned on and biting their lips as they watched Monique. Given what she deserved, her French tones lapped the walls as she was fucked in front of them, her groaning acceptance as they opened her up having all the women wet below.

The showers that morning after breakfast were erotic – after giggling through their morning meal, hungry eyes stared, letting each other know who liked who and who was accepting as they washed next to one another, hands following soap… following curves.

The strapping over the intendant's knee outside the room did nothing to warn or quench their hunger, their sister's wanton tones echoing up and down the hall as she groaned under the intendant's hand, making them worse.

All day, the intendants were maddened as, time and again, they tried to give harsh examples, willing audiences viewing the discipline and hoping they would be next, hoping treatment would be theirs.

The library echoed as strap met ass… howls of correction bringing hunger to all as countless women were bent over and disciplined… it didn't work.

Becoming truly angry, the intendants grew cruel, these new slaves' virtues tested as they were taken to treatment rooms, but frustration kept growing, the intendants strained on and pushed to madness as their efforts were absorbed.

The wings inside echoed with correction, desperate efforts to bring the women under control meeting irritated failure as groaning want marched with professional training… the women could handle it, and the intendants knew it.

Knew it as their hands fell harder, as their straps grew quicker, but wanton replies as asses reddened only signaled their failure, the failure of their disciplining exposed and embarrassed by those they had trained.

Outside, the Mistress and a throng of intendants were busy, occasional smiles coming from them as screams slightly louder than usual came from the wings, drifting over the rear grounds at times, the Manor's own soundtrack accompanying them.

Sports Day… so it was declared. Women were harnessed, women were leashed, crawling, begging, raced, and subdued… it was correct procedure. Like everything else in the Manor, it was not some aimless chase of pleasure on the staff's part, that came at night; instead, it was programmed behavior modification. Years of experience had the intendants more than aware of what the women would do after their night together. They knew how they'd have to bring them back down from their newfound high, from their will for each other, from their wanton acceptance. They knew discipline, for a time, had to be harsh again as they brought them to order, pleased that their chastity-driven acceptance of female virtue had been a success, but irritated that they were made to work harder to curb their indiscressions.

Outside, the Mistress laughed as frustrated intendants had women on all fours at times, their groaning struggles competing with the screams from inside as they were openly fucked in full view on the lawn. No longer embarrassed, they came over implements, intendants sweating under the afternoon sun. With corseted waists grinding in strap-on correction, no one was quite sure just who was being punished, intendants rising in shattered frustration under the pressure from the Mistress to keep her will and control.

Julie was a lost case as they were raced over the grass, disciplined again as they were run back and forth over a hundred meter dash, two at a time, having the wind knocked out of them. It was a necessary step, and the intendants knew they could not change this newfound hunger for each other – nor did they want to, as they simply wanted to maintain control, the breakdown of discipline at this stage a fearful waste. A waste of their training, a waste of their time… retraining at this stage being quite impossible now. And so it went on, intendants running the games, groups of women teamed together and raced over the lawn. From the library above, slaves cleaning windows watched them run back and forth, intendants corseted and shouting, demanding 'faster' at each end. With intendants howling and the Mistress watching, winners were counted and team scores were tallied, the losing groups facing forfeited tortures, grunting bodies strained by powerful thighs fucked hard on the grass, exhaustion delivered…

Control re-established!

Those like Julie, who simply wouldn't be downed,

faced a new form of discipline, a new form of holding… shame.

At this stage, the women didn't view correction as embarrassing, more turned-on and pleased to be the center of attention, playing up to their audiences, showing their strength in their discipline, frustrating intendants and forcing hands to work harder.

To the right of the race lines, though, a new form of control was introduced – women of such stamina were bridled! Literally suited as a horse… teeth burdened with leather as they were bridled and lashed, hands secured behind a saddled garter strap imposed, twenty feet of leash given out from their intendant at the center. The center of a circle, a length of fire making them run… a bullwhip!

Funny at first, humor soon was gone, it leaving with the whip, its licks bringing screams! Forced out as she ran, forced on through her bridle, each running victim circled by her intendant, her embarrassment paraded with determined cruelty shown, her handler's skill her own wanted prize.

The intendants who knew how to train in this way took enormous pride in their abilities, and at length. With their corseted audience, they showed years of training, the whip kissing asses gently, stinging at times, others being savage and loud, screaming torture brought forth.

The skill was in the landing, the delivery honed over years. Some was from the wrist, some was from the drop, the arm all important – not a throw, but a drop. Sent out as the charge ran, finding her at twenty feet was impressive, but more so was the landing in just the right spot. The slave was not told how to run, or to canter; she was taught with the whip, her legs forced to lift as it dropped. Almost on instinct, and with her nerves fired after each lash, the skill of this correction was obvious to all. After a time of screaming and fear over the unknown, the slave was settled as she ran under directed lashing.

Intendants watched, envious of the skill as the slave was controlled, learned to lift and run. Without words, it became obvious to her quickly, failure meeting leather, misattention meeting lash, embarrassment bringing tears as she ran in front of her audience… and cried as they laughed. More skill displayed, her thighs brought higher as the whip kissed atop them, just under her ass, the lash bringing immediate lifting, her running turning to a canter, her tears whipped away. Not away from her face, as they ran in the sun, but away from her mind, the bullwhip's fire dominating her thoughts, the thoughts being of collapse, of giving in to sure beatings taken away by its landing, from her handler controlling her. Her experience told as she watched her face, watched her bite down on her bridle as she ran, saw the embarrassment emerge, the thoughts of giving in to the stress… taken away in an instant fire delivered across her cheeks!

It went on till exhaustion, the eventual slowing and pulling in, the slave forced into final submission following direction to her knees, utterly embarrassed as she was unbridled. With tears running freely, she tried to hold back crying, about to give in fully as she was raised to her feet… and cheering!!!

All at once, the intendant audience erupted in congratulations, the slave still crying in bemused confusion as she watched all around her encourage and cheer her while her nerves were shot through, crying on as she smiled, the encouragement infectious as she was given over to her group….

Then on to the next… trained in canter, she too was brought to tears, her ass reddened and punished under the afternoon sun, her audience's approval on leaving the circle confusing her utterly as she cried through the encouragement. The confusion came from her happiness… how could she be happy as she cried? Pleased, after such embarrassment?

Because she was a slave…

And they were making sure that she knew it….

It was the intendants' will that she be brought down and controlled, and they cheered because they were truly happy with her performance. Had they wished to break her and leave her a dribbling mess, they were more than capable of achieving this quickly, but that wasn't their aim, nor their wish for their charges. After such great work and fantastic learning, they did not want them damaged or harmed; they wanted behavior and etiquette. They wanted their work to shine through.

The night with each other had given a worrying change, the women now prone to mischief after becoming familiar with their want. Reminding them of discipline, then, of house order, was necessary. They had to be brought down from their high to a more manageable level, like prize racehorses indeed, as they were stabled and valued, fed well and trained, the intendants not wanting to harm, but simply maintain their form and learning.

Raced together over the grass, Jennifer was run again for the umpteenth time; she was tired out, the intendants determined to keep order over them, their reputations at stake as the Mistress looked on.

It was with Andrea this time, and did she ever try to keep up, her attraction for Jennifer more than obvious despite repeated attempts by the intendants to bring her down. They worried over her behavior, their tolerance for the women now obvious, familiarity with each other after their night together having limits. The intendants, and more over the Mistress, though understanding and pleased that their forced change in the women had worked, would eventually deal harshly with those who tested their patience too much.

With screaming in their ears from leather-clad audiences at each end of the grass circuit, the two turned at the top, almost bumping into one another, Andrea laughing aloud as they stumbled back down over the grass, the two determined not to be bridled for lack of effort. Running so hard, the screams encouraged them on as the two were really enjoying themselves as they gasped for air, reaching for the finish, their team mates depending on them as they came… before they fell in front of them!

Fell over the line in gasping collision under cheers from intendants, appreciating their effort, the two collapsing in a heap and overjoyed with their praise. Struggling to rise, Andrea stumbled in exhaustion back down on top of Jennifer, their giggling infectious… and then it happened.

Completely on instinct, Andrea kissed Jennifer's

lips! Being so close to her, with her yearning attraction, and having bathed her in affection throughout the night, she couldn't help it, her body reaching out as it had done through their time before.... The cheering stopped.

Pulling her lips away, Andrea quickly shared Jennifer's shocked expression, and for a moment, the audience was silent as they took in this utter breach of etiquette.

With the added pressure of the Mistress in witness, Jennifer's intendant group flew into action… utterly embarrassed by their women, they descended like wolves, seizing their charges and dragging them away.

The Mistress herself was speechless as she watched them being dragged away across the grass, the women quickly taken inside… straight down to the fourth level!

With Andrea crying as they went down the stairs, the women waited for their group's angry chastisement, but none came. Not able to look at Nadia, for the first time, Jennifer truly feared her, the expressions on their faces all matching Urst's. Stony silence as they dragged their tears past bemused intendants, themselves passing on the stairs. Silence from the handlers because they were worried, as the slaves' waywardness was their failure – it reflected their training abilities as intendants. Right now, they were worried about the Mistress's response toward them rather than their slaves, this dominating their thoughts, there being no time to be angry toward them… that would come later.

For right now, it was damage limitation, as without words they dragged their stricken charges straight off the last stairs and up the left wing, right to its end, through the last door and to their fate. Entering inside, there was only a short pause to close the heavy iron door behind them, this allowing the women to see a confused site, the slam of the door snapping them to attention as they looked on a small square room with a half circle at the far end in front of them. Curving away from them and evenly spaced along the circular bay recess, five dull black steel boxes were secured on the curve, seven feet high, under two feet deep and under two feet wide; these lay before them. The walls were stone, horrible and unfinished, the light above a flat panel mounted in the ceiling's center, dull and unintrusive, illuminating the stone floor like the wall, rough under the women's feet, this truly being the bowels of the Manor… but not quite.

In the room's center, a circular dusty black lid curved upwardly, laying flat and shut over something underneath, Andrea beginning to cry again as Jennifer followed her attention to Urst, who now moved into the room's circular bay end and opened the back of the second dull box, it sitting a foot off the floor and a foot short of the ceiling, like the others, the heavy back side swinging open with a grind, revealing a bare box structure inside, empty, and just big enough… for a person.

Dragged forward, Andrea burst into screaming as Valerie and Urst heaved her inside, grappling with her arms as they held them to her sides, forcing her face to the wall as she screamed in sheer terror, the slam of the door sealing her inside, her muffled panic barely audible as it was locked behind her.

Inside the box, Andrea immediately had a breakdown, screaming in total darkness as she felt the cold steel under her feet, banging her face off the steel wall in front of her, the steel door freezing her ass from behind as she bashed her back with her wriggling, screaming in terror as she realized what she was in. Unable to move her arms but for a wriggle, she screamed in the steel coffin, bashing off every steel side, the pain unnoticed at first as she howled in terror, screaming for release and begging for the intendants, but none came, Andrea left in terror as she broke down on her own, locked inside with the darkness.

Outside, her muffled shrieking was barely evident, Jennifer appalled, looking to Nadia, a strong look sent back – a look that made it worse for her, as she didn't look angry… she looked worried.

Worried as Urst drew back the hatch from the floor, a hole three feet across leading to pure darkness below, Jennifer's panicked look up to Nadia meeting concern…. They had to do it to her.

From the ceiling, Carly reached up to the dropping hooked fastening at the end of a steel winch cable, even she looking concerned, seeming not to want to look at Jennifer, the cranking turning of the winch cable let out by Valerie, who was stony–faced, from its mounting on the wall to their left.

In front, Urst squatted down carefully, unhooking a solid steel fastening from a massive dull brown steel bracket on the stone wall, just inside the hole, before standing to her feet with it, drawing up a second steel cable attached to its end. Carefully, the two women stood to either side of the hole, gingerly connecting both ends of their brackets to each other before gratefully moving away from the danger in front of them, both cables now one and left to Valerie on their left.

For a second, muffled shrieking became the focus in the room before cranking turning brought the cable up from the hole. Looking at the hole in terror, and then to Nadia and then back again, Jennifer heard the cranking turning of the winch run on as Valerie, powerful as she was, struggled with the effort, winding up and up. Jennifer's fear built inside as time passed, no end seeming to come with the cable still rising. To Nadia and back as the cranking rolled by, a look of sympathy emerging as she watched Jennifer begin to crack, terror in her eyes as she realized how deep the hole was, guessing easily what was about to happen to her.

Finally, a form worrying Jennifer more as its flat mottled brown steel lid came into view from the darkness, solid, a strong six inches of gap all around it as it rose into the room with its steel bars ready… for Jennifer!

The cranking finally stopped, Jennifer's heart pounding as Andrea's muffled bubbling behind her was almost unheard, the stress fading her out as she looked down in front of her, eyes wide on her own fate, winched up over the hole.

Resembling a giant bird cage, with a circular top of inch-thick steel, bars ran around its edge, three inches apart, four feet down to its base, another inch-thick circle of steel with a curious raised edge, an inch higher all the way around it on top at the outside, walling in all the bars' bottom ends, welded to the base….

Without any explanation, Urst reached forward, opening a door in the cage which was raised off the floor and above the edge; it swung open, hinged on one of the dull brown bars itself, a foot wide and only two feet in height, a small entrance now open and soon to be sealed for hours.

Jennifer thought about talking as Urst reached for her shoulder, thought about crying out as she sent a fleeting look to Nadia, not asking for mercy, but asking for something, for acknowledgment… for love.

Pushed inside, she had to turn to go through, had to crouch in a sitting squat, her ass cold, meeting dusty steel, its uneven mottled surface rough but not sharp. Her hands were crossed over her legs by Urst in an almost caring gesture as Jennifer pulled them defensively to her chest, Urst looking into her eyes for the first time with cool Nordic stillness, closing the door and locking a huge old padlock. Retracting the key, she let it bang heavily on the door, stepping back as the cranking started over again, Valerie lowering her down, the room lifting away above her as she quickly looked to Nadia for one last time, an honest look of sympathy coming back to her, forced by Jennifer's terror written on her face… and no one ever spoke.

Her world fell black as the cage entered the hole, Nadia disappearing from view, the last thing she saw as she thought about screaming, joining Andrea above as she burst into tears. Crying openly to the cranking of the winch which faded above her, hardly any sound left at all – just the feeling of the dropping now. Lower and lower, her look up was just useless, the steel roof blocking any view and the room's light above now gone, seeming to not want to enter the hole with her.

Crying out, she burst into anguish as she felt the cold bite still harder, worse with every few feet as she was lowered further to the Manor's depths, thirty feet down, a final bang of rough steel meeting stone signaling she was where she would stay while her fate was decided.

She couldn't hear the fumbling of the cables, Carly and Urst separating them again, and couldn't hear the winch's end secured back to the ceiling, but the final crash of the steel lid coming down vibrated up and down the hole's stone walls, Jennifer certain what it was as it was locked into place… she fell to pieces.

Above her, Andrea had screamed so much she was hoarse – she slumped against the left side of the steel box, crying helplessly, her head sore on her prison wall, her face bruised, her back sore, her ass freezing and her feet numb, her crying tones echoing off the steel tomb all around her in the darkness. She couldn't see the slit gap atop the seven foot box, designed in a double-hook formation near the wall so that light couldn't easily find its way in, and with the room's shabby light turned off as the intendants had left, locking the iron door behind them, it didn't matter. As far as Andrea was concerned, the box was sealed – darkness, silence, and air running out as she thought, her anguished cries weak from effort as she sobbed on the steel wall beside her.

For Jennifer, it was little better; after a long cry on her own, she sobbed in the darkness, pulling her legs in tight for the heat. Even colder where she was, it was the darkness which she feared, her silence its ally. Eventually, she began to feel the roughness of the steel finish with her toes, her feet next, as she slowly explored her confinement, boredom a curious company as she met the edge of her prison. She could feel the individual bars with her toes in the darkness, between them the raised lip – an inch high, like a small steel castle wall holding them in, its length smooth between each bar before her toe found the next one, rounding it as she went. Shivering, she cried out quietly, pulling herself together as she reached out to the bars, feeling her confinement in the dark… and silence. It was frightening, Jennifer fearing inside as she gently let her hands run through the bars by the side of her waist, down gently to what she'd find beyond them, fear causing her to jump as she touched the cold stone beyond the bars, quickly pulling her hands back up before curiosity got the better of her. Gingerly, she touched the stone again – rough, dusty… empty. She walked her fingers gently around, expecting at any moment to feel something scamper across her fingers, something that would have had her die of fright, but there was nothing. Even down here, the house was well kept, she thought, her hands jumping back as one of them found the wall, a surprise even though she knew it was there. Six inches from her cage, all around her in the darkness, her hands found the wall, the rough stones unfinished in true castle style, Jennifer mapping her confinement in the silence below the Manor.

Exploration finished, the boredom returned, Jennifer sobbing for a time and feeling sorry for herself, huddling together, holding her legs against her in the dark. It wasn't even her fault she was here, she thought, becoming angry at Andrea for putting her through this…. Andrea… she thought to above her, remembering her screaming in the steel box. She wasn't strong – locked inside that coffin, she might go to pieces, a part of Jennifer feeling she deserved it for doing this to them, but her inherent good nature taking over quickly and forcing her into worrying about her… she did like her.

She thought of her bubbly Irish accent, her voice singing with her charm, her smile and mischievous eyes, innocent but wanton… Jennifer even smiled in the dark… but then something came over her….

In the cold, alone for what must have been hours now, she had no way of telling that something unpleasant was stirring beneath her… inside her… she had to go!

To the toilet, she needed to go, realizing the ridiculousness of it all as she reached forward in the darkness to the bars, cold dusty steel meeting her hands as she suddenly wondered when they were coming back… could she hold on? Another twenty minutes, and the unpleasantness grew worse, she being cramped in a squat; the design was intentional, its makers knowing this would force nature on quicker, there being less space for the victim and the growing natural waters inside. With the cold on her lower regions making everything worse, Jennifer's uncomfortable rocking back and forth wasn't helping anymore… she had to go…

Anger, sorrow, self pity all came through her mind as she reached for the bars, finally taking them in hand… and letting go…

A sobbing mixture of relief and self pity, she half-laughed to a cry as she felt the warm fluid gush out below her, quickly filling her steel floor, a full load as she'd tried to hold off for so long. Crying on, she released it, all the warmth building around her on her feet and her cheeks, welcomed heat in the darkness below the Manor, but the smell repugnant and strong in the air around her… it had no place to go. Like her, it was a prisoner, a real one as Jennifer suddenly realized why the inch high lip of steel was around the base, raging in anger at them as she realized they'd meant it, she being forced now to sit in a pool of urine, the smell having her scream her anger out in the darkness… she hated them.

After a time, the warmth around her grew cold, Jennifer disgusted by herself as she sat in her efforts, the smell less of a bother, but the cold growing all around her as she tried to sit still in her mess so that the waves didn't lap against her.

Above her, more shrieking had occurred in the second of the holding boxes, Andrea also forced to let go from the cold under her feet. She'd cried helplessly as the warmth ran down her legs and filled a pool at her feet. Standing trapped in her waters, the smell was worse for her in her cramped confinement. Crying feverishly, she'd finally slumped again on the left of her tomb, the walled coffins designed so that doors opened two inches above where she stood, ample room for a fine pool beneath her. Unknown to her, she'd filled well the space below, the pool reaching up through the cracks in the door and escaping out behind it, and dripping to the floor. On the stone beneath her wall box, her release spread out below her, the intendants having found much mirth with this set-up over the years of treatments before hers. In the olden days, when once they had checked on the prisoners, they would wall up five women at a time, waiting for all five puddles to appear, only then considering the release of the muffled wailing inside, they who went first facing Jennifer's predicament soon after, once and whence satisfaction had been had that all five had released.

Over the years, weaker slaves suffered significant

mental damage from this process, and under pressure from the backers, this procedure was scaled back, clients truly unhappy with some of the results upon release… it was now only used for extreme misattention.

Hours…. Jennifer couldn't find comfort over them; her head resting behind her on the bars grew painful, so she moved to one side till pain forced her to the other, and then more had her droop her head to the front, the smell of stale urine meeting her from below. Crying had stopped, and anger, too… she was just tired and cold… oh, so cold.

The lurch upwards startled her, as she'd heard nothing above, the waves of cold urine rocking back and forth around her body as some escaped over the lip, the cage rocking slightly as it rose and Jennifer instinctively steadying herself, grabbing for the bars in the dark before pulling her hands back, thinking better of it. Rocking again, she put them down through the urine, steadying herself with the floor, fearful they would catch on something outside the bars as the cage raised up the hole.

Soon, the cranking came into earshot, Jennifer never having heard a more beautiful sound as, tired, she prepared her face, her submissive look, not wanting to incur any further correction and just needing to sleep… she was so cold.

Light! Real light began to fight its way down around the cage edge, her eyes lighting up with its arrival, so happy for the company, her senses waking up, running to the sounds and the sights, Jennifer having to remind herself to hold her look as she prepared her eyes to fall on Nadia.

Cresting the edge of the hole, the light flooded Jennifer, her look moving to excited happiness for a second before stealing back its practiced stance, her eyes excitedly falling on… the Mistress!

The Mistress, in her full terrifying glory, waiting for her, her eyes seizing Jennifer's immediately from the other side of the bars as she was raised to her from the edge of the hole, caged, freezing and cowering in a pool of her own urine as it lapped at her feet.

The Mistress's angry glare dropped to the pool, the smell and her accusatory look back to Jennifer making her feel weak and dirty… and she couldn't help it… she burst out crying.

Her own intendant group, all four, stayed back, holding expressions of stone as the Mistress watched, unmoved, though happy to see the hole had done what it always did, another slave now broken down in front of her… easy prey to manage.

"There, there, dear," the Mistress whispered condescendingly, running her nails threateningly up and down her cheek, Jennifer luckily so down that she didn't resist. "Don't worry, we're going to fix this, make it all go away…" She ran her nails around Jennifer's cheek, a finger extending under it, the sharp feel of her nail menacingly pulling Jennifer's face up gently with its sharpened edge.

Sobbing, Jennifer shivered before her.

"This wasn't your fault, was it?" The Mistress's eyes widened slightly, her head cocking some as if looking for an answer, but knowing Jennifer was too shocked to offer it. "It was that other girl, wasn't it?" She nodded her head at Jennifer as the slave looked back fearfully.

Jennifer thought of what to do as time stood still, the Mistress holding her chin with her nail in the gentlest threat, waiting for an answer.

Jennifer buckled under the pressure, gently nodding on the nail.

"Well, she'll be dealt with, don't worry, but you, my dear, were involved." The Mistress looked at her more accusingly, her nail pulling slightly, entrapping Jennifer's attention to her. "A good slave should have pulled away, looked for direction from her trainers; you're to do nothing without their direction, are you?"

Jennifer watched the Mistress cock her head, drawing out her answer, Jennifer slightly shaking her head atop the Mistress's nail.

"Well, good then, you know that you've done wrong – that's a good sign." She took away her threatening nail, going back to running the backs of her fingers up and down Jennifer's cheek like she was some pet she adored. "It's a sign your training's taken hold, that you know you've been wayward, and we all know what that means in this house," she paused…. "Correction…."

Jennifer's sudden look of unfairness changed the Mistress's stance immediately as she drew away her hand, staring seriously down at her and leaving her feeling trapped and vulnerable, her naked body back against the bars behind her.

"Do you think this is an unfair course of action?" the Mistress asked rhetorically, Jennifer saying nothing as her tone rose threateningly. "You think this was your punishment?" The Mistress looked around the cage and back to Jennifer, both knowing she sought no answer. "My dear, this was just to allow you to think on your wrongdoing, to focus your mind on your lack of control… it's obvious from your attitude that you've not found the right answers to these problems yet, so you'll need more help in finding them, won't you?"

Jennifer could only look up, fearing as the voice grew harder.

"Well, at least you know not to answer back; I am encouraged by that, at least," the Mistress seemed to calm. "But this attitude I can see on your face, this unfairness you think we've brought you – you should know by now that it's our decisions that matter for you, it's our decisions that are best for you," the Mistress growled angrily, glaring at Jennifer.

A long pause allowed the Mistress to stare at Jennifer, making sure the last of her resistance was gone as her eyes and voice pushed Jennifer back down to the fearful state she preferred her in.

"Do you think you know better than me?" the Mistress asked in a sudden condescending sweetness that Jennifer dared not answer. "Good then, we're in agreement…. I know best and what's best for you…" she trailed off to a growl, glaring at her before walking off, her guard already told where to bring her as they began to unlock her cage.

Chapter 25

Example

The Mistress was unbelievably angry at assemblance in the ballroom, her disappointment in the lack of control obvious as her voice pushed at the walls containing it. Just in case anyone missed her displeasure, the box had been brought in and sat in the middle of the room, its presence having all slaves in fear.

Their initial chastisement over, they waited as the Mistress moved out, everyone waiting, as they knew what was going to happen, the incident on the grounds now everyone's knowledge, and everyone knew… they were in for it.

Standing beside another in silence, Andrea's tears ran freely, totally shaken by her experience on the fourth. Jennifer, too, was badly scarred, her memories fresh from the hours below.

Both with head down in full submission, they heard the boots approach, each tack toward them thundering like a storm inside them…. Andrea's breath was shaking.

"Why?" The Mistress asked, her tone one of real regret as she began to question the condemned. "Why did you do this?… How could you do this to them?" She asked, referring to the intendants, the two slaves remaining head down. "After all they've done for you… after all they've given… you want to throw this all away because you want one another?" the Mistress charged, Andrea frozen in fear, tears running down her face as Jennifer, face down with her, shook her head for both of them. “Well, I don’t see I’ve any choice…” the Mistress asserted loudly “I have to consider dismissal” Jennifer finally lifting her head at the statement, suddenly shocked at the decision.

Meeting eyes with the Mistress, she saw that a serious expression looked back like that of an accountant… not angry, just processing, seeming to be cleaning house, taking care of a problem. “What would you have me do?” the Mistress gave ground, as if offering a way back.

Jennifer stood, eyes wide and shocked at the possibility that she was about to be dismissed; her Mistress would be shattered with the failure, embarrassed, and she could lose everything, after all she’d been through….

“Well, if you don’t know, then you leave me no choice…” the Mistress suddenly turned away, walking back to the center, Jennifer suddenly shocked into action…

“Please…” Jennifer heard her own voice echo in the hall, shocked at how loud she’d spoken out, her nerves causing the loss of control…. The Mistress stopped, pausing but not fully turning, as if waiting for something else.

“Please, Mistress…” Jennifer suddenly remembered to complete her address of her properly, this having been another slip of etiquette in front of the group.

Turning back, the Mistress moved solemnly, relief over her face, as if bringing their virtue.

“That was difficult for you,” she spoke caringly, standing with them as if meeting them on the street,

Andrea now looking up, still with fearful tears rolling. "Oh, Jennifer, how could you let this happen, how could you fall at this stage… and Andrea, what happened out there – how could you do this to her?"

The two women looked back, shocked that their names were being used openly in the great hall, a thing that rarely happened in direct address, usually only in relation to lists of correction for the purpose of shaming ; the Manor's slaves were to have nothing but the direction of the intendants each morning. Each day, the house complement would rise to the virtue:

"Without burden without baggage
without direction theirs to follow."

A familiar teaching in-house, it was drummed into them in each morning's assemblance, an example that they were to have nothing but what was decided for them, never clothed and never named, never complemented and never praised.

Here, then, the women were shocked as the others looked on, Andrea's tears even seeming to stop, the two unsure of how to respond.

"I know…" the Mistress spoke. "I'm shocked, too." She dropped her head before turning, looking out across the circle. "The fault is obviously not with the intendants," she declared, a familiar mantra ringing out. "I just wonder how two professionals like you can make such a mistake."

Shock again, all around, as another house taboo was broken, praise being used on the women!

"I've thought about it a lot," the Mistress continued, stopping with her back to them, almost at the other side of the circle. "The fault not with the intendants, and not with the lack of learning, that effort obvious." The Mistress praised again!

"It leads me to believe we might have special cases on our hands," she turned with a look of appreciation on her face, eyeing the two fondly. "There are times that this happens, over the years." She swung her mane, addressing the rest of the women who were gob smacked at her praise for the two women standing with their mouths open in disbelief. "Like athletes in training camps, there are occasionally one or two who rise, who stand out against the rest," the Mistress moved back slowly, the two women uneasy as they watched her… something hiding in her look, fighting with the praise. "When this happens, the trainers are pleased, as they realize they have something special on their hands… pleased, as they have some that stand taller than the rest, that are better… " she trailed off.

The audience, still in shock, stared as she paused.

"NOT IN HERE!!!!!!!!!!!!!!"

The Mistress's scream shattered the room, all slaves jumping with nerves, even the intendants surprised by the savagery, the two women baulking in terror as a raging Mistress glowered over them. "Do you think you're a special case?" She screamed, the women shrinking where they stood. "WELL??!!"

Andrea thought of crying and Jennifer didn't know what to do, the two completely unable to answer as a raging expression pressed hard on them from in front.

"They train you, they teach you, they guide, they fuck you, and yet, still this is how you repay them!!!" She bore down, struggling to hold back her rage, her voice breaking into a hiss as she glared into them. "Well, if your bodies are that hungry for more attention, then special cases like you should get it, then," she declared. "Far be it for us to stand in your way with our lowly program; we'll just have to look up and hope we can be as good as you someday," she glared, the circle no longer confused as they looked on in understanding that justice was about to be done.

Almost shaking with anger, the Mistress remained where she was, a look of certainty on her face as she looked into the eyes of the pair in front of her.

"You needed to be with each other… needed each other's company so much you were prepared to declare it in front of us," the Mistress accused, glaring down at them as they listened to her voice growing stronger, her anger with them staggering. "In this house, it's only the intendants' company you need!!!!!" She declared, roaring in on them as they shrank further in front of her. "And since you seem to have forgotten that, and it's company you desire, then you shall certainly have it, and with it, maybe your memories shall return…. TAKE THEM!!!" She screamed, and with arms seizing them from behind at once, the women were shocked over again as they were marched out of assemblance, their fate unknown and awaiting them.

"This latest breach of etiquette is almost unforgivable at this stage," the Mistress sighed as she took the hall back under her command, the intendants' boot steps falling off in the distance. Shaking her head as she dropped it, she turned her attention back to the room. “Think of the work my staff have put into you all these months, and some of you still fall wayward like this… disrespect them in this way…” she lamented, raising her full brunette mane in fury, her eyes seeming to scan around the circle for a victim. “Well,” she slowly growled, “I won’t allow you to disrespect them,” her voice grew steadily angrier as she moved toward her favorite implement, the women realizing it wasn’t for Andrea and Jennifer after all as they suddenly felt new terror in the circle. “I told you before that the failure of one is the failure of you all, and you shall all suffer together,” she declared, confirming their worst fears. “I will make sure that, when you leave our care, there will never be a time when you embarrass our staff or bring this great house’s reputation under threat…. BRING HER!!!” She suddenly demanded, pointing at a face.

The women stood bolt upright in terror, each realizing many more examples would be made as they watched a frightened slave being secured to the box. With her beautiful ass held high in front of them, it would soon show the Mistress’s anger in stripes, this wrongdoing to be punished and shared by them all.

Leather strapping complete, the Mistress took her place on the right, the example secure as an intendant took a position on her left, a black cane in hand, arm poised to deliver….

“You are all progressing full well into submission, but this newfound respect you’ve gained from my professionals around you shall not be allowed to go to your heads – you are slaven!” the Mistress bellowed.

“Born to Serve! And

Discipline will be maintained!!!"

And with the sharp raise of her head, the cane was brought down for the first time over the slave's ass, her scream beginning the day's lesson in the great circle for them all….

A lesson they would never forget….

Chapter 26

The Forest

It was afternoon, the sun warm as it peered through the canopy, catching her bare skin at times as she followed Urst's gorgeous gym-toned ass deeper into the woods at the rear of the Manor's grounds. Naked but for her collar, she felt the gentle jarring of her leash, Nadia's soft booted footsteps beside her as she crawled reminding her to heel nicely. A command like others she'd learnt in-house, the Mistress's legion of intendants passing down her orders to lowly slaves like Jennifer, as Nadia had when they'd entered the foliage, now no longer heeling, but heeling nicely.

Held for weeks now at considerable cost, they lived life in-house in constant owned circumstances, nothing hidden, nothing nasty, all knowing this was their place and the life they had chosen. Chained to their beds in the dorms at night, they could smell the scent of their sisters around them, the occasional whimpering of hot tortured cheeks making some reach down to ease the pain while still others where left in jealousy as intendants arrived for their night time activities.

Everything had been going well; she'd taken her learning and gained her etiquette, even attracted the attentions of one of the most highly thought of intendants, leaving her feeling the luckiest slave alive, the burning jealousy around her in the dorm proof of that. But she was a little forgetful sometimes, having so much to do, and she missed some things, but it was none of that that had caused this to happen… it was

Andrea. Jennifer had felt it to be unfair when the Mistress had singled her out with her in front of everyone in the ballroom. Forced into the middle of the hall by intendants, she was humiliated in front of everyone, naked and made to recite her failings… she'd felt ashamed. Standing with Andrea, she'd been made to feel that it was her who had done so much wrong, when in fact it had been Andrea. She'd been terrified by the Mistress's threat of dismissal, and couldn't understand why she'd been so harsh with her… she knew she was hard, but had she no understanding?

She did… she just couldn't show it in front of the others, having to maintain ruthless control at all times. What Jennifer didn't realize as they moved through the forest was that she was experiencing the Mistress's understanding. While she was treated to a day in the calm sunlit afternoon and a humiliating but nice crawl through the woods, she was so far from the ballroom now that she couldn't hear the screams from within it behind her… nor the screams that would come from it later… from Andrea.

She had thought she was going over the box when they'd arrived in the ballroom, and found it waiting for them, her screams of anguish to be in full view of all to complete her humiliation, but was surprised when the Mistress ordered the intendants to take her away. Surprised more when Nadia and Urst had seemed to calm as they left the ballroom, and had become happy, even playful as they left sight of the Manor. She'd worried, even nervously looked up at Nadia as they cleared the rear grounds, Jennifer made to heel all the way across, Nadia glaring at her nicely, reassuring her favorite that everything was okay, encouraging her to resume submission. There had been no explanation yet, but with the Mistress's words ringing in her ears about how they'd been so wanton, that they'd get what they deserved, Jennifer worried as two ultra-fit powerhouses took her deeper into the woods… her correction was to be intensive.

At the time, she'd felt lucky to have avoided the box, but now as leaves crumpled under Nadia's boots beside her, she worried about what was going to happen. Worried, but took great heart from Nadia's fun mood, Urst still stone–like, but her care seemed to be telling her not to worry, as well. She knew they had no choice, their reputations put at stake by Andrea's failure, too, and she promised herself not to cause them trouble as they put her through whatever the Mistress had decided for her. Crawling behind Urst, catching her powerfully built physique, at times, did make her worry, though. Looking up at Urst's boots as she walked in front of her, powerfully built thighs clad in lace met her eyes with black panties and the matching corset straining to hold her in as she moved, a rucksack over her shoulder obscuring her blond Icelandic hair. Inside the rucksack was a small tent, lubrication, and all other implements they would need to give her the Mistress's learning, her grace gifted thoroughly that she may be forgiven after acceptance. The sharp tug on her leash confirmed that Nadia had noticed her looking up, bowing her head in servitude as she adopted the appropriate pose, heeling nicely, knowing Nadia's stunning Venezuelan eyes were now squinting down on her. From above, Nadia's gaze looked down hungrily, her gorgeous short brunette hair fixed on her favorite below as she decided what to do with her behavior, her little misattentions, her personal care. Determined to protect her from her own mistakes, she also had to show care, aware of how Jennifer felt as she, too, knew she had done nothing wrong, and that Andrea was to blame, but aware also of the Mistress's impatience and the conniving of the other intendants, all only too happy to see her favorite suffer. Her punishment, then, would be learning, Nadia already making it known to Urst that she was to be instructed, not harmed, Urst having difficulty going against the Mistress's stronger recommendations, but having a loyalty to her group, she herself having had favorites in the past. Jennifer was right to be worried about Urst, though, as she was already more than determined to protect her reputation, and, like the Mistress, had ran out of patience with the indiscretions of her group's women… Jennifer's fate, then, really was in Nadia's hands.

Still holding her leash and squinting down at Jennifer after her look up, seeing that her head was now bowed again as Nadia had instructed, she took it no further. Taking it no further because, although she was going to protect her, she still knew it would take all her strength to go through what they were about to do to her, and she wanted her to know she was on her side. That, and they had reached the very rear of the woods now, the huge wall coming into view behind the foliage as it pushed hard against it, Jennifer having to fight hard with curiosity not to look up, Nadia being pleased she was winning the battle. The fight for Jennifer was all the harder as she could make out a doorway in the wall, her eyes still able to make it out from her bowed state as Urst moved toward it. Almost hidden among the dense foliage, it was obvious it wasn't used much,

Urst retrieving a large rusting brown key from her backpack and, with great difficulty, finding its path into the old door's look. The doorway was made of old oak planking, vertical and flaking in places with age, but solid, as if part of a castle, Jennifer thinking of the walls in the hole as she watched Urst's equally solid Icelandic body wrestle with the handle, her muscles heaving against the planks as she tried to push them aside. After a few attempts, Urst's heaving forced the door backwards, her underwear straining to contain her exertions as her implements flailed loosely around her hips, Jennifer's mouthwatering for a second before Nadia's sharp tug on her leash dropped her head; she'd soon get to feel Urst's exertions….

The doorway creaked open, and she was taken through to real forest and the freedom beyond! She felt it, became excited as she heard the doorway creak closed and the sound of the old key lock it behind them. As they pushed deeper into the thickening forest, Jennifer was truly lost, and wondered if her escort knew where they were taking her, the feeling of freedom amazing as they went. For months, all she'd known was the Manor and its ways, and now to be crawling through an unknown world, she felt… free!

How right she was, for she was outside the Manor's grounds, which meant her contract did not apply and, effectively, she was now being held illegally and against her will. If she had a mind to she could have made a run for it, that is if she had wished to, at this stage that was no longer a reality and why this procedure would never have been carried out in the early months of training. This decision would never burden her mind though, because although she didn't know about her sudden change in circumstances, the intendants certainly did, which was why Nadia was so attentive with her leashing… there'd be no escape.

After almost half an hour, they came to a small clearing, cramped but with sunlight clearly coming through the canopy, a beautiful scene offered below… about to witness Jennifer's struggles. Forced down to her side, Nadia had her hands and feet bound in moments, feeling no need to tie her off to surrounding trees, the chance of her managing to flee being about the same of her outrunning her intendants before they brought her back for what would certainly be worse. Nadia being one of them, Jennifer had no intension of running away anyway, and so she lay on her side, as her love had left her hands bound to her feet, awaiting her learning. Lying comfortably, as Nadia had made sure she got to watch with rising trepidation, her curiosity giving way to alarm as she watched the set-up of the arena of discipline before her.

Unloading the rucksack, the intendants prepared as Jennifer watched a small green tent being erected to one side, Nadia and Urst laughing and giving Jennifer more ease with their fun, easygoing attitudes. As the sun bathed down, she listened to their carefree enjoyment, seeming to forget about her predicament as they blew up a small inflatable mattress, pushing it inside before following it in with more laughter, before this was broken sharply by hammering. The hammering of tent pegs like those they'd used to pin the tent to the ground, Jennifer unable to see what was going on inside and left confused as they continued preparations… she'd find out later.

Finished, they left the tent, moving a short distance

away, Jennifer watching as they hammered two tent pegs firmly into the ground, parallel to one another, before moving a little forward and doing the same thing again. When the fifth one went in at the front of the two sets, mid-way between their spacing, it was obvious they were for Jennifer, the slave feeling the strain suddenly of the collar around her neck.

After clearing the ground, Urst began bringing oil and other implements, Nadia standing up and displaying her beautiful figure in the sunlight, her eyes matching as she turned squarely on Jennifer, taking her in with them. Soon her boots were softly approaching, Jennifer's punishment about to begin. After being untied, Jennifer was led forward and turned into the middle of the pegs, the tent now in front of her and to the left as she knelt on all fours. Urst smiled as Nadia bent down beside her, assisting with the ankle restraints, the padlocks snapping, cool leather coming tightly around her ankles, alarming enough, but heightened all the more as stainless steel ankle snaps attached to the leather were fastened to the tent pegs hammered in the ground. Soon, she began to feel her heart pumping as her wrists were secured in the same way, sumptuous comfortable leather around them, taking her calm as the steel eyelets attached to them snapped shut on the front tent pegs.

Obviously worried, Jennifer's expression heightened further as Urst, to one side, began attaching the standard Manor harness with black matching her latex, oiled and secured to her front. Caught off guard, Jennifer started as Nadia took her collar in her hand. Looking up for support, she saw Nadia's beautiful brown eyes looking caringly down on her as she attached a steel locking clip to the eyelet of her collar, leaving it dangling free as she drew a hand adoringly over Jennifer's cheek, out of sight of Urst. Her worried looks seemed to calm with Nadia's support as she offered what she could, stroking gently down her back, pointing forward as she handled her as softly as possible. Smile tolerated, Nadia smiled back, motioning with her eyes as her care followed her direction, leaning forward, letting her take her neck clip. Jennifer breathed out heavily as Nadia stroked her back, easing her down to the fifth peg below. Slightly worrying aloud, Jennifer felt Nadia's hand rest on her ass, encouraging her poise as she snapped her into place. Nadia releasing her, a frightened gasp escaped as she felt the restraint on her neck, Jennifer shocked as she pulled and couldn't move, the collar holding her fast. With the sudden shock, her hands tried to wrench as she felt how tightly she was down, Nadia's gentle spank holding her in line as the intendant ran a hand supportively up her back. Held down with her worry, and Urst watched as she finished, her harness now tight and ready. She waited, though, patiently watching Nadia bend down to Jennifer's ear, the slave's fright soothed by her words as she ran her hand back and forth, gently over her back. Over and back, her fingers glided, soothing Jennifer, supporting her love as Urst looked on, moved by the care. With final encouragement, Jennifer nodded, breathing properly, Nadia allowing more time before lifting, having calmed her.

Jennifer watched what she could, helped on by Nadia's care, listening to one side as Urst mused, gently laughing. Waiting patiently, their calm seemed to help her as Nadia was handed the remaining Manor harness.

They hadn't even punished her yet, she thought, as she watched them lube the dildos, confused as she tried to work out why. But that was just it – they wanted her ass free from blemishes, so there were not going to be any whips today, no lashes or canes, nor strappings either, it finally dawning on Jennifer… they were going to punish her anally. For the first time, Jennifer got scared, looking at Urst's powerful thighs and remembering how she'd forced open the old door with them, and realizing she was far away in the forest, and no one could hear her scream.

Walking behind her, soft booted steps brought dread as Urst's knees nestled between her calves, her legs held open helplessly before her as, behind her, Nadia kneeled against her left, facing Urst, both women's hands now enjoying their charge, slowly moving back and forth over her ass and up her back. A standard beginning, it was to show her she was helpless, to put it firmly in her mind that there was nothing she could do. Maddeningly, with all the fear and trepidation, her body still responded to Nadia's touch, Urst smiling at Nadia's favorite glistening for her underneath, showing she truly was hers, Urst bringing forth the oil to add to her vulnerability above. Jennifer fought with squeals as Urst's fingers descended into her crevice, the feeling of wetness lubing up her rear before she felt the soft blunt end of her punishment descend between her cheeks. Jennifer's vulnerability was penetrated almost instantly, her ass opened up by Urst as she gently forced her walls under Nadia's direction, the other intendant insisting her beginning was easy as she reached forward underneath, taking Jennifer's face in support. Jennifer moaning out,

Nadia squeezed, wrapped her hands around Jennifer's back in support, gently squeezing her love as Urst opened her up.

Jennifer could feel the support and the gentleness of the entry, moaning out as she pulled back on her neck brace. Held fast to the ground, she felt the huge member push inside her, moaning louder as she opened, gaining strength from Nadia's care, Urst gentle as she started slowly beginning her needed learning.

Soon, Jennifer could hardly feel their hands around her, the soft feeling of the dildo inside her all she could focus on as it strained her walls, its lubed thickness forcing her ass, Jennifer gasping as it filled her, Nadia stroking in support. Halfway in, she began to groan and shake, Urst's powerful thighs beginning to push past opening, forcing entry inside to fulfillment beyond. Groaning loudly, there was no restriction on her efforts, supporting hands continuing to stroke her. Struggling openly in the forest, Jennifer's deep growling continued, her straining freely flowing as the sun bathed down on the gorgeous scene below. Slowly filled and supported, she was allowed to come to terms with it, her punishment handled slowly and with care as she was stroked. Tended well, and groaning thankfully, she knew her assailants were made wet listening on to her thanks as she growled with their handling. Nadia was so proud as she watched her take her learning, smiling at Urst across her charge below. Groaning for both of them, Jennifer clenching her teeth, Nadia wrapping her arms around her, almost groaning herself as she listened to her struggles. Jennifer was indeed struggling, unsure if they were just being easy with her, as all intendants were when they started this. Usually not for their benefit, the slow start was simply to make sure they didn't injure a slave as they entered, leaving oil to take effect so they could continue longer sessions. She'd learned in house that, unlike men who can feel a woman's soft insides through their members, women haven't this advantage, leaving them no way to know what's being felt through a dildo. They cannot feel when they are pushing too hard against one wall or another, they cannot feel pressure and softness, acceptance or pleasure. For women with dildos, there is always the chance of hurting someone because of this lack of sensation; a normal woman can instruct, reach back, talk… but in house, a slave cannot and daren't. So in order to prolong treatments, education, or punishment, intendants had been trained in the practice of strokes. Easing themselves in, they got thrusting correct, natural like men before, going heavy with learning, leaving a slave no way out to avoid direction through injury. Groaning out, Urst rotated her powerful hips slowly, filling Jennifer completely, the slave's closed eyes popping open on Nadia's waiting for them, the woman having moved down to see her. As she looked down hungrily into Jennifer's eyes, the charge groaned back, not embarrassed as she struggled with the load, seeing Nadia's support. It showed her they were trying to help, that they were caring for her through it, Jennifer realizing this and groaning out, deciding to give them what they wanted.

Leaving her supported, Nadia moved back to face Urst, both intendants' hands slowly peeling Jennifer's ass cheeks apart, the soft dildo able to glide freely in and out of her now, Urst taking hold strongly on her hips as Nadia still held her cheeks apart, Jennifer starting to groan as her ass was filled. Unable to reach back to place a hand between her and Urst, Jennifer could only groan as Urst pushed deeper inside, Jennifer losing her breath as she was purposefully filled, her body struggling aloud, confirming the Mistress was right.

Struggling, pulling on her restraints, Jennifer gasped, losing it, crying out as a sharp spank from Urst told her to behave, to take it as she filled her, working her professionally from behind. Her legs began to shake uncontrollably, her body trying to pull away as Urst's powerful thighs gave her what she needed, her helpless cries slipping out, leaving her waiting for another spank, but none was to come. Instead, the striking smell of Nadia's hair filled her senses as she nuzzled in beside her head, almost flat on the grass with her, gently telling her…

"Come on, Jennifer, take it, you can do it."

"Come on, that's it."

"Take it for me, make me proud."

"I'm here for you, I'm going to get you through this, but you have to work for me, can you do that?"

Jennifer groaned in acknowledgement, still not receiving permission to speak, something strange about Nadia's voice, she thought, whispering so quiet, as if she didn't want Urst to hear, but quickly that was at the back of her mind, Urst beginning to fuck her deeply, Jennifer imagining her muscular thighs flexing back and forth as she cried, almost losing it, Nadia quickly offering encouragement.

“Heah, come on, you can do it.”

“She’ll be finished soon.”

“Come on, you can take it.”

“Take it for me, huh?” Her voice was tender, her beautiful brown eyes looking into Jennifer’s for an answer. “Take it for me?”

Jennifer nodded as best she could, her collar snap holding her down as her ass was held high for Urst, still working behind her.

It went on for what seemed like an eternity, her legs vibrating uncontrollably as Urst’s final pull out had her moaning uncontrollably, the swelled head’s slow path up inside her straining her walls with an unnatural feeling inside. With its final leaving straining open her asshole, she gasped as it left, her body pulling shut. Her rest, though, wasn’t to be… no rest, no break, Nadia immediately taking her turn, sliding in where Urst had left off, taking hold of her firmly.

Jennifer felt betrayed as she felt her own intendant’s latex cock slide easily in after Urst’s. Betrayed as she lost her breath, waiting to cry out, Urst now down and talking with her at the front, not caring like Nadia, mechanical like an intendant.

“Take it…. You have to learn.”

“It’s the Mistress’s will for you.”

“You have to serve her….”

But she wasn’t concentrating on Urst, as she kept waiting for Nadia, now fully inside, to begin fucking her hard, to begin punishing her as Urst had, to pound her, but she wasn't doing it. Instead, she was gentle, handling her softly, care in her movement… as a lover would fuck. She wouldn't force her, Jennifer could feel that, moaning as she managed her, Jennifer feeling her respond to her struggle, easing as she groaned, shallowing as she strained.

She was fucking her good, it feeling different from Urst's, Jennifer unsure at first, but relaxing into Nadia's rhythm. She wanted her, of course, but still worried, restrained between them. Urst smiled, looking back at Nadia, the show of want groaning from below, slightly embarrassing her as she reddened under Urst's stare. Reddened further as suddenly Jennifer felt something different inside, unsure at first as the feeling rose. Already straining at the limit, she didn't need more pressure, but as it welled up inside as she pulled hard on her collar, the familiar feeling was taking control with the unnatural entry from behind. Flooding back, she screamed uncontrollably as both feelings married inside her, the orgasm feeling like the first, with the strength of the spasms as she gushed out her want. Her handlers were stunned at the gift, Nadia soaked, holding her from behind, both intendants wide-eyed upon her descent into crying, her body jarring, restrained over feelings too strong to take. Collapsing into hysterical tears, Jennifer screamed out as she showered Nadia in love, screaming on beneath her. Momentarily stunned, Nadia couldn't help wrapping around her, showing her care and support, Urst sheepishly pulling back, staggered by the display.

Jennifer sobbing beneath her, Nadia cared and consoled her slave, a quivering wreck crying on between them, sobbing out, Nadia insisting she replied,

Urst watching on as love paraded in front of her.

It went on longer, her intendants still having to do their job, although both were obviously shaken. Jennifer truly groaned in regret when Nadia pulled out, straining on her ankle cuffs to push her ass back toward her, showing she was hers… Urst visibly affected by the display.

Not long after, strung up between two trees, Jennifer was subject to a session of spanking and pinwheels paddling and else, but her intendants had been thrown, such had been the ferocity of her display. Jennifer spread eagle and standing between the trees, they couldn't deal with her as usual, Nadia's love getting in the way of her duty, itself shattered by Jennifer's screams for her on the ground. Urst, too, but in a different way, having no one in her life… she looked on in wanton wish… she was suddenly lonely between them.

Looking deep into her eyes, Nadia meant something to go between them as she took hold of her from the front, nestling her cheek in beside hers, responding to her tiring as Urst continued from behind.

"It's okay, it'll be over soon…" she whispered to her ear, her embrace one of love, Jennifer easily feeling this as Urst's flogging continued.

Urst landed more drops on an already well-punished ass. Held still for her by Nadia, the pain mounted, making her wonder if she'd read Jennifer right as she squirmed and cried through jolts from behind. Held expertly by Nadia, Jennifer's cries seemingly ignored, Urst went from the long lashings to stepping back, just allowing the tips to snap at her ass, the pain intensifying on her cheeks, each snap causing her to cry out in Nadia's ear… but she still held her.

They were making sure she got it right, making sure she had dominance, both intendants rattled by Jennifer's screaming and worried their performance had been affected. It seemed like a lifetime before they finally cut her down, taking her to the tent, Jennifer unable to offer any resistance as she was almost carried by Nadia. Truly under her care now, she was completely at her mercy, her captors still unsure of their discipline and their feelings of sympathy for her… it was unnatural for them to feel such care for a charge… it unnerved them. Taking her into the tent… the sun had gone down as a small fire crackled outside, setting the scene on the final direction. Jennifer moaned as she felt her ass stinging, laid on her back over the mattress they had arranged earlier, the hammerings figured out now as her arms were raised back over her head. Her wrist eyelets were snapped onto tent pegs, two hammered through the plastic tent to the ground underneath. Totally vulnerable and tiring from her ordeal, Jennifer moaned out fearfully, starting to cry at the session's length, Urst suddenly seeing something wrong as Nadia rushed to her aid.

She didn't punish the complaint or direct as she should, her eyes flooding with care as she laid over Jennifer. Taking her in her grip, it was gentle, the emotion felt as she kissed her and cared for her, Jennifer brought around to her gaze.

It worked… Jennifer saw the emotion, responding to Nadia's rush, her silent direction obeyed and trusted… but it was wrong… as this wasn't dominance.

Urst's natural instincts to punish such insolence rose inside her, but met a fearful barrier, making her step back as it came. Made her fear because the barrier came from inside her, not from a threat from Nadia, but a care for Jennifer from herself!

Urst worried and decided to take immediate action, pushing it away as she tried to treat her professionally, Nadia seeing it as she came, their looks exchanging over Jennifer as they paused their power above her.

Nadia could see her worry, and Urst could see her love… without uttering a word, Jennifer watched a quiet understanding being exchanged above her, Urst warned to go easy and Nadia reminded of her duty.

Entering the punishment's final phase, Jennifer growled as Urst's powerful Icelandic body entered inside her, the strap-on opening her femininity below, Jennifer feeling aggrieved as she looked to Nadia beside her, feeling she was hers and this an outrage. This staggering breach of etiquette should have brought sanctions immediately, but all the women's directions had been thrown by the emotion. Working on, Urst's determination had even vanished after watching the love in the pair's eyes, even she feeling this was wrong, that she was stepping where she shouldn't. Her huge thigh muscles united with the rest of her body, over Jennifer, they could easily deliver more power lying down… but they didn't. Jennifer moaned out as Nadia lay by their side, gently stroking her hair. Urst was shaken and didn't continue long, Jennifer's emotion throwing her off, the last part of her learning finished with one intendant unsure how to continue, and another smitten and unable to begin. Urst made a final effort to push her feelings aside and grind hard into Jennifer, but her sudden panicked moan reached deep into Nadia's heart, her coming immediately to Urst's shoulder… it was over. Nadia couldn't watch this happen to Jennifer anymore, her eyes not angry at Urst, but definitely telling her… Urst withdrew.

Nadia took over… Jennifer confused and not objecting, but feeling aggrieved again as another intendant tried to finish her, tried to obey her professional demands within her and finish the treatment.

Jennifer cried under her, realizing she had to do it, that it was the way of the house, but all women could feel it as they lost a fight with something stronger.

Nadia tried… years of training fought for control in her to thrust into Jennifer as she knew she should… but she couldn't. Under Jennifer's tears, Nadia instinctively fell on her, tongue finding hers, thrusting coming to an end, Jennifer moaning below as their love passed between them. Nadia didn't withdraw… she couldn't. Instead, as Jennifer's crying audibly changed from pain to love, Urst was left uncomfortable beside them as the two fell to love in front of her. Jennifer's body had been pushed all day, sore inside and limp with fatigue; it was Nadia's love, though, that took her to it. Her care felt all over, and within, it took nothing after Urst for Nadia's movements to bring a last screaming gift from her. Showered again, Nadia held her as she screamed, unable not to grind as she held her loving agony. Shaking to a cry, Jennifer sobbed with her love, the two women shattered emotionally, Urst finally making her mind up to leave, but her look caught by Nadia as she went, her hand arriving on her shoulder.

Caught looking longingly at their relationship, feeling an emptiness at not having her own, but Nadia stopped her from leaving.

Urst looked confused as she saw the look in Nadia. Stunned by the offer, she didn't know what to do, Nadia looking down at Jennifer while holding Urst from leaving left Jennifer stunned, as well; she wasn't telling… she was asking.

With the emotions they had been through all day, the three women all wanted to be close to someone, Jennifer initially confused before realizing what she meant, seeing Urst's loneliness above her and Nadia asking her to sooth it, drawing a finger over her cheek, suggesting. Jennifer, seeing Urst's need and Nadia's love above her, was touched by the display of care… she smiled her acceptance.

Nadia's offering of Jennifer between them almost moved Urst to tears, Jennifer's look up of warmth finally releasing them as she was broken by the offer… after everything she'd done to her.

Roles reversed for a time, Jennifer uncuffed and teaching as she felt a care in Urst's touch, a care she'd never felt before. Nadia held back jealousy as she watched her teach her lessons. Urst's learning that night would lead directly to her future, when a care of her own enrolled, she able to bring her to her heart after learning how to treat her from Jennifer.

Instead of being punished through the last of the lesson that night, Jennifer was secretly loved by her intendants. Against the direct will of the Mistress, she was given pleasure from the one she loved and from another she'd come to respect, the three sharing a night they would never forget.

Chapter 27

Ballroom

The Mistress had finally had enough of Andrea, standing early that morning before the rest of the house rose as she was held by her wrists in the entrance to the ballroom. Her two leather-clad assailants looked ahead as usual, as if trained in some military establishment, no one talking as, in front of them in the large oval-shaped room, six more intendants squatted down, their gorgeous stockinged thighs mouth-watering under their leather corsets.

The room's soft cream walls and ornate cornicing did nothing to calm Andrea as she was forced to stand naked in the large doorway at the entrance to the room. In front of her, the intendants squatting down were busy lifting steel rings up from recesses in the wooden floor, these having been barely visible as they worked them out with their fingers. Finally lifting them all, two stood up, one moving to the back wall, the other nearer the doorway, making for the wall-mounted hand cranks that had held the curtain on that fateful day. Besides them, two more ominous looking intendants who, all the while, had been standing directly across from those holding Andrea, never flinched, eyes fixed squarely on her. With the bay windows behind them, they stared at her from the other side of the room as if trying to hold back anger with professionalism as they glared.

That meant ten intendants in all were in the room, Andrea suddenly realizing as the hand cranks began to turn the reason why she was here. Above, two steel wires with attachments at the end began to lower from the pulley system through small holes in the ceiling. Unnoticed before, they came down accompanied by the sound of winches, these hidden away above the roof, out of sight. Listening to the gentle trundling, Andrea began to get nervous as the wires came within reach of the four intendants, all still squatting down. For some reason, they had remained in a square arrangement on the floor – the two on the left, one behind the other, now reaching up and taking the attachments, and guiding their descent onto the steel rings, attaching their fittings as Andrea suddenly realized what she was seeing.

Within their dorms at night, the intendants, while securing, took great pleasure in letting rumors slip, half to frighten the women to submission and half to torment as they kept control. Andrea, like many others, had heard the rumor of a punishment reserved for slaves who had pushed the boundaries of the house's patience. Slaves like her who, after all this time, still had slip-ups of mind. She wasn't an unruly patient… she just had trouble focusing for long periods of time, her fun and carefree nature, which had everyone warm easily to her, getting in the way of house procedure. This had been seen by the Mistress many times before Sports Day, even she letting it slide as she saw the potential in Andrea's form. It wasn't so much that she couldn't concentrate, and there certainly wasn't a lack of commitment – she just had to be focused more on her environment. Letting her slip-ups go, the Mistress – because she had warmed to her like everyone else – blamed herself for Andrea's wayward attitude. Had she simply dealt with her on instinct, in a harsh manner from the beginning, this would never have happened, and this approaching procedure would never have to have been carried out. Realizing this, the Mistress had revised to correct this mistake, and fallen back on her own assuredness, the harshness coming back to her, hand over Andrea, the correction she surely needed. Without this sudden shock, the subject would continue carrying this misattention with her, it burdening her further as she travelled her chosen path. This would not do because, as they advanced her training, this attitude would only get in the way of delivering her back to her Mistress, the house's reputation given ill with the delay, so something had to be done….

With that in the mind of the Mistress, Andrea was jarred suddenly as the intendants at either end of the room had swapped gearing in the pulley system, and had begun turning again, bringing a second set of steel wires dropping down between the first. Watching on, the clicking of the winches echoed round the room from their hiding place above the roof as the final set of steel wires was brought between them, the first set already connected to the floor rings by the intendants. As the new steel came within reach, two of the four intendants still squatting on the floor stood up on the right, leaving two still waiting for the falling wires, their work almost at a close. Moving off for the back wall, Andrea watched the two who'd risen, their movement in steps of perfect form, swaying hips as corsets glided.

Andrea began to shiver, looking at the two intendants directly facing her, as the two walking away from her passed them. Silent all the while, they were clothed differently from the others. Still in corsets, their uniforms had something different, something the women had come to hate, fear growing as Andrea realized… they were in chastity.

Finally, Andrea knew why they looked so angry – they had been worked up. This was a house term for intendants who were used to punish unruly slaves. Not content with their professionalism, the Mistress would sometimes insist on the raw desire-driven rage that could be brought out among her staff and used to heighten a slave's correction. To achieve this special working, rooms off limits to the house patients were used. These rooms on the third level had large circular leather racks where intendants, spread eagle, would be secured, already naked. The racks resembling huge table tops, one at either side of the grey tiled empty room would then be raised to face the back wall, the intendants chosen having to reluctantly accept their duty as sisters around them readied them further. The intendants chosen for this procedure were fitted with house chastity – the Mistress, if possible, finding the most reluctant participants to guarantee their anger. The belts with their special construction ensured the virtual impossibility of any feeling within, even the experienced staff knowing no way to deal with them. This, then, rendered it a miserable experience for intendants, used to being in full control and having satisfaction at their fingertips. Once secure and elevated, the chosen, for the next half hour, would watch the large screen on the room's back wall where the Mistress's dictation, recorded earlier, would detail her wishes on procedures to come. The recording would show the slave in question, explaining her crimes and what was to come of her, making sure, in no uncertain terms, that the intendants knew that it was her failure that had brought them this torment. After this, a selection of mouth-watering adult entertainments would be played for the next two hours, the intendants suffering through it, only having their belts unlocked at the end to allow relief of any restroom issues. Finally, their belts would be secured a second time as floor mats where brought in, and a selection of intendants performed live in front of them, their groaning pleasure completing a last half hour of torture.

Standing now in front of them, Andrea could see the desire in their eyes mixed with anger, and the wish to carry it to her. In front of them, the two still squatting on the floor held the second set of wires, these no longer dropping as the winches rested silently, hidden above them. Their rest, though, was short-lived as, again, their winch gearing was changed and their handles were turned in reverse. The first set of wires connected to the floor rings now rose, the slack in the cables' length quickly taken up as an ominous sound now joined the room. The clunking sound hidden above signaled the winches straining as they hoisted the cables, a sharp cracking sound from the floor below revealing a secret that a slave learn. In the floor below the cables, a fine line appeared, hidden before, cracking open, showing a ten foot by eight foot rectangle hinging up on its right side, hoisted up and away by the winches above. Andrea looked on, stunned as a thick wall of wood lifted on its hinged side, revealing a frightening sight waiting for her below. Her eyes fell on the rumor, the one they'd laughed at and argued about over meals. Looking into the shallow pit, she saw a large rectangular steel box waiting underneath. Shivering, she watched the remaining two intendants attaching the second set of wires to steel rings, lifted from the rumor below, to the door of the forgotten prison!

The intendants had laughed in the dorms, securing them some nights, Andrea and the others feeling sure they were just trying to frighten them. They'd listened as they heard talk of a secret chamber, the forgotten prison. Buried somewhere under the house's floors, it was an extreme measure for a failing slave. They'd claimed this eight feet by six feet chamber was only one and a half feet high, built that way so that a slave secured in it, spread eagle, would be forced against two angry intendants secured in with her to the dark below. Buried under the floor, they laughed as they claimed, sometimes, they were forgotten about, the slave getting much more punishment than intended, and hence the chamber gaining its name over the years of use. Laughing, they had talked of slaves' terror as darkness fell on their masked confinement. The Manor not being content with just sealing them in, for added effect, slaves were face-masked, not hooded and restricted as with the Mistress's pleasure, but left able to hear and scream, simply unable to see at all. An unnecessary addition, as they were in darkness anyway, the mask simply used to add pressure to the charge and to ensure one other vital thing… to hold their mouth open. Held for hours and secured, this forced opening would bring fear, but was actually for safety, no one able to see or assist for those hours as two crazed intendants might get carried away… hopefully. Under the floor, their muffled cries would be unheard through a steel door and a floor above them, their angry tenders sealed beside them, having no mercy after being driven wild.

There was no laughing now, though, as Andrea

heard the winches raise, the second set of wires above the pit, the steel door below lifting up like the floor before it. Opening, the door hinged up on its right side, old hinges grinding as the fear inside was revealed at last…. Andrea stared open-mouthed at the small interior, its floor of padded rubber revealing restraints at each corner. The restraints would give their occupier the position of complete vulnerability. Trapped spread eagle on its floor, the slave would experience the steel walls on either side, strewn with countless implements, from wheels to crops from wands to lotions, all neatly secured in leather strapping and within easy reach for those inside.

With the door almost fully lifted, the two squatting intendants reached inside, their hands bringing forth house strapons, their black lengths soon to glisten as they were attached. Slowly standing and moving to the worked-up intendants, they fitted their tools of correction as they continued standing motionless, glaring at Andrea before them. Fitted and secured in place, Andrea watched the hourglass figures of the intendants move to the back wall while the first two came back, giving her gentle eye contact, lulling her into a false sense of security as they feigned care. Soon, that faint notion flew from her as Andrea saw them squat at the pit, reaching in to the implements inside, bringing forth a black leather face mask.

Andrea began to whimper as they approached, the slave struggling a little in her intendants' grip, her wrists held fast, whimpering all the more as the mask was wrapped on her, the world falling black. Inside the mask, she squealed as a black plastic gum mounting found its way into her mouth, filling her front gum line almost completely, forcing her cheeks to follow its form as it held her mouth open. With it being comfortable and designed to stay away from the back of her mouth to ensure no sensitivity or inadvertent vomiting, she was still easily able to swallow, but the fear was its forced opening. Forced to bite down around its edges, she lost the fight immediately as leather straps were secured behind her head, her breathing secured and made safe, but her mouth held open for those who'd be in with her.

Her struggles were ignored as she was firmly moved, now feeling four sets of hands lift her, securing her down into the box, the environment pushing her nerves over the edge as she started to cry. Panicking as she felt the leather restraints wrapped round her wrists and ankles, crying gave way to breathing heavily as she heard two ominous sets of heels sharply tacking on the floor toward her, the sound echoing around the box.

Suddenly, pleasure and fear engulfed her as two silky forms began to touch her, sliding in beside her, one on each side, immediately starting to kiss and stroke wherever they wished, Andrea's senses thrown to panic. About to scream as hands explored between her legs, and a suddenly clang signaled her sealed in, the door closed on her and her captors, a scraping of steel signaling a padlock making sure. Nerves screaming, she pulled against her restraints involuntarily, her captors smiling at her panic between them. As she screamed in the dark below, those above could barely hear her, the steel door holding her struggle within. With the slow clunking sound above echoing through the box, her struggles were snuffed out completely as the floor lowered down above her,

Andrea pulling in terror as the gravity of what was happening set in.

Above, eight sets of heels connected sharply with the wooden floor, driven by eight corseted leather forms as they left the room peaceful and empty behind them, the quiet beguiling the terror going on underneath it….

Such was the secrecy of the house that no one but the Mistress and those intendants involved knew, not a chance of hearing anything either as, within twenty minutes, an intendants' ball had started, the intendants laughing and drinking, bringing their charges for the day in, discussing all of that week's advances, the music blaring as some began to dance, their thighs straining to the music.

Straining of a different kind going on underneath, though, Andrea screaming at times, her captors running wheels up and down her, reveling in her discomfort. They had endless energy, pushed by endless desire, having been worked up and left utterly horny in their chastity. There was nothing they could do to relieve their desires… nothing but make her suffer for them.

Chapter 28

The Party

In light of the recent breaches of etiquette at such a late stage, and with the Mistress finally calming down after her punishment had been given out, she became concerned with the house course, wanting to make sure they would deliver well.

Her solution, as usual, was unexpected, different, and brilliant… a party.

In this, she sought to insure the slaves knew their place, not only as the intendants' muses, but of their role when they left the house, the parties they held occasionally excellent simulation of real gatherings on the outside which would come to them later.

To keep them as realistic as possible, great fanfare was made of them, the knowledge of their arrival made common, the women encouraged to look forward and prepare to behave, to show their skills in learning proper, to impress with their professionalism.

Impressive, too, was the party dress – many intendants, although not all, leaving behind the fine corseted house uniform in favor of dressing in costumed finery, the nights sparkling and intense, always surprising and fun.

It was encouraged among staff, but not admitted, that their behavior was to be toned down, their standard harsh corrections not to be employed, the women to have great enjoyment in these events. Repeated immersion in this way trained women to look forward and view events as huge fun, a real chance to let their hair down, leaving them ever willing to go to more… good training for their leaving… good behavior implanted gently.

Nadia smiled at Jennifer, stroking her face with the backs of her fingers as she sat dutifully on her knees in front of her in the Ballroom, Nadia holding her leash as intendants passed, giving impressed looks, nodding to Nadia at Jennifer's fine behavior, leaving her proud of her favorite. Nadia had seemed to guard her more after the incident, seeming to worry about her feelings, talking quietly with her as the music played on, behavior not common for staff. It was more than worry, though her smiles at Jennifer were unable to hide her truth, all seeing it as they passed, no one even attempting to put their hands on Jennifer as slaves around her were used for pleasure… no one dared.

Noticing Andrea being missing, Jennifer inquired, where could she be? Not knowing she was kneeling right over her with Nadia, and Nadia laughed when she asked, now tolerant of Jennifer's interest, but giving her a sharp spank to her ass just to satisfy anybody watching. Responding to Jennifer's hurt look, she grabbed her after it, feigning anger while telling her why she'd had to do it… for the audience around her, telling her not to worry about Andrea before parting her panties, her own wine drinking and the screams of pleasure around her arousing her want. Pulling Jennifer forward and down by her leash, her legs were open to greet her, satisfaction her job now, Nadia getting off on the knowledge of what was going on right beneath them aware what the Mistress had decided because of her closeness to her unlike most of the other intendants milling around them. Jennifer unaware of Andrea's struggles beneath her, this hidden by the music, was made to concentrate on Nadia, her tongue reaching out to her silken work, groaning against the moistness as a playful spank was delivered to her rear.

The party was great, the women having fun, the time of their lives… some even given champagne, giddy with the offering, the Manor's rules relaxing as their behavior improved… all except one…

Jennifer couldn't understand why she was absent, but daren't ask further… for now, she had been instructed to wait in the west wing of the first level near the showers with Carly… she'd been left with the jackal. Not understanding, she stood quietly in form, behaving… Carly did not.

Champagne telling she had had fun with Jennifer, Nadia no sooner out of earshot, and her hands were wandering. Pestering her for fun, she teased and worked a now constant victim after her refusal on the grounds… Carly just wouldn't let it go.

Jennifer tried not to smile, though, as Carly moved back reluctantly to form, the sound of Nadia's boots approaching in the distance showing who was the wolf.

Boots approaching, Jennifer stayed on, keeping form, her look down, not challenging, not looking in the direction of the arrivals. After such a good night, she wanted to make Nadia happy, perform for her love, show her commitment… it would at least keep Carly in check as she watched the devotion, knowing it went both ways. Jennifer couldn't see the irritation on Carly's face, but knew it was there – she could tell by the way she was standing, her drooped head watching Carly's body language as all slaves had learned to do over the months… she had to fight hard to contain her smile.

With head drooped, she didn't see or hear the approaching answer to her concerns, her bare feet making no sound as she approached between Urst and Nadia, suddenly coming into view between their leather finery.

She almost looked up, but fought it down, Nadia smiling as she watched her, proud of her struggle.

"Jennifer...."

Jennifer lifted her head to the Latin music, it washing through her ears as her eyes gave all.

"You are to help Andrea, as she's been through a lot," continued Nadia softly, Jennifer seeing a strange Andrea... not crying, just tired looking.

As the strange scene played out, Jennifer was given Andrea's hand, she worryingly not looking up and Jennifer knowing full well what the look meant, having seen it on Linda times before... she was close to cracking.

"Take as long as you need," Urst informed softly, it seeming strange when she tried to be so gentle, Jennifer correctly guessing that Andrea was in a bad way as she looked for confirmation, Nadia nodding.

Instinct taking over, she correctly acknowledged Nadia's wishes, carrying them out as she guided Andrea to the showers.

Intendants remaining outside, they were out of earshot quickly, and sight, too, as Jennifer rounded the front wall, ensuring she took Andrea right to the back, a strange obedience following her hand.

With the waters running now, no one could hear them speak. Even the cameras hidden above had difficulty when the water ran, the intendants behind them satisfied to watch and observe, it obvious how things were going as Andrea suddenly fell to pieces in Jennifer's arms as she took her between them.

Pulling back, Jennifer had to seize her, Andrea slapping her and trying to fight away as she bawled in her arms, her experiences trying to make her run. Sobbing and strengthless, she was now back where it all began, doing what she'd been told not to, what had got her what she'd been given. Punished and broken, she sobbed in Jennifer's grip, her tears flowing with the showers as intendants watched the agony from above.

"You don't know what they'll do!" Andrea sobbed, trying to pull away one more time, but with no strength left from her treatments, Jennifer determined to hold her close.

She listened to her agony, tried to console her as she spoke, Andrea shaking on, only barely hearing her voice as she replied… she was so scared.

Jennifer was enraged, and she came out of the shower finally, holding Andrea by the hand, her anger so great at them that she had to let it out… she didn't care. She glared straight through Carly, even challenged Urst, the intendants stunned for a moment and not sure how to respond, Nadia watching and seeing the anger in her charge. Jennifer saw her hand lift, motioning the other two, holding them off as she looked on at her, Jennifer concerned at the raw emotion. Trying hard not to give her the same, Jennifer tried not to glare at her, but only barely held it off as she held a broken form by her hand beside her. As Urst reached for her, Jennifer suddenly pulled her back, Andrea sobbing as she did so, Nadia's hand raising once again.

A long pause, the intendants shocked at the

display… a stand-off.

It took great experience to manage these situations. Over the years, the intendants had seen countless breakdowns, had been responsible for most of them, and they knew full well when people were on the edge.

"It's time to go to sleep…" Nadia finally said softly, Jennifer struggling to respond properly, not able to look at her completely, angry at every house uniform for Andrea's condition standing beside her…. "We should walk down together," she looked enquiringly at Jennifer, not telling her, just offering… a look of understanding on her face.

Jennifer calmed slightly, responding to her voice; it was a voice she had grown to trust, if that was possible in the program. She watched Nadia motion with her hand toward the hallway, down the wing.

Jennifer looked at Andrea, still holding her, looking back enquiringly, Nadia nodding… the two allowed together as the three corsets followed behind.

As they went slowly on, the intendants above looked shocked at the cameras, two slaves in company with their intendants following their lead… this wasn't right.

The Mistress, upon the report, almost exploded with the news, but it was hers who saw it happen, hers who had made it true. She would never lift a hand openly to Nadia, but she'd pushed her this time to the very edge, and the fight they had in her chambers the next night was there for all to hear, the rage sounding through the Manor like a war from high above.

Right now, though, it was below that was the concern, the procession followed closely on the cameras, Jennifer escorting a still sobbing form forward, the cramped nature of the level in bringing her down the dull amber darkness triggering her fear, Jennifer having to console her, twice stopping to hold her from running back.

When they finally got inside, she wouldn't let her go. Another stand-off in close quarters, Nadia in quiet command, the room witness to the power of someone special in your life. All the power in the world, and there was nothing she could do to her. Everyone watched as Jennifer finally and, for the first time, openly challenged Nadia in front of them, saying nothing, but not releasing, not following Nadia's direction. Nadia looked at her, a look of quiet anger, as she had wanted Jennifer to calm Andrea, and thought it best it was her, to sooth the pain they had been through, to show them it was over and that they'd been forgiven… but she hadn't expected this.

Standing angry at the challenge, she looked at Andrea still there tearful beside her, and looked back at Jennifer, holding her hand, shielding her under her empty protection, Nadia weighing up what to do with her. She hadn't realized Andrea was quite so bad off, hadn't realized they'd done this much damage. She thought of wrenching the two apart and imposing order… of forcing Jennifer's submission, that the room could watch her downed. She thought of the result and the outcome… of Andrea, sure to leave, and she thought of Jennifer and her feelings… of their love for each other now.

She left that part out in her battle with the Mistress, had to scream of her strategy to stop the pair of them leaving, the Mistress enraged and knowing full well about Jennifer. Not an idiot, and totally in control, nothing in house escaped her. Her show of force on her Nadia evident the next day, both with bruising marks, but Nadia's worse. She would show her how to dominate, show her the correct course of action, correct her failure in-house, the whole staff baring witness to it.

Nadia knew this would happen, knew it as she stood there weighing up what to do, whether she would carry this burden for her and whether she really was in her heart… she would.

Jennifer would feel so sorry for her when she saw her injuries, but she was strong and shook it off when they were alone, and Jennifer tried to care… Jennifer would never again question whether her feelings were real.

The injuries came from Nadia's decision, her open defiance of the Mistress's course. Shocking Urst and Carly, too, she had them shackled together on Jennifer's bed, the very position that had started it all and the very reason it had happened…. it worked.

Andrea didn't leave… drawing strength from Jennifer's help and seeing the battle with those around her, she was more devoted than ever to her side… just more careful… sharper.

Nadia may have been able to have those under her see her weakened, but the Mistress would certainly not, the house bearing full witness to why it was her will that led them forward, Nadia's body her standard, bared. Her open challenge on her wishes was met with pain, Nadia reminded of her place, held between them, the Mistress making sure she understood and making sure the house knew, as well….

No one would have dared do as Nadia had done…

No one would ever do it again….

Chapter 29

Held Below

The house was tense, picked up by all that had gone on that morning, and the women desperately tried not to put a foot wrong.

Even the morning's example that day accepted her punishment with such grace that the women were in awe at the learning. Secured by two, as usual, her acceptance of her direction through anal measures was heard purring around the dorm, the fourth intendant's guarding unnecessary as powerful thighs convulsed rhythmically, bringing her home.

The tightness didn't lift, all the way through breakfast and showers, and on to the main hall where intendants stood rigid, the women fearing what that must mean as they waited in assemblance.

Together in their circle, the intendants could be seen snapping to an even tighter stance than usual, pulling on their invisible reins, forcing their charges to do the same as the Mistress swept into the room under guard.

"Well," she began with a short but pleased survey of the room. "It seems I have before me some of the finest examples of femininity ever assembled in this house."

Praise was usually followed by punishment, and the women steeled themselves for what must come now, the Mistress slowly parading in front of them.

"Shame, then, I have to do this to you," she said with uncharacteristic concern. "Your training is entering its final phases," she explained. "Soon, you will go forth carrying the banner of this great house with all the responsibility that that brings."

The women, still reeling from such praise, stiffened more at the candor, sure they'd be soon paying for such a rarity, a usual insistence of the Mistress.

"With that, then, I feel no guilt with what I'm about to do with you," the Mistress went on, confirming the women's belief in her way of strength over charges. "With this house's reputation at stake, you must and you will be steeled against all you must go through as you endure the happiness you have chosen through the honor to serve."

The Mistress spoke in riddles sometimes, never quite giving them details about their day, it being a known delight of hers to watch the fear on the faces, her verbal torturing given freely as it wrapped them up in worry, their contemplating the hardships to come.

Not just sadism, but recognized control of the highest standards, compared to the unprofessionalism of those wielding just whip and brute force… bad form and an example telling of an amateur. True domination was subtle, coercive and invisible, yet strong, words wielded, not whips; slaves bound in-house with emotion and with subtlety, with chains they could never undo, the Mistress's reins never leaving them.

"And so, to lessons you must have," the Mistress assured them, pausing and looking along their display. "Lessons that will shock some of you… lessons that will disgust some of you!" she assured the women, actual regret showing for a moment in her eyes, bringing fear to their order. "I want you to understand that I feel for those who are about to struggle with this, but it is necessary for you to fulfill all your duties of servitude and provide all the happiness that your owners may require from you as you travel with them on that road to fulfillment."

The Mistress's true showing of reluctance for them now had minds cased in fear, whirring through all the devices and rooms, all the equipment and tortures, and what could possibly still be brought on them now which they hadn't seen before….

Men!!!

Relief was palpable, but met confused looks, smiles encouraged by intendants as they delighted with them in their laughter. It was explained that, over the next week, the women were to be put through what the Mistress believed to be horrific, her hatred of men in general seeing her very much absent that week, direction left almost entirely to the intendants.

As the Mistress had predicted, a few who shared her virtues were disgusted at what they were put through, truly disturbed and needing great management, at times, from the intendants. Others, too, as the Mistress had described, were shocked at the depth of this training, the intendants putting them in every position and multiplicity, every gut-wrenching and screaming defilement, their bodies offered and filled in every conceivable way that they believed was necessary.

This shock did not extend to all the women, however – many being appalled as a few truly enjoyed themselves, Julie in particular, that little slut!

She was, though, to the womens' delight, reined in one evening, the intendants themselves irritated by just how much fun she was having, and thoroughly used as an example to certain others, to maintain professional behavioral standards in house. Even the following day, Julie found herself being the morning's example, a very thorough dealing with by the intendants hearing her groan through half of breakfast after what they did to her, a clear message to all that:

"Standards would be maintained!!!"

And so, to evenings of hurting inside in peculiar ways, ways forgotten almost with their confinement having gone on so long, smiles brought to some with the memories given, irritation to others at this thrusting unprofessionalism. Irritated at the enjoyment of the life, tools as the intendants called them, the men's grunting enjoyment after the supply of their bodies and the hurt they left angered even the deepest of submissives at various points.

Such was the irritation that the cool professionalism of the intendants' punishments and directions, when necessary, over wayward attitudes in those weeks, were suddenly seen in a new light, and with respect! Such was the skill and experience they had when compared with the grunting buffoonery of the life tools that the women felt at peace after being dealt with by them, instead of in pain from these groaning neanderthals.

Such was the contrast between the two sides of this endurance that week that the intendants suddenly came to view a huge surge of appreciation for them and their cool professional direction. This was not a surprise to the intendants, their having seen this many times before when the women in house were given a taste of the real world they were going back to, with all its frailties and nonsense… but they did appreciate it.

It was lucky they did because the appreciation poured fourth in their outright submission to the intendants, utterly unmistakable for the first time, there being no resistance at all and the women truly happy to be under their stewardship. The intendants noticed, their smiles and laughs back and forth to each other coming easily at the incredibly good behavior, effort by the women giving way to nods of appreciation, intendants' hands then stroking and caring for the first time, unable to hide their own appreciation as the women came to truly look up to them.

This caring, though, extended only to the women, the intendants also irritated and even angered by the male enjoyment of their charges, silly noises of pleasure with them seeing them meet out some incredibly strong punishment. Indeed, the women themselves were shocked at the displays of savagery, the intendants seeming to have no care at all for the males' suffering as they dealt with what they termed:

"Disrespect in house."

New screams of pain, true hurt and fear in pleading

voices, echoed around the wings, women wincing at times as they witnessed true terror in some of the men, they having no training to deal with it like the women had gained over the months.

Having no understanding of the way or paths, no correct etiquette or submission routes, they had no way to manage or deal with the intendants' unbelievable savagery. Reduced to screaming tears and begging pleas, their howls were drowned out under screams of anger as groups of leather fury fell like lions on prey.

More than once, men were carried away, saved only by the eyes of the control room intendants hurriedly sent to pull them free of savage violence, groups of intendants descending on them in frenzies of anger after untrained behavior and the breaking of rules.

Even the house psychiatrist, so good with the women, remained tight and unhelpful. At times, she was present in hallways as bawling creatures were taken away amid screams of angry intendants, these women held back by others, raging at not being able to continue their onslaught. Blood and tears of the men on the marble tile seemed to bring no natural care from the psychiatrist, Jennifer observed, even sure she'd seen her smirk one night when a truly broken male was carried away. Her guess was that the psychiatrist only had to be present to satisfy legal concerns in house, and had no intention of helping the males… and she was right.

And so, then, to her appreciation of the intendants; just like the others, it began to gush forth undeniably through her utterly wanton submission, and this day would see one given total devotion.

Nadia smiled as she saw Jennifer struggle to

maintain herself among the others that morning, after Nadia had whispered during unshackling that she'd be responsible, personally, for her learning that day… just the two of them.

Through breakfast and assemblance, she had to fight hard to keep her practiced dropped look of submission while, inside, her body strained in anticipation as she thought of her intendant.

Nadia leading her through the Manor to the stairway was the hardest thing to deal with, her tight-toned Hispanic curves teasing with every crack of her heels, sending shudders through her muscle, the strain under the leather like Jennifer's beside her. At one point, Jennifer even considered doing something wrong, such was her wanton desire, so that even Nadia's fury would have brought her to flow, but she thought of Nadia's reputation, and instead kept her head bowed and showed respect.

They were to go to the lowest level for today's training… but they never made it…. Unknown to Jennifer, Venezuelan lust was raging through Hispanic veins which suddenly turned off at the second level, heading straight to a room she knew was vacant.

With the door locking them in darkness, Jennifer was almost smashed to the ground as a torrent of Spanish she couldn't understand ravaged over her, the sound of leather ripping off joining it and the feel of warm skin as the body she'd begged for wrapped itself around her. Almost immediately, her femininity was jammed against a soaking Nadia, another torrent of Spanish bringing fingers and want, Nadia savagely ripping at her, forcing her love down on top of her as Jennifer's groaning acceptance drove her wild, the two women writhing in darkness and screaming in passion.

Nadia kissed her like she'd never been kissed before afterward, held her like she'd never been held before, and all she could smell was her… all she wanted was her.

Leaving the room, Jennifer had to maintain her slaven face, but Nadia didn't…. She laughed teasingly as she watched Jennifer's training kick in, and guided her playfully as they descended to the fourth level.

Nadia was truly troubled by Jennifer's trepidation and her timid look as they came off the final stairs, but the charge couldn't help it – every time she'd entered this place, a new horror had awaited.

Through its dark, musty cold west wing, the odd and dull sickly light fought weakly from an overhead covering, through the grime over its square plastic, barely giving enough to light the rubbish and debris under it, the wing and the rest of its junk strewn along the floor remaining in darkness, the lights like small beacons to move toward in the gloom.

Nadia fought to reassure her as she led her Jennifer. "This is an easy day; don't worry…. it's not you who'll be doing the screaming," she smiled.

With their passing debris and old-looking fabric, the cold dark atmosphere did its work to frighten the charge as she held tightly to Nadia's hand, the fabric brushing off her naked legs as they moved. She could hear her own breath, squeezing Nadia's hand harder as she guided her through the labyrinth of darkness, screams of pain heard at times, but not from slaves… from men!

Turning finally to a steel door, Jennifer could only just make it out as Nadia rapped on the door with the palm of her hand. A short pause later saw it finally crack open and out toward them, the shuddering sound of old hinges turning joining its creaking weight, worrying Jennifer further as a hand on her back quickly pushed her inside.

With the door closing behind them, Jennifer's eyes widened… a jail! And more, directly ahead of them, ten from the door against the right wall, an intendant sat seated at a small table, a monitor in front showing three infrared camera views of both directions down the wing, as well as the outside front of the door they'd just come through.

Immediately to her left, an open door led to a sight that stunned and frightened Jennifer, as a naked, terrified man had two intendants, completely ignorant of his fear, attaching electrodes to every part of his body. Stood upright and secured to an apparatus resembling a steel mattress, small units displaying his heart rate and vital signs were on a table below him and to his right. His terrified eyes pleaded out to Jennifer, as if daring not to speak as she watched one of the intendants squat down between his legs and attach electrodes to his testicles, one already being wrapped around his penis as the door suddenly closed on the scene, the other intendant pushing it shut from behind.

A passing smile to the guard from Nadia brought a malevolent and disturbing smile back, the guard clearly amused by what was happening in the room across from her.

Behind the guard, on the right wall, another door stood slightly open and let laughter escape as busy boots could be heard moving around, as if arranging something inside.

Beyond the wall, a large open area recessed into the right wall with one desk and intendant sitting behind it was faced by an area on the other side of the room, this filled with older and worn uncomfortable-looking apparatuses and implements. Nadia would explain later that male comfort was not their concern, and fine new expensive leather implements would not be wasted in beating men when needed, as she put it, harshly.

Jennifer was taken aback as she looked right from these rooms toward the back wall where her eyes fell on an olden-style barred prison facility, eight feet wide from the left wall and running twenty feet back to the rear wall. The bars ran from floor to ceiling, and inside, Jennifer could make out a dozen men or so, the same ones used during this week's training, lying on wooden benches, battered and bruised and clearly suffering as they sat or lay quietly, still cuffed inside the cell, under blankets and rags.

"Here to sign for number nine," Jennifer heard Nadia say as the charge remained shocked, staring at the suffering.

"He's still quite fresh, even exhibits misbehavior at times; he's really not been properly broken down yet… are you sure you don't want a hand, just in case?" the guard replied, fishing for paperwork and handing Nadia a pen.

"No, just have him delivered and secured in room 2, and I'll manage from there," Nadia assured her, already starting to sign the paperwork laid in front of her.

"Showered?" the guard asked.

"Yes," Nadia confirmed. "See that he's cleaned up

before securing, please," she replied, and in such a matter of fact way that it drew Jennifer's attention as she finally signed all the paperwork and turned around to her, breaking into a smile and giving a little excited twitch of her eyebrows as she approached, as if…

"Shut Up!!!"

A screech followed by a savage slap suddenly came from the open doorway, Nadia looking at Jennifer with a mischievous smile as she took her by the arm and guided her to the open door, their eyes falling on another terrified man inside, one side of his face bright red. Inside the horrible concrete room with the slightest tinge of green on the walls, one solitary light bulb hanging from the middle of the ceiling fought to reveal more. Below it, a fearful man lay naked on an old wooden table, this being at waist height and eight feet long, its solid wooden construction boasting a three foot width, and the man's hands secured by the wrist to each leg at the top while his ankles were settled just the same at the table's bottom. Around him, four intendants were busy preparing something, their excited mirth betraying a relish for something that was about to happen.

Two stood crouched to either side of his head, including the glaring one who'd just slapped him, to his right, while two stood to either side of his waist, one fumbling with something Jennifer just barely saw as she put it back in her garter pouch… lubricant.

"A ha ha!" The intendant on the left side of his head exclaimed as Jennifer saw the one on the left side of his waist begin a rhythmic motion with her arm that could only mean one thing.

A squeeze from Nadia brought Jennifer to her mischievous smile as she pushed her by the waist, a little closer so that they could see clearer inside.

The man groaned.

"What did I just tell you!?" the one at the right of his head threatened.

"Oh, let him groan," the other immediately opposite her condescended, pretending to care. "He's going to be doing a lot of it soon, aren't you, darlin'?" she laughed in the man's face with the other one as the man looked back in terror. A strange look, Jennifer thought, being as they were doing something so nice for him, it seemed; what were they about to do to him, she thought, as the rhythm of the arm increased.

Another groan.

"That's it, sweetie, come to me," the other intendant across the waist from the one supplying the rhythm had all the intendants laughing as she waved her half-clenched hand over the now terrified looking man, and with glee. More groans as the intendant directly across from her brought him closer, skillfully working his member in between them, the man beginning to groan out more and more as the intendants' smiles increased, as if waiting for something. Rhythm increasing, the sound echoed around the room as the man began to pull at his restraints, his body beginning to convulse as he groaned out, only making the intendant work harder on him, his groaning getting louder as he pulled at his restraints, one of the intendants unable to resist reaching out and squeezing his nipple and the other smiling in delight as the man suddenly lurched upward, groaning as his restraints held him down, the hand working feverishly on his member as he groaned on to the intendants' delight… all watching his member with huge smiles as he groaned beneath them, the feverish hand suddenly bringing a huge lurch as the man lost control, moaning out as the speeding movement brought a huge stream of semen up and across the room, his moaning uncontrolled as the intendants' cries of glee matched the feverish hand working harder, forcing huge streams of semen up and out from the wrenching man, trapped and screaming now as the hand knew no mercy, the man even banging his head as his body lurched, the semen petering out of his body, unable to give anymore, his member becoming utterly sensitive – the shuddering pleasure too much and now becoming painful as his body tried to pull away by itself, but was held fast by the restraints, a tired feverish-handed intendant suddenly flicking an evil grin to an equally evil one across from her as she nodded, releasing the sensitive member to a brand new, fresh intendant arm! The feverish pace on the member now tripled and more, the man crying out in agony to the glee of the intendants screaming over him. Jennifer's eyes widened from the door as the hand now got even faster, the man screaming in agony as he was forced into a punishment orgasm! His member now utterly sensitive and needing release, he was forced to continue, his body releasing an excruciating feeling of uncomfortable internal sensitivity as he screamed in agony, hands wrenching, feet pulling, head banging as intendants shrieked with laughter over him. Screaming in agony, and the feverish hand knew no mercy, increasing its fever as he screamed below, his muscles inside and his stomach now totally contracting on themselves as if squeezed in a vice, his body desperately trying to make him stop, but tied spread eagle so that he couldn't as the intendants forced him on, his muscles wracked in agony at the waist and his body convulsing, head banging, and the intendants shrieking, the hand quickening with his head banging against the table over and over and over till, finally… silence.

Not a sound, but just the feverish hand still going for a time… and then….

Screams of laughter!!! Intendants falling over his limp, lifeless body.

He'd Fainted!

Laughing like hyenas, the intendants high-fived, laughing at the goo.

"One minute, nineteen seconds!" one near his head called out with glee.

"Well, I'm going to beat that!" assured the other across from his head who'd slapped him originally.

Jennifer watched, open-mouthed and stunned at the coldness, the cruelty of what she was seeing, as she'd never seen intendants act so horribly to the women.

"Awww aw oh ha ha!" the intendant at his head alerted the three others, busily cleaning and arranging new lubrication at the man's waist as he came to, shaking uncontrollably, bewildered and frightened.

"Glad you're back," the only one now at his head condescended, pretending to care again, stroking the terrified man's face. "It's time to go walkies again!" she laughed into his face as the man's look turned to terror.

"P…Please… Please… I'm sorry… please, no more…."

"Shut Up!!!!!" the intendant who had originally slapped him, and was busily arranging his lubrication, suddenly slapped his legs savagely before going back to her work beneath him.

"Yeah, shut up or we'll stop using oil!" one of his feverish tormentors threatened from between his legs, to the laughter of the other two.

"Walkies," the one at his head announced with glee as she watched the terror mount in his eyes, sticking her tongue out and licking the side of his cheek just to show he was trapped; he was going nowhere….

A look of glee was also in Nadia's eyes, she being clearly amused by the suffering, but it was muted by Jennifer's look of concern for the man as she guided her away.

Approaching the door, they saw that the guard had left the desk, the door to the room with the electric apparatus left ajar, muffled struggles and gagged cries of pain signaling more good intendant-learning going on.

It finally tipped Jennifer as she almost broke down with what she was seeing, Nadia quick to contain her, grabbing her by the face and glaring into her eyes angrily before slowly releasing her as she felt her come back. A semi-angry point at her boots on release signaled Jennifer to submit, her head dropping dutifully, her practiced submissive expression coming on as she obeyed and stood waiting for further instruction.

"Guard!" Nadia shouted.

The guard appeared hurriedly from the electric

room, a sickening smile on her face as she nodded, reached to the desk, and pushed a button releasing the door from the inside before running straight back to where she had come from, carrying her sickening smile with her as they left.

Chapter 30

Slave To Slave

Nadia briskly guided them along the fourth level, her eyes and memory able to nimbly take them around the debris and the gloom no barrier to her as she tried to remove Jennifer from what she'd witnessed, as well as calm her in a vacant room before her training.

Unseen, Nadia grimaced, able to feel Jennifer's hesitancy, feel her shaken and disturbed, about to cry.

Her grimace, though, wasn't for her – it was for herself as she fought with her own turmoil, her natural trained dominance demanding coldness and uncaring, to force Jennifer on while a beating heart inside her was weakened by feeling, demanded else.

Finally, with Jennifer almost tugging back on her hand, Nadia brought them to a stop in the darkness, knowing infrared cameras could see them here but not listen, though she whispered all the same, pulling Jennifer in. "What's wrong?"

Jennifer almost bubbled over in the gloom as she started, Nadia feeling the shock through her body. "That man… that poor man!" she stammered.

Nadia took her in her arms. "It's necessary," she began. "It's…"

"What!?!" Jennifer almost screamed, trying to pull from her arms.

"Jennifer!!!" Nadia screamed, seizing her, Venezuelan anger searing down the wings and Jennifer freezing instantly under the power.

Caught for a time under an angry glare, she could

only barely see that Nadia tolerated her fearful resistance as she pulled her back in, her shaking final breakdown to tears softening her rage.

"How could they do that to him?" Jennifer sobbed, shaking in her arms and remembering the fear and terror, the utter disturbance and suffering in the man's eyes. "How could they be so cruel!?" she broke down completely.

Nadia pulled her in, hugging her gently, rocking her as she cried and letting her get it out as she squeezed with understanding… "Oh, Jennifer," she said softly into her ear… "I want you to listen to me… can you do that?" she spoke with care.

Nadia continued softly, gently tugging Jennifer for a response as she sobbed into her chest, nodding dutifully but crying on, truly disturbed by what she'd seen.

Still rocking her gently, Nadia laid it all down – the function the men had in-house as tools for learning with, their confinement, their unbelievably cruel treatment, and what had made this necessary… the deaths.

Initially, there had been no men at the Manor; for years, this part of life had been ignored, not a part of the Manor's program, but constant requests and client complaint had eventually made it necessary, however reluctant the staff were to acknowledge this part of life.

When the Manor's reputation became in danger of falling, the program was changed to include a general training of male familiarity, as the brochure stated.

In effect, it became understood, upon the clients' insistence, that their property be returned to them able to deal with all eventualities that they would find necessary, or to put it bluntly – to handle anything at a party.

The change had actually seen the previous Mistress of the house be discharged, her inability to alter and accept this new direction pushing her to move on after two decades at the helm of the Manor. As usual, despite the house's rules and customs, in the end, the Manor was a business, and its backers would not accept its standing or profit margin being unduly affected by even its highest authority, their present highest authority taking charge after being voted in upon the other's departure. With her own despising feeling toward men being all to real, even their Mistress would rather this training did not occur, but her own determined lust for power saw her tolerate this particular client-wish, even though she would generally be absent when it was carried out.

Jennifer listened, still head-down, as Nadia described the initial treatment of the men as fair and luxurious, an understanding given that they had no training themselves, the intendants' seeing their vulgar, disturbing, and sickening attitudes being tolerated in order to use them for the task.

As much as some women hated it now, in that time, it had been far worse, men able actually to enjoy the pleasure of the slaves, even talk – Jennifer raising an eyebrow coming around to this point as Nadia spoke.

Both the women and the intendants had worked through gritted teeth as these buffoons, as Nadia put it, had enjoyed themselves over their good work, obviously affecting it negatively, their presence and boisterous attitudes upsetting the cool mood ever-present in the Manor.

This was made far worse upon their leaving each time, each new batch acting in such submissive terms as to be selected for the task, only to turn into smiling cretins on entrance to the great house, their behavior worsening with each year that passed. The word was getting out, and getting worse with each leaving, that this great house full of trapped women needing male attention was a great place to be if you could act weak and fool the selection process.

With constant complaints from women and intendants, and eventual complaints from clients unhappy at the stories from their slaves on return, the Mistress finally acted… badly.

Her decision to institute harsh discipline on untrained males, some of whom had actually been in the Manor more than once, backfired when unrestrained males were actually disciplined by intendants, setting off their natural dominant urges.

The intendants themselves were horrifically injured, and what could only be described as a riot ensued, the men unhappy at a gradual crackdown and final beating of their colleagues, defending one another and attacking the staff in house. Feeling justified after the intendants' attempts to dominate and subdue them over the beginning days had left them angry at what they saw as ill-treatment, and they lashed out, banding together and returning treatment of their own that Nadia stopped short of describing.

Unlike women, men could not be isolated and broken down… unless shackled and contained as this was carried out. Unlike women, men would not forget ill-treatment and get on with the same people just a short time later, seeking a way to move forward, but instead they would cling to the instance of the act, and exact revenge for it no matter how far back it went.

This notion of revenge had built up in many of the males that year as the Mistress had had the intendants crack down. Unknown to them, as they thought differently, the house had become a powder keg of resentment, the intendants thinking they were doing their job and only vaguely aware that something was brewing, and certainly not aware of the danger they were in.

Quartered in rooms, unguarded and not confined, the men would talk openly at night, their experiences of training that they viewed as ill-treatment convincing many that something had to be done, their instinctual feelings of dominance over women just raised higher, the harder the intendants tried to train them.

Finally, the storm broke one afternoon as three intendants tried to beat one down in front of two others for a house infraction, the two others charging the intendants and releasing their anger on their screams.

Despite the best efforts of other intendants who arrived, the men had been raised to the state of animals, lashing out at all attempts to contain them and inflicting horrific injuries, and showing no signs of stopping. As they pushed through the Manor, the danger became obvious, other men beginning to join them; eventually, nine male animals, incensed and not responding to reasoning, started hunting down intendants and beating them mercilessly, all while watched on the screens above.

After the screams of a final two stopped, their having been beaten unconscious and left bloodied in the wings, the Mistress gave instruction for the final control to be used.

They had to be shot before it was contained; seven would succumb to their injuries in-house while another two were dealt with by the house's backers, the other males luckily below at the time and unaware of what had happened, that being all that saved them from the backers.

Nadia squinted at Jennifer's naivety when the charge mentioned the police…

"The people behind this house don't like that kind of attention," Nadia explained, frowning at Jennifer. "Their own people deal with these things."

Jennifer stared, swallowing and trying not to show it, for the first time realizing this was not a game, and the lengths the staff were prepared to go to. Her questions about the firearms met stony silence from Nadia, Jennifer having never seen any evidence of them, and up to that point unaware they were even present in-house.

"We are in charge."

That was all Nadia would say, glaring at her as she started another question, making her fall back to listening as she finished.

After the incident, reviews over the house's program reluctantly found that client insistence meant male training for women was necessary. Not being able to remove this element from the program, it was decided that 'New Policies' regarding male management were to be carried out. These included many new safeguards, including strict manacling for males in-house at all times, selection to be carried out on a basis of unfamiliarity; in effect, no males admitted were to know each other beforehand. Only weak males would be admitted – no athletic or physically able specimens were to be allowed in, ensuring easier management. No males were allowed to speak, a strict rule ensuring no rapport could be built up among them. The males were also to be kept strictly on their own when used; no other male was to be present when they were utilized.

As well as this groundwork, it was found that the reputation of enjoyment for any male gaining entrance to the Manor had to be dealt with, and would be through a targeted response on the males admitted. In effect, they were to be brutally treated at all times, beaten for the slightest infraction of the rules, ensuring not only that no enjoyment was had, but that upon release, this knowledge would spread in the community.

This, then, would accomplish three things in the Manor's favor :

1 :Only real male submissives would apply for this work, other males who were time-wasters looking for fun and not committed submissives surely staying away with word of this new brutal regime in-house.

2 :These harsh measures would ensure not only female safety in house, but actual male safety, as well, though not comfort.

3 :Women in training would no longer be put off by inappropriate male behavior, ensuring better training and eventual client satisfaction.

This, then, played right into the Mistress's hands, the backers giving her free reign to unleash her insistence of unspeakable suffering on any poor man who dared enter the Manor, under the guise that it was for everyone's safety.

Jennifer tried not to look disagreeing as Nadia finished her defense of why these men were being put through this. She smiled, as she easily saw it on Jennifer's face, but did not react over much, pleased that Jennifer was not openly disagreeing with her and thus respecting her authority, and more, that she was now holding herself together, ready for her training.

Before this next learning, though, they took a step through a door on the left before the end of the wing. Inside, a dark and foreboding room with grey walls meeting grey floor, and a dim black-shaded lamp nestled in the left corner by the door, this giving the grey rectangular platform box which was a length's ways from the door on the right an evil look. Stopping Jennifer and leaving her in the middle of the room, Nadia moved to the right wall, her eyes used to the dark as she gathered what Jennifer slowly saw were implements hanging there.

As her eyes adjusted to the light, Jennifer could make out the wall now, and what looked like hundreds of implements hanging there, right across its face, as she gazed right at the box, its wrist and ankle restraints on either end, Jennifer realizing this was a house of horrors for whoever ended up here.

Shivering, she listened to the chinking of metal clips and sliding of leather as Nadia chose what they needed, another sound being faint in the background behind the wall, Jennifer sure a man was screaming, at times, as she stood there naked.

Sharp boots approached from the wall, the Hispanic beauty with pain in each hand… wheels and ties and a look of intent, Jennifer's mind ablaze as she gazed at her smile.

And so, to their task, Jennifer still unsure if the implements would come her way as she followed Nadia past the stairs, hand in hand as they turned to the left and through the first door that came.

With the door swinging inwards, away to the right Jennifer was pulled into shattering light. So sudden, the change from the dark foreboding wings, that she was taken aback as they left cold gloom for warm bright, white kitchen-like freshness.

With Nadia releasing her to move and close the door behind them, Jennifer was stunned, the sight routing her to the spot as she looked on. In front of her, a ten foot long, ten foot wide by ten foot high, bright white square room met a white polystyrene-tiled suspended ceiling, the feel like a cross between a kitchen and an empty office block. Nothing on the walls and white-tiled marble floor left the doorway on the left wall closed to them as they entered, a curious and strong feature, there being no door present in it, and it being darker in that space, their eyes having difficulty penetrating, such was the brightness where they stood. Square office-like lighting buried in the polystyrene ceiling above made it difficult to look up, but right now, that wasn't a problem for Jennifer as her eyes were fixed on the left wall past the doorway, and what was hanging through it… a man's penis!

Through a small hole in the wall hung the entire equipment of a man, his testicles and all the only thing that stood out in the otherwise smooth white room, Jennifer taken aback as she heard Nadia finish locking the door, her arms soon around her waist and taking her fully through the doorway.

Through the doorway there was another ten by ten by ten foot room, only lit by the light coming through the doorway at first, but which was soon bathed in warmer light, Nadia switching on a small black-shaded lamp in the far left corner, a warm glow in the black-walled room having to fight the dark to reveal a tan colored floor of wood, and a man!

Again, Jennifer was stunned, looking on at a secured form, the back of a man absolutely welded, face-first, to the wall by leather buckles and strapping.

In the exact center of the wall, his legs were held two feet apart, black leather cuffs wrapped and padlocked around his ankles and secured to steel mounts on the wall. Only getting up to his knees before there was more, two more black leather harnesses secured around them, hard padlocked again and secured to wall mountings. Only a short ways higher, at his thighs, the same story with large leather straps before a large solid-looking harness went around his waist, eye-wateringly tight, and had him absolutely pinned by his waist to the wall, no possibility of pulling even a millimeter back, as it was secured with large steel padlocks to either side of him, his body squeezed hard at the waist, uncomfortably so, Jennifer thought.

As Jennifer watched, Nadia stepped forward, almost ignoring the man as if he was some piece of meat, more intent on checking the harnessing, especially the waist, before she moved upwards to the next harness, three quarters up his back and again far too tight-looking, Jennifer thought, before proceeding to the cuffs around his arms. His arms were spread out like his legs below him, and he made no sound as Nadia inspected the tightness of the three respective cuffs on each arm's shoulder, elbow, and wrist, pulling each padlock and ensuring it was tight before finally moving to a cruel-looking neck brace. Tight around his neck and forcing his head straight and against the wall, it – like the harness around his waist – had padlocks to either side, and to the wall, Nadia carefully inspecting each one. Careful because, on either side of the black leather neck brace, an attached strand of black leather led away from the brace to the wall, where mountings with padlocks had them secured. It was on the inside of these strands, facing in toward the neck, that one had to take care, as small sharp steel spikes like the teeth on a wheel protruded from the straps. This was obvious encouragement to keep the charge facing forward, and way more than necessary, Jennifer thought, the slightest turn left or right bringing instant pain to their neck, and probably cuts… cruel.

Seemingly satisfied with the guards' efforts at securing, Nadia paid some final attention to the waist strap before turning, unable to hide a small smile that was emerging as she led Jennifer by the hand, back into the bright white of the adjoining room… and to the penis.

Moving to the back wall, she turned back with a

white rubber matt, unnoticed before as it sat against the back wall, and she laid it out on the floor below the penis. Dropping to her knees, she gently motioned Jennifer to kneel down on it beside her on her right as she smiled and explained that, today, she was going to be taught the mechanics of the male genitalia, and how it worked.

Jennifer listened, still stunned, not starting to quite smile yet as she listened to Nadia explain its various parts, watching as she reached forward, lifting the penis gently in her hand and exposing the testicles below as she pointed out various nerve points. Jennifer couldn't help beginning to smile, setting Nadia off, too, no correction given for this apparent loss of slave-poise, but instead, almost an encouragement as she explained that women were naturally given to curiosity regarding the male genitalia. After a short introduction to Jennifer's hands to familiarize her with it, and allow her to get the smiling out of her system, Nadia almost laughed at Jennifer's obvious interest, it being so long since she had held one. As she explored on, they both smiled hugely as it started to grow in front of them, Jennifer having to hold back a laugh, and Nadia, too, as she playfully stroked her fingers off of Jennifer's cheek in a pretend slapping gesture to get her to pay attention. Still growing in front of them, the penis became almost fully erect, something the male was certainly about to regret, Nadia only allowing it because she wanted it to keep holding itself up so she could begin working on the testicles beneath without having to hold it herself.

Her smile dropped significantly, Jennifer feeling the mood change and it throwing her a little as Nadia took on a more work-like attitude, producing a very sharp-looking wheel from the bundle of pain she'd brought with her.

She smiled evilly as she noticed Jennifer's confusion at just how sharp the wheel was, her eyes by now, after so long being in-house, easily able to see it was much worse than those occasionally used on them, almost as if it had been made that way intentionally.

The first touch of its teeth on the exposed male testicles brought a shifting from the other side of the wall, but no sound, Nadia stopping and her smile fading completely as she seemed to listen for any sound at all. Satisfied there was none, she proceeded, first moving over the left testicle, the shifting increasing and then fading away as she moved up the skin, clear of the testicles and on to the shaft itself, Jennifer confused when the shifting didn't return. She watched intently as the wheel proceeded slowly up the shaft, apparently bringing no discomfort, the shifting from next door remaining absent until she neared the top, the white skin leaving for the blood-filled head turning pink and almost reddening as the wheel rose higher. Almost immediately, the shifting returned louder than before, the first groan of pain sounding as Nadia moved the teeth under the rim of the head, this more painful, and there was groaning as she moved sideways along the rim, allowing the teeth to find their way under it, and there was the first bang against the wall as the man's forehead impacted it, Nadia smiling as she continued. With a motioning of her eyes, Nadia made sure Jennifer was watching as she lifted the wheel up and over the edge of the rim, the slow cruel movement forcing the penis to move by itself, convulsing with the captive's discomfort, Nadia smiling as she slowly rolled the wheel to the tip, bangs and groans signaling the male's pain and Nadia's pleasure.

Soon, it was Jennifer's turn, Nadia showing and explaining that the nerves in the testicles and the head where incredibly sensitive, especially to sharp objects, and she smiled as Jennifer flushed. She also smiled at Jennifer's confusion with the sack holding the testicles being much less sensitive, and at her real difficulty with understanding the shaft had very weak sensitivity, Jennifer truly confused as she ran the wheel up and down it, getting very little response. Where she wasn't confused was at its tip, Nadia explaining and showing her the nerves, especially as, around and more under the rim, the areas were especially sensitive, forcing contractions in the muscles, in the penis, as Jennifer began to delight in running the wheel under it, having it seemingly jerk by itself as the male groaned on. Eventually, Nadia grabbed hold of the penis by the shaft, the male quieting as she began to squeeze, the end reddening further, but to Jennifer's surprise, there was no sound from the male. She was amazed as she saw the muscles slowly flex tighter and tighter in Nadia's arm as she put the penis under incredible pressure, in a vice-like grip, but the man stayed silent. Releasing it, she looked at Jennifer, smiling mischievously as she raised her hand to the head, cupping it gently before beginning to squeeze with hardly any pressure at all applied before the groaning started. With her smile increasing, only a small bit of extra pressure brought the banging back as the male began to cry out, Nadia taking the wheel from Jennifer, her look turning deliciously evil as she ran the wheel's teeth over the tip of the penis head, the man crying out in agony for the first time, his head banging more and more. Taking the wheel away, she squeezed on for a time, seeming to enjoy the man's discomfort, Jennifer finding that, soon, you could feel his body's struggles on the other side of the wall as you held the penis, the struggles making you smile uncontrollably as you held the man's pain in your hand.

Soon, with her turn to learn, she had the man crying out, Nadia encouraging her to push her hesitation aside, her natural feelings of sympathy for the man getting in the way of her training and bringing a scowl from Nadia as she insisted that Jennifer push further. With the man crying out regularly now, Nadia forced her to begin from the testicles, all the way to the head and on to the squeezing, until she was satisfied that Jennifer had a good understanding, the man now crying out regularly and increasingly.

Jennifer was confused as to why the man stayed excited and erect through all this agony, Nadia explaining that the penis was outside of the man's control, almost with a life of its own, its own mind purely programmed to respond to female attention in almost any way. It was absolutely needing of female attention, so much so that, with even the slightest of touches, it would remain erect and in search of pleasurable feeling from them, tolerating quite large administrations of pain. The penis, itself, Nadia explained, as long as the pain wasn't overly painful, would remain erect for them while the man behind the wall would be left to tolerate and deal with the pain… such was the selfishness of the penis in its need for their attention. Far, it would seem, from a man's best friend; at times, it would seem to be rather cruel to him,

Jennifer still confused and somewhat unbelieving that she herself would remain excited with the application of such agony to her privates as she, again, began running the wheel to the man's struggles.

Louder and louder were his groans, Jennifer beginning to truly enjoy herself as the music of the male struggle rang out from behind the wall, Jennifer beginning to laugh as she learned where to put the wheel to bring louder cries, and where else to run it as she squeezed it tightly in her hand to bring the banging of the forehead, Nadia laughing on with her… until the man finally cried out just once too loudly….

Nadia's smile disappeared as she rose, scowling, her finger instructing Jennifer to remain put as she watched the same hand move to her hip, drawing her cane as she moved angrily into the other room.

Her anger was frightening as her voice filled the room behind them and the first strike of her cane brought a scream from the man, followed by six more, Jennifer freezing and her feelings of enjoyment disappearing as she felt so sorry for the man, the landings savage and not instructional, but pure torture meant to hurt.

Returning, Nadia tried to force a smile over her rage, her cane still drawn at her side as she surveyed a frightened Jennifer, doing her best to holster her anger with her cane as she knelt down, taking her place beside her.

Jennifer followed Nadia's gaze to the penis now in front of them; finally overwhelmed by the body's pain, it had dropped down, now only half at attention and leaning to one side. Nadia's forced smile at the sight became real, bringing Jennifer around a little, one beginning to emerge on her face, too, as she looked on, confused, as Nadia seemed to begin to care for the penis, gently stroking her fingers under the head before tickling the man's testicles and gently running her nails up and down the shaft, making sure she gently caught them under the rim each time. Jennifer looked on in amazement as, despite the man's obvious continued suffering behind the wall, this silky gentle caring movement of Nadia's fingers and nails brought him back to almost instant erection, his penis flushing with blood as Nadia continued her pretense of care.

Eyes widening, Jennifer watched as Nadia closed her hand gently around the man's shaft and began masturbating him, his penis becoming rock solid with her touch and Nadia smiling as she rhythmically worked on him. Jennifer watched as shifting of another kind could be heard starting on the other side of the wall, the man – though stinging from savage cane strikes that he was unable to tend to – clearly enjoying Nadia's attentions. Jennifer watched, confused, there being no way she would be brought to enjoyment like this after such a savage beating, and she squinted, looking at the penis… it truly was selfish!

Nadia laughed as Jennifer told her what was going through her mind before Nadia began to explain what she was doing. She explained that there were different ways of arousing a man in this way, as her hand continued to demonstrate. By her having a light grip, the man would feel the incredible care of gentle femininity wrapped around him, relaxing and enjoying him, Nadia explaining that, if this continued, and if the man was secured and unable to move, he would after a time have one of the most powerful orgasms a male could have… but that wasn't to be.

Squeezing tighter, the shifting next door was instant as Nadia began to squeeze hard and increase her stroking dramatically, there coming a small bang as the male hit his head in pleasure against the wall, it happening as Nadia smiled, working harder, the penis's end reddening further as she continued to tighten her grip. She explained, as another bang came through the wall, that the male mind had now changed, and if she continued in this way, as the male wanted and definitely as the penis wanted, the orgasm – although strong – would not be as devastating as the gentle touch, as the penis's nerves were now under pressure and the blood was restricted through the tubes inside. Jennifer's confused look brought more explanation as Nadia taught her that the male could feel the fluids, especially the orgasmic ones when they finally flowed at the end of this procedure, their passing through his equipment. If, she explained, the penis and testicles were under no pressure, the blood and fluids would be allowed to fill all the tubes inside and flow unrestricted at speeds over the nerve endings, bringing a vastly more powerful orgasm as they flowed out. The male, in this case, leading up to this explosion, would feel little from the gentle touch on the outside as it brought him there, as pressure on the nerves inside from out would be light. On the other hand, if large pressure was brought by the grip on the shaft or elsewhere, the nerves inside would be pressurized from outside, bringing increased want from the male at the female's insistence, but with a price. The price being that the increased pressure, bringing want as she brought him there, would then restrict fluid speed and pressure over the nerves, reducing the power of the orgasm itself.

Nadia laughed as Jennifer asked whether it was better, then, to have a strong grip until he was almost there, and then release and be gentle.

“You don’t want them enjoying it too much,” she laughed on, explaining. The male, although not having women’s abilities with emotion, did have feelings, and suddenly changing action would bring confusion to the male mind, it not good with sudden switchings of neural messages like that. “If,” Nadia suddenly frowned as she said it, “one did want to bring the male the most pleasure, it was better to stick to the same action from beginning to end, the orgasms, though being different, would be stronger themselves than if split by two actions.”

“The male mind just isn’t advanced enough to handle two things at once,” she smiled. “Even in the thing they most covet,” she condescended, her shifting captive on the other side of the wall.

Jennifer looked on as Nadia showed her a final trick, explaining that if it was necessary to have a male complete his action, then a fast way of achieving this – even if he was tired and limp – was possible, Jennifer frowning at the curious statement.

She watched as Nadia directed her eyes to her hand as she worked up a little higher and, instead of securing the penis by a mid-grip, she secured it three quarters higher, Jennifer expecting that the male was about to be tortured in some way. Instead, to her surprise, there was almost immediate increased banging, and the definite slipping out of groans, Nadia’s eyebrows raising in disapproval at the sound, but tolerating it for now as she taught Jennifer.

Looking on, Nadia showed her that, as she raised her hand each time, she was gently catching the underside of his head where she had run the wheel, the increased sensitivity under there entirely welcoming the catching of her fingers under it as they passed up and over the head before coming back down, raising and catching underneath as they passed over once again, a definite groan escaping from next door as they did so. Still tolerating the male's insolence, she increased her grip and slowed still more, catching under the head, although the shifting began calming behind the wall and the groans stopped. She showed that the male was still entirely receptive to the catching action, but able to tolerate it and control himself, the crushing of the nerves and restricting of the blood flow inside bringing him poise and some self-handling of his emotion. Smiling, she made sure Jennifer was watching closely as she released her grip, bringing feminine gentility to the action, catching under the head in a soft silky movement and almost stroking the penis as she increased the speed, the shifting instantly returning and the man groaning loud as Nadia worked him on, her hand becoming feverish. With groaning from the other side as the penis became rock solid in front of them, Nadia suddenly took her hand away and placed the shaft in Jennifer's, closing her fingers around it. Jennifer's eyes widened as she felt his pulse through his shaft, his blood pumping as it thundered away, his shifting body on the other side still obvious with want as she held him mercilessly, teasing on, giving no relief to his starving hunger. Still holding on, Nadia smiled as they listened to his shifting increasing, Jennifer holding him further, the two smiling as his shifting increased, the penis rock solid now, but receiving no relief from Jennifer, the two smiling on and listening to his struggles on the other side as they held him in delicious torture. Jennifer's eyes widened as she smiled, almost laughing out, as Nadia pointed to a small fluid emerging from the tip of his penis and remaining like a tortured lake at his tip… precome… such was his desperate torture now.

Nadia explained as they ignored his plight that his head was now filled with desire, all other thoughts now pushed aside, themselves being all he could think of, the male mind unable to hold much more than one thought at a time as he was now in bondage by their attention, feeling chastity by hand. Their cruelty continuing as they held his want, Nadia explained that frustration like this was utter torture to a male, like being in pain and not being able to focus on anything else because it was so intense that he, too, was now in the same, such was his deep internal need for their attention that his body was starving, focusing all his attention on his want. On Jennifer's frown, Nadia asked her to imagine a hunger like she'd never felt before, total and unceasing, her body starving… past tears, past caring, and now collapsed on the ground, desperate for food, and now someone holding her down and dangling the most delicious of meals just out of reach in front of her, laughing on as she starved beneath them. For a second, Jennifer realized the cruelty they were giving, her enjoyment leaving as she still held the male, but quickly brought back to her learning as Nadia saw the struggle in her, quickly changing the subject to the fluid. Precome, she explained, came from the over-excitement of the penis, it having a mixing chamber of fluid inside where semen raised from the testicles to mix with other male lubricants which would carry it deep inside a woman's superiority. Normally held in check until the final act, if the male mind was stimulated enough or physical stimulation of a gentle manner was applied, or both, the male penis would be unable to prevent a leaking of these other fluids to the surface, the two women now openly laughing as it signaled the male's loss of control, and how deeply they had his attention in their hands!

A groan… a sympathetic forlorn groan of pain brought on by their laughter, such was the male's suffering at their show of chastity… a mistake he'd soon regret!

Almost immediately, Nadia raised her cane, whipped from the side of her hip, her anger surging forward as she brought Venezuelan rage to the man, his thinking soon of nothing else but her pain!

Jennifer winced, pulling back upon feeling the first savage strikes with her screams, through his penis, the jolts of pain unmistakable through her hand as the man's screams followed Nadia's, her savage beating filling the rooms, Jennifer releasing the penis in horror and covering her mouth as his cries of agony filled the air.

Tears of pain met searing anger as Nadia roared into his ears, standing right against him, demanding control and behavior. Threats now… evil promises of utter agony with Jennifer squeezing her mouth as she cupped it, reeling back as she listened to what Nadia promised to do to him if he failed to give her what she wanted.

Still covering her mouth, she listened as the man

cried, desperately trying to bring his feelings under control as the searing burns now striped across his rear begged for care, Nadia giving none, just glaring into his left eye from behind as he dared not look at her, his tears flowing.

Sharp boots seemed to thunder off the walls, Nadia returning with Jennifer's shock at the beating heightened as she saw the glinting of definite dark fluid on the intendant's still-drawn cane, it held in a hand shaking with rage… and blood.

Trying to bring herself under control, Nadia grimaced, motioning Jennifer back to the matt, her hesitancy for a second bringing scowling ire from her as she tried to holster her cane, her shaking anger making it difficult.

The man was in agony… that being obvious as a now completely limp member drooped in front of them, Nadia squinting and glaring more in anger that she now had to excite it again in order to continue training Jennifer, stuck in sympathy, the male's suffering being obvious.

Seeming to disregard any notion of sympathy, Nadia roughly took Jennifer's hand forward, lifting the penis like it was some kitchen food stuff and placing it in her palm, forcing her hand to close around it. As Nadia sorted through the implements she'd brought with her on the floor, Jennifer's sympathy grew with her feeling the man crying through his penis, the shaking movement obvious, silent but unmistakable. The penis, too, seemed to care for its owner, its selfishness gone, it grew none in her hand… his pain too great, his beating too savage.

Nadia seeming to calm, her shaking stopping, she

grimaced at Jennifer's sympathy, obviously annoyed as she roughly pointed at his testicles, raising her hand and keeping the penis held out of the way.

From her hand, she produced a small rubber ring, Jennifer watching as she proceeded to take the man's testicles and stretch the ring over and around them; they were now held proud in front of them, flushing with blood.

She explained that now that the blood had difficulty getting out, the area was expanding in size, bringing a form that would calm after a while, but the swelling meant the nerves were pushed against tissues, heightening their sensitivity.

As if to prove her point, she flicked only her finger against his right testicle, Jennifer feeling an immediate and unmistakable jolt of pain through his penis, any recovery in her hand now thwarted as Nadia flicked it again, the jolt coming more noticeably and Jennifer squinting confused.

"How could such a small tap feel so bad to him?" Jennifer asked, truly confused at the huge pain she was feeling through his penis in her hand.

"The nerves," Nadia answered, a smile emerging on her face, her mischievousness replacing her anger slowly but surely as, still held in Jennifer's hand, the charge felt another jolt as Nadia tapped the left testicle.

Jennifer's confusion abound, Nadia laughed at her expression, the tension breaking as she explained how sensitive the male testis were and the reason they hung outside the body. So sensitive were they that even their semen couldn't stand the temperature inside the male body, and had to hang in the cooler air outside... "Where women can get them!" she assured Jennifer mischievously, her eyes lighting up as she laughed at the idea, Jennifer finally laughing, too, the mood in the room lifting.

Still holding the penis, Nadia encouraged her to flick the testicles and feel the jolts of male discomfort through the shaft. Her confusion mounting at such obvious intense pain, Jennifer listened as Nadia likened it to a toothache, explaining that the flicking left an afterglow of pain that was not obvious to women, but was caused by the swelling of the nerves under such sharp quick trauma. As Jennifer squinted sympathetically, Nadia explained it would go away after a short time, but that any huge trauma like a kick or a punch would see the nerves swell uncontrollably, deep inside the male body, the whole area connected, and seeing the male in internal agony capable even of bringing on a blackout or heart attack.

Jennifer's confusion continuing, Nadia explained that a kick would see the external nerves at the testis in agony, but immediately superseded as the nerves would send signals eight to ten inches diagonally up inside the body, toward the underside of the stomach, having the male feel a pain akin to a car sitting on the underside of his stomach. Jennifer frowned… Nadia telling her to imagine being kicked full-force in the stomach, and then telling her to imagine that pain travelling further inside her stomach, and then telling her to imagine that it grew to the weight of a car on her stomach… then telling her the horror of the male body.

She listened as Nadia explained that, although she could hold her stomach and nurse the pain, the male – because these nerves were so deep inside – could not get to touch or care for them in any way, but instead had to suffer the pain that the swelling of the nerve endings would cause for hours, he unable to nurse them, and instead having what, for women, would feel like the deepest of awful cramps, like the weight of a car inside them on their stomach for hours.

Looking on incredulously, Jennifer couldn't understand when Nadia explained that the initial shock of such an assault removes the male ability to speak or breathe, this being what can bring blackouts or heart attacks to those unfit enough to handle such agony.

Jennifer couldn't understand or believe it was that bad, and began to resist tapping the testicles in front of her, but Nadia forced her on, explaining strongly as she glared at her: "Either you learn quickly or his torture continues till you do…. If you truly want to be kind to him, learn quickly."

Of course, 'quickly' meant 'harder', Jennifer eventually and reluctantly bending to Nadia's insistence, forced to tap the head, as well, which definitely hurt him, Jennifer feeling that, still holding him with one hand as she tapped with the other, but not hurting as much as his testicles, the jolts not being as strong. Still, it confused her, Nadia's explanations doing little to facilitate her understanding of why such a small tap to the swelled head's endings would cause such pain. In any case, Nadia pushed her on, seeing her tap in various places and under the rim to his extreme discomfort, as Jennifer felt before she was finally allowed to leave his head in peace, but this meant the torture headed elsewhere.

Jennifer was forced down again, as Nadia seemed determined to learn her well as another round of testicle-tapping brought shifting and cries, not groans, as the man finally began to lose control. Seemingly uncaring, Nadia didn't smile, but seemed to be concentrating on maximizing his discomfort, pointing out where to tap next, the man crying out at times as she found a particularly sensitive spot…. "Practice," Nadia assured Jennifer. "That's how you find those spots."

Finally, the man cried out one too many times, Jennifer horrified as the rage returned, Nadia reaching back for her cane and about to rise when Jennifer's look of pain caught her eye. Squinting at her in an almost disappointed way, her feelings for her seemed to stop her rising, Jennifer's begging look for sympathy for the male finding reception as Nadia brought her hand back, seemingly not wanting to upset her, though caring nothing for the male.

Finally, she relented, satisfied that Jennifer had learned, and giving the poor captive a welcome break, even seeming to care as she gently eased the ring from around the male's testicles, his groan of relief tolerated as they swung freely for a time.

But only for a time, Nadia bringing forth the next suffering for him as she brought out a long thin tie of leather and wrapped his balls in a figure eight pattern, Jennifer watching as the elegant tying brought immediate swelling and discomfort through her hand, it still holding him, and she being sure she could feel his head strain against the wall at times as Nadia tightened the strip around his balls… she could.

In a matter of fact way, Nadia explained this obvious light torture was for his own benefit, as the restriction of blood flow to the testicles would make it more difficult for him to orgasm, and if he did before she wanted him to, he would be made to suffer. She cocked her head and her ear toward the doorway, mischievously, in an obvious gesture showing she wanted him to hear that… she was controlling him… although her threat was very real.

Catching Jennifer's look of discomfort as she watched the man's suffering through his swelling balls, Nadia explained that, as long as the tie wasn't on too long, there would be no long-lasting effects for the male, and as long as they took it off after a time and allowed full blood flow back to the testicles, they would remain undamaged. This, then, Nadia said, looking hard at her, was up to her to learn quickly, as she would not remove the tie until she learned, and so his length of torture was truly in her hands.

Jennifer nodded, resolving to learn quickly, Nadia smiling and realizing that Jennifer was also under her control, knowing she would now apply greater pressure to the male, despite his discomfort, in order to bring about a faster end to his suffering.

With a slow re-emerging of life in the penis, Jennifer had felt it recede under the tying, believing she could feel real fear in the male as Nadia had tied his testicles, but now under her gentle care, its selfishness had returned, as it had started swelling in her hand.

Suddenly, though, it was in different hands, Nadia taking it from her and Jennifer wondering if the man was suddenly in fear behind the wall, certain she would be, but then something amazing happened – something she couldn't believe… Nadia kissed it!

After torturing it and its owner incessantly, she now delivered such care and tenderness to it through her warm moist lips that, almost immediately, it swelled completely upon her attentions! Jennifer was stunned at its selfishness, seemingly ignoring the agony its owner had been made to feel by Nadia as it swelled toward her, wanton for her attention, Jennifer truly confused; how could it want its torturess?

Nadia smiled as she took it in her mouth, sucking hard on its end, seeming to truly enjoy herself before catching Jennifer's glance and releasing it, smiling more at its rock hard attention for her, still held in her grasp, and having to fight hard not to laugh at Jennifer's confusion at the care she was now showing, her anger absent.

She explained again that females were pre-programmed to enjoy this act, and although she shared the Mistress's anger and irritation toward men, it did not stop her from enjoying this natural act on them… as long as they behaved. Still smiling, and now with Jennifer catching it, too, she seemed to be unable to help herself as her smile descended into mouthfuls of the male; at one stage, Jennifer's eyes widened as Nadia seemed to push herself up against the wall toward the male in wanton lust! Catching her confusion, Nadia seemed to have to fight herself off the male's member, instead presenting it for Jennifer, it still being in her steely grip as she insisted a smiling Jennifer open her mouth and give the first taste of her own care to the male, the man groaning on the other side of the wall to their surprise.

"He likes you," Nadia assured Jennifer. "Awww, it's because he could feel you caring for him earlier," she laughed, the male obviously very pleased with his savior's attentions, unaware she had saved him from beating number three.

Encouraged to learn the penis's sensitive areas, Jennifer was soon sucking and licking while holding the penis, feeling the pulse and other feelings as she poured pressure and then kindness, biting and then sucking on various parts as Nadia taught her. She showed that sucking too hard on the poor male's testicles brought obvious discomfort, the male feeling they were being stretched off of him inside, whereas a gently sucking brought warm affection, Nadia quite happily tolerating his male music from the other side of the wall as it taught her charge.

Again, she showed her that teeth on balls, with their sharpness, brought pain, but immediate attention if necessary, and she laughed. Again on the shaft, Jennifer's confusion persisted at how such a large part seemed quite immune to her biting, this until she bit just too hard, the nipping of his skin bringing a jolt against the wall as the women laughed at his motions. At the head, Jennifer now showed her learning, able to guess where sharp teeth would bring worried attention from the male, the top back under the tip seemingly especially sensitive, and Jennifer laughing as it jolted away from her nibbling, having to chase it at times as the male groaned in semi-discomfort. She laughed as he seemed to fall out with her, his groaning growing unhappy, and then she brought him back with caring attention, Nadia smiling, allowing her to suck for a time, gauging his mood by his groaning behind the wall.

Finally, she showed how you could suck up and under the rim of the head as you rose, the catching movement increasing his arousal and bringing him closer and faster to finishing, a final large suck on the head after the catching lift over the rim, though being uncomfortable for their cheeks with the pressure, bringing unmistakable thanking groans from a happy male behind the wall.

Jennifer well versed now, Nadia stopped their attentions and had Jennifer place two fingers on the large vein along the penis, the pulse obviously thundering beneath, harder and faster than Jennifer had felt so far, Nadia not having to teach her what that meant as she gently reached forward and began to untie the male's balls. His groans of pleasure leaked out as he tried, to Nadia's pleasure, not to annoy her by holding them back as she removed their leather bondage, and let them hang free, Jennifer smiling huge and biting her lip to hold back a squeal as she watched them pulse with want after their attentions.

"Now for some retention," Nadia whispered as she rose Jennifer, the charge following her Hispanic curves as they sexily swung from side to side in their leather, her sharp boots moving to the other side of the wall, Jennifer listening.

A shivering slave couldn't help quivering as the full power of leather and Hispanic passion pressed against him, pushing him harder into the wall as she wrapped around him, feeling his fear and want as she purred into his ear.

"You've been a good slave," her delicious tones silkily washed inside his ear as she brought her exposed thigh up and under both of his, letting her warm thigh nestle between his exposed cheeks and against his body. "There's one more thing I have to teach my slave," she informed him. "And you're going to help me, aren't you?" she whispered, the male nodding slightly, his head bumping off the wall. “You are not to come until I command you, do you understand?”

The male nodded against the wall.

“Yes?” Nadia asked for confirmation.

He nodded again.

“You’ll wait for my permission?” she asked, putting her hand on his side, the man shaking as she pressed her nails sexily into his skin, the threat obvious.

Deep strained breath and a nodding head brought Nadia her answer as she strained him slightly further for her want.

The sound of leather separating from skin filled the room as the male had to fight, feeling the gorgeous warm intendant’s thigh pull away and leave him alone on the wall, her attentions now moving to his front.

Smiling on, the two on the other side laughed as Jennifer took him in her mouth and showed what she had learned, the male groaning now in pleasure, his head banging off the wall not in pain, but in pleasure as he listened to Nadia order him to hold off from the other side.

“His pulse is so quick,” Jennifer giggled between mouthfuls, pouring on the pressure as Nadia warned him, standing above her.

“Slave! Don’t you dare!!!” she shouted strongly as his moans grew.

“Don’t you dare!” she demanded as Jennifer poured on her learning, starting to catch under his head each time she rose, the man groaning out under the pressure, desperately trying to hold off as Jennifer pressed him on.

“UGGGHHHHhhhhh!!!” came a strange groan, unheard to this point….

"No!!!!!" screamed Nadia in response, Jennifer excited by his struggles, catching him more as she sucked and absolutely squeezing his head with her cheeks as she determined to suck his semen to the surface.

"UGGGGHHHHHHhhhhhh!!!"

"NOOOOOOO!!!" screamed Nadia.

"UGGGGGHHHHHHHHHHHHhhhhh!!!"

Suddenly, Jennifer felt the head swell in her mouth, far larger than it had before! Catching her by surprise, it seemed to fill her inside, pressing down on her tongue as she excitedly clamped down on it, giving an unbelievable tight suck and finally forcing his balls to release, her mouth engulfed in male fluids as she felt it convulse again and again, fluids surging into her mouth as she half-choked, but held on, clamping down and drinking his gift hungrily, determined in her excited state to empty his balls completely, sucking harder and harder as it surged out of her mouth and down her chin. Across her cheeks and flying everywhere, and he groaned in forced ecstasy as Jennifer put all her day's learning to full use, and forced the semen from his balls, his member pumping her with everything it had as she sucked on, never releasing him for a second as the waves of male gratitude filled her throat and washed warmly down to her stomach, the male shaking, becoming sensitive as Jennifer worked him on, his head banging against the wall as she remembered the tortured orgasm earlier, but she couldn't stop her want for the male, gratitude so great after all her work that she wanted it all, and determined to suck it out of his balls, no matter what it did to him!

His head still banging, her hungry slopping sucking

sounds were only stopped by a restraining hand from Nadia, who'd stood back till now, the male still groaning on the other side and Jennifer expecting to turn to Nadia's smiles for her great learning, only to find a scowling anger waiting for her.

Slightly stunned and hurt after all her effort, Nadia squinted at Jennifer, her own confusion answering Jennifer that it was not her who was in trouble, Nadia's forced gentle stroke along her shoulder telling her this much, reassuring her before reaching back for her cane.

Open-mouthed and dribbling with male warmth, Jennifer realized he'd come without permission, that Nadia's final lesson was spoiled and no amount of begging looks were going to stop her this time.

Jennifer looked on as Nadia finally lost her battle with her anger and made to move to the other room, her hand almost on her hip… when a sudden knock stopped her.

Unable to speak, Nadia was so filled with rage, Nadia turned as two intendants opened the door from the other side, the atmosphere stopping them at once from their timed collection of Jennifer, now passed, and bringing them to make sure she was well. Sizing up the scene immediately, they realized it was not Jennifer that was in trouble, and gently motioned her to come from her knees to them, staying silent as they witnessed Nadia's rage. Jennifer's look for permission from her teacher brought a movement of her hand toward the door, all she could give in her current fury, Jennifer gingerly rising and making her way to the waiting intendants while Nadia was seemingly frozen in rage as she bit her teeth behind closed lips, glaring at the doorway to the other room.

Led away by the other two intendants, Jennifer looked back, catching a brief glimpse through the doorway as it closed, Hispanic fury standing perfectly still with a look of solid anger on her calm face, a look Jennifer and the others in her group had grown to fear… a look that signaled she had truly lost her temper. As the door closed, she saw Nadia finally draw her cane from her hip, her eyes cast squarely on the opening that led to the helpless male.

Jennifer felt so sorry for him….

Chapter 31

Understanding

Breakfast… and, oh, what a breakfast – the women alive with delight, their morning stories all abound, crossing tables with mischievous smiles and devious eyes, delighting in what they had done.

Stories of male pain and begging, suffering, had the women engrossed, their laughter unkempt as they swapped tales of trials and pressures kept high.

"Eventually, he cried!" Linda vaulted out, her eyes widening as she told the group.

"So would I if they'd done that to me!" exclaimed Julie from across the table.

"Oh, I doubt that," quipped Suzanna from the end to Julie's pretend scowl, the table laughing on.

"Did you hear about the beating one of them got in the hallway next to the library?" asked Andrea.

"Was it that bad?" frowned Monique.

"I'll say," came a voice from the table to their left. "We saw it from the library; he wouldn't keep his head down, wouldn't stop looking at the women – I think he was new."

"They almost killed him, I heard," returned Andrea.

"Almost," another voice replied from amidst the group opposite them. "Another group of intendants came running to stop it or they would have!"

"It's not right what they're doing to them," defended Amandine, she having difficulty, like some others, with the sheer suffering that was being given them.

"Why?" quipped Samantha, having been beaten badly herself in the early days and now quite hardened to it. "They know the rules; it's their own fault if they can't obey," she regurgitated, the intendants' learning deep inside her now.

"Well, that's just it, they don't," argued Diane. "They haven't had any training, so how can they expect them to act right?"

"Well, if they don't, they end up taken downstairs," Heather lamented, Carly having let slip to her in glee about the procedures for dealing with misattention by males.

"What's it like?" asked Andrea, staring at Jennifer, she the only one of their group to have seen it so far.

"They're all taken downstairs," Jennifer looked down, clearly disturbed as the memories came back. "That's where they keep them," she trailed off, not wanting to answer any further.

"They have to control them," Samantha defended the intendants' hard efforts, thinking over her own months, the reasoning now plainly obvious.

"It's more than that," Suzanna came down on their side sympathetically, but stopped from going any further, the eyes above her doing their work.

"It could be just a strategy," bubbled Julie, trying to lift the strain from the table. "They could just be seeming that hard on them."

"Do you really believe that?" asked Diane. "With what they say they do to them?" she threw another question out after the first, she herself having been informed by intendants of their program, something the rest didn't know yet.

"They can't be that bad to them down there," Andrea joined Julie's side. "It must just be fear strategies to control them… you couldn't be that cruel to someone," she looked over at Jennifer as if for an answer, the rest of the group following her stare.

"They don't care," answered Jennifer finally, conscious of the camera above them, it stopping her answering further and the group staring at her for more, seeing the struggle on her face as she dropped her eyes to the table.

"It can't be that bad," Julie finally uttered, breaking the silence, herself having been in most of the Manor's learning suites, as the brochure called them.

Jennifer struggled to find an answer for them, the camera above having her under pressure as Nadia's eyes burned her from inside, coming through in the memory from the fourth level wing when she'd raged at her questioning, leaping forward….

"It's not for us to question the ways of this house…."

Above in the control room, smiles broke out at Jennifer's answer, the intendants looking on sure to congratulate Nadia later on her fine work with her charge.

The sour note over breakfast didn't last long, laughter soon filling the room again with sickening excitement, some women truly angry at men over their lives' events, now reveling in the chance to see them suffer. Backed up by those who didn't want to go through this part of the house's training at all, their alliance together formed the majority in-house, and with the intendants also sharing this view, the few feeling any sympathy had no significant voice in the wings.

Soon another day began, women taken to this side and that, to the library and outside, to the academy and the cleaning rooms, and then others taken to more specialized appointments… like Jennifer's… taken downstairs, to her horror… a third day on the fourth!

She couldn't have realized it, but it had been at Nadia's insistence. She hadn't been scheduled to receive her final bout of learning with the males for a few more days yet, the time for her mental state to recover a usual timeframe in-house, but Nadia had insisted.

During their morning rise, Jennifer had seen fit to push her liberties with Nadia as she'd bent over to uncuff her, the usual morning whispers of want replaced that morning with a worry about the male, with a question regarding his condition.

Nadia had been irritated, used to being her center of attention each morning and used to such lapping, like some pet reaching up for her, and here today Jennifer had put a male in front of her instead… she would learn.

Taken down by intendants from Samantha's group, there were no platitudes, no ease or familiarity, Jennifer steeling up and not putting a foot wrong as she performed with perfect poise on the way down. Her learning protected her as she moved in tandem with them, no direction required. Her training, her control, and Urst's advice with her as she moved, watched for the slightest error by her guard, foreign group intendants only too happy to instruct another group's women.

Arriving on the fourth level's fearful wings, their cold gloom didn't have to be endured long as she was escorted right from the stairs and on to the first door on the right, Jennifer's heart jumping as she realized what it was, the room with the wall of implements she'd seen before… the house of horrors!

As the door opened to its grey interior, barely lit by the lamp on the floor to the left, the intendants smirked at Jennifer's hesitancy, her wall of professionalism finally breaking under the pressure, the two behind her having to nudge her forward to follow the two in front, her fear their prize.

The door never closed; instead, she was brought to a halt in the center of the room, the grey platform box menacing to her right, the intendants behind her now, smirking further as they felt Jennifer tense upon seeing its wrist restraints open and ready for use to their right.

"Okay, get her ready; it's number four and he's new," said one of the two intendants in front of her as she came back, passing her and leaving with the two behind her, the last intendant in front reaching for her hands.

Shivering, Jennifer's slight resistance brought an immediate slap to her right hip, the intendant barely knowing her and having a no-nonsense approach to foreign groups' slaves. As she began to attach wrist restraints to Jennifer, their cool black leather softness saw her attention drawn for a second, a vicious slap landing on her right hip and dropping her head back to immediate submission.

Then, a new sound along with the slap… the sound of sharp tacking heels on tile, a sound Jennifer had come to know instinctively, a form coming out of the darkness where the implements hung to the left.

Unseen before, with the weak light and her fear on entry, a familiar sight emerged from the darkness, carrying a scowl straight to the other intendant, her own hands pausing on its arrival and not needing any more direction from Nadia, the hands becoming gentler as they worked.

"Well, slave," Nadia shifted her attention to Jennifer as her restraints were attached, small padlocks sealing them around her wrists. "It's time for you to learn," she said, a coy smile held in check at the edge of her mouth, an official tone only just hiding warmth.

Jennifer showed the proper respect, her head staying bowed and awaiting direction.

"You're about to learn what you must," Nadia said, reaching for her chin, pulling her look gently toward her before eying the grey platform on the other side and gently tilting her head toward it.

"Learn well," Nadia instructed as she brought her chin gently back toward her, "And you only have to learn once."

Jennifer's eyes widened, the cryptic message doing little to calm her, though she knew Nadia was caring for her.

Knew, too, did the intendant finishing her cuffs, her eyes squinting as she listened to this obvious show of care, her objections to how Nadia seemed to train her group obvious, she being actually irritated she was here at all, but still she knew better than to make issue of it.

"What you take from today is up to you," Nadia continued cryptically, "it can be painful, or instructional… my advice is to enjoy the instruction;

that way, your questioning…" She grimaced slightly, trailing off in thinking of Jennifer asking after the male's welfare that morning. "…Will at least be answered." She raised her eyebrows, still gently holding Jennifer's chin like some pet as Jennifer gently nodded onto her fingers.

"You won't enjoy this," said the other, the intendant having moved down to secure ankle cuffs to Jennifer and finally unable to stand the care being displayed anymore, her group employing more traditional methods of control on the women. "Although you won't forget it," she laughed gleefully as she rose, ready to tease Jennifer further when her smile came up against seething anger, waiting for her as she stood.

A short exchange of looks saw her smile leave as she moved off, Nadia irritated by her treatment of her favorite, this being common knowledge in house now, and seeing her angry defense of Jennifer coming forward.

Jennifer had to fight not to smile as the other intendant cowered at the head of the grey platform, seeming to fumble with the wrist cuffs and other objects below its top and out of sight, her head drooping slightly under Nadia's glare.

Turning back to Jennifer, Nadia tried to stay professional as she saw Jennifer's obvious show of emotion, her feelings bubbling for her in her eyes.

"You have to see the difference," she said to her, Jennifer almost frowning, but holding her composure with Nadia picking up the point and answering Jennifer's unspoken question. "Between professionals and…." she grimaced, thinking of men, her irritation toward them strong and welling up. "Amateurs…" she finally finished, cocking her head slightly and raising her eyebrows, asking if her charge understood. Jennifer bowed her head dutifully and respectfully, more than aware an explanation was far more than any normal slave got, much less a care that she understood. Nadia then released her to the other intendant's care, the woman's heart jumping as she watched Nadia glare at her, the message clear, before the senior intendant moved off and left the room.

Taking Jennifer by the shoulder, the remaining intendant led her to the top of the box, her ankle cuffs snapped to waiting attachments near the floor at its head before she was bent carefully forward over the platform, the door still open in front of her and to her right. Her hips nestling between the platform's open wrist cuffs, Jennifer watched as her own wrist cuffs were attached three quarters of the way down the platform to steel eyelets just under its edges, one being every six inches along its length at either side. Snapped neat and secure, even the padlocks were applied with care, the intendant seeming not to dare hurt her and Jennifer fighting hard not to smile as she felt Nadia's love protecting her….

Secure and held, Jennifer watched from the platform as the intendant moved off, out in front of her, sharp tacking boots and leather uniform swinging powerful hips across the room, the sound continuing through the door and disappearing down the wing.

For a time, Jennifer was calm, but that quickly faded as she was left alone with her thoughts, her slight shifting in her holdings showing her just how tight they were, the barest of movements possible with only her head able to survey her surroundings.

Silence, dull grey walls barely lit with her platform, the door in front of her even darker, left open to the wing, Jennifer shivering at the sight and uncomfortable in the gloom. Slaves didn't like being left alone – they needed constant attention and encouragement, like any needing pet, as they needed direction and praise, correction and strength, this giving them their place in life and a feeling of belonging.

Right now, only shivers belonged to Jennifer, the cold air creeping in from the wing and leaving her feeling vulnerable and uneasy, now her mind realizing that anything could come through the doorway, no one here to keep her safe.

Looking right, she saw the gloom hid the leather-strewn wall, shapes of implements melding together in the dark, leaving Jennifer with no clue what was to happen in the room, the sharp glint of steel here and there sending thoughts racing, fear increasing as she waited.

Silence… worry… fear… Jennifer felt her vulnerability, bent over and ready for anyone who came behind her… number four, they'd said… she knew they'd said… what had Nadia meant? That she could take instruction from this… from what?…. Surely they weren't going to let him…

"You won't enjoy this!"

The intendant's words who'd cuffed her rang out in her ears as she looked down her platform, realizing the position she'd been secured in, the realization dawning on her what was about to happen….

Then they came! The sound of tacking heels, low at first and echoing up along the wing, louder from the right as they came, Jennifer knowing that's were they kept the males and slightly pulling on her wrist restraints as she realized what they were bringing. Her pulls were useless as the heels got louder, and multiple heels meant multiple intendants, only grouped when they guarded, guarding a charge they were bringing to her….

Trying to remain calm, Jennifer bowed her head to the table, her eyes still fixed on the doorway, heels echoing as the first set of leather corsets swept into view, their in-house uniforms coming straight to Jennifer, a no-nonsense approach as she caught the first sight of the naked male among them!

Frightened, she fought hard to keep her head, the door finally being closed behind the last two as they entered, the other two continuing on, escorting the male behind her, holding his wrists as they came. Jennifer squirmed as she felt the heat from his body close behind her, making her tighten up inside and making her want to cry – not wanting what was coming to her, this not what she'd come here for!

As she fretted with the horror running through her, she watched the intendants at the door lock it! Lock it from the inside, her mind suddenly racing as she remembered the other time a door had been locked on them from the inside, and what had happened after that, her whole body screaming as they finished and moved toward her!

Totally strained in her cuffs, she listened as the male was instructed behind her, warned that the slightest deviation from their instruction would bring immediate savagery to him, Jennifer feeling like crying as she heard two sets of boots move toward the wall of implements.

She waited in absolute horror, waited for what was about to be done to her, knowing no one would stop it as the two sharp sets of heels tacked back from the wall, the sound of sliding leather filling the silence as an implement was passed to someone behind her.

Screaming inside, Jennifer listened as all the heels present moved off to her right, the intendants seeming to turn and remain in line, the darkness shrouding them in her vision and the room now silent but for the screams inside her head....

"Begin!"

The blow was savage!

"AAAAAUuuughhhhh!" Jennifer heard herself scream out, her nerves unable to hold her composure as this final stress across her ass cheeks broke her.

Then another!

"AAAUgghhhhhh!" Jennifer blurted out again as leather straps landed on her like a car crash.

"Slave!!! Composure!"

Came a threatening demand from her in-line audience. Jennifer grimaced as she heard a cat of nine tails being taken through the air behind her in clumsy fashion, the wielder obviously having no clue how to wield it.

Slam!

Jennifer groaned, but held her scream, no more instruction from the intendants who were seemingly satisfied with her effort. Then another Slam and another, Jennifer's muffled groans filling the room as she suffered the landings of this fool!

'What is this idiot doing?' She thought as yet another clumsy landing found her cheeks, her audience silent as she struggled in front of them. The landings were stupid, amateurish, the wielder having no subtlety or understanding as to what she was feeling, it being obvious from the blows that he couldn't empathize, much less control her, no skill to show direction or flow. Another blow and another, Jennifer letting out a yelp before containing herself better, the intendants offering no correction at her outburst and seeming to understand she couldn't help it.

Unknown to Jennifer, they were similarly disturbed by the ridiculous display by the male charge, it being offensive to them, but worse was still to come.

Watching on as Jennifer struggled, they grimaced in the dark, out of sight, their rage and irritation finding them scowling and clenching their fists, this the reason they were in the darkness, so that the male would not be put off by their objections.

It was not just Jennifer being tortured, but they, too, as they watched one of their charges being beaten under their care, this amateurish attempt at direction being necessary and part of her training, but painful for all to watch. They grimaced further as the lesson began to take hold, the male beginning to smile and enjoy himself, their rage at this hidden in the darkness… his silly mind not realizing how he'd pay… how they'd make him suffer for this later!

Another cry echoed off the walls, this tolerated by her guard as Jennifer endured another stupid land, her ass becoming sore but not stinging, just sore, her cries leaking out more and more as she, too, realized the idiot was enjoying this. Struggling, she listened on to the male's breathing, it being that of enjoyment, his lust increasing with his landings – that much obvious, his attempts at skill leaving Jennifer angry… and seeing her grimace. Grimace more and more at his stupidity, it growing painful with his enthusiasm, each strike seeing her audience wince now as they watched a beating, not a session.

Crying out with the fool's enthusiasm, Jennifer realized as she suffered through it that her horror was unfounded, and that she wasn't to receive what she'd feared most. She realized as the beating came that this was to show the difference… the difference between teaching and fine instruction… between correction and idiocy.

Groaning as her ass bruised, as they let it continue, not watching the strikes but her face as they suffered to in the darkness beside her. Unknown to Jennifer, it was her expressions they were watching, not for learning or for suffering, but for anger and for rage.

Usually, these feelings were discouraged, corrected out by intendant training, their will that of fear and submission and their authority meant to be absolute. Today, though, they had to step back, allowing this procedure to flow in front of them, something they had to endure, it being something the Mistress could not.

Beaten on, Jennifer was corrected verbally more than once, her cries becoming hopeless, and then angry, and then what they wanted. Groaning under the bruises on her rear, she was allowed to moan out as they brought an end to the display. Unable to hide her anger, Jennifer seethed at the male now in front of her as they took him to her right, to the center of the room.

With him manacled in front of her, the intendants watched her expressions as they secured him, satisfied that Jennifer was ready for the next stage. No correction was offered to her scowls, her usual submission replaced by anger with her ass hurting hard behind her. Watching, Jennifer grimaced, her heavy breathing signaling pain, no care offered to her, bruising seemingly ignored as the intendants formed up, unlocking the door to the wing beyond Jennifer, almost growling as she watched them leave with the male among them.

Wounded, she struggled hard in her confinement, uselessly pulling on her restraints, her ass begging for attention, for soothing hands, for application of lubricant, but nothing came… just her groaning increasing as she was left alone with her pain.

Her ass continued hurting, growing in agony, her tissues swelling as she was soon in tears, trapped alone. Her cries echoed through the doorway, down the wing, the soft flow of cool air flowing inside and seeming to try to sooth her, but her entrapment seeing her scream instead, seeing her cry out helplessly.

Her ass hurt, but hardly stung – it was hurting from the fool's blows, from his silly beating. Left to endure the pain, she started hating him and started thinking of how Nadia had dealt with the other one, started to feel he'd deserved it, and how this other deserved the same.

This was, of course, her training… not the beating, not the fear, but the showing of the difference between a professional and an amateur, and of why the males were treated how they were. Jennifer seethed as she remembered his enjoyment behind her; how dare he enjoy doing this to her, she thought, and his silly attempt at correction… he didn't have the right to deal with her at her level, she thought on… he was beneath her… how dare he…. She was learning well.

Eventually, over the rest of the morning, her tears dried down the tracks of her face. Exhausted from the pain and slumped down now over the platform, her pitying herself had fallen away, replaced by anger as she'd remained confined….

Watching this transformation from hidden cameras above, the intendants saw their work had been successful and went to get her… after lunch.

Taken to a familiar room down the east wing of the fourth level, Jennifer bore witness to some correction on the rack; still angry, she was surprised how she could watch so easily, the charge's screams not disturbing her like before. Guarded by two of the intendants from the morning, her hands were cuffed out in front of her as they stood watching. It seemed that they were to make sure her ass continued to hurt her as they waited, Jennifer too angry to care what was coming next as she listened to the wayward screams of the slave lying out in front of her, the wand snapping along her body… she deserved it.

Jennifer suddenly snapped to, herself, as she realized what she'd just thought, Samantha's uncaring attitude from the opposite table at breakfast coming into her mind as she realized what was being done to her…. she was being hardened.

Not sure she liked this, Jennifer thought on as the screaming continued, the shackled slave seeing her misattention bringing her here, the intendants expecting more from them now, and quite ruthless in their demanding of it. True, it seemed heartless, but they did work hard on them and were probably quite rightly offended after such hard work if a slave didn't try hard enough or if they continued being wayward… No, Jennifer thought as she watched the slave writhe and struggle in her restraints, screaming out again as the wand came down along her length… she knew the rules by now… she deserved it!

In the west wing along the fourth level, something else deserved was being prepared. Unknown to Jennifer, her other two intendant guards had just walked into a room directly across the wing from the male holding area… from the prison.

This room was behind the wall of implements Jennifer had observed that morning, behind that wall and across from the prison, and had been the place Jennifer thought she'd heard the screaming males before… she had.

A strange room, having cream walls brightly lit from flat ceiling lights buried in the office like suspended tiles that made up the roof above them and gave a business feel, the room itself being oval and disorientating.

Built intentionally this way, when one occupied its center and the door was closed, craftsmanship in the decorating meant the door itself could not be seen, the room completely oval and leaving one difficulty in seeing any way out. The floor was soft maple and melded perfectly to cream walls and ceiling above, no fixed point for eyes to seize on, the feel bewildering after just a short time inside.

There was only one fixed point, number four's eyes widening as he was shackled towards it by his stony-faced intendants, he at least learning by now not to struggle.

With the door sealed behind them, leather corsets marched a trapped male straight across the room, their echoing heels reverberating off the walls with his fears as they came toward the large device he'd never seen before but which was at the center of the room… a pain stand.

A soft oval rug, cream colored, greeted the male's feet as they marched him to the center, their boots stopping, tacking as he felt the last of the comfort he'd know that day. Eyes widening further, he felt a rough jolt from the intendants pulling his shackles and, irritated at his hesitancy, they saw him brought unsympathetically to the end of the rug and turned toward the device, the door they'd arrived through now directly to their left, but invisible in the wall, the disorientation already beginning to take hold on him.

Looking down at the form in front of him, the male stared at a steel pole, two feet high, and then a large bracket; he saw a wooden box found at its top… at waist height.

The box was rectangular, its length facing away from him, a small hole on the face at his side with some sort of hinged fixture underneath and around it, the shape concerning him as his eyes looked at large fixed wrist cuffs, black steel with black leather lining, one to either side of the box… bolted on.

As the intendants had dropped and busied themselves with his shackles, a sudden pull at his ankle restraints saw his attention come down to their no-nonsense working hands, business-like and firm as they proceeded to seal him in to a point below.

Looking down below the box, bracketed to the pole, he saw that its three feet steel of led down to a large rectangular structure on the floor. The pole found another large bracket at its center, from which four flat steel lengths, four inches wide, went out at left and right, two feet long, and at front and back, four feet long… the end of each flat steel length bolted to a rectangle of flat steel, these again four inches wide and enclosing the structure in the middle of the room.

The sheer weight of the device's steel structure saw it push deep into the rug below, the male becoming worried even more as he saw, at each corner on the enclosing steel rectangle, bolts securing it through the rug and directly into the floor below.

Only beginning to realize the severity of the situation he was in, his downward gaze, half-ignored by the intendants, suddenly saw them securing his ankle cuff eyelets directly onto fixings on the long length of steel leading from the central bracket, his way and out, behind his feet to the enclosing rectangular structure around him.

In only seconds, he was padlocked by his feet to the structure, having hardly time to feel fear as the intendants rose around him, their speed at confining him a tactic to confuse and disorientate, having him secured before he realized what was happening…

before he had time to call out. Their business-like stony-faced ignorance of his increasingly fearful expression continued, their taking his hands like he was meat, his hesitant struggle overridden as two intendant hands on each wrist saw them brought to steel cuffs at either side of the box, their metal sound of locking complete with small padlocks, making any escape now impossible.

Then… calm….

The intendants visibly relaxed, slowing down, one moving forward and even passing a small smile to the other as she stayed to the male's right, his confusion continuing at their seemingly eased attitude toward him. It was as if, now that he couldn't get away, they were at ease, as if with the heavy secure work finished, they could now relax… he was wrong.

As he watched the one in front of him, a sudden wave of pleasure passed through him as the intendant's silky soft hand beside him found his member. Looking to his right, he was surprised, this being a move sure to bring a beating, but he was further surprised to find a warm, smiling face, the intendant gently masturbating him as she smiled into his confused eyes with the show of warmth.

Then, he heard it….

It was a tactic! Simply to draw his attention from the one in front and keep him calm as she'd reached under the box on top of the pole in front of him, the sharp sound of a locking latch reverberating around the silent room, seeing his eyes fall back on the other intendant, as she opened the box…

He looked on in confusion as the rectangular box's left side swung open just in front and out of reach of his fingers, on a hinge at its far corner, almost halving the left side in two and revealing a circular comfortable-looking leather-padded lining on its inside. As he continued looking down in confusion, he hadn't even noticed that the intendant to his right had stopped masturbating him and simply held his erect member while the other in front of him reached down and flicked a small black switch on the bracket below the box, allowing a twenty-four volt current to find the small red light inside the box.

Suddenly, more confusion as the tiny lightbulbs sheathed in plastic guards let a crimson glow escape the box, coming from their positions inside on the box's end nearest the male. Inside, the mahogany box was bathed in red as tiny bulbs low down in the corners of the box's nearest wall glowed off the leather lining of the now open-hinged left wall, the male watching as a smiling intendant moved her hand inside. His attention was taken by the other intendant, the two now crowding in on him, worrying him as, for the first time, he pulled back on his restraints, the intendant nearest him smiling as she felt it, the attempt hopeless and the male fearing as he felt how tightly he was secured.

Not giving him time to think, the two suddenly increased speed again, the male fearing as he felt the hands of the intendant nearest him pull the flat circular hinge on the box end in front, swinging it down. Suddenly, the opening, the small hole in the box became larger with the hinge falling away as she immediately took his member forward, a waiting hand seizing it from inside and pulling him strongly in! The other intendant's hand squeezed hard on the male shaft from inside the box as she beamed into his eyes, watching his fear. Her gaze into his eyes as she squeezed the hungry penis was yet another tactic, his attention shifted to her as she reached further down, seeming to pleasure him as he felt her explore his vulnerability, taking his balls in her hand and gently tugging them forward, all the time keeping his attention fixed on her with a hungry look . He only dropped his eyes from her as the hinge came back up, under his balls beneath him, his feeling his whole equipment now trapped inside the box, the hinge's half-moon circular shape tightened firmly underneath him, escape now impossible as another small padlock from the intendant's garter was snapped shut on the hinge's fixing.

Looking back up as he felt the hinge squeeze menacingly on his most vulnerable part below him, his fearful look met cruel enjoyment, the intendant in front having to fight hard not to laugh as she gave his member a final squeeze before releasing it, and closing the box on his vulnerability.

Crowding in on him fast now, his worried breathing brought enjoyment to them both as they pushed their leather dominance in on either side of him, their sultry uniforms and silken skin bringing no excitement… just fear as hands writhed around him, his head looking all around when a sudden searing slap across his rear erupted…

"Eyes Front!!!"

Obeyed… and Slam! Another searing strike across his rear from the other intendant,

"Down!!!"

Obeyed…. His head drooped down as he suddenly realized how vulnerable he was, the intendants suddenly stopping their smiling, their control tactics no longer necessary to distract him and their work completed… it was back to despising him now….

As the male feared, realizing it was all an act and there would be no softening or friendliness over time among them, he felt them work on to secure him even more. Reaching down for a steel eyelet below his shackled hand on the box, securing a thick black holding strap to it, and then its cool soft leather almost covered his whole rear as they wrapped it around him, pulling him tight against the box, almost uncomfortably so as it was snapped on to the eyelet on the opposite side.

A short survey of their work, a pull on this fixing and that ensuring tightness, and they were finished, a glare of utter contempt and revilement from them into his drooped and quiet head being the last of their work before they left, his head never rising as their boots left the room.

His head didn't lift, but he tried to move a little in his confinement… he couldn't. Not uncomfortable, but tight, he breathed heavily, squeezed hard against the box with its heavy steel bracket and securing mount below ensuring only his ankles could move slightly in their restraints, his hands free to move, but sealed hard at the wrists.

Eventually, he couldn't help it, looking around the room in silence; he couldn't see a door or anything else, the stillness maddening.

How long was he there? Half an hour, an hour? No way to be sure… only his breathing to keep him company; bored, but he was new in house, and didn't appreciate this rare pleasure… he'd soon know it didn't happen often.

A crack and a door opened in front of him, a little to the right on the oval room, his head lifting in surprise; he'd known there was a door on the left somewhere, which they'd come through, but hadn't even noticed there was one out in front of him, and now four stony-faced intendants – the same guard from the morning's lesson – came tacking through, a leashed subject crawling on the floor among them.

He watched as they came in, his disorientation clearing as he recognized the crawling subject, her look angry and resentful… Jennifer!

Suddenly he pulled back, inadvertently, as he realized exactly what the box was for, Jennifer leashed straight toward him as his eyes filled with fear!

With her moving toward him, there was no screaming, no savage demands or harsh punishments, but four smiling intendants clearly amused at the fearful look, having no intension of letting him hide it as they crowded in on him at the box, starting to laugh with glee as they teased him, daring him to talk and annoy them. Watching his growing fear, they laughed as it heightened with a crawling Jennifer now being secured on her knees on the opposite side from him. Laughing on, they let him watch as her ankles were secured like his to the flat steel length leading from the bracket on her side, her hands secured to it, too, her wrist cuffs padlocked to more steel fixings on her side.

Then, the laughter was subdued, a building quiet around them now as they all watched his face, one of them reaching down under the box, a sharp clicking like before seeing the left side open again, the laughter returning at his face, the procedure moving on… to another face

To a very angry face, her ass still hurting from the morning, still in pain and bruised, worse now, memories sharp from her hours of suffering, having been left on her own over the box all that morning, and now determined it was her turn! Her turn as the male feared, looking down as a raging twisted Jennifer, her head gently coaxed out to the left of the box by the intendants, laughing on at a terrified male as they let him watch them slip her head into the box, sealing the left side behind her… sealing her in with his member!!!

"Bye-bye…. See you in the morning!" They laughed with glee, intendant etiquette falling away as they witnessed his fear, cajoling each other with their fine work as they left in rowdy disarray to the control room above where other intendants waited in mirth, all ready to watch the pain below!

Inside, a raging Jennifer was momentarily stunned by the sight in front of her, a sight to behold, and she even felt herself getting horny, the smell of raw trapped male in front her doing much to bring her around. Her glowing red cage complete with male fun almost had her smiling at the sight, but then she felt her ass hurting, still untreated from the morning, and moved forward with her teeth reaching out for him for the first of many times!

The screams were panicked cries at first – not pain, just fear – Jennifer having difficulty getting hold of it, awkward without her hands, but get a hold of him, she would! Finally irritated, she lunged at it, the effort bringing the first of his many pleadings, asking her to…

“Stop!”

That he was…

“Sorry!”

Well, he hadn’t been sorry that morning, Jennifer remembering how he’d enjoyed it, Samantha right, she thought as her teeth clamped down on his shaft for the first time, hard… they deserved this!

“AAAAAARRRRRRGGGHhhhhh!!!!!! Please… AAAAARRRRRRGGGhhhhhhhh!!!”

His panicked cries and struggling reverberated through the mahogany to Jennifer, seeing her just bite harder, the tears of laughter in the control room having to be subdued by the intendants on duty as they watched the once sweet Jennifer go to work!

“That’s your girl!” an intendant shouted gleefully to Nadia as she stood watching, too proud of her favorite’s savagery!

“Huh Uggghhh AAAAAAARRghghh uggh uughh….”

The man struggled above Jennifer, clutching pointlessly at the box, his wrists secured to it as she worked on him inside. Strange, she thought, that he felt calmer, as if he was getting used to it, his penis becoming even harder, she noticed… how could he be…. Jennifer suddenly realized that his fear had dropped, that he was enjoying it! Well!!! She raged, remembering her lessons from the male secured to the wall as she eyed the rim under his head and raised up, making sure her teeth found their way under it…

"AAAAAAAAAAAAAARRRRRRRRRRRGG GHHHHHHHGHHHHHHHHH!!!"

His panicked cries filled the room, shattering around it as he wrestled hopelessly with the pain stand, Jennifer delivering unbelievable pain inside as she bit her revenge into him, howls of laughter filling the control room above!

"AAAAAAAAAAAAAARRRRRRGGGGGHG GHHHHHHHHHHHHHHH!!! PLEASE!!! AAARRRGHGGGHHHHHHHHHHH!!!"

He begged in utter agony, Jennifer being a woman and unable to understand the pain she was delivering, or the fear she had him in with this attack on his most vulnerable and prized possession. Inside the mahogany box, she worked on as, outside, the male's cries bounced off the walls, his eyes having nothing to focus on in the echoing oval, his mind only able to focus on the pain, this being the real reason for the structure of this maddening chamber….

"AAAAAAAAAAAAAAAAAAAAAARRRRRRRR GGGGGGHHHHHHHHHHH STOP!!! PLEASEE!!! AAAAAAAAAARRRRRRRGGHHHHH!!!"

Nadia was stunned as she watched her favorite work, her sisters howling with laughter around her as Jennifer gouged into him again and again, the man screaming in terror as she felt him struggle against her, pain and the stand having him helpless and having to suffer his agony inside. With the screaming muffled, Jennifer suddenly felt something else, something unexpected as she worked, something between her shackled legs… wet… she was turned on!

Turned on, as he screamed and tried to pull away from her, as she chased his penis around the box, it slipping from her grasp at times, only for her to chase it into one of the box's corners, trapping it and getting it in her mouth again, her teeth clamping down, she only wishing she had her hands as the male screamed on above her!

He'd pay for what he'd done… oh, how he'd pay, she thought as she lost her grip on him once again, the male screaming and shaking the structure they were locked into, as such was his fear of her as she chased him, his balls gently slapping her chin as she went… his balls!

Jennifer suddenly realized that, in her determination to catch his penis, she'd forgotten about them… and how sensitive they were….

Suddenly, the panicked male screamed his way into begging!

"NOOO, NO, PLEASE, NOOOO!!!"

As he felt Jennifer move down, concentrating on the poor vulnerable balls who could not get away, like the selfish penis, Jennifer's eyes widened as she took the first one in her mouth, the male screaming in panic as her teeth came slowly down…

"AAAAAAAAAAAAAARRRRRRRGGGGGGGG HHHHHHHHHH HELP!!! PLEASE!!! NOOOOOOO!!! AARRRGGHHHHHHHHHHH!!!"

Shrieks of laughter came in the control room, the staff on duty unable to control anyone anymore as they, too, knew what the short pause in the male's suffering had meant, and how his now truly disturbing screaming was a sure sign that Jennifer had his balls!

"AAAAAAARARRRHghghhGGHhgh!!! PLEEASE!!! AAAAAAARGGGHGHH!!! PLEASE!! AAAARRRGGHHHHHHH!!!"

Jennifer listened as she applied her lessons of pain, now to the second of his balls, the male unable to even speak properly anymore as she made him pay, still angry over the hours of hurt he'd left her in, in the House of Horrors, a Horror of her own now being given back as she clamped down on the second ball!

"AAAAAAAAAARRRRAGGGHGHGGHHGHG HGHGGGHH!!!!!!!!" He wrestled in agony against the stand, his screams coming back at him from around the room as he grew disorientated and begged, even lurching forward over the pain stand soon, Jennifer having his first ball again as he shot bolt upright, screaming in agony….

"AAAAAAAAARRRRRRRRRGGGGGHHHH HHhhhHghhhghghhg!!!!!!!!!" His face was white! Terrified and in shock! Nadia watching on above was, for the first time, not sure she liked Jennifer having so much power, or what she was doing, but the other intendants in the room were more than sure….

"Go on, Jennifer, do it!" an intendant voice screamed at the screen.

"Remember what he did to you!" came another, then another and another, Nadia squinting, unsure as suddenly….

"Jennifer! Jennifer! Jennifer! Jennifer! Jennifer! Jennifer! Jennifer! Jennifer! Jennifer! Jennifer! Jennifer!"

Nadia, for the first time, looked at the fear on the man's face on screen, his terrified cries being drowned out by her sisters' sick and repugnant laughter… for the first time, feeling unsure of what they were doing to him, but she wasn't going to stop it.

"AAAAAAAAARRRGGGHGHGGGHHHGHGH GHGHGG!!!!!!! Please pleasee Plaswe AAARARRRRRRRHHHGGGHGGHHHHH!!!!!"

Jennifer had become bored with his balls and made her way back to the penis, determined to punish its selfishness, it still remaining hard despite her efforts as she trapped it once more against a corner and seized its bulging end.

"AAAAAAARRRRGGGHhhhgghhg… no no

no…. Please. No no… AAARARARGGGAAAAAAAGGGHGHHHHHHH!!! ”

The male screamed in agony as Jennifer found her way under the head again, getting very good at it now, the penis raw from her attacks but she having no intention of stopping, the box’s solid mahogany structure doing its job to dampen the male’s cries and leaving Jennifer not fully aware of just how much she was torturing him….

Screaming went on, both in the maddening oval and in the control room above, the male aware he was trapped and in real mortal danger, but with no one aware of his location, no one to stop these crazed women from going too far if they chose, a crazed one clamping down on him inside as he screamed out, his heart racing with his tears!

Yes, tears… tears of embarrassment, of sorrow, of suffering and fear, as a once male submissive was brought face to face with the true realization that there really was no care for his suffering in this place… that there was no escape, as he was trapped!

“AAAAAAAAAARRRGGGGGGHHHH!!!”

His panic raised all the more as he suddenly realized, like the other males, that this was not some sexual game and that the staff of this place really had no concern for him at all, as a sudden bout of savagery from Jennifer took his pain to new heights, her teeth finally breaking through his skin with her efforts!

“AAAAAAAAAARRRRRRGGGHHHHHHHHH!!! No, NO… Noooooooooooo!!! AAAARRRRRGGGHHHHHHHHHHHHHHGGHH HHHH!!!”

Blood!

Blood running down his shaft with searing stinging under his head as she continued biting him, unaware, his screaming reaching huge heights and reverberating off the walls as he wrestled in panic, this new pain searing inside him with the rest as Jennifer continued on, the male panicking and becoming light–headed, begging for mercy!

Jennifer could feel that something had changed; caught up in her determination to deliver her payback, she could feel the male's sudden increased struggles and hear his voice reach new heights through the muffled mahogany, but didn't know why, and yet her teeth were sinking down once more the fluid unnoticed with her anger and chase….

"AAAAARRRRRRRRRRGGHHHHHHGGHH HHH!!!"

He was red-faced and panicked, with clutching hands, wrists manacled with useless cries for mercy, and there was the delight of the howling audiences above as the final male collapse began, the mind caving in as he collapsed in tears for all to view….

Jennifer could hear the tears… at first, they didn't affect her, she being still angry, and then she finally tasted it… blood!

Her first reaction was for herself as she pulled back, reviled and fearing disease… and then she calmed and remembered the Academy… the information on how all house guests were screened.

Her hesitation, though, had stopped her attack on him, the pause allowing her to hear the male's searing tears above her, the blood running down his ripped member in front of her, a crimson picture of her savage cruelty on him….

She was suddenly consumed with guilt as her truly caring and submissive nature returned, no longer blinded by her anger as she instinctively tried to reach forward with her hands to care for him, to show sorrow for what she had done… but she couldn't.

Her hands trapped, her face fell as she listened to the bawling male above her, his emotion real, his suffering unbelievable at her hands, as she had to face what she'd done in front of her… how could she have!?!

How could she have done this to him, she thought, as his tears bawled out above her, guilt consuming her below as she began to hate herself for this act against him. Again, she tried to reach out, to care as the suffering male's cries filled the box around her, magnifying what she'd done to him, and the guilt, but there was no way….

The guilt! As it filled her body, it brought the memories of the male's suffering in the prison to her, the memories of the male savaged by Nadia against the wall, the realization that she was now part of it, of their pain, and that this poor male would lie suffering in agony in the freezing night on the prison floor because of her…. She couldn't stand it….

As he cried out in true agony above her, crying for help and for mercy, she was consumed with hatred for herself… for them, the intendants…. They'd made her do this to him, made her this horrible bitch like them, her anger seeing her terrorize this male and now hate them as he sobbed above her after what she'd done to him. It made her want to cry, herself, as she looked on at what she'd done to him his quivering tears visible in the shaking of his savaged equipment in front of her….

She wanted to reach out her hands, though trapped, wanted to say she was sorry, wanted to care for the sobbing male, and suddenly, almost on instinct and out of guilt and caring, she had him in her mouth again!

The male shrieked at first as he realized it wasn't over, the first sting of saliva meeting ripped skin seeing him convulse to attention, Jennifer having him all the way in her mouth now, the man gripping the sides of the box and steeling up, preparing to scream as the teeth came down… but they never did.

Instead, a confused surge of pleasure washed through his body, this mixed with a gentle sting, the pleasure more, and smothering as Jennifer gave of her sorrow now, the male close to fainting, his emotional rollercoaster having seen fear, terror, hopelessness, and now pleasure run through him, his senses shot in the maddening oval room as the first moans of pleasure drifted out. Trapped like him, inside they gently glanced off the oval walls, Jennifer gently caring for him below, feeling him come around and calm with her attentions as she made her sorrow known with all her training, her first strong sucking apology bringing a groan of thanks from above.

Happy at the sound, she apologized more, tasting blood with other fluids, but those other fluids were growing stronger, Jennifer sure she was making her sorrow known. She was reaching up for his growing end, and he groaned on with her stinging sweetness, her attentions light on his wounded member, determined now to make her apology felt.

The male's tears had fallen away, Jennifer able to feel his nervousness lift as she worked firmly on him now… strange, she thought, as she sucked down; if the male had done similarly to her and then offered her pleasure, to say sorry, she certainly wouldn't have accepted. That's just the way males are, she reasoned with herself, sucking him down, an obvious grateful groan sounding out above her… they always need what we can give them, always are grateful for our attention.

Soon, the male certainly was, his member swelled and filling Jennifer's mouth, now the small sting from his open wound almost nothing when compared to Jennifer's giving. Her time at the wall remembered well, she gave it all to this grateful male, his soon struggling and heaving at the box giving Jennifer warning as she felt his pulse quicken….

But she wouldn't turn away, wouldn't stop saying 'sorry' hard… sucking stronger with each raise on his head as he swelled up, Jennifer taking him there, his groans loud and completely uncontrolled as Jennifer felt the first stirring from his balls within, more fluid appearing as she felt the convulsing start. A new torture now of pure pleasure, hard, the male clutching the box and unsure of how much it was to take this, Jennifer increasing her grip on him, groaning pleasure signaling the first taste of real semen as he began to lose control. The next shattering convulsion saw Jennifer sucking hard still, the male groaning out with no choice but to take her sorrow now, Jennifer losing control as she excitedly brought him home, his groans heaving off the walls and his member surging forward, Jennifer filled with grateful semen and her mouth bulging as she took him in! New groans filled the room as Jennifer fought to keep him in her mouth, awash with male warmth, his penis bathed in the slippery surge. Jennifer sucked down, her stomach filling, her mouth overflowing with male warmth surging out around her lips, his balls emptied to her torture, her attentions hard and tightening on. Coated in his own gratitude, his member slippery inside her mouth now, Jennifer choked happily on his warmth, washing her sins away with his surging thanks now. Pulsating on, and her mouth filled fully, unable to contain the grateful wash, it shooting out as pressure built. Shooting up her cheeks and across her mouth, it suddenly found her eye, stinging hard as she groaned, but held on, still determined to show her sorrow for him.

Groaning out, Jennifer sucked him on, letting him pump his warmth rhythmically down her throat and taking it all inside, showing she was sorry, his groaning loud as he delivered his last, a hungry torturess determined to empty him fully. Collapsing over the stand once more, the male groaned out, as Jennifer wouldn't let up, sucking his balls dry from beneath, her attentions tightening as she fought for his last.

With passions dropping, Jennifer's eye began to sting more, really hurting now as she released him, more concerned with her pain and there being no way to stop it. Really hurting, Jennifer was suddenly irritated by his groaning above her as she realized this was the second time, despite all she'd done for him, that he'd made her sting, and now her eye stung so as she looked forward… at a vulnerable member.

Just like on the wall, the selfish penis lay before her, tired-looking; it had shrunk, beginning to lean to one side as if going to sleep after all it had done. It had caused its owner so much pain, and caused her the same, too, and now it was selfishly going to sleep… well, Jennifer didn't think that was fair!

Suddenly, the man raised up off the stand as he felt things change below him as Jennifer chased the selfish penis, the man calling out as he felt her trying to seize it with her teeth again, but it was so slippery now with its semen coating it, annoying Jennifer more as it slipped away from her, making her more determined as she finally trapped it, seizing it with her teeth and making it pay!

"AAAAARRRRRRRRGGGGGGHHHHHHH!!! PLEASE, NOOOO!!! AAARARRRRRRGGGHHHHH!!!"

Another round of begging screaming had Jennifer finally release his member, satisfied she'd made her displeasure known, and with the effort to hold onto it now with its slipperiness so tiring, she finally let him go….

She eyed it in front of her as it grew limper and smaller, the selfish penis finally going to sleep after all the pain it had put its owner through, Jennifer not sure she wanted to let it get away with it; why should it, she thought?

Again, she thought of biting it, but it was so slippery that she couldn't be bothered as her eyes shifted to the male's balls, and she thought about them… but she had been very mean to them, and they didn’t annoy her like the penis… instead, she sighed and let her head rest against the side of the box, a small smile emerging on her face as she looked at the equipment in front of her and realized she was horny, and then realized something else… he had had pleasure, and was satisfied, and she wasn’t! Jennifer had no possibility of orgasming – instead, she was trapped and horny, and her eyes where stinging… why should the man be allowed to get away with this, she thought… why should he get pleasure and she not?

Another round of screaming on the pain stand, then!

It didn’t last long, though, the man being very lucky that it was Jennifer, the stand having seen the breaking of many men before, with women inside who were not as caring as her. After a short time, she began to care for him again, both beginning to get on as Jennifer couldn’t help sucking on him, her state now moving from angry to caring to horny… she needed to cum and, as long as she couldn’t, the male would get no rest!

This was supposed to be another part of the stand’s torture – with the female unable to cum and bathed in the scents and sights of male vulnerability, it was meant to keep her attending to him in whatever fashion she chose, all night, until merciful release in the morning found the male utterly savaged… but that wasn’t Jennifer’s way.

Instead, the male only had the lightest of tortures from her once her initial anger had been delivered to him, the two actually beginning to truly enjoy each other's company....

This was not the same in the control room above, and soon doors opened to approaching heels, their session cut short with intendants angry at the pleasurable display, this not being what the room was for.

Still, the two waited as the sound of opening latches bathed Jennifer's wincing eyes in bright light, the rush of cool air making her dizzy as she was pulled free, her eyes finally focusing on her Nadia, come to get her.

She looked angry, but not at her, giving a glare at the man still trapped, two intendants now upon him her look over the scene jealous, almost furious, Jennifer guessing she'd watched their time together on the stand from hidden camera's above.

With a short glare at Jennifer, Nadia soon had her by the arm, Jennifer unsure what to think or what awaited her as she took her out into the corridor beyond.

Nadia's anger boiled over quickly as she seized her, halfway up the corridor again, knowing they couldn't be heard, like before. "Enjoying yourself?" she glared at her in the gloom. "Well!?" She demanded, Jennifer unsure of what to say.

"I..." Jennifer stammered under Nadia's anger.

"You, what!?" she raged. "You had fun!"

Jennifer cowered as she realized what she'd done, Nadia seething with jealousy in front of her, her own face still covered in male-driven guilt.

"Look at the state of you!" Nadia growled, angry at the male's attention on her. "You were supposed to make him suffer; did you forget what he did to you this morning!?" she raged, embarrassed that the other intendants had watched the lesson descend into pleasure between them on screen.

"I did…I…." Jennifer broke off, starting to cry her, emotions as usual ripping one way and the other, the pressure of everything over the day straining on her now as she didn't know what she was supposed to do….

Nadia watched as she started crying, her head dropping between them in the cold wing, the intendant's rage offering little sympathy after such enjoyment. As she held Jennifer under her glare, happy she was hurting after what she'd done, she realized at least that she didn't have the power she'd been sure of her having as she'd been watching on from above… at least this was still Jennifer, still the one she'd fallen for.

After a time, Nadia could contain her anger more, taking Jennifer in her arms as she made her look at her, made her apologize, made her show she was hers. Some more sobbing and promises of better effort… some more crying, and arms softened, Jennifer knowing she'd done wrong and feeling the anger willing to forgive her, and take hold of her again… she wouldn't make the same mistake again.

Nadia talked her down, even answering her concerns, happy as Jennifer seemed to understand why they were so heavy on the males in house now.

Nadia explained that they couldn't have a repeat of what had happened before, that the backers wouldn't tolerate it, so their program had to be savage, efficient and effective, its five stages having been honed to perfection over the years.

First, males were deprived of protein in-house, fed

on mainly vegetables, as this meant their brains did not have the nutrients to maintain healthy cerebral functions, and over time would cease to function properly, leading to confusion and an ease of control, this being a common trick in cults, Nadia explained.

Second, males were like the women, kept naked, but routinely embarrassed in front of each other, making them feel small and, again, inferior, a feeling nurtured by further embarrassing them, this freely given by the intendant staff. This, of course, was meant to break down their egos, a source of male confidence that the house staff slowly chipped away at, males getting little confidence from their looks once their egos were brought down.

Third, males where milked, as Nadia put it, during training sessions with the women, not for their own pleasure, and were severely beaten if found to be enjoying it too much, Jennifer remembering the poor male on the wall… but no, it was for more practical reasons. With the male semen amounts kept low, they were easier to handle, less aggressive, and less able to resist the mental changes that were being inflicted on them, and of course they were more useful, as they did not climax quickly when being used as tools for training.

The fourth stage was made up of house treatments like the ones Jennifer had seen in the prison, and elsewhere on the fourth level. This was begun once the male ego had been sufficiently removed, ensuring maximum damage mentally, especially if witnessed by the other males, this being a further crushing blow to their male egos as they were made to cry out and show weakness in front of the others, Jennifer only realizing now why the doors had been left open so that all in the prison could hear that day.

Then came the fifth stage, the last and most sinister of all, this being comprised of the beatings males received. They were intentional, most in the program not for the pain, but for the damage it did mentally. Jennifer's eyes widened as Nadia explained that research gained from studying males in confinement showed that, with every fight a male lost, his body produced more of a hormone called cortisol. This cortisol had a pathetic effect on his body's physical and mental well-being, eventually leading him to the male feeling sorry for himself, and it was this line of thought that saw him unable to fight back, the suppressive effect of this cortisol on his anger so total as to nullify any probability of eventual attack from him. This horrific and intentional damage to the male's mental state being the condition the intendants sought, and the stage at which, when reached, the house would define him as…

BROKEN!

Jennifer winced at the thought as Nadia explained on, that at this point, a male could take as much as forty years to recover from this damage… if he ever did at all… the suppressive effect of the hormone imbalance after that much pressure being such that it was unlikely, and hence, an utterly dangerous procedure for any male to go through… something certainly not described or warned of in the Manor's brochure.

Nadia's explanation of the in-house cruelty on the males, brought out by her jealousy at what she'd witnessed between Jennifer and the male, seemed to cut back Jennifer's beginning understanding of why it was done, Nadia suddenly realizing she'd made a mistake.

"We need tools," Nadia declared. "If we could use plastic ones, we would, but that wouldn't do," she announced, Jennifer for a second hearing the Mistress in her tone.

"But what about them afterwards?" she asked, thinking of the mental damage the intendants were doing to them.

"They're only men," Nadia frowned in complete seriousness, no care for their wellbeing at all; not needing anything from them with the course she'd set in life, she displayed the callous disregard other women had to hide as they went alongside men through life, but not here…. In the Manor, women could observe their natural traits freely….

Seeing her mistake in explaining too much, Nadia didn't tell Jennifer what was about to happen to him as they left, for fear it would upset her, her seemingly incessant and unnecessary care for their welfare irritating her once again….

Instead, Nadia teased Jennifer as they went, explaining they'd watched as she'd worked… that he'd really enjoyed most of it, that he was a professional slave and probably didn't think much of her performance, Jennifer not believing her, however, sure she'd felt a connection with him. Nadia insisted, though, skillfully pushing the morning's pain he'd cause her, again and again into Jennifer's mind, making her angry again… making her the way Nadia wanted her, unfeeling toward them.

Jennifer was irritated, wishing she'd been harder on him now, but Nadia told her not to worry, that next time, they'd arrange a slave in the stand with him who wasn't. That they'd leash her up to the fool, letting him think it was going to be more of the same, before locking her in with him and only then telling him… she was an intendant!

"He definitely won't enjoy that," Nadia said, smiling as she saw Jennifer give the look that she'd wanted, the look that she'd learned… the look showing she believed that they deserved it. "He'll have the longest night of his life," she assured her.

Before that, though, he was to have another time he'd never forget; behind them as they left, Jennifer had assumed the male was being unshackled and probably taken back to the confinement with the others… but he wasn't.

Two of the intendants from Jennifer's morning lesson that had arrived with Nadia and had remained tending to the male, as they'd left, were still there and tending to his shackles… making sure they were tight.

As the male, forgetting to droop his head after his time with Jennifer, dared to look into the face of the intendant in front of him, she returned a serious, still, and unfeeling look, watching him as he was still confined, the box's left side hanging open from Jennifer having been removed.

Confused, the male hadn't noticed the intendant behind him finish checking that he was tightly secure, or noticed her reach for her hip, the first strong sound of swishing air alerting him as he turned to see her practicing her stroke through the air with her cane behind him.

Almost immediately, he was drawn back to his front, his eyes widening on into a serious face clad in leather, coming closer, reaching into the box's open left side and taking his balls with her hand, and straining them toward her as the heavy practice through the air stopped behind him.

Peering into his eyes with venom, his vicious assailant strained his vulnerability with her hand below, tightening her grip on his balls as her sister drew back her cane one final time, and then they began….

Chapter 32

Rhythm Of The Lifestyle

Jennifer awoke as normal that day, to the sound of gentle chinking as her sisters were uncuffed, and then the patient waiting as the morning's example was dealt with before them. Soon, breakfast and quiet talking, then showers and the day's working.... it was all so normal.

No one fretted, no one questioned.... this was life now, and this was the life they'd wanted... this was what they'd trained for.

The house resembled a well-ordered machine, everyone knowing their place and what was expected of them, everyone performing their duties, no more complaints now.... It was all so civilized.

It was of the occasion now, not the norm, that a slave was found wanting, the treatment rooms having fallen quiet, seldom used to guide their behavior, minor indiscressions rare now.

This, of course, was the sign that their training was nearing its end. With little to do now, and almost boring familiarity, the intendants in-house more resembled executives than exotic teachers. True, there was the odd occasion when some had to be reminded and nudged back on course, but in the main, they were just filing paperwork over the days, one report mirroring another as the sun set again on cuffed dorms below.

The normality became their work then – weeks went by with no end in sight, the women missing the excitement of old, even the frightening times... at least their minds had been stirred then, unlike now. This, of course, was part of the program, the intendants themselves having to work hard to maintain the normality, they too, truly bored, but having to look at that as satisfaction, the women left to grumble their want, their torture.

It was all designed to have them feel exactly as they did… bored.

Women could not handle this situation… devoid of occasion to use their communication and sounding abilities, they were like animals in a cage, pacing back and forth, the wings seeming to become shorter on a daily basis.

Truly missing their harsh teachings, they watched jealously on the rare occasion when one was dealt with in-house over those weeks.

Rare, because of programming, the intendants wanton, too, but having to work differently, to sustain the boredom. Instead, waywardness met restraint, the women now embarrassed more at being dealt with, examples being put on display instead of punished, something they all tried to avoid.

With their training came their confidence, and true belief that they were better than… hence, those left immobile in the hallways, gagged and spread eagle over hours' time, were brought to tears, their confidence shaken with their sisters passing them throughout the day.

This was the new control over those weeks… display.

It was embarrassing, to be left for hours with your own thoughts, tied spread eagle between pillars or window frames, one's femininity on wide display and saliva dripping from the ball gag left tight.

Some cried, others despaired, but all hated and tried to avoid it, a favorite for display being the library, the intendants' meanness still able to leach out over the women there… their true nature ever finding a way. This was for those found more wanton than most, left displayed not in the hallway or in the wings, but taken to the library, the quiet boredom utterly crushing. Outside, the rounds of fitness on the steps below had occasion to glance backwards on a sister, spread eagle between the windows.

Displayed fully for all to see, running tears had to beg mercy from those below, their plight not witnessed, the tears too far up to be seen, unlike the charge's body, left to be shown over hours with her boredom unattended above.

Not only did this shake confidence, but it left a feeling of unfairness, the women believing rightly that they were trained professionals now, and truly better and above such treatment… but the boredom continued on during those weeks, all pervasive and unabating….

At night, strict attention was paid to dorms, wandering fingers not allowed between thighs, swift punishment leaving wanton women to be taught, the few who accidentally climaxed during this teaching paying heavily, and watched by all the following day… the library being the new horror above.

And so it went on… and on.

The morning that they were told the news, it released a wave of relief throughout the Manor.

They were to graduate.

The news lifted the stress, the boredom easier to deal with, but still the tightness went on throughout the nights, the suppression heavier than ever, the women realizing something was going on.

Like the nights before, when they had been introduced to each other's femininity, they felt themselves being driven to a wanton state, all knowing something was coming now, and all wishing that so could they….

Chapter 33

Graduation

That night, they knew… knew from the way intendants shackled them, knew from the tightness in their poise and the professionalism in their stance. Over the months of training, they had become adept at sounding out the intendants by now… intuitively, they could feel how they worked, their hands, the subtle changes in their speed and strength, their motion almost talking to them… it was to be the next day.

All knew it and no one slept easy… there was no need for nightly instruction and no intendants came as the women drifted nervously in and out of sleep, all sisters sensing each other's unease as they listened to each other shifting on their cotton cages throughout the night.

Half worried and half wanton, they found that sleep was hard, the word 'graduation' on everybody's mind, it sounding like such a good thing… but so had other terms… and so had other days.

Toned and stroking thighs slid on crisp and cotton sheets, the scent of wanton women turning, cuffed in dorms again with worries stealing sleep; at least the morning would bring an end, the dawn their relief.

It brought fear!

Fear as they were uncuffed, the intendants stony-faced and utterly professional, no morning's example made, a no-nonsense approach to their raising!

Breakfast was mechanical, the women truly worried as memories of another day repeated out in front of them, all slaves showered and brought to line – the full complement of intendants noticeably up and guarding them before the march… straight toward the main ballroom!

Boots echoing up the wing to the main hallway had no sympathy for worried feet, naked and marched directly as the women had before, toward the room that had seen so many leave, to the room that had broken so many sisters….

Turning behind the main stairway, they were marched straight through the open door, the speed alarming them as the first inside had their nerves reach for the ceiling, a full phalanx of intendants waiting for them in line on the opposite side of the room, and there! There were the tables!!!

Rubber tops were stretched over and set like before, but no separating curtain this time as they were brought into line, directly opposite leather-clad power, a line of strength meeting a line of fear….

The last inside entered the line, even their guard now moved to the opposite side, forty fully dressed intendants in curved leather and corseted, fear now opposing the women's worried line… but the door was not sealed….

To their right, a frightened line had an escape route ready. Minds full of frightened anguish saw memories of Julie running for it on that day, and what had happened to her after meeting its locked handle… but it wasn't locked… it wasn't even closed.

Amidst blistering sunshine from the midday sun, submissive worry was suddenly drawn to attention, the

Mistress's deep tone finding them from inside the wall of leather. "Well!"

Minds snapped straight with bodies!

"Look what we have here..." her drawl waved over them as she moved out from the corseted army, her own black leather more grand and powerful looking than the uniforms around her. "It seems we have real professionals on our hands," she eyed threateningly as she moved toward them. "Seems they don't fear even the full house company," she turned back to the intendant wall, eyebrows raising and smiling, drawing theirs. "Well... it looks like they've learned after all," she said, turning back and now walking up the line, arm's length from the fear standing before her. "What are we to do with such arrogance?" she asked aloud, her tone surprised. "Should we just let it be... let them get away with it?"

Confident women felt first day trembles as she moved down their line, each fearing she would reach for them.

"If they're that confident, then it must be the result of their training," she announced louder, nearing the end of the line nearest the windows. "Must be their teachers are just that good... we should be proud of ourselves," she smiled, glancing at the leather smiling across from her. "It's not every day we have such incredible specimens walk these hallways," she announced, turning at the line's end and walking back up. "We should enjoy them!" She announced, the women fearing falling under her stare. "They have, after all, been waiting so long for enjoyment, themselves, and after such effort, I feel reward has been rightly earned...."

The women watched as eager looks crept over their opposite line, leather want on naked worry.

"Of course, this house is not without respect," the Mistress announced, her tone higher, but condescending into disapproval. "Should any slave not wish our most generous offer this afternoon, she will not be punished for leaving." She cast a glance at the open doorway, the women confused as she turned away from them, back to her own.

"She will, of course, be left, though…" she stopped in the middle, between the two lines. "Left in the hallway… for hours… hours with her want… her desires… as she listens to her sisters and their wants… their desires… listens as they are fulfilled, entry back into this room of want today not permitted to any who wish to leave… not till we're finished…." She turned, eyeing the women hungrily.

Silence…. No one moved, and the door lay open… but no one went for it… minds fearing and then becoming confused, held now by the Mistress's tone and words fighting with want and worry, the worry of the tables and leather smiles all in front, with the want of days, of tight restriction, with the need for physical attention.

The Mistress's look fell from its threatening stare to a coy mischievous look, playful as she approached again, her threatening stance gone like their worry before. "So… we have a bunch of slaves after all," she looked warmly at their number, her tone reassuring with her look. "I suppose we'd better cancel the rest of today's learning…" she announced, smiling, reaching gently out to Julie. "Looks like we're going to be busy," she beamed, Julie unable to help smiling back….

No one left… and there was no rush of hungry leather surging in on them from the other side. Instead, warm smiles and teasing laughter saw intendants and slaves having the times of their lives, the women realizing they were there, at their destination… that training was over.

And so, screams all afternoon… screams of pleasure, want. Tears, tears of joy and pleasure…. Pressure gone, pleasure replacing it, their final test passed and the open door meeting no takers.

The women groaned unrestricted, watched the Mistress smile, beam with pride, shattering orgasms and want delivered….

Intendants moved around, having who they pleased… restraint unnecessary, a simple bother now. Their charges gladly fell over tables for them, legs dripping with oiled wantonness, tired bodies groaning into evening sunshine… tired, more falling to writhing groans below.

Those with lust and tired longings wanted more below, among the tables, the leather hunger widening eyes as uniforms loosened and fell around them… first intendants' panties and then corsets… half-leather powerhouses dragging ever more down among them, among their want, their lust wrapping charges around them, tongues made to pleasure another, trapped in thighs and else, wanton scents and groaning out….

Soon, for the first time, there was the shattering sound of the Mistress's orgasms, heard there among the throng below… naked, wanton, and writhing leather… a mass of groaning pleasure… bodies reaching… walls heaving, female lust consuming all.

As the sun fell on relief and groaning, all were

tired, but had order brought over them… house discipline failing and barely possible… but smiles of want held line with a half-dressed Mistress. With intendants around her, beaming out alongside her, she announced they'd passed, that all restrictions were lifted.

Shrieks of joy and wanton laughter, some falling with their sisters, hungry to the floor, others leaving for lower quarters, no one alone and no one themselves. Around the house, celebration broke out everywhere, the house club even having willing visitors, intendants struggling to round them up, the house filled with countless Julies!

Even through the night, the women dormed and left uncuffed had intendants on cameras smiling. Laughing out aloud, they watched their antics below, the pressure lifted now, and the women playing it up. Smiled all the more as they were openly challenged through the cameras, the women playful and breaking rules, all so strict before, but now relaxed. Intendants shook their heads and tried not to laugh as they were teased down from the control room above… eventually, discipline was granted.

The recurring nightmare of the first time in the ballroom was put to bed in the women's thoughts, a process wholly supported by the house psychiatrist, who believed in repairing psychological scars by teaching the victim to remember what had happened, but through a differing and stronger perspective, bringing closure and a new strength for the future ahead.

There was, though, one area of the house that wasn't swept up with joy, and felt hard to a few who had truly bonded with their captors. Tearful scenes played out in private quarters and quiet places as special couples talked about their coming parting, one pair in particular sobbing in each other's arms. Both promised special places in their hearts for each other as they returned to their Mistresses, Jennifer for the first time able to match Nadia at something as their tears raced each other for the floor….

"How can I go back to her after all this?" Jennifer sobbed. "How can I be told by someone after being given all this training…."

Jennifer cried on as Nadia told her she could still be strong under someone else, that submission could be given in love and not weakness, her own body giving away her grief as she shook, holding Jennifer, her words hardly heard.

Jennifer would not be joining the parties below that night, never having been secured tighter in her life, held by Nadia's most gentle grip….

Chapter 34

Hand Over

Rising was different that day; there was no morning's example, no stress as some were uncuffed, and smiles, intendants smiling everywhere as they got them ready…. they were proud.

For months, they had worked on them, molded them… taken away bad thought patterns and put in their own proper lines. They had watched a bunch of scared wayward amateurs turn into strong confident professionals… their professionals… their charges. Now, as they made sure they were dressed for the first time since they'd arrived, that confidence beamed back at them. The women beamed out shocked smiles and surprised laughter as they were dressed in the very uniforms that had held them down for all these months.

The Mistress's graceful leather corsets gripping perfect training, her brood turned out in house finery, the women almost salivating as they felt for the first time how good the boots felt, these that they had crawled after and feared under.

Jennifer almost burst with joy when Nadia looked across at her, her expression of knowing how she felt in the uniform obvious as she fought to contain her pride, looking at her.

And so it was as twenty-three more sets of heels joined the echoing strength up the wing that day. Their pride sounded out with their footfalls now, beaming eyes following intendants true, a tacking line of polished finery sweeping into view through the ballroom door, the Mistress stunned as it snapped into line with no instruction needed.

A short speech saw interruptions being accepted, no heads turning as perfect training had all eyes focus on her direction, their own Mistresses – not seen for months – escorted into the room behind them, confused on them not turning. Confused but understanding as their final assemblance proceeded, the months of training displayed in front of them with perfect poise, perfect attendance, not one foot wrong as they showed training in all its splendor.

Those waiting in line at the back of the room brushed at tears as they watched their own move from the great circle's edge, one after the other, with a grace and motion they'd never seen them carry. Moved to the Mistress at the circle's center, accepting the house blessing in perfect etiquette, bowed faces of professionalism sustained, emotion held as they took their reward in one hand and the Mistress's hand in the other, then giving a curtsied finish of effortless poise and control.

The women listened to care in the voice of the Mistress after they each received the Honor Of The House, an award that carried not just a scroll with their name in gold leaf, but the knowledge that their name was now entered into the Manor's records, meaning they had the right and privilege to carry its name. This right gave connections, opening doors worldwide, their training and ability making them literally worth their weight in gold to those who knew what their training meant. In short, they would never want for anything again… even a split from their owners meant nothing now, as the world was theirs… and teaming with offers.

The Mistress's tones rolled this out over the room, making sure owners were left in no doubt of this, her own unique way of caring for her brood.

Worried looks and conferring waiters addressed their fears as they wondered quietly aloud. Wondered who they were with this confidence before them, this elegance having been unseen, now giving this shattering performance.

Tears fell on the last instructions, joyous cries loosed as she sent them off… back to their owners… back to their lives… nervous hands reaching out as they came.

Leather finery over familiar eyes, arms wrapping together as they finally came home….

Chapter 35

The Final Lesson

The gentle squeeze and look of warmth from her Mistress saw to Jennifer's return, the same as her entrance in fashion, the elegant car pulling away from the Manor, gently crunching gravel under its path as Jennifer looked understandably back at her disappearing home, the darkening forest surrounding them as the sun set behind their car. She stared sadly at the great house, her fear on arrival now confused with grief at her leaving, her mind drifting on whether she'd ever see it again, or the others, or… and there! There was Nadia under the arm of the Mistress, both sitting against the Manor's walls, watching as she left, a coy smile on Nadia's lips as Jennifer suddenly realized what she'd been telling her! Suddenly realized what she'd meant, and that if someone as strong as her could submit to someone and still remain that strong, then so could she!

Realizing this, she passed a quick look at her Mistress driving before quickly looking back, her last glimpse of Nadia before the passing trees took her away, leaving Jennifer sure she'd seen her smile grow, sure she'd realized Jennifer had learned, that she knew it was possible.

Jennifer turned to her Mistress, her heart beating as she realized that, before, she had not been able to submit to her because she'd felt weak and bullied, but now it was different; now she could submit to her…

O b_H [hil

Because she'd been made strong enough to do it…

A word about the author…

I once toiled in a dead end job that bled away my dreams over years as I suffered the lies and mean minded rubbish that pervades the minds of those who would hold back the ones given to imagination.

Imagination leads to discovery, on life, on one's self and if it is married to travel…..it leads to freedom.

"Travel teaches us to see"

The final breaking with my old life led from a chance encounter with a friends colleague. After listening to me bemoaning the rut I had gotten myself into over the years she announced my difficulties on a bar room table.

She put her finger on the table and announced…

"You spend most of your life at your work",

She drew her finger diagonally left a few inches across the table and continued,

"And you hate your work",

She then drew her finger diagonally back right across the table and completed,

"So you spend most of your life hating your life!"

That chance encounter changed my life as I determined to devote it to travel managing to leave that job and career forever a few years later and take to travelling extensively around Europe gaining experience in the finer things in life that decade of experiences in those places leading to the writing of "The Manor".

I hope you enjoy and discover where happiness awaits.....time is short.....travel.

www.ingramcontent.com/pod-product-compliance
Lightning Source LLC
Chambersburg PA
CBHW060750030726
47503CB00002B/221
* 9 7 8 1 5 0 9 2 2 8 1 0 2 *